MW01124586

Out of the Blackness

Carter Quinn

OUT OF THE BLACKNESS
Carter Quinn

Cover design by Scott J. Latimer, SJL Graphics, LLC

Printed in the United States of America

Carter Quinn Books
carter@carterquinnbooks.com
carterquinnbooks.com

Dedication

This one is for the *Fusionistas*. You all made my GRL 2012 experience something I will treasure for life. Thank you for the love, laughter, and friendship.

Acknowledgements

This book wouldn't exist in any form without the help of some wonderful people. I really do have the most amazing friends. Special thanks to Lara Brukz, Marie Sexton, Marilyn Blimes, Scott Latimer, Janet Sidelinger, Aniko, Jan, and Whitney. Without your input and hard work, Avery's story would still be nothing more than a Word file on my laptop. You're all incredible.

To those of you who purchased, read, and/or reviewed *The Way Back*, I offer my deepest thanks. You all made a dream come true.

Lastly, to Avery, my little Whisper Boy, who literally started out as a susurration in my brain. I feel you, free and happy, in my heart. Thank you for letting me know and love you over these last two years.

Table of Contents

Author's Note

I am not a psychologist, nor do I play one on TV or the internet. This book was a labor of love, but also an absolute work of fiction. It is not meant to provide any real medical advice, nor is it meant to be an accurate representation of any state child care facility or practice. Any mistakes or inaccuracies are either unintentional or designed to forward the story.

Chapter 1 - November

It takes a minute to realize the scream comes from me. I cut it off with an extreme effort and force my eyes open. The bedroom is dark, save for the slivers of blue moonlight that force their way around the old-fashioned shade pulled firmly over the window. I gasp and pant for breath, even as the nightmarish images are already fading, but the terror stays very, very real.

The bedroom door opens and I squeak in alarm at the massive shadow in the doorway. My trembling turns to outright vibrating and the panting becomes sobs.

"Oh, Aves," I hear Sam say on a sigh. He crosses to the bed and envelopes me in those steel-strong arms of his. I lean into him and sob against his t-shirt-covered wall of chest. He holds me until I begin to calm, then leans back and caresses the tears from my face with gentle strokes.

Even though his are the only eyes I can look into without fear, I can't do it now. My eyes flick up no higher than his mouth before going back to study the steady rise and fall of his breathing. "I'm sorry," I whisper, ashamed.

He tilts my head up with a curled index finger under my chin. I fix my gaze on his nose, crooked from many breaks, but still my favorite nose ever. "Hey." His soothing voice washes over me. "There's nothing to be sorry about." He starts to lay me back down, but I yelp in fear and cling to him. "Shh," he coos, brushing his thick fingers through my longish dark hair. Trembling again, I finally force myself to meet his gaze. He must see the terror there, because he grimaces slightly and pulls me off the bed with him. "C'mon," he says, indicating the door with a jerk of his head. "Let's go get some hot chocolate."

It's code and I know it. But I also know Sam is in Calm Avery to Sleep mode again, so on trembling legs, I follow him into the kitchen, grateful to him—for him—as I have been since the day we met fourteen torturous years ago.

I sit at the kitchen table while he heats the milk on the stove. One of Sam's rules is that milk must never be microwaved. He has only turned on the light above the range, so I can pretend I don't know he's crushing an Ambien tablet into powder. It mixes well with the hot chocolate so I don't taste it in the final product, but we both know it's there. Even though they're prescribed for me, I won't take them like normal people do. But then, there's nothing normal about me.

I feel hot tears bubbling up from my belly, but I force them down, hugging myself against the cool night air. I refuse to let myself think about the reason I have that Ambien prescription. Of all the painful memories I have—and I have few that aren't, and all of those involve Sam—those are the worst.

Sam's gentle hand on my shoulder brings me back to the present. He hands me my mug and I get up and follow him to the living room where we settle together on the couch. I curl up against him as he turns on the television.

"Sorry," he says when I duck my face against his chest to avoid the too-harsh light of the TV. He quickly mutes the sound and changes the setting from Dynamic to Movie, making the picture on the screen dimmer and more appropriate for the low light in the room.

He swings an arm over my shoulder and gives me a brief squeeze. "Wanna talk about it?" he asks gently.

I shake my head no, clamping down hard on the resurgent terror. "I—I don't remember," I whisper. It's mostly true. I rarely recall specifics from my nightmares, just the overwhelming terror of them. Sam knows this, but he always asks. He's there to help me pick up the pieces, just as he has from the beginning.

I sip my doctored drink and he copies my actions. I know we'll both be able to sleep, thanks to Dr. Sam, but until then, I let myself absorb the comfort my best friend and roommate offers.

I hate being small. The only times I don't hate it are times like these, when I'm on the couch with Sam as he watches television. At five-four, I'm eight inches shorter than Sam, short enough my shoulder fits under his armpit while his arm wraps around my shoulder. My head rests against his shirt and I can hear his heartbeat, feel his chest rise and fall with his breaths. Sitting here with him like this is the only time I ever feel safe. Loved, too, but I know that's an illusion. Sam is my older brother, not by blood, not by legal adoption, but because he took care of me when everyone else decided I was a punching bag. He rescued me then and he still thinks it's his job to keep me safe. I snuggle in closer to make myself smaller, to avoid the assault of those memories, and his huge hand slides up and down my thin arm, petting and comforting me. I curl further around him, almost into a fetal position, and his other arm comes around to hold me tighter to him. He knows when I need this and he never turns me away. I feel his lips in my hair as he kisses my head and whispers, "It's okay. I won't let anything hurt you." I nod against his chest even though I don't really believe it. I know he'll try and I am incredibly thankful to him for it; but I also know I shouldn't have been born and the world has been trying to fix that situation since that very moment. It will win in time—when I've hurt enough, when it has punished me enough—no matter how much Sam tries to protect me.

***

The next day at work, I'm even more grateful for the almost-full night of sleep. It is crazy busy, especially for our small store. That hateful pre-December shopper's holiday is almost upon us and it seems like the whole city wants to give books as presents, and they all want them right now for the lowest possible price or less. I'm able to escape to the stock room most of the day, unloading cases of books and loading them onto carts for Molly or Brian to shelve. On high volume days, Walter, the elderly owner of the store, allows me this escape because he comes down from his office overlooking the sales floor to mingle with the customers. He thrives on crowds, where I want nothing more than to escape them.

Molly is as Goth as she can get away with and still be in uniform. Instead of the black pants we're supposed to wear, she dons a long, flowing black skirt. Her makeup is still dark and artfully, if liberally, applied. People stare at her all the time, but she doesn't seem to notice most of the time. When she does, though, she somehow manages to make the gawker feel embarrassed for judging her. I don't know how she does it. Aside from Sam, the woodwork is my best friend. I try to blend in with it as much as possible. If no one notices me, I'm less likely to take a fist to the face or a boot to the ribs.

Brian is Molly's opposite in every way. Even after working with him for two years, he still makes me uncomfortable. He's blond and jovial, and it's obvious he's a jock. What he's doing working in a bookstore is beyond me. Actually, that's not fair. When his scary and loud as hell jock friends come in, one would swear they only know six words between them, most of them variations of "dude" or "bro." But when those guys aren't around, it's obvious Brian enjoys words. He's read enough of the classics to be helpful, but his favorites are science fiction. Most surprising is that he loves comics; not the usual suspects like Batman or Superman, either. No, his favorites are cutting edge and cult classics most people have never heard of.

Molly and Brian burst into the stockroom in the midst of an already-heated argument about the merits of the Nabokov translation of Mikhail Lermontov's *A Hero of Our Time*, and I involuntarily recoil against one of the large stacks. I listen to them go back and forth for a minute before Molly turns to me with a disgusted look on her face. "Would you tell him, Avery?"

I look between them, taking in the swiftly throbbing pulse points in their necks and shake my head. I back away from both of them and go around the stack, the tall bookshelf, placing it safely between us. "I—I'm going outside," I stammer, heading for the door.

"You see what you did, you big dumb oaf," I hear Molly practically screech before the heavy metal door closes behind me with a thud … and a click. I bite back the groan at my own stupidity. I was in such a hurry to escape the argument I forgot to place the wedge in the doorjamb. Now I'm locked out and will either have to hope Brian or Molly hears me pound on the door or go around front and wade through the masses of customers. Neither idea is particularly appealing.

I sit down on the smoking bench beside the door, though I'm not a smoker, and catch my breath for a few minutes. It's only an hour before lunchtime and already I want to go home. I really wish this holiday would hurry up and be over. At least it's not snowing, I think, realizing I'm shivering with cold.

I'm about to blow on my hands, thinking the cold metal of the door will hurt less if I pound on it with warmer hands, when I see him. He's a mountain of a man, at least compared to me. He's dressed in fashionable blue jeans, with a short leather jacket over a button-down flannel shirt, and he's striding down the alley toward me. He's chattering away on his cellphone, so if I keep very still, maybe he won't notice me. I try to make myself smaller on the bench, knowing a beating from this guy would take weeks to heal. I cringe inwardly when he pockets the phone a few feet away from me. I keep my eyes on his feet, ready to run at the first sign of intent. It'll be pointless, but I have to try. He never breaks stride, just calls a jovial, "hi," as he passes. I nod slightly, so as not to anger him, which either ignoring him or speaking is likely to do. I watch him in my peripheral vision as he continues on by. When he is far enough away, I let myself look in his direction. I only have a second to notice what must be the finest butt in the Western Hemisphere before he turns around, now walking backwards. I'm almost too startled to notice the nice heavy package in his jeans—almost—when my gaze, practically compulsorily, cuts up to meet his. He grins beautifully and waves before turning again and mounting the stairs beside the dock of the furniture store next door.

I hear someone yell out, "Yates!" just as I spring from the bench and sprint in the other direction. I need to get inside where I'm safe.

***

Sam gets home late, which usually means he's at the gym, but I can tell by his face that isn't the case tonight. When he looks up from taking off gun belt and sees me in the kitchen, his expression changes from contemplative to something I can't quite make out. He quickly stashes his service piece in the gun safe in the coat closet, crosses both rooms and envelops me in a hug so tight I have trouble breathing.

"What's wrong?" I ask, my mouth smashed against his chest.

The sound of my voice seems to break whatever trance he's in and he steps back, letting me go. "It was just a really bad day at work," he answers, reaching into the fridge for a bottle of water. He twists off the lid and sucks half of it down before I can even wonder what that has to do with me. Of course, maybe it doesn't have anything to do with me. Sometimes even Sam needs comfort—that he gets some of that from me is still surprising, but at least it makes me feel less bad about leaning on him so heavily all the time. Unfortunately, when a police officer has a bad day, that's generally not a good thing for anyone. I'm about to ask again if he's okay when Sam finishes his water and tosses the bottle in the recycling bin.

He sniffs the air appreciatively. "Dinner smells good. I'm gonna go take a shower."

"It's almost ready," I say, turning back to peer through the window in the oven door.

"Okay. Listen, Aves … If you think you'll be alright on your own tonight, I think I'm going to head over to Kira's place. I may spend the night."

"Of course," I lie. "I'll be fine." I keep my back to him so he won't see the fear I know is readable in my eyes. Some comfort he gets from me, some he gets from Kira. I know their relationship is serious. They've been dating for a year and a half and they're clearly madly in love. I also know that means someday soon I'll be on my own. The thought absolutely terrifies me, but I know times like these are good practice for when that happens. "Are you going to eat dinner first?" I ask lightly.

"Of course, champ," he says, ruffling my hair as he walks by. "I'd never miss your Spanish chicken and rice."

After we eat, Sam sits on the couch and pats the cushion next to him. "C'mon, let's get in some serious bonding time before I have to go."

I want to say no, but we both know I need it. Maybe he does, too. During dinner, I kept catching him looking at me, but he wouldn't say anything other than it had been a bad day. I know he's protecting me again, but I don't know what from this time. Instead of questioning him, I curl up next to him and breathe in his fresh, reassuring scent.

The next thing I know, I'm being lowered gently onto my bed. My sleepy gaze locks with Sam's as my head settles into the softness of the pillow. He smiles slightly and whispers, "Go back to sleep. I'll stay for a while."

I nod sleepily and close my eyes. As soon as the bedroom door clicks shut, though, my muscles are riddled with tension. I try to relax them in individual groups the way one therapist tried to teach me, but it's no use. I lay there, stiff as a board, until I hear the apartment door close behind Sam some time later.

I wait a few minutes in case he's forgotten his wallet or something. Once I'm sure he's gone, I get up and cross the room to my chest of drawers. Inside are my pallet supplies—two blankets, a pillow, and a nightlight. I plug the nightlight into the oddly-placed but convenient socket and, for a moment, almost get lost in the soft blue LED glow. I keep one of the blankets folded in half to act as the mattress, then place the pillow at one end and drop the other blanket accordion-style along the other wall. I've found it's easier to pull across my body when I do it that way.

Once my Sam's-away bed is complete, I move quietly into the kitchen and prepare a mug of extra-doctored hot chocolate. I know I shouldn't double-dose the Ambien, but it's important that I sleep through the night. Having a nightmare without Sam here would keep me up all night, terrified of every sound and shadow. The anxiety would carry over throughout the day and I would be a useless mess at work. Sam doesn't know I do this and I hope he never finds out. I don't want to see the sadness and disappointment in his eyes. Even more than that, I don't want him to feel guilty about leaving me on my own. I'm almost twenty-three; a grown up. I should be able to handle being alone in the safety of my own home.

But the sad truth is the nights have always been the worst. The cover of darkness lowers inhibitions and allows people—men, especially—to do things they would only dream about in the daylight. I've learned that the hard way. It's the reason I've only been able to sleep with the light off in the last year. Even now, sometimes a nightlight isn't enough and I have to leave a lamp on.

I drink half the mug before I even make it back to my bedroom. I lie down on my pallet but quickly get back up again. From the nightstand next to my twin bed, I grab my low-end cellphone from the charger. I glance at the time—10:14—and make sure the alarms are set. I can't afford to be late to work tomorrow. I lie down once more atop my makeshift bed and drain the last of the chocolaty goodness. I place the mug on the carpet outside my space, then reach over and draw the closet door closed, secure in my little space inside.

***

Tuesdays are the slowest day of the retail week and that is definitely true today. I look out over the store from the cashier's stand ten feet to the left of the front doors and see nary a soul. Apparently, present-hunters only think of small bookstores on weekends. Molly and Brian have scampered off to the break room for their customary Lovers Luncheon, leaving me to man the register.

I'm contemplating what an odd expression that is and how it scarcely applies to me—I feel more like an energized bundle of nerves than "a man" most of the time, and what does feeling like "a man," well, feel like?—when *he* walks in, the guy from the alley.

It's been three days since I've seen him and I've managed to completely put him out of my mind. But here he is again, live and in the flesh. My breath catches at the sight of him and I look quickly away. I don't want to antagonize him by looking at him. Some straight guys seem to think that any time a gay guy looks at them, he's thinking about him sexually. It isn't true, of course, especially in my case, but it's been three months since my last trip to the hospital and I really don't want another trip there today.

That first quick glance at him did provide some details, though. He's dressed similarly to the way he was on Saturday, but this time his blond hair is covered by a stocking cap, the kind with the retro yarn ball on top. As he comes toward me, I realize he is truly huge, with broad shoulders, a trim waist and what Brian's friends would call ginormous guns. He's bigger even than my 6'2" brother, and that scares the hell out of me. When the time comes—and it will, I can feel it—he's going to do a lot of damage.

I keep my gaze at the level of his chest—never look them in the eye, rule number two for survival—and take three steps back from the counter, out of fag-bashing range, even for arms as long as his. I fumble for my phone on the counter behind me, hoping I can get a call out to Molly or Brian before anything happens. I realize my heartbeat has kicked up in anticipation, adrenalin coursing through me like crack. My breaths are rapid and shallow and I'm already trembling. He's between me and the break room, so I can't escape that way. And if I dash outside, how many members of his posse will be waiting? Running is certain suicide, so I realize it's going to be a take what's coming to you moment. He stops at the counter and I cringe, waiting for the impact or the taunt that sometimes, but not always, precedes it.

Except when he speaks, his voice is gentle and laced with something like concern. "Hey—are you okay?"

I nod vigorously, studying the black buttons on his blue plaid flannel shirt.

"You're trembling. Are you diabetic? Do you need some orange juice or peanut butter or something?"

I shake my head no and force my voice past my lips. It vibrates almost as much as my body does, but at least the tears haven't started yet. "N-no. H-how c-can I help?"

"Are you sure you're okay? Maybe I should call someone?"

Once again, I shake my head and repeat the question. He seems less concerned about making road kill out of my face than about my health, so I force myself to relax enough to forestall hyperventilation.

"I'm looking for a present for my little brother," he says, that note of concern still in his voice. "My name is Noah Yates, by the way. We kind of met the other day. Are you sure you're okay, dude?"

I see his hand come at me and I yelp and jump back, ending up half-sprawled across the back countertop.

It's just then that Molly comes around the corner and sees everything. "Hey!" she yells, charging up to stand between me and Noah Yates, intimidating in her instant fury despite being a good eight inches shorter than him. "What are you doing?" she demands of my would-be basher.

"What?" Noah Yates asks with an astonishing level of surprise in his voice. "I—nothing—" He stops, takes a breath and continues with a different tone altogether. "I was offering to shake hands." He sighs. "I'm Noah Yates. I work next door and I came over to look for a comic book for my little brother, but I don't know anything about them, so I was hoping for some help."

"You weren't trying to hurt Avery?" Molly clarifies, menace still in her voice.

"No! I would never—look, maybe I should just go. I don't know what's going on here, but I'm sorry I scared you, Avery. You have nothing to fear from me, I promise."

"Avery?" Molly demands.

"Y-yeah?" I squeak.

"Are you okay?"

"I-I guess so?" I reluctantly climb down from the counter, feeling foolish, but keep my distance from Noah Yates. He sounds sincere, even contrite, but I'm still wary.

"Okay," Molly says. "You," she points to Noah Yates, "I'll meet over there at the comic books section." She indicates the wall adjoining his store with a nod of her head. "You," she swings on me now, "go keep Brian company in the break room. And for Pete's sake, calm down."

As they walk away, I hear Molly start to tell him about the guy who, a few months ago, tried to punch me because I had just sold the last Blu-ray copy of *Twilight.* I wait for them to get well out of change-your-mind range before practically sprinting for the break room.

"Oh, you do want some?" Brian asks when I come through the door. "I didn't think carrot cake was your thing."

I'm too busy trying to catch my breath and calm down to pay much attention to him. He notices my agitation and stands.

"Avery? What's wrong?"

I shake my head and put out a stilling hand. "Nothing. I overreacted, that's all." *But he's* so *big*, I think, and wonder when the last time a guy that big was nice to me. For all his muscles, Brian isn't that big. He's probably five-ten, which is way bigger than my five-four, but Noah Yates must be at least a foot taller and 100 pounds heavier than me.

Brian is still looking at me. I can feel it. Finally, he says, "Are you sure you're okay?" At my nod, he indicates a chair at the empty table.

"Have a seat, man. Help yourself to some cake. I'm gonna go check on Molly."

After Brian exits, I sit at the table and try to collect my badly scattered wits. What just happened is extreme, even for me. I know the almost endless nightmares of the last two weeks are affecting my judgment. I will always be afraid of guys the size of Noah Yates, but usually I can control my terror a little better at work. I want to cry at the hopelessness of the situation, but instead, I heave shuddering breaths.

I don't know how long it takes me to calm down, but a few minutes after I feel like myself again, Molly walks in the door with a huge smile on her black-painted lips. I narrow my eyes and turn away, afraid she's going to make fun of me. Molly is probably the person I trust most after Sam and his girlfriend Kira's brother Kaleb, and she's always been considerate of my feelings, even without knowing the full story of my past.

Instead of making fun of me, though, she sits across from me and takes my hand in both of hers. I try to tug it away, but she holds fast. Anyone else and I would flip out completely, but I know Molly won't hurt me.

"Avery," she begins quietly, "can you tell me what happened?"

I shake my head again, not that I won't tell her, just that I don't know how. "He's so big," I say instead.

She nods. "He didn't come here to hurt you, Aves." My eyes flick up to hers and I see the teasing glint in them to match the smile once again on her lips. “He came in because he thinks you’re cute. Apparently you almost met in the alley the other day?”

I stare at her in shock and confusion. “H-he thinks I’m cute?” I cringe inwardly, thinking of all the ways that simple statement could lead to more hospital bills. Tears spring to my eyes and I ask desperately, “Did you tell him to stay away?”

I see several expressions cross Molly's face in quick succession, but I’m so bad at reading them—avoiding eye contact has its own consequences—that I have no idea what they mean. “Oh, Avery, why would I do that? He seems like a really nice guy. He was so upset about scaring you it took all my considerable charm to get him to stop apologizing.” She squeezed my hand once more before letting go and standing up. “You should give him a shot. I invited him over for lunch tomorrow.”

***

The rest of the day passes like it’s standing still. By the time I clock out, I’m ready to climb the walls. As much as I often relate to Rogue and her inability to touch and be touched without causing pain or death, I would so much rather be Spiderman. Better yet, I would love to have the ability to freeze time or explode bad guys like Piper from the old TV show *Charmed.*

I quickly walk the two blocks to the parking lot, shivering from the cold despite my heavy pea coat. The sidewalks are quiet at this time of day, which always surprises me. An hour earlier and the buildings are filled with businesspeople and shoppers. But come six o'clock, everyone has better places to be.

I insert my key into the lock of my ancient Honda—it's a rust bucket that looks like it's held together with electrical tape, but it runs relatively well, certainly good enough for what little I use it. I paid $400 for it four years ago. I've got my money's worth—when I hear my name on the wind. My head pops up at the sound and I see Noah Yates loping down the sidewalk toward me, a cautious expression on his handsome face.

Immediately, the adrenalin screams "*Flee! Flee!*" I jump into the car, lock my door and promptly drop the dang keys. By the time I gather them in my hot, trembling little hand, Noah Yates is standing by my car door. He's bent over, peering in through the window, but my gaze is caught and captivated by the bulge in his jeans. They're so tight, I don't have to wonder if he's cut. I will never admit it, but the feeling that surges through my brain is very definitely not fear. I'm unaccustomed to feeling lust. For someone my age, my sexual history is, well, nonexistent.

Noah Yates breaks into a radiant smile that makes me want to forget all my troubles and fears. He sits down on the cold cement outside my window so my head is above his—something no one but Sam has ever done—and quietly signals he would like me to roll down the window.

All I can see of him is his handsome face and those broad shoulders, so I force my eyes to the knob and roll down the window about two inches—enough to facilitate conversation, not that I'm going to talk, but still closed enough that I'm safe. I turn my head back in his general direction but keep my gaze focused on the interior of the door, which could really use a good dusting. With so much of his body below my sight line, I have to keep my eyes on something inside the car or I'll inadvertently make eye contact.

"Avery," I hear his gentle voice coax, and I nod in response. He heaves a heavy breath and I fiddle nervously with my keys. What could he want with me? If he were going to attack me, he could easily have done that before I got in the car. So, why is he here? And why am I just sitting here instead of making a mad dash home?

"Avery," he tries again, "can you look at me?"

I shake my head very slightly, the fear bubbling up again. This is such a mistake. I start to rock slowly in my seat to keep from vibrating. My arms seem paralyzed. As much as I want to lift the keys to the ignition and drive away, I can't.

"C'mon, buddy, it's okay. I'm not going to hurt you." Instead of the impatience or hatred I expect to hear in his voice, all I hear is a coaxing sincerity. I'm so shocked that my gaze cuts to his for a brief second before refocusing on my lap.

Hazel. His eyes are hazel. *A light green with shots of pale brown, enough to mix the two colors*, I think wildly.

I hear his surprisingly sweet laugh and one of the hundred knots of tension in my stomach releases. "Hey, you looked at me! Even if it was just for a second, I'm going to count it as a win!"

My eyes close to ward off the pleasure in his voice and I thumb the keys in my hand, searching for the one that will take me away from this confusing moment. I look over when I hear his fingernail tap on the glass beside me, focusing on the thick, long digit. An involuntary shudder runs through me at the reminder of how much pain he could inflict on me. He says he won't, but I've heard that too many times before. The only person who hasn't hurt me is Sam and I wonder frantically why I'm still here, why I've let myself be put in such a dangerous situation again.

"I'm going to come over for lunch tomorrow, okay?" he asks, but it's more a reminder than a question, as if I could possibly forget. "Don't be afraid, buddy. I promise you can trust me."

Those words galvanize me into action. I have the car started and backed out of my slot before he can even get his feet under him. I hear his startled, "Okay, bye," as I slam the car into drive and roll the window up. My little Honda doesn't make the fastest getaway known to mankind, but it gets me out of there. I had been fairly warm with the early-evening sun shining through the windshield, but now I'm chilled to the core. I wrap my coat more firmly around me and race home.

Trust. What a lie that word is.

***

Over dinner, I tell Sam about Noah Yates. By the end of my story, Sam's face is creased with concern, but his words catch me off guard.

"You haven't been taking your anxiety meds, have you?"

My mouth opens and closes twice before I mumble a "no" in the general direction of my lap.

Sam rises from the table, crosses to the cabinet beside the refrigerator and comes back with a brown prescription bottle. He pops the lid off, shakes a pill into the palm of his hand, and places it on the table next to my water glass.

"They make the nightmares worse," I protest quietly.

His big, comforting hand covers mine where it rests on the table. "Is that why you quit taking them?"

I nod slowly, swallowing the lump of regret in my throat.

"Aves," he soothes, "you need to tell me these things. We'll get you something different. In the meantime, you can't just stop taking meds. You know that."

I nod and mumble, "I don't know why I have to take them at all. They never do any good."

"You have to take them until you're strong enough not to need them anymore. You were almost there before—"

He hesitates and I recoil, wrapping my arms tightly around my stomach. I don't need him to remind me. Every time I glance in the mirror, I'm reminded. It's one reason the mirror on my bedroom door is covered by a huge poster of Rogue.

"—August," he finishes clumsily. He sighs. "I'm sorry. I know you don't like to be reminded of it, but I have a dangerous job. I'd like to know you're healthy and happy in case something ever happens to me."

My wide eyes flick to his and an all-consuming terror rises inside me at the thought of being alone in a world without Sam. I know I couldn't make it. History has proven that. And I have no wish to find out if anything has changed. If the time comes, I won't even try.

Sam reaches out to squeeze my shoulder. "Don't worry, kiddo. I'm careful. I don't plan on leaving you for a long, long time."

I nod, only partially reassured.

"You want me to swing by around lunch time tomorrow and meet this guy?" he asks with another squeeze of my shoulder.

"No," I say, hoping he will anyway. Or maybe I'll take my lunch out of the store. There's a small coffeehouse down the street that makes an okay Panini. Even though it's only mediocre, at this point I'll do anything to avoid Noah Yates.

I spend the rest of the evening in my room, relaxing with the only thing that truly makes me happy, working jigsaw puzzles. Finding and placing the precise pieces in the only spot they'll fit appeals to my need for order. I can get lost for hours just placing piece after piece together. It doesn't matter the picture, although I favor nature scenes, it only matters that I'm making sense out of chaos. Several of the most complicated puzzles I've completed hang on my walls. When Sam did whatever magic he did to make the first one stick together, I nearly cried from the pure joy of it.

I'm not avoiding or punishing Sam because he brought up August, and I think he knows that. Sometimes—most times—after being surrounded by people all day at work, I just need to be safe and alone. Solitude is as much a security blanket as it is a torment. I have to have it, need it immensely, but too much of it is debilitating. When Sam comes in around 10:30 with a mug of hot chocolate for each of us, I give him a grateful smile and we talk a little as I drink it. It doesn't take long for the Ambien to work its magic and I know Sam is as pleased as I am that my sleep is dreamless.

***

I am able to spend most of Wednesday morning in the stock room organizing the day's deliveries. Walter always has high hopes for Christmas holiday sales, so we get in veritable mountains of new books. Thanksgiving is still two weeks away, so the real shopping craziness hasn't started yet, but it's only a matter of time.

Walter was one of us once, but now he has his own family. Like Sam and me, he grew up without parents, so he sort of understands me, even though he doesn't know my full history. No one but Sam knows that much about me, and he only knows because he was there for most of it.

As I unload a box of nonfiction political bunk—incongruously huge sellers, so somehow required stock—an unusually colorless cover catches my eye. I place the latest repugnant propaganda carefully on the cart next to me and reach in for the odd book. The cover is a mellow cream color with a black-and-white photograph on the lower two-thirds below thick black text announcing the title, *The Orphan Trains.*

My hands tremble slightly as I turn back the hard cover and read the description on the dust jacket. For seventy-five years, ending in 1929, orphaned, abandoned, and homeless children, ranging in age from newborns to older teenagers, were packed into what amounted to cattle cars and sent by train from coastal cities in the East to the Midwest to start new lives. For some of those 200,000 children, the move worked out. For others, it meant separation from siblings and other loved ones, or worse, indentured servitude to the child's new "family." The book details the history of some of those children.

Before I can think twice about it, I find a corner between stacks, sit down on the cold, dusty concrete floor and start reading. Somewhere around the twentieth page, the story in my mind morphs from that of a nine-year-old boy in 1910 being crowded onto a train car to my own memories.

My earliest childhood recollections are few and those that remain are vague at best, but they seem to revolve around a small me giggling down at my smiling, happy mother from a great height. Over the years, I've been able to piece together that my parents were once happy together. I remember my father as a presence and a force more than a face. He liked to hoist my little body on his great shoulders and chase my mother around the house while one or both of us shouted "Toro!" as she waved a tea towel at us. He would bend over and I would make finger-horns atop my head, giggling like mad as we crashed through the towel.

And then, suddenly, I would be peaking over a cold, steel-colored edge to see my father dressed in his only suit, asleep inside a pillow-lined box. No matter how much I cried or pleaded with him, he wouldn't wake up.

The next memories are the first that truly seem to belong to me. There's my first beating at age five and then the one that always sticks out in my mind. I'm barely six when I inadvertently walk between the television and Carl, my mother's boyfriend. As soon as I do it, I realize what I've done and start crying, begging for his forgiveness, promising it'll never happen again. But Carl's face is contorted in rage and hatred and he silently beckons me to him with one crooking finger. I hear my mother yell awful things at me, wondering how she would have such a worthless, stupid kid. I look over at her through my tears, silently begging for help. I see her standing at the edge of the kitchen, screaming and gesturing with a wooden spoon in one hand, my diaper-and-stained-shirt clad almost-toddler little brother on her opposite hip, his little face scrunched up as he prepares to wail his own fear. I'm almost hysterical by the time I get close enough to Carl's chair for him to reach me.

He grabs a handful of my brown hair and yanks me close, yelling in my face about what a useless piece of shit I am, even as I bawl my apologies and promise it won't ever happen again. He doesn't even acknowledge my words, just holds my hair in one fist while he draws back the other. He waits. I know the drill. I look up into his hate-filled brown eyes and then his fist crashes into my face so hard my entire body spins around, yanking out giant clumps of hair. He releases me and I slump to the floor, already tasting the blood pooling in my mouth.

I hear Carl bellow, "Boys!" and his own sons, two and three years older than me, run into the room. "Get this filthy dog out of my house!" he orders them. I curl into a ball, knowing what's next. It doesn't matter to them, though, because I feel their boy kicks rain down on my already bruised body for a long time before one glorious blow to the head knocks me out.

I wake up to darkness hours later. My entire body protests against any movement, but I slowly, painfully crawl out of the sweltering heat of the doghouse I've been thrown into. Outside, the grass is cool against my sweaty, broken skin. I lay on it for a while, and then drink from the bowl of warm water they've left for me. I try not to cry about the beating, because I know I deserved it, but I do allow myself low whimpers from the pain.

I don't realize I've curled into a fetal position in my small corner of the stockroom and am crying my heart out until I feel a light touch on my shoulder. I jerk away and slam my eyes open to see Molly crouched down beside me, one hand over her mouth, the other still stretched out toward me. Her eyes are wide and her face reflects absolute horror. I recoil until I hear Sam's voice, then I launch myself at him. He catches me and holds me tight as I sob into his neck. "Why won't it ever go away?" I cry desperately.

Sam gathers me tighter and stands up, carrying me. I hear him tell Molly he's taking me home and I cling to him, my last lifeline to sanity, hoping he still has patience and strength enough for both of us.

***

When Sam gets me home, I fall into a fitful sleep, awakening only at the sound of him returning from his shift at work. We talk most of the evening and late into the night. As we work a puzzle together, I tell him things I haven't been able to before, mostly about my life before he came into it. I had already been in the group home for a year before Sam arrived. It just so happened he showed up on a day that Tommy Blevins had decided to make mincemeat of my face for the second time in a week.

Tommy was eleven to my nine, and he and his gang of teen terrors had singled out Joey Wirth and me to beat on whenever possible. On good days, Tommy and his minions stole our lunches and tore pages out of our school books. On bad days, Joey and I would be surrounded and pummeled until we were bloody. None of the adults cared enough to stop it. If bruises were visible, Tommy forced us to tell them they were from clumsiness or games or fights at school. Otherwise, we would face even worse next time. Three days before Sam arrived, Joey hanged himself with Tommy's belt. It was his only way out and I knew it would be mine, too, as soon as I found the courage.

But then Sam arrived, bigger and badder than Tommy Blevins ever hoped to be. Sam had been in the system a long time, but hadn't made it to our group home before. He's never said what made him drag Tommy off me that day, but most of the thrashings stopped with Sam's arrival. Once in a while, Tommy or one of his boys would still manage to get to me. When that happened, the boys responsible were punished with Sam's own fists.

Sam was once moved to a different house. It was the longest two weeks of my life. During that time, Tommy unleashed a year's worth of beatings he'd been saving since Sam showed up. Somehow Sam was able to get back to our group home. He's never said what stunts he pulled or what whistles he blew, but I'd never been so glad to see someone in my life.

When he got back and found me bruised and bloodied with yet another broken arm, Sam had marched right past the caregiver and dialed 911. Tommy was taken away that very afternoon. It was a strangely anticlimactic ending to three long torturous years. The caregivers were quietly replaced and life at the group home slowly improved. I didn't see Tommy again for almost ten years.

I finally tell Sam why I never fought back against Tommy and his gang. Sam never knew about my mother's boyfriend, Carl, and how often he and his sons beat me. He only knew that mom had dropped me off at a firehouse one day and the hell I'd gone through at the group home. But finally, I allow myself to share everything.

I tell him about the time I dropped and shattered a plate while drying dishes. Without even thinking about it, I repeated the word I'd heard so often around the house. I had no idea what it meant, but it was the first time my mother slapped me. I was five. Carl had seen the slap and it had opened the floodgates. That very night was my first experience with physical abuse. Of course, for as long as I could remember, the whole lot of them—mom, Carl and his two boys, Junior and Darrell—had been telling me what a worthless excuse for a boy I was. Aside from the physical pain they inflicted, I still think the worst part was being forced to look Carl in the eye as he beat me. He demanded it. If I couldn't do it on my own, he would yank my head around until my eyes met his of their own accord. And then it would get worse. Once I tried to block a blow with my left arm. Carl had wailed on it until he broke it, swearing that if I ever raised a hand to him again, he'd break my neck. There was never a doubt in my mind that he would make good on that threat.

So, as traumatizing as it was, it was somewhat of a relief the day my mother marched me into a firehouse and told them she never wanted to see me again. She told them in front of me—as she had told me so many times—that I was an abortion that didn't work and she'd finally grown tired of dealing with me. It's hard to argue with a woman who hates her child before she's even met him; much less spent his lifetime wishing aloud that he was dead.

I've never seen any of them again. The only regret I have about that is that I would like to have a picture of my father. The only good memories of my childhood are of him. It would be nice to be able to see his face.

Sam talks and talks, wheedles and cajoles until I finally give in out of exhaustion. This week, Sam will speak to someone at the department and find a therapist who specializes in cases like mine. I'm not sure I like being described as a "case," but Sam is convinced he can find a therapist who will help me put to bed the living nightmare that is my past. I don't share his optimism. He keeps telling me that none of the things that happened to me are my fault. I know he genuinely believes that, but I don't. It's impossible to think that way when I've been told over and over from practically my first memory—and by almost everyone but Sam—that I never should have been allowed to draw breath.

Sometimes I wish I had Joey's strength. I've heard people rant and rave about how selfish and evil suicide is, but until those people have endured the physical and emotional living hell Joey and I have lived, they can't possibly understand. What happens when the "temporary problem" they always talk about isn't temporary? Try telling the seven-year-old me that the beatings would eventually come less frequently but never stop, because he would never be worthy of that, and see if he wouldn't rather swing freely from the end of a rope. If only I were convinced I wouldn't mess it up, I'd do it right now.

Of course, I know that would hurt Sam terribly and render all his years of protecting me pointless. And the last thing in the world I want to do is hurt Sam. Maybe that's the real reason I haven't followed Joey's lead. Sam doesn't deserve any more pain, and I've grown accustomed to it. I know it will win in the end, just not by my own hand. Probably not, anyway. Definitely not today.

Chapter 2 - November

I return to work more than a little embarrassed. When Molly sees me, she extricates herself from a chatty customer and wraps me in a giant hug. We cling to each other for a moment before she remembers herself and steps back.

"No more reading in the stockroom," she commands sternly, like she's the boss. Then her black-lined lips part in a cheeky grin and she amends, "Unless it's "*The New Joy of Gay Sex*."

I grin half-heartedly after her as she moves off to field a new customer's query. I head back to the stock room to complete yesterday's task, but find it already finished *and* cleaned up. On one of the rolling carts, I see the book that started all the mess and glare at it. I know I shouldn't. I know it could start the whole process all over again, but I'm compelled to open the book again.

"Oh, no…!" The wail is ripped from my soul as I see what I've done. Desperately, I flip through page after page. Each one shows the same thing. Somehow in my agitated state, I managed to draw in the margins of almost every page. Train cars and dog houses, over and over again. I don't even remember doing it, but I know I did. I'm the only one here obsessive enough to bring my own pens to work. Walter supplies ones with black ink, but for some reason, I have to have blue. Tears slide down my cheeks as I confront the evidence of my madness.

Angrily, I dash the tears from my face and take the book out to the sales floor. I find Molly behind a cash register and wait silently until she's finished with her customer. I toss the book on the counter and reach for my wallet.

"I ruined it," I say in answer to her questioning look.

"What?"

"Yesterday. I drew in it. I don't remember doing it, but I did. It's all over the insides." Still shaken by the discovery, I look at her through watery eyes. "Please just ring it up so I can throw it away and forget about it."

Quietly, Molly scans the book into the register and places it in a bag as I slide my debit card through the reader. "Maybe you should hold on to it for a while," she suggests, her expression showing her concern.

I nod silently, take the bag and walk away. I want to throw it away, but I can't bring myself to do it. I've never thrown away a book in my life. Instead, I stow it in my backpack and wonder what possessed me to deface it like that in the first place. I haven't drawn since I was a little kid. Back then it was the usual stuff, a bright yellow sun in one corner shining down on a house with a big green yard. Sometimes I would try to draw a little boy and a dog, hoping mom would take the hint and get us a puppy who could use the big dog house in the back yard, but she never did. After Carl came along, the sun was replaced with rain, the grassy yard became huge water puddles, and the puppy disappeared because the doghouse was really meant for me, until finally I came home from school one day to find my pictures had been taken off the refrigerator, torn up and thrown away. I never drew again. Until yesterday.

I force the thoughts from my head and go on about my day. Several stacks on the floor are in severe disarray, so I spend a few hours straightening, re-alphabetizing, and dusting them. Between customers, Molly entertains me with an ongoing narrative of yesterday's high and low points. When she mentions Noah Yates, I start to fidget. Just the sound of his name in the air makes my blood pump a little faster. I recognize the sexual interest even through the innate fear, and it continues to confuse me.

Sure, some people would find him attractive. He's obviously tall, muscular and good-looking, none of which bode well for me. He has only been kind in our two—three, if you count the alley—brief interactions, but those *were* brief, so who knows what sort of monster lurks beneath that placid façade. I've been fooled before, although not by someone so gigantic. Still, there is something about him that makes me want to step outside the fear box.

Molly mentions his name again, but I forestall the conversation I don't want to have by telling her it's time for my break. I grab the last Starbucks Mocha Frappuccino from the fridge in the break room, pull on my coat and slip out the backdoor—remembering to wedge it open this time.

I sit on the bench and sip the cold, sugary coffee drink. I'm still tired from the extended, emotionally draining conversations with Sam yesterday, so I lean my head against the brick wall and close my eyes, inhaling deeply to keep from falling asleep. It's relaxing out here in the alley. We're in the middle of the block, so the sound of traffic on the side streets is more rhythmic than overpowering. Luckily, there are no restaurants bordering this alley, so the trash rarely smells. Occasionally, I can hear the yells from the rambunctious furniture guys next door, but they seldom venture out here unless they're loading a truck for delivery or receiving a new shipment of stock. When they are, I immediately go back inside. I may know my fate, but I feel no desire to tempt it.

I realize I've dozed off with a half-empty bottle in my clumsy hands when a softly called, "Hey," jerks me awake. How is it that I already recognize that voice? I look for the man and see him leaning casually against the building on the opposite side of the narrow alley. He has one foot propped against the building and his thumbs are hooked in his pockets, leaving the rest of his fingers to nonchalantly outline the gift area in his jeans. I croak out a weak, "Hey," and watch him nervously as I bring the frap bottle up to drink from it.

"I missed you at lunch yesterday," Noah Yates says as he slides down the wall to sit on the ground, those long, thick legs stretched out in front of him, crossed at the ankles. Even his feet are huge.

I nod, mumble, "Sorry," and study the pattern on the soles of his boots through my lashes. I don't have to remind myself to keep an eye on him. It's instinct. I'll need to move the instant he does if I hope to make it inside unscathed.

"Molly said you weren't feeling well," he says. "I hope you're better today?"

I nod slightly and wish he would just go away.

"Good," he says, sounding genuinely pleased. A strained silence enfolds us for forty heartbeats before he says, "I've already taken my lunch today, but when I saw you out here, I had to come say hi. I'm really glad you're feeling better, Avery. I'm off tomorrow, but maybe we could have that lunch together on Friday. I mean, if you're working."

Although most of my usual complement of fear is still with me, I have to struggle to suppress a smile. He got all that out without pausing for breath. My eyes flick up to his muscular, plaid-encased chest before I force them down again and offer an almost imperceptible shake of my head.

"Oh," he says with what I would swear is disappointment. But why would he be disappointed? "So you're off Friday?"

Again, I signal no. It is so extraordinarily difficult to talk when I'm not in control of the situation, or at least can pretend I am. Books. I can talk about books and comics to my customers with very little trouble—unless they're the size of Mt. Man-Everest over there. But these supposed "social" situations everyone seems to crave just freeze my vocal cords. It's frustrating in times like this, when all I want to do is plead with Noah Yates to leave me alone. But I also know it's a perfectly valid and necessary defense mechanism. The chances of being backhanded into next week are greatly diminished by my silence.

"Oh," Noah Yates says, interrupting my train of thought. "Hey, if you're working the evening shift, I could bring over some takeout from Nick's. You like Italian, right?"

It's all too much. Surprisingly, I'm neither shaking nor vibrating, but he's coming at me nonstop and all I want is for him to slow down. "Please," I plead, barely over a whisper, but it's enough to grab his attention.

"Oh, hell," I hear him groan. "I'm sorry, Avery. I'm coming on too strong, aren't I?" He sighs and I shudder in relief. "Listen, I'm really sorry. I know this kind of thing is difficult for you and I understand; I really do. I don't mean to frighten you. I'd just really like to get to know you. We'll take it as slow as you like."

His words, as much as the sincerity and remorse in them, catch me by surprise. How is it that in less than a handful of meetings this giant of a man has already figured out the force that drives me away from people like him? Just how much has Molly told him? And most importantly, what does that mean? Is he pretending to be nice so he can get close enough to do maximum damage? Or could he really be a nice guy? The thought startles me so much I don't have time to stop it; I look into those hazel eyes of his for a split second and see the enormous grin that spreads across his face in the same instant.

"Win number three," he says with a note of pure joy in his voice. I may not know facial expressions, but I know vocal tones. The happiness in his surprises me yet again.

I stare down at my feet and bite my lip to hide the smile. I notice the frap warming in my hands and drain the last of it in a quick gulp.

"Okay, buddy," Noah Yates says softly, "my break is over, so if you want to be inside before I stand up, you better get a move on."

Hurriedly, I twist the cap on the bottle and move to the door. Halfway through it, a thought crosses my mind and I turn back to him—where my gaze absolutely does not inadvertently land on his bulging crotch. Nope, not at all. "Three?" I question quietly, hoping he will follow my disjointed thoughts.

"Yep." I hear the grin in his voice. "Number two was when you didn't run away at the sound of my voice." His long legs start to fold at the knees and I quickly duck all the way inside, pulling the door locked behind me. I hear his delightful laugh through the metal and realize there's a genuine smile on my lips for the first time in weeks.

***

The week passes slowly. Monday I have an appointment with my doctor, who chastises me for the way I stopped taking my anxiety meds. She's a nice enough lady and she takes her job seriously, but she doesn't get me at all. After two years, she still seems befuddled when Sam answers most of the questions she poses. Some of his observations surprise even me, and I realize again how much attention he pays to my moods and health. It makes me feel vaguely guilty for taking up so much of his energy. In the end, Dr. Farris agrees to change my anxiety meds to something that shows the nightmare side effect further down the list. Just in case, though, she also issues three refills for the Ambien after Sam assures her I am not abusing it.

Noah Yates continues to haunt the fringes of my work life. I see him Friday, Saturday, and Tuesday for a few minutes each. Sometimes I notice him trying to stifle a laugh while pretending to shop when he's really listening to the almost incessant banter between Molly and me. I know the quality and spontaneity of my sense of humor dims when Yates is around, but it's out of self-protection. Sometimes he engages Molly or Brian in conversation and tries to drag me into it, but I'm always careful to keep just enough distance from them I can just walk away when he tries that. He seems to keep a close eye on the alley and feels it necessary to at least say hello when he finds me back there. He hasn't talked about having lunch together again, but I know it's coming. Molly seems absolutely taken by him, which doesn't seem to bother Brian in the least. I'm the farthest thing from an expert on heterosexual relationships, but Brian's lack of jealousy surprises me. Is it because he knows Noah is gay?

Wait. No one ever said Noah Yates is gay. Yes, Molly said he thinks I'm cute, but puppies are cute, too. Maybe he means cute in an entirely nonsexual way. That would be good, actually. Not that it's possible anyway, but the last thing I need is that big galoot thinking of me and sex in the same sentence. The very thought nearly makes me hyperventilate my potato soup.

Instead of contemplating the possibility of Noah Yates wanting to have sex with me, I allow my mind to touch on the very real threat of my upcoming therapy appointment. I've done it before, this head shrinking business. It was a less than successful venture. In fact, it was an unmitigated disaster. After they took Tommy away, the state insisted I submit to counseling. But even at that tender age, I already knew that the second surest way to end up bruised and bleeding was to speak.

The shrink stared at me for hours while I concentrated on twisting my fingers together in my lap—all of it in complete silence. After five seemingly endless sessions, the doctor had declared an end to the experiment.

Years later, after Sam rescued me from the last year of group home living, he insisted I try again, with absolutely the same results in only three sessions.

I know this time will be different because Sam has found this psychologist, a Kendall Moorhead, through the police department. He has already briefed her on some of my past. She has even given permission for Sam to sit in with me as long as I was comfortable with it. I know I won't be able to keep silent with Sam there. Even if I don't answer, he can. He knows everything about me—well, all but the darkest thoughts that suffocate me.

The chime on the door interrupts my train of thought and I look around the edge of the stack I'm straightening for the thousandth time this week to see Yates standing there scanning the store like he's looking for someone. Idiotically, I think to call out to him in case it's me he's looking for, but then sanity takes hold once again and I move to out of his line of sight to continue my straightening. Against my better judgment, I am beginning to believe the man doesn't want to hurt me, but a decade and a half of training have taught me not to listen to those little voices inside me. Even if he doesn't want to hurt me at this moment, once he realizes who I am, sees the real me, he'll be just like the rest of them. It's the way of my life. So I have to concentrate on the reality—Sam, Kaleb, and Molly are the only people

I can completely trust. Everyone else I have to keep at a safe distance, both physically and mentally.

"Hey."

The sound of his voice is loud enough to break through the cacophony of thoughts scrambling my brain. I'm startled enough I push the book I've just placed all the way to the back of the case, causing the ones on both sides of it to collapse onto my arm. Surprised, I jerk my head in his direction and see the smile on his handsome face and the twinkle in those stunning hazel eyes before I force my own back to the mess before me. "Hi," I say softly, getting back to work.

"Avery." I hear the pleading tone in his voice but choose to ignore it. He's leaning against a short stack that runs perpendicular to the tall one I'm working on, keeping several feet and hundreds of books between us. I'm thankful for the safety that provides and I wonder for the second time if he knows this is what I need, or if it's just happenstance.

I sigh and turn in his direction, keeping my eyes on the shelves of books he's leaning against—science fiction, authors G – I. "Yes?"

"How are you? I haven't seen you for a couple of days."

I shrug and nod. I still can't figure him out. If he doesn't want to use me as his own personal living punching bag, why does he keep coming around? I've said maybe two dozen words to him in all of his combined visits, so it's not like he's fascinated with my conversational skills. He's observant enough to know his very presence drives me to the edge of my nerves, yet that doesn't keep him from coming around repeatedly.

"I'm glad to hear it. I've been worried about you." I hear the smile in his voice and wonder what put it there.

I frown and turn back to my job, absolutely at a loss about what to do with that new information. "I'm fine," I say, my voice barely above a whisper.

"So how about that lunch then?"

Immediately I begin shaking my head no, terrorized by the mental image of being alone with him. I back away from the stack, silently calculating my escape route.

"Avery." Yates's voice is low and soothing, just the right tone to arrest my flight for a moment. "Molly and Brian can be there. I don't want to scare you, but I *do* want to spend time with you somewhere other than the alley."

I've known this was coming, as much as I've tried to deny it. No matter how much I want him to, it doesn't look like Yates is going to leave me alone any time soon. I have three choices—have Sam come chat with him, deal with it, or find another job. But where will I find another job where I won't be the freak? How will I possibly survive the interview process? I was lucky that Walter knew Sam, so I had two things in my favor when I found this job—Walter was one of us and Sam could tell him a little bit about me before we met. I know I won't have that sort of luck again. And working somewhere without Molly around to kick butt for me? It wouldn't be nearly as much fun, not to mention the damage it would do to my already fragile grip on sanity.

I manage to rein in my runaway thoughts long enough to notice Yates is still standing there awaiting my response. "Why?" I ask, risking another glance in his direction.

I see the smile spread his gorgeous lips before I force my eyes away. "Because I like you, Avery, and I think you might like me, too, just a little bit, if you'd give me a chance. I don't want to hurt you, buddy. I know you don't believe me yet, but you will. I'd like very much to be your friend."

I feel my head shaking no, but I don't remember setting it in motion. This is everything I've feared since Yates sat down beside my car. He's going to break me one way or another: if not physically, then surely emotionally. I can't let him in, even if I want to, which I don't. No one but Sam and Kaleb can see the real me—especially not Noah Yates. Even Molly only gets to know certain information. Because as much as I will deny it if pressed, Noah Yates seems to be a decent person, but even seemingly decent people kick dogs and throw out the trash. And as soon as he figures out who I really am inside, that I shouldn't be breathing, I know he'll make me pay for it. Instead of saying any of this—because really, how can I?—I say, "No, thank you."

Very carefully, I force myself to study the pattern in the carpet as I walk away into the stockroom, keeping my ears alert for pursuing footsteps. He doesn't follow me. I turn back to look through the stockroom door windows to see him grinning at me, holding up four fingers. *What the heck did he win this time*, I wonder.

Chapter 3 - November

I stare resolutely at my hands clasped tightly in my lap and wonder if this could possibly be the world's lumpiest couch. It's certainly not comfortable, but I suppose that's sort of the point. It's therapy; it's not supposed to be comfortable.

Sam and I have been sitting in Dr. Moorhead's office for twenty minutes while she gets basic information about me from Sam. I can't speak; the terror is just too close to the surface. I realize this woman isn't here to hurt me, but eventually she's going to want to delve deep into the recesses of my brain and dig around for my most painful secrets. I want nothing more than to get up and leave, but I know Sam won't let me. I'm at least grateful Sam didn't find a male therapist. I know I would have already bolted if he had. Dr. Moorhead—Kendall, she insists—is a tall, thin woman with long waves of red hair. It's not a brassy red, but something darker and richer, the color I'd like to have if my hair were red. Luckily, though, my own hair is a thick, dark brown. I cut it so it mostly hides my eyes, especially when I'm looking down, like I am now. I can feel her gaze on me as I fidget and I wonder what color her eyes are. Probably green, but certainly not the same hazel as Noah's.

Most of the get-to-know-you session passes without me saying a word and I remember practically nothing from it, just the impression that Dr. Moorhead is calm and relaxed. She's clearly in control of her world but doesn't seem to feel the need to make sure everyone knows it. I wonder how many sessions of silence I can get away with before she dismisses me like the ones before her have done.

After the initial session is over, Sam takes me to Chipotle for a burrito, one of my favorite things in the fast-food world. Unfortunately, I'm still too anxious from the session to be able to eat it. At home, Sam works a puzzle with me like he sometimes does, and lightly quizzes me about my impressions of the shrink. I try to give vague affirmative answers but he knows me too well.

"She's here to help you, buddy. I know you don't really believe that yet, but it's true. You know I wouldn't ask you to see her if I didn't think she was going to help, right?"

I nod, concentrating on the puzzle so I don't have to see the disappointment in his eyes. Ever since the book incident, when I told him everything, he's been on a crusade to fix what's broken in me. He doesn't understand that it's not something inside me that's broken, it's me. I'm broken.

***

"Avery," Dr. Moorhead finally says as she leans back in her office chair and readjusts the legal pad on her lap, "I'm here to help you. You know Sam found me. You don't think he would send you to me if he didn't think I could help, do you?"

Reluctantly, I shake my head in the negative. Of course she would invoke Sam's name and practically his very words—the one sure way to get me to cooperate. It's two days after the first session and I'm reluctantly back again. We've just spent twenty minutes in silence. I've concentrated on wringing my hands together in my lap while she stares at me.

"Okay, then." I can hear the ring of small victory in her voice, but for some reason it doesn't offend me. "Sam has given me some of your history, but I'd like to verify some facts and get the rest from you. Can you do that for me?"

I nod slightly and begin to answer her questions. Yes, I turned twenty-two on April 23. Yes, I spent most of my childhood in the Englewood group home. No, I didn't have any friends except Sam and Joey. Yes, I remember my mother dropping me off at the fire station. No, I'm not going to talk about that or what came before.

When I become visibly agitated at the mention of my mother and younger half-siblings, Dr. Moorhead very graciously backs off and says we can talk about them in another session. I don't bother to correct her. Instead, she probes around into my history at the group home and my relationships with Joey and Sam. I answer all her questions quietly, with as few words as possible. I don't know this woman. I'm not about to offer up my darkest secrets for her to judge, even if Sam found her. When she asks how Joey's suicide made me feel, I'm done for the day. Without a word, I get up and walk out of her office, ignoring her calls. Fighting back the torrent of tears, I brush past Sam, who has risen from his seat in the outer office, and continue right out into the hallway.

I'm somehow able to hold myself together until I get to the stairwell. I burst through the doors and break down sobbing. I find my way down to the lowest level, where I tuck myself into the corner, as far under the stairs as I can get, curling up to wrap my arms around my shins and bury my face between my drawn-up knees. Those horrid questions have brought it all back so clearly. I can practically feel every bruise Carl ever left on me. My heart feels split in two and bleeding agony just as it did when I first learned of Joey's death. And just like then, I hate Joey for not taking me with him. And I hate myself for hating him. Joey was my only friend before Sam. I loved him and he loved me. We were the same. Together, we could face anything, even Tommy Blevins and his gang of thugs. Together, we would doctor each other's wounds and pretend we would one day be free of all the pain. Except now, Joey really is free of it. And just like my father and my mother, Joey hadn't loved me enough to keep me with him. He'd found his escape and left me here to suffer more and more. And I know Sam is preparing to follow suit. Sam, who has protected me for more years than I have fingers, is only a few short months—if that—from leaving me, too. I know it. He will marry Kira and I will be alone again. But this time, I will really and truly be alone because Sam will have a happy new life without room for a severely damaged little brother. I want to damn Joey for leaving me, but I can't. I feel the pain of his absence every day, but he was smaller and even more fragile than me. He deserves his blessed relief. All I deserve is whatever's coming to me.

***

Later that night, Sam and I sit down to dinner at the tiny table in our small kitchen. As soon as we got home from the therapy session, I threw myself into cooking. I do it often, but I don't have the greatest variety. Still, Sam never complains that dinner is usually one of the same ten dishes. "At least I don't have to look forward to Meatloaf Mondays every week," he said once when I asked him about it. So, of course, for the next three Mondays, I made meatloaf. The third Tuesday, he presented me with a new cookbook. That night I selected one of the chicken enchilada recipes. I make the same one tonight.

Sam silently fills both our plates from the baking dish in the center of the table. I feel his eyes on me and I know it's just a matter of time before the questions start. He's a good cop; he knows how to interrogate a suspect gently. Before he can start, though, I clasp my hands together in my lap and watch my thumbs circle each other, first one direction then the other.

I feel the hot flood of tears leap to my eyes but I don't even try to contain them. After the disaster at Dr. Moorhead's office, I should be cried out, but apparently there is still moisture in my body, ready to spring forth at the slightest provocation. As two gigantic drops splat onto my thumbs, I take a shuddering breath and whisper, "I'm sorry, Sam."

I hear Sam's fork clatter to his plate and suddenly his big, strong arms are wrapped around me, holding me tight and safe. I bury my face in his neck and sob as he makes the appropriate hushing noises and strokes my back. It is a repeat of the scene under the staircase when he finally found me, but this time there's no judgmental psychologist watching in the background.

"Are you ready to tell me what upset you so much?" he asks gently, pressing a brotherly kiss to my hair.

I shake my head and tighten my arms around his neck, but I do try to get my sobs and breathing under control. As much as I hate to talk, Sam is the one person in the world I know I can say anything to—well, almost anything. I know I can never tell him how much I want to go be with Joey because I know how much that will frighten and hurt him. And really, I don't want to die every day, just sometimes.

Eventually, I gain enough control I can push back from Sam a little bit. He keeps one hand on the back of my chair and brushes back my hair with the other. I heave one last sigh and place my hand over the enormous wet spot where my tears have soaked into his shirt, embarrassed even after all these years to leave that kind of evidence of myself on him. He covers my hand with his. "Don't worry about it," he says gently, reading my mind. "Tell me what happened?"

"Joey," I whisper, unable to put sound to my words. "She asked about Joey." And just like that, the tears start flowing again, but this time silently, without the wracking sobs.

Sam squeezes my hand where it still rests on his chest. "What about that upset you? You've talked to me about Joey plenty of times."

I shake my head. It's not the same, nowhere near it. "She doesn't care about him, Sam. To her, he's just another dead kid." Now the sobs start afresh. "But he's my Joey. He was a real person…with dreams…and fears—and so many…bruises he couldn't…take it anymore." I wipe my face violently with the backs of my hands, my pain and desolation turning to anger. "She doesn't want to know about Joey. She just wants to talk about his death and how that makes me *feel.* How do you think it makes me *feel,* Sam?" I glare into his eyes in pained defiance, something I've only allowed myself to do a handful of times in all the years I've known him.

"I know how it makes you feel, Aves." Sam's calm voice and sad expression actually help soothe the spikes of my anger. "You feel lost and alone, and confused and angry, and you're desperate to keep ahold of at least some part of him."

I nod along with his words, grateful that he understands.

"But, Avery…." He hesitates. "I think there are two or three more emotions you feel that you really need to deal with. And that's what Kendall is there to help you do."

This time, my eyes met his with fear, not of Kendall Moorhead, but of those other emotions Sam just mentioned. As much as I really don't want the answer, I need to know. I need to hear if Sam knows me too well after all. "What other emotions?" I ask.

He strokes my hair again and I lean into his touch. "You really want me to say them? You don't want to wait for another session with Kendall?"

I shake my head, my breath coming more shallowly. He knows, I think. He knows me too well to have missed it, even though I've never said the words aloud.

Sam closes his eyes, takes a deep breath and begins to speak as his eyes open again. "I think you're a little bit jealous that Joey's pain has ended and yours keeps recurring. I think you're angry that he would leave you alone to face that situation without him—and you have every right to be, Avery. And I think you're afraid that the only way for your pain to end is to do what Joey did."

With those few words, my best friend and protector has laid my deepest secrets and fears out on the table between us. I feel the tsunami of panic rush in, ready to destroy me and everything in its path. I try to push away from Sam, but I don't need to. He recognizes the panic and lets me go. Blinded by tears and lack of breath, I stumble blindly down the hall to my room. This isn't an I-need-to-be-outside-to-get-oxygen panic. This is a laid-bare-to-the-world-must-hide panic. I stagger into my room and directly to the closet, where I pull the door closed behind me, curl up in a ball in the corner and bury my face in my knees, my body wracked by dry sobs and violent shudders.

***

I shiver from the cold, only somewhat enjoying my break. I'm in the alley again. I contemplate taking up smoking so I have a genuine reason to sit on this bench as much as I do. I won't do it, of course. It's smelly and expensive and not nearly as sexy as it apparently was fifty years ago. Geriann, the last smoker to work at Flip the Page used to tell me how she just fell in love with Marlon Brando and James Dean because of the cigarette packs rolled up in their t-shirt sleeves. She used to sigh longingly talking about Natalie Wood puffing away in *Rebel Without A Cause.*

I spend far too much time contemplating smoking, but anything that keeps my mind from reliving yesterday's therapy session is a good thing. My next appointment is tomorrow, a thought that turns my stomach. I know Dr. Moorhead will be intent on finding out why I ran out of the last session, but it's the last thing I want to talk about. Joey is a very special memory and I don't want to share him with anyone else. Sam knows about him, of course, because when I first met Sam, it was only three days after Joey's death and I was keenly feeling the loss. I talked about him then, back when the loss was still fresh, my grief overwhelming. But as time passed, I locked him away in my heart, unwilling to explain him or us to anyone else, even Sam.

I hear the crunch of rocks under boots and jerk my head to the right, where I see Noah Yates approaching on the far side of the alley. I force my eyes to the ground before me when I realize they've stopped to take in the sight of his strong thighs moving under tight, worn denim. I don't understand what it is about him that turns my thoughts to his body. I'm not a sexual being. I know intellectually I would prefer a sexual relationship with a man, but I certainly have no intention of actually experiencing any sexual acts with anyone. I rarely even masturbate, though lately, when I have, my traitorous mind has conjured images of a gloriously naked Noah. I wonder if his chest is as hairy or his belly as flat and ridged as my fevered fantasies have imagined.

"Hey, buddy," I hear Mr. Fantasy say softly as he takes his customary place across the alley from me. "Are you having a good day?"

Still staring at the ground, I nod and force myself to speak, as difficult as it is. "It's okay."

His soft chuckle warms me slightly. As ridiculous as it is, it feels like approval. "It must be," he says. "I didn't even have to drag those words out of you."

I shrug and hide the small smile that plays on my lips, unsure how to respond to the tease.

"Well, my day's been horrible, but it's looking up now."

Despite my best efforts, I'm curious. I've never seen Yates in anything but a happy mood and I wonder what he could possibly consider a horrible day. My eyes flick up to take in his solid chest, encased today in a blue plaid flannel shirt under a lightweight green jacket bearing the furniture store's logo. "What happened?" I ask, surprising both of us.

"Corvo and I were out delivering an old-fashioned buffet to this couple in Olathe. I'm not entirely sure how, but Corvo left one of the thing's legs on the end of the truck, so when I went to lower the lift-gate to take us all down to street level, the thing pitched forward. It weighed about 150 pounds more than me and caught us by surprise, so neither of us could stop it once it started to go over. In a heartbeat, the customers had three thousand dollars of spankin' new firewood in their driveway."

"Oh, no." I am so caught up in the story I jump at the sound of my own voice.

Noah laughs. "Yeah, they were really great about it, though. We called back to the store and Alvin, the store manager, promised to order them a new one at a discount. Corvo's in hot water. Alvin's making him clean out the staff refrigerator." He laughs again and I find myself wanting to smile along with him. "That thing is a health hazard. The CDC could probably discover a whole host of new bacteria in there." He draws his long legs up and wraps those muscular arms around them. "Your turn. Tell me about your day."

I'm so shocked my gaze actually meets his before I slam it back to the ancient concrete between my feet. I shrug uncomfortably and concentrate on keeping my breathing under control. It's a simple question. I should be able to answer it without panic rising in my chest. "It's okay," I say again.

"Yeah? No crazy furniture-delivery guys coming in asking about comic books?"

The panic recedes a little at his teasing. It's almost comfortable in a strange way. "He's harassing the help on his break," I answer, hiding a stupid smile behind my hand. I keep my eyes on the cement between my feet. It takes him a couple of heartbeats to react, but when he does, it's with a full-bodied laugh that actually elicits a giggle from me before I clamp down on it.

Finally, Noah gets his laughter under control. "You're a quick one, little Avery. I kind of suspected you would be, but that took me by surprise. I thought I'd have to wait a lot longer for you to turn your sense of humor on me."

I can't fight the rush of warmth that spreads through my body at his praise and I glance up through the curtain of my bangs to see a broad smile lighting up Noah's handsome face.

"That's an official fifth win, buddy. You keep this up and I'm going to run out of fingers to count them on."

I open my mouth like I'm going to respond, but my train of thought is derailed by Molly crashing noisily through the door. "Avery, we need you," she says, then smiles widely as she catches sight of Noah. "Oh, hi, Noah. Hey, why don't you swing by for lunch on Thursday?"

My startled eyes meet hers in a silent plea. She gives me that "get over it" expression and smiles again at my stalker—new friend, whatever he wants to be called. I know neither of them cares what I think, so I slip past Molly and leave them to it.

***

What none of us realized when Molly stuck her big fat foot in my mouth is that Thursday is Thanksgiving. For those of us in retail, that particular holiday begins Hell on Earth. The Day After Thanksgiving brings thirty days of the crankiest, rudest shoppers imaginable, all searching for that one—or one-thousandth—perfect gift to celebrate the season of joy and love and giving. I giggle a little at the thought, but quickly control myself when I feel the stares from others in the waiting room. They probably think I hear voices now.

It's Wednesday, time for therapy session number three. Sam sits beside me paging through a three-month-old *People* magazine whose cover story wonders if Kate could be the new Diana, whoever that is. Sam's fidgety, nervous, I suppose, about my appointment. His case of nerves certainly isn't helping mine any. I don't want to be here, don't want to go through all this.

"It's going to be hard," Sam had warned me last night as we ate left-over chicken enchiladas. "It's going to be painful; I won't lie and say it won't be. But you need this, little brother."

I nodded then and nod now, reliving his words. I don't know what he hopes I'll gain from this. It's not like Dr. Kendall Moorhead can suddenly flip a switch and change who and what I am. I know I'm a cosmic punching bag, an abortion that failed. She can't change that and there's no use pretending she can.

My musings are interrupted by the sound of the great doctor herself calling my name. I look up to see her smile and gesture for me to follow her back to her office. I glance pleadingly over at Sam, who looks so confident and safe in his police uniform, but he just smiles, ruffles my too-long hair and nods his head in the doctor's direction. "Go on, little brother. I'll be right here."

I nod stoically, forcing my chin not to tremble, and rise to follow the doctor down the long hallway to her office. My knees are weak so I feel even more awkward trying to get my legs to function properly. I ought to be grateful because that amount of concentration forces the wildly unsettling thoughts out of my head for the moment. It is only when I've taken a seat on the World's Lumpiest Couch that my fear rises to the surface and threatens to undo me.

Dr. Moorhead positions herself in her office chair, legal pad on her lap and faces me. I see all this through wavering, rapidly tunneling vision. I hear her gasp seconds before my world goes black.

***

Sam's worried face is the first thing I see when I open my eyes again. He smiles slightly with relief as I take in my surroundings without moving my head. I know immediately what happened and I feel stupid—and maybe a little hopeful that Sam will realize what a bad idea this therapy experiment is. Maybe he'll agree that I can stop this foolishness now.

But before that hope can take root, Sam frowns and urges me to sit up slowly. He takes a paper cup of water from Dr. Moorhead's outstretched hand and presses it into mine. "Sip it slowly," he cautions before turning back to the shrink. "Kendall, can you give us a few minutes, please?"

I hear the concern in her voice—*real or pretend?* I wonder—as I stare at the lukewarm liquid in the cup. "Of course. Let me know when you're ready for me to come back in."

As she closes the office door behind her, Sam takes a seat next to me on the World's Lumpiest Couch. My head still feels woozy, but the intense anxiety that caused me to pass out has receded to its usual level, spiking just a little bit in anticipation of Sam's next words. I don't want to hurt him, but even more than that, I don't want to hurt *me*, which is why I really don't want to continue this experiment. I know all my demons so well I've given them nicknames. They're part of me and I'm, well, if not okay with that, I'm at least resigned to their presence and influence in my life. I know that to try to exorcise them will cause me unimaginable pain. And to what end? I'll still be me: the walking target, the one who shouldn't draw breath.

Sam sighs heavily and I flinch slightly when his hand comes up to stroke my hair out of my face. "Did you forget your anxiety meds this morning? Or are they not working again?" he asks gently.

I replay the morning in my head, but I honestly can't remember. It fits both ways. I can see me taking the ugly little pill, but I can just as easily see me forgetting it. So much for I-witness testimony. "I can't remember," I confess hesitantly.

"Okay," he says. "I'm going to have to keep a better eye on that, I guess. Your medicine is just as important as the therapy. You're going to need both if we're going to heal you."

I close my eyes and nod. Apparently Sam isn't giving up on the therapy. I turn pleading eyes to him. "I don't want to be here, Sam. I don't want to do this. Please don't make me."

"Avery…." The disappointment I hear lacing my name hurts. "I know this is going to be tough, but you've had a lot of really horrible things happen to you that you need to learn how to deal with in a healthy, constructive way. You blame yourself for things that are not now and never have been your fault. You need to learn how to stop taking that blame and then figure out how to love yourself for the totally amazing guy I know you to be."

I flush and stare again at the cup of water I've been nervously rotating in my hands.

"Did you know I went to therapy, too, Aves? In the time between moving out and coming back to get you, I saw a counselor." He chuckles slightly at my look of total astonishment. "Oh, yes, I sure did. It was tough, but absolutely necessary, just like for you. The difference being, I'm right here to give you support. I'm here to tell you what an incredible little brother you are and how much I love you. And I'm here to hold you while you cry when it's hard and to cheer you on when it starts getting easier.

"Right now I know you're doing this because I asked—okay, coerced—you to, but pretty soon you'll be doing it because you're feeling better about yourself and you're putting your demons and doubts in the past where they belong. I promise you that as painful as it is to start the process, you'll be so much stronger and feel so much better after a while. If you can just hang in there until then, you'll be so very glad you did."

I never knew, never even suspected that Sam had undertaken counseling. I can't even fathom such a thing, but I know he would never lie to me about it, which also means he wouldn't ever lie to me about it making him happier and healthier. The questions for me are both simple and complex. Can I force myself to go through this? And what happens when I'm done? Sam has always tried to convince me that the things that were done to me, the beatings and abuse, that all those things had more to do with my abusers than with me, that I wasn't responsible for any of it, that I never asked for it to happen. As much as part of me wants to believe him, I've always known better. It was and is because of me. Because I am not supposed to be here.

I don't believe that therapy can possibly change that fact, but maybe the good doctor can teach me ways to cope better when it does happen again. Maybe Dr. Moorhead can even help reduce the level of fear I feel every day in every situation. And maybe, just maybe, she can help end the nightmares. That alone could make it worth going through emotional hell three times a week.

Slowly, I meet Sam's eyes. "Okay, I'll take my meds like I'm supposed to and I'll give this head shrinking stuff a try."

I'm rewarded with a relieved smile and a tight hug. *If only I could stay safe in my big brother's arms always*, I think.

When Dr. Moorhead returns, she smiles slightly at me and retakes her seat beside her desk. "We're going to try something a little different today, Avery. I can see with my own eyes that you're still very distressed about coming to see me, so I'd like to explore some options that might lower your stress levels. Are you okay with that?"

Still somewhat embarrassed by my panic attack, I merely nod, keeping my eyes on the carpet in front of me.

"Good. First, I think it would be advisable for you to take a Valium about thirty minutes before our sessions are scheduled to start. Now this isn't something I want you to make a habit of, but I think for the next few sessions, at least until you get used to being here and talking with me, it will help to alleviate some of your anxiety about being here. Are we agreed?"

I smother a smile, wondering why I hadn't thought of that. I don't really like to take the Valium because it seems like another crutch and it sometimes makes my mind foggy, but in this case, it's the perfect reason to take them. "Okay."

"Excellent. Now, tell me something that makes you happy, something you enjoy doing more than anything else."

Surprised, I glance at her green silk blouse before finding the carpet again. "Puzzles," I croak. "I like to do jigsaw puzzles."

She writes something on her notebook and I cringe, waiting for the judgment. "That makes sense, actually. You're already making order out of chaos, which is really what therapy is all about. In our case, instead of creating a physical picture out of jumbled pieces, we're taking the fragments of your memories and fitting them into the proper ways of dealing with them. That's good, Avery. Is there anything else? Do you like to write or draw?"

My hands clasp each other so tightly my fingers have gone to sleep. For some reason the answer has me back on the verge of tears. "I used to draw when I was little."

"Do you think you'd like to start again?"

"No," I whisper, the image of my torn and discarded drawings fresh again in my mind.

Dr. Moorhead leans back in her chair. "It's very important that you have an outlet for the emotions we're going to be sorting through in our sessions. I usually suggest that my clients keep a journal of their thoughts after each session. Many people find it helpful to work though their thoughts and feelings while writing them down. But I think visual images might be a better way to go for you. I'd like you to visit the art supply store down the street on your way home. Pick up some sketch pads and colored pencils or crayons or whatever you'd like to make pictures with. Then, after each session, I'd like for you to draw your emotions. You don't need to try to make a pretty picture if that's not what you're feeling; just let the pencil and the moment guide you. This isn't for a grade and I'm not going to judge you for any of it. I won't even look at it if you don't want me to; but you will need some way to let it all out. Give yourself a time limit if you like, say, thirty minutes. When your time is up, you can either finish what you've started or leave off right there. You'll feel a lot better about our time together and you'll get to rediscover something you once loved to do."

I nod imperceptibly, remembering how I'd vandalized the orphan trains book. I wouldn't have imagined ever drawing again, but obviously my subconscious was way ahead of the good therapist. I suppose it won't hurt anything to try at least.

Somehow I make it through the session with Dr. Moorhead. Out of stubbornness, I refuse to call her Kendall. If I'm going to be coerced into therapy, I'm going to hang on to a few of my own thoughts. Perhaps because of the traumatic beginning or because that caused a truncated session, I think she goes easy on me. There are no major dark secret questions and she doesn't ask about Joey. I wonder if Sam warned her that would be a bad idea. Whatever the case, I walk out of the session on my own power without another round of tears. Sam beams such a huge smile my way that I can't help but feel like I've accomplished something.

***

Inside my closet, I stare at the blank sketch pad with an equally blank brain. What am I supposed to do now? Draw something. Draw what? When I was little, I drew the usual kid stuff, houses and sunshine and rainbows, but I felt those things. I don't feel anything now. So maybe that's the key. How does one draw blankness? How does one draw his emotional state when he hasn't the foggiest clue what that is? I blink away tears of frustration and grab the first colored pencil I find.

Of course, it's the black one. *Okay*, I tell myself, *you can deal with that. It's just a doggone drawing. It's not rocket science.* But it seems as complicated and as alien as rocket science. I haven't held a colored pencil since I was six years old; it doesn't even feel right in my hand.

Hesitantly, I put it to the paper and draw a line across the top of the page. I stare at the line, connect a few more to it and I have a box. I start to shade in the box and completely lose myself in the process. *Yes*, I think, *this feels right. This feels like me.* Without letting myself think, I simply let the pencil work across the page, letting it fill the entire space with blackness.

When it's full, I frantically flip to the next page and repeat the process. I give in to the process and force it all out through my pencil. I can practically feel the energy flowing from my body onto the page.

The alarm on my phone startles me out of my trance. Aware once again, I stare at the half-finished page. What I've finished is completely black. I flip back through the pages and realize I've done the same thing on the four previous pages. Shaken, I toss the pad into the far corner and scramble out of my closet.

Four and a half pages of nothing but blackness.

Fighting back tears, I stumble to the kitchen and grab two pills. I know I shouldn't mix the valium and the Ambien, but *four and a half pages of nothing but blackness!* I skip the grinding up of the Ambien, skip the hot chocolate, and just swallow both pills with a half-glass of water. I don't want to think about it anymore. I want to sleep, need to sleep. And until I sleep, I need to be able to calm the demons inside me. Forcing my mind to blankness, I stumble back to my bedroom and collapse in tears on the bed.

Chapter 4 - November

It's Thursday morning, Thanksgiving, and I have no idea what I'm going to do. My years in the group home taught me to hate the two biggest holidays of the year. Thanksgiving serves to remind people who have nice, happy families that they should cherish the ones they love and be thankful for all they have. For those of us whose families abandoned us as children, it's merely the first of two times a year we see lots of strangers who wished they had children of their own, but take none of us. Around this time every year, the guilt begins to weigh heavily on the more fortunate—those blessed with families or wealth or both—and they begin to bring us "poor orphan children" food and gifts, not the gifts Joey and the others wanted most—a warm, safe home with a family who loves them—but material gifts the bigger and older kids beat us up for anyway.

Not once in all the years I spent in state care did I hold out hope of being adopted by some mythical happy family, not like the other boys did and do. I knew those people could see the real and true me, the one who doesn't deserve to be loved, the one whose own birth mother tried and failed to kill him, and then categorically rejected me. Instead, Thanksgivings and Christmases were merely further reasons for Tommy Blevins and his gang of thugs to beat the holy heck out of me and Joey and the rest of the smaller, younger kids.

Sam, of course, has tried almost desperately to change my view of those two holidays. He thinks we can reclaim the spirit of them by creating our own traditions. Basically that means I have to play nice with Kira today while the three of us fumble around the tiny kitchen making Chinese food. Why we can't just order in like the rest of the non-turkey-eating world, I don't know.

I glance at the clock and groan quietly. It's only seven a.m. I'm tempted to roll back over and try to reclaim sleep, but I know that's a useless endeavor. Instead, I force myself out of bed and into the shower.

After scrubbing myself clean twice under water that is almost too hot to stand, I dress in jeans and a hooded sweatshirt, the gift of the clothing gods. I plaster a smile on my face and head into the living room expecting Sam and Kira to already be there reveling in holiday...revelry or whatever.

Instead, I find a note from Sam taped to the television. I cross the room to read it and breathe a little easier. *"A – Gonna try something a little different this year. Be back by eleven. Do not eat anything after 10. Loves – S."*

I make myself a fried egg sandwich on toast and actually remember to take my anxiety meds. I know I'll need them today. As much as I like Kira I can't help but resent her just a little bit. After all, I know she's about to take Sam away from me. They'll soon be a happily married couple with children of their own to provide a better life for. I know Sam wants to be a father something fierce. Heck, he's been training for the job since the first day he met me. I know he wants to adopt, to create a family for some kids like us whose biological families didn't care enough or didn't have means enough to support kids. I know he'll be a fantastic father and Kira will be an awesome mom. I just wish their happiness together didn't mean leaving me to my own devices.

The thought of being alone so scares me that I realize I'm starting to hyperventilate. I force myself to control my breathing while concentrating on the mental image of Sam walking around the apartment. Eventually, I calm down enough to hit the cupboard for another pill, one of the Valium I rarely allow myself to take on days I don't have to leave the house. My anxiety levels should be low enough at home that I don't need extra help, and usually they are, but today is not one of those days. It's Thanksgiving! I swallow the pill with the last of my orange juice and turn to wash my few dishes by hand. Whatever it takes to make the time until Sam gets home go by faster.

***

Rogue and Bobby have just touched for the first time at the end of *X-Men: The Last Stand* when I hear Sam's key in the lock. I quickly dash the tears from my cheeks with an embarrassed laugh. That scene always gets to me. I'm almost ashamed of how glad I am to hear Sam's return; I hate being alone in the apartment. I jump up from my cozy nest of pillows on the couch as I hear his deep voice rumble through the wood. When Kira's lighter voice responds, I cringe momentarily. The sound of her voice reminds me that the jig is almost up, as they say. Before my mind can run away with itself again, the two of them elbow their way through the door carrying an assortment of food containers, none of which even remotely resemble the shape or scent of Chinese.

"Avery!" Sam calls, a smile spreading wide across his face when he catches sight of me. "Happy Thanksgiving, little brother. We brought food!"

I watch him cross into the kitchen, Kira trailing behind with a matching smile. It catches me off guard when she stoops to press a Chap Stick-y kiss to my cheek. Like her brothers, she's tall, slender, and beautiful. Her long, dark hair curls elegantly to just below her shoulder blades. "Happy Thanksgiving, Aves," she says. She has warm brown eyes and I know they must sparkle with holiday happiness.

"Thanks. You, too," I say, surreptitiously wiping the weird wax from my face. I follow them into the kitchen and stare helplessly as they spread out the bundles on the counters. "Are we not doing Chinese this year?"

Sam stops moving long enough to shed his coat. He takes Kira's off her shoulders, pressing a kiss to her neck. "Nope. I thought we'd go traditional this year." He gestures with his free arm. "Behold! Turkey, dressing, mashed potatoes and gravy, some hideous red thing Kira swears is delicious—"

"Spiced apple rings, you ungrateful brat!" Kira laughs at him, and then turns to me. "They're *so* good, Avery. You'll love 'em."

My head is practically spinning. If pea soup is hiding among the offerings, I know I'll be in trouble later. Taking it all in, I merely nod. "Wh-where did it all come from?"

Kira pauses in mid-reach for the oven thermostat. She turns to Sam, scowling. "Sam, didn't you talk to Avery about this?"

His gaze drops to the floor and I marvel, as always, at her ability to turn the big, confident cop into a scolded schoolboy with just one look. "I thought I had, but I guess I forgot," he admits.

Kira reaches up to smack Sam upside his head, but stops at the last minute, as her eyes meet mine. Hers widen in shock and mine find the floor. It's only then I realize I've taken two steps back, out of the room, away from the violence. In my heart I know Kira is only playing with Sam. She'd never hurt him and he'd never allow it. But exchange the loving teasing for simmering hatred and I'm back in my mother's kitchen, about to witness—and possibly, probably, be the subject of—a beating.

"Oh my god, Avery, I'm so sorry!" I hear the absolute horror in Kira's voice and, though I know it's genuine, I take another two steps backward, my eyes trained to the living room carpet, my arms hugging myself tightly.

In seconds, I feel Sam standing before me. I can see his ugly brown shoes, but still I don't look up. "She wasn't going to hurt me, Aves."

I nod. I know that, I do. But still, this is too much. I'm not ready for this. I start to shake my head, wanting the memories to go away, willing the sight and scent of blood from my brain. I hear the coats hit the chair as Sam tosses them off to the side. Then his big, calloused hands are on my cheeks, gently tilting my head up.

"Look at me, Avery."

I clench my eyes closed, but the bloody image on my eyelids forces them back open again. I feel Sam stroking my hair and it begins to calm me enough I can look at him. I know the plea is there in my wet eyes, but I have no idea how to vocalize it.

Sam continues to stroke my hair as he draws me slowly into his embrace. "It's okay, little brother. It's you and me and Kira. Avery and Sam, right? Nothing's going to hurt you here, buddy. I've got you. Just relax and breathe for me, okay?" Without conscious effort, my arms wrap around him, stealing his strength and calmness. "That's it, buddy," he whispers into my hair. "It's okay. Breathe."

After a couple of minutes, I feel my heart pulsing at its usual tempo and realize my breathing is back down to normal. I give Sam a quick squeeze to let him know I'm alright. He lifts his cheek from the top of my head and loosens the embrace. "I'm sorry," I whisper, embarrassment rising to the surface as it does every time I midjudge or flake out over nothing.

"Never apologize to me, Aves." Sam strokes my hair one last time. "You know Kira would never hurt me, right?"

I nod solemnly.

"You know she would never hurt you, either, right?"

I shake my head slightly, because what was I gonna do, lie? Of course Kira would hurt me. Perhaps not right this minute, but given any change in her relationship with Sam, she is just like everyone else. Sam misinterprets my answer, perhaps intentionally, and steps back, a half-smile on his face. "There ya go, then," he says. "Not a reason in the world to worry about this again. It's all okay."

Again I nod, ready to get on with the rest of the day. Actually, I just want to go to sleep, but I know that's off the table. Sensing my mood like he always does, Sam suggests I lay down on the couch while he and Kira reheat lunch. I nod again and Sam lets go of me completely. Seconds later, I'm wildly asleep on the couch.

***

It's summer. The heat of the day beckons me to come play. The neighborhood kids are next door, playing on Andrew's new Slip-n-Slide. I meticulously check my room to ensure that all is clean. Clothes are either hanging neatly in the closet or folded crisply in the dresser, dirty ones are tidily folded in the hamper in the closet. All dust bunnies have been chased away and my bed is as well-made as a seven-year-old can do. Nervously, I check to make sure the bedspread is even on all three sides. That was what set Carl off last time—the foot of the bed was uneven. By the time he was finished teaching me how to do it correctly, I couldn't sit for several hours. I was covered in bruises and welts from the middle of my back to just above my knees. I desperately want to avoid that now. All I want in the world is to go play in the Slip-n-Slide. The shouts and giggles and screams from next door threaten to make me sloppy, but I know one mistake is all it will take to ensure I can't go outside for weeks—certainly not in just shorts.

I open my bedroom door just as I hear Carl come into the house. He's been in the garage all morning, working on his car, no doubt drinking lots of beer. It's always worse when he's drinking, but I tell myself this time it'll be okay. I've done my chores and cleaned my room perfectly. He can't find fault with anything. Today I can prove to him I really am a good boy.

I try so hard.

I should know better. I've been told I'm a worthless, pathetic bastard enough times it should have sunk in by now. But still I have to hope, because I really do want to be a good boy. I just want Carl and Mom to love me, even when I make mistakes. Because that's all they are, mistakes. I never *try* to be bad or wrong, it just sort of happens and I have no control over it. I know I can do better. I just have to try harder.

I'm two steps from the kitchen when I hear the jeering tone in Carl's voice as he mocks Mom for something. I can't make out the words, but I should know by now to disappear. Unfortunately, the siren song of the Slip-n-Slide is far too powerful for a seven-year-old to resist. It overpowers my sense of caution. Besides, I know I've done everything right for once. Still, my breathing goes shallow and the buzz starts in my ears. I know they're going to fight and I know I should avoid that kitchen at all costs, but...please. I just want to play with the other kids. Please. It's so nice outside and I've been a good boy, I promise.

The roar in my ears drowns out their words, but I hear Mom and Carl shouting. My feet keep moving me into the kitchen out of that desperate need to be a regular little boy for just one afternoon, for just a few hours. Please, oh, please.

Just as I enter the kitchen, Carl backhands Mom with all his might, sending her stumbling back several paces right into me and the wall. I hear glass shatter and I know there's my mistake. I was in the room when it happened; therefore, it's my fault. I watch, absolutely vibrating in fear as Mom pulls her bloodied hand away from her face. My eyes immediately focus on the glass shards sparkling innocently on the linoleum floor, almost willing them to jump back together so I can avoid what is unquestionably coming next.

"You ungrateful little son of a bitch!" Carl bellows venomously at me. "You made your mother break that glass! *Look at me when I'm talking to you, boy!*"

I'm already bawling when I feel him grab a handful of my hair, wrenching my head up so I have no choice but to look at him. I feel more than see his arm cock back. The instant my fear-filled child's eyes meet his hate-filled adult ones, his fist smashes into my cheek.

***

"Avery!"

Sam's voice chases away the nightmare, but it takes a moment to realize I'm still screaming and crying. *Will these nightmare memories ever go away?* I silence the scream, but bury my face in Sam's shoulder as I continue to cry. I'd forgotten that particular beating, but I remember it vividly now. It was the first time Carl broke my orbital bone, but it wouldn't be the last. Two days later, Mom took her "clumsy" boy to the doctor. I'd fallen out of a tree and landed on a rock, of course.

Who wouldn't believe that of a boy who'd already broken his arm doing the same thing?

Sam holds me tightly, rocking me until I finally cry myself out. He doesn't need to ask. Only two things make me scream in my sleep—Tommy Blevins and Carl. Sam's hands are gentle as he caresses my back and strokes my sweaty, tear-dampened hair.

It's only when Kira hands Sam a glass of water that I remember she's there. The embarrassment I'd felt earlier intensifies tenfold. I struggle fiercely to pull myself together. I know Carl can't hurt me anymore. He has no idea who or where I am. And Tommy…well, after August, I'm almost sure he knows better than to cross Sam again. I repeat the mantra over and over in my head: I'm safe. With Sam, I'm safe. When I've said it enough times I almost believe it, I disengage from Sam's protective embrace. I shiver slightly without his warmth enfolding me, but force a tremulous smile to my lips. "It's okay. I'm sorry."

Sam ruffles my still damp hair and rises from the couch. "No reason to be sorry, buddy. Just remember all of that belongs in the past. You're safe now. And today is Thanksgiving. Let's spend the rest of the day being thankful we have each other. You, me and Kira, the Big Three. Seriously, let's put some joy into the day so we can get more out of it, okay?"

I nod, not really sure what he's talking about, but it sounds better than sitting around thinking about Tommy or Carl.

Sam ruffles my hair again. "Go wash your face, little bro. You're a mess. Then come into the kitchen and get some of this amazing grub. Everything will look better on a full stomach."

Chapter 5 - December

If I can count on nothing else in my life now—aside from Sam, of course—I can still be grateful for Tuesdays, the slowest day of the retail week, even in the midst of holiday shopping. And so it is today, with only eleven shopping days left until the greatest of all charades, Christmas. And, of course, I still haven't yet purchased the few gifts I feel compelled to give each year: Sam, Molly, Kira, and her brothers Kyle and Kaleb. It's a short list, but those are the people to whom I owe something, some token of acknowledgement in this crazy holiday season.

I stare at the cappuccino maker in the break room, trying to remember how to get the beast to work. Not because I want one, but because I can't remember the steps. Molly has shown me the thing a handful of times, but I just couldn't ever summon enough will to commit it to memory. But now I think the new meds Kendall Moorhead has had Dr. Farris put me on are eating away my brain. They sometimes make me feel detached and as if I'm looking at the world through a fog, which makes it harder to access the stuff stored in my brain. I need to pack as much stuff in my leftover grey matter as possible.

Dr. Moorhead and her brain-eating pills have had at me for nine sessions now. The woman is absolutely certifiable herself. She has repeatedly assigned me homework—homework! From a shrink! Until this last project, I've been able to complete them without much effort. But I know she knows that, so this latest assignment is my punishment. As such, I'm avoiding it with every fiber of my being. Just the thought of what she wants me to do has me wishing I could find a melon baller for what's left my brain so I could just scoop out the memories she so desperately wants me to write about. She wants me to write down the most important memories of my childhood and then tell her how I feel about them, the lessons each taught me, et cetera. She even gave me a stack of index cards with the questions she wants me to answer about each memory. It's going to be a long process; she wants me to concentrate on five memories each week.

These sessions have been difficult and painful, just as she and Sam promised they would be. Dr. Moorhead claims that with each appointment I keep we're making progress, but I don't see it. The only things I know for sure are that my anxiety levels top out before Sam arrives to drive me to the good doctor's office and that when the sessions are over, I'm so emotionally wrung-out that I go immediately to bed to nap for several hours.

Dr. Moorhead feels it is her mission to discover every one of my painful, buried memories. She claims that only by exposing them to the light of day can she—we—learn the real lesson from each of them. She is convinced none of the abuse Carl or Tommy or even Mom meted out was my fault. She claims Mom started out with all the right intentions—to be a good wife and mother—but that something outside of her control changed and she coped as well as she could, which, unfortunately for me, wasn't nearly good enough. I know Dr.

Moorhead thinks my dad's death was the catalyst for this change, but I don't know. I can't remember.

I don't know how she can know these things considering she's never met the woman who so reluctantly gave birth to me, but if it makes her feel better to say so, then who am I to argue? In my opinion, the sheer number of times my mother told me she wished I'd never been born refutes Dr. Moorhead's opinion, professional or not.

Finally, I give up trying to figure out the cappuccino machine and head back out to the task I'd abandoned a few minutes ago. The social sciences section needs straightening and restocking as badly as I need to stop thinking about my therapy sessions.

It is just Brian and me for the moment. Molly is off today. Tracy and Matt, the new seasonal part-timers are at lunch down the street. The sound of a familiar voice breaking into laughter causes a hitch in my step. Involuntarily, I look toward the checkout area.

Noah. It's been almost three weeks since I told him I wasn't interested in being his friend. In that time, I've seen him maybe half a dozen times, but only for a fraction of a second each time. The first time was in the alley, as usual. He was walking from the parking lot to his dock, just like the first time I'd seen him. Just like that first time, he was chattering away into his cell phone. And just like that first time, he slid it into his pocket just a few feet from me. But so very unlike that first time I laid eyes on Noah Yates, I felt no fear. I didn't try to make myself smaller so he might not notice me. Just like the first time, he didn't break stride. He merely offered a quiet, "Morning, Avery," as he walked right on by. I had breathed a sigh of relief laced liberally with disappointment. It had taken me days to recognize that second emotion. No one would ever confuse me with someone who desires attention, but I realized I've grown accustomed to being cheerfully hounded by the man. Even if I wanted—no, still want—him to leave me alone, his sudden and complete compliance with that request continues to surprise me.

Truthfully, as much as I would deny it to anyone who asked, I sort of miss the man. He is relentlessly perky and as persistent as a bad rash, but there's also something very Sam-like about him. As enormous and obviously powerful as he is, there is within him a gentleness that chips away at the majority of my fears and anxieties. Honestly, I could have worse-looking men trying to give me their attention, not that his looks have anything to do with anything.

Since that first sighting after he agreed to leave me alone, the most acknowledgement of my presence he's given is a slight nod in my direction or a casual wave as he walked by. One voice in my head screams that simply isn't good enough, while another begs me to just let Noah Yates fade into my past before we find out about the flip side to his gentleness. It's there, that flipside. It has to be; it always is. While I silently agree with the voice urging me to ignore Noah, I am somehow unable to do so.

I almost give in to the urge to look down at my feet as they propel me toward the registers up front where Brian and Noah are in conversation. I resist only barely, and only because my eyes are so greedily taking in the sight of him. He's dressed differently today, in khaki slacks and a deep brown turtleneck sweater that hugs his body like a second skin, showing off the width of his shoulders and the sleek narrowness of his waist. The huge biceps that a month ago had me recoiling in fear just look powerful and strong today. The things those slacks do for his butt should be criminal—or a requirement for every pair of men's slacks. Surprised at the track of my thoughts, I round the corner to the safe zone behind the counter and feel heat rising to my face. I glance over as if I'd only just noticed the big galoot is there. I force a shy smile to my lips before I turn and bend over to look in the cupboard behind Brian for…Ah! Windex. Yes, I'm in search of Windex. To…uh….

I've totally tuned out their conversation, though I'm vaguely aware it has something to do with *X-men.* It's only when I hear Noah tell Brian it's time for him to leave that I realize my mistake. I'm facing away from him with my head hidden away in a cupboard. Not exactly the easiest way for him to begin a conversation. But by the time I pull my head out of the cupboard, the front door is closing behind him.

My stomach drops to my shoes as disappointment almost overwhelms me. I lean back against the counter, the Windex bottle still in hand, and try to stop my head from spinning. *This is what you wanted, Avery,* I tell myself. *Stop flaking out and be glad. Remember how much it hurts when they finally figure out what you're good for.*

"Man," Brian says, "I don't know what you did to him but you should try to fix it."

"What?" I'm so taken aback I actually meet Brian's blue gaze. "I didn't do—I didn't do anything!"

He frowns. "Really? Because he was just fine until you showed up. Then he bolted like a spooked horse."

I meet Brian's gaze again and hold it for a heartbeat longer than last time. Kendall Moorhead would be so proud. "His break was over?" I offer by way of explanation.

"Dude, he isn't working today. Didn't you notice? No uniform."

My mouth opens and closes a couple of times, but I have no words to offer. Instead, I shrug, put the Windex down on the counter and stare at the worn pattern of the carpet. "I didn't do anything," I repeat, more to myself than to Brian. But I wonder if maybe I did.

***

"So what do you want to do today?" Sam asks over breakfast.

Unsurprisingly, he was up and around before me. Typical of those mornings, he made us breakfast. Banana pancakes, bacon and hash browns. Orange juice for me, water for him, so his peanut butter-slathered pancakes don't stick to his mouth. How he eats that stuff, I'll never know. I keep to the traditional maple syrup, which I also pour liberally all over my hash browns, much to Sam's disgust.

At his question, I chew faster, swallow hard and ask the stupidest question of the day. "You're off, too?"

Sam smiles widely. "Yep. And I've scheduled Avery Time all day."

It's ridiculous, I know, but I have to be practically glowing with happiness. Aside from Thanksgiving, which doesn't really count because of Kira, this is the first day we've had off together in months.

It's not that I resent Kira for taking up so much of Sam's time, because I really don't. He deserves to be happy and Kira helps push him over into that almost-giddy zone. But I do miss being able to spend large blocks of time with him. After all, not counting the year he was away before liberating me from state custody, we've practically been joined at the hip since the first day we met.

Not in any sort of sexual sense. Sam has always been the straight older brother in our relationship, where I've been the asexual younger one. I've always known I'm gay. It was never a question, strangely enough. Just as it has never been a question that I won't—cannot—act on the vague interests I have in men. There is just no way I can possibly let myself be that unguarded. With only a few exceptions—Sam, the K's, and Molly—touch means pain. Tommy Blevins taught me the final lesson Carl's beatings had been building up to. And then there's August to try to forget.

Before I let my mind carry me into those dark memories, I force all bad thoughts from my brain and concentrate on the really important thing—that Sam and I get to spend the day together, just us doing something fun.

I beam a smile at him. "Can we go to Go-kart World? And the comics shop?"

Sam nods with a smile. He knows me so well. The only time I really let loose is at Go-kart World. And I only want to go there when I'm already in a great mood. Sam's always up to go there, so it's an easy sell.

"And maybe have dinner at IHOP?"

Sam laughs. “Easy, slugger. You and I both know that by the time we get done at Go-kart World, you won’t have room for dinner.”

I agree with a shrug. In addition to the go-karts with three awesome indoor tracks, the gargantuan complex also has mini-golf, bumper cars for the kids, and the best cotton candy I’ve ever tasted. Right next to the video game arcade is a pretzel shop with amazing hotdogs and corndogs. It isn’t the kind of place I go often. Most days it’s chock full of people, from toddlers to Q-tips, the white-haired brigade of grandparents, with a majority of the patrons being in their teens. But every now and then, with sufficient pharmacological preparation and a good enough mood, I’m able to find enough strength to enjoy all the offerings.

***

The noise. The crowd. The thrill. It’s all so unlike me, but I so seriously love this place, if only for a few hours at a time. There’s just something about the control I have when I’m in one of the go-karts. It’s one of the few times I get to be in total control. The huge, heavy helmet conceals my identity from the other racers, so no one knows it’s the human punching bag who just smoked them in the race.

It’s my time to relax and have fun. I know I’m safe here. Not just because Sam is with me, but because Kira’s two brothers own the place. They love Sam almost as much as Kira does, which means they watch out for me just like Sam. It’s strange and it made me nervous the first few times we were here after Sam and Kira started dating, but now it's almost like having three Sams.

But for some reason, when I walk in here, none of that matters. My only concern is getting Sam and me into suits, helmets, karts, and a race as soon as possible. I would never consider myself a competitive person, but when it comes to karting, it's like Avery disappears and my dad's son comes out. He named me Tucker after his grandfather, some big war hero. Here, in this building, about to go to go-kart war, I feel more like the Tucker my father must have envisioned when he named me than I ever did growing up. The kid with mental and physical scars from a lifetime of beatings seems to fade. It's a thrilling release, even though I know it's only temporary.

Sam squeezes my shoulder and I turn a big smile up at him. "Race, cotton candy, race, hot dog, golf, race. Is that about right?"

I laugh. "And maybe a race in the arcade before we leave?"

Sam laughs this time. "Alright. I'll meet you at track three. I'm going to go say hi to Kyle and Kaleb."

I nod and take off to the equipment rental counter. Maybe one of these days I'll buy my own suit and helmet, but not quite yet.

***

There's more to racing a kart than hitting the accelerator and steering the corners. A driver has to learn or know when to coast, when to break and when to hit the accelerator again. But most of all, he has to be aware of the other drivers and the barriers at dangerous speeds up to fifty miles per hour.

Usually, Kyle gives the racers a brief rundown and last second safety tips, those he hasn't already given the novices in their pre-race training, but today that's Kaleb's job. He laughs and rolls his eyes at me when he sees me bouncing on the balls of my feet. I smile back at him, ready to get the show on the road. I've already smoked Sam in the first two races. Now I'm looking for complete victory. I know this one will be tough. This is the course he always beats me on, but today I'm feeling lucky. I know I'll win.

Five minutes later, Kaleb comes by to check my seatbelts, a huge smile on his face. "You ready, kiddo?" he asks, tugging on my shoulder strap.

I nod enthusiastically under the heavy, hot helmet.

He draws back to look at me and I meet his blue gaze without a second thought. "When Sam marries my sister, are you gonna come live with me? I'll take good care of ya." He winks to show he's joking. I laugh and shake my head. Kaleb always flirts shamelessly with me. If he wasn't already in a long, happy relationship with Josh, I might worry, but Kaleb is the one man besides his twin brother Kyle who I know is low-risk enough I don't have cause for concern. Neither is as harmless as Sam, but I know they care and they look out for me.

Noah.

I shiver as the thought of him slams into the front of my brain. Harmless is definitely not a word that would describe him. He may be trying to show me his beatific side, but anyone that powerfully built is definitely not harmless. Even Sam has had to prove on occasion that he can and will inflict harm on those who cross his carefully drawn lines. It makes my skin crawl to know that most of the hurt he has put on others is because of me.

Kaleb starting my kart's engine startles me out of those dangerous thoughts and I turn my brain back to the race. Lifting my hands to the steering wheel shows they're trembling slightly. I take a deep breath and roll my shoulders back, trying to keep loose and relaxed. When the light flashes green—go!—I slam down the accelerator.

This race is five laps along a twisty path that resembles a Formula 1 track in Spain. It's by far the most nerve-racking and fun track here. It takes incredible concentration and nerves of steel to avoid the other eleven drivers, the walls and pylons. Sam and I exchange leads on the first two laps before another driver overtakes us both and I completely forget about Sam. It takes everything in me but I catch up to the third driver on the next to last turn, pass him on the outside of the last one and put a kart length between us by the end of the last straightaway. *Victory! Heck yeah!* I beat Sam and this mystery driver!

The driver unbelts himself and steps out of the kart. He is enormous, tall and muscular. I hope he has a sense of humor. I unbuckle my helmet, watching his efforts mirror mine. Sam's huge hand clamps down on my shoulder as I lift the heavy helmet off my head.

"Great race, champ! I can't believe you beat me!"

I grin at him over my shoulder and glance back at my nemesis from the race, the devilishly witty comeback dying in my throat at the sight of Noah Yates's stunned expression.

His surprise gives way faster than mine. A huge grin spreads his lips wide for a moment before I see his eyes flick to Sam. He crosses the empty area between us before I can fully comprehend he's here. He kneels a few feet away, stopping to redo the perfectly good loop in his shoelace.

"Nice driving, sport," he says, grinning up at me.

My gaze finds my feet and I take notice of my racing heartbeat, much more the product of seeing Noah than from the excitement of the race. "Thanks," I say quietly. I realize with a shock that I'm not feeling afraid, only shy.

"I'm Noah Yates," he says to Sam.

My gaze flashes between the two of them and I swear I see two feral animals taking each other's measure.

"Sam Kenyon. How do you know Avery?"

If the earth opens and swallows me whole right now, my only hope is that it doesn't take these two with me. I know I'm not imagining the hostility in Sam's voice, the extra pressure his hand is using to grip my shoulder.

But Noah only grins disarmingly. "I work at the furniture store right next to Flip the Page. Avery and I met a couple of months ago."

I feel the recognition hit Sam's body, but his grip doesn't loosen and his stance doesn't soften. "I see. Those were some pretty slick moves," he says, meaning the race. Or at least I think he means the race.

Apparently Noah doesn't think so, because he chuckles. "Don't worry. My only slick moves are on the kart track." A new thought seems to slam into his brain. "I'm sorry. Are you two together?"

"No!" I answer the same time Sam does.

"Yes."

My gaze finds Noah's confused hazel one for a split second before I mumble in the direction of the floor. "I—I mean Sam's my brother."

Noah finally rises cautiously to his feet and I recognize once again just how tall he is. Strangely, though, in this setting, with Sam by my side and Kyle and Kaleb nearby, Noah's immense size doesn't fill me with terror, not even with my usual wariness. Here, it's just nice to see another friendly face, even one I've just whipped soundly in a race. He moves closer and slowly extends his hand to Sam. "It's very nice to meet you, Sam," he says.

"It's nice to put a face to the name," Sam concedes as he shakes Noah's hand firmly.

Noah flashes me a cheeky grin. "You've been talking about me?"

I don't know what comes over me besides the heat of a blush, but I roll my eyes and say, "I might have mentioned that you keep bugging me on my breaks."

Noah laughs delightedly, while Sam simply stares at me in shock, surprised, I suppose, that I would talk to a relative stranger that way. "I'll take any win I can get," Noah says and I know he's talking about more than the race.

"Listen," Sam says, "Avery and I were about to go get another hotdog. Would you like to join us?"

I turn surprised eyes to my brother, who merely smiles down at me like it's the most natural request in the world, and maybe it is—in someone else's world, but not mine.

Noah seems to sense my mood again. "I'd love to, but that was my last race. I really need to get going. Maybe a rain check?"

"Absolutely," Sam says, extending his hand again. "It was very interesting meeting you, Noah. I look forward to seeing you again."

Noah grasps Sam's hand. "Likewise, Sam. Take good care of our friend here. See ya, champ." He lightly tousles my slightly damp hair, the very first time he's ever touched me. My scalp tingles where his big hand touched it and I gasp, not in fear, but in complete surprise. With a quick nod in my direction, Noah turns on his heel and departs. I can't stop watching him walk away. It's like the sway of that perfect butt has me hypnotized.

"Earth to Avery."

"Huh?" I tear my gaze away from Noah's behind just as he rounds a corner out of sight and focus again on Sam, or try to. My mind keeps replaying Noah's retreat in vivid color.

"*That* is the guy you were all worried about a while ago?"

I frown, trying to follow the question. My scalp still tingles from Noah's touch, so I run my hand through my long, dark hair to fix that. "Oh. Yeah."

Sam looks down at me, a mysterious tilt to one side of his mouth. "Interesting." He nods in the direction of the food court. "Why don't you go get us some food and I'll meet you there in a bit. I want to have a quick word with Kaleb."

A few minutes later Sam straddles the stool across the table from me. I push his hotdog and fries at him without looking up. "I don't think you have to worry about Noah. I think he's one of the good guys."

Startled out of my thought of Noah, I gape at him. "You can tell that from five seconds of conversation?"

Sam laughs. "I'm a cop. It's what I do. Actually, I asked Kaleb about him. It seems they've known each other since they were little kids. They grew up across the street from each other. Kaleb considers him one of his best friends."

"Oh." I'm not sure what to make of this new information, but it surprises me that Noah knows the K's. It shouldn't; for all its population, this really is a small town. I roll my eyes again, desperate to change the topic of conversation. I never intended for Sam and Noah to meet. Now that they have, I want to erase him from Sam's mind as quickly and completely as possible. "So after we eat, do you want to try winning a race in the arcade?"

"Geez. You're relentless today!" Sam shakes his head in mock disgust but takes a big bite of his hotdog and I relax a little, knowing the competition is back on.

***

The rest of the day goes by so fast. Sam and I stop off at the comics shop where I spend a small fortune. We have an early dinner at IHOP so I can indulge my love for stuffed French toast. And through it all I only think of Noah Yates when Sam asks about him. And every third minute after that.

It was such a surprise to see Noah outside of the bookstore. It's almost as if I had convinced myself he didn't exist outside my store and his. I rarely run into people from the store outside of it, and it always catches me off guard when I do. I'm always at a disadvantage when it's a purely social moment; in the store, I have knowledge, so I have some sort of control. But Noah…Noah catches me off guard all the time.

Sam laughs and points out how I blush when I talk about Noah. It's true. I recognize that he's managed to get me to lower some of my defenses and that absolutely petrifies me. Sure, he may be a good guy. He may even be Sam-quality good. But I'm still me. Sooner or later he'll figure out what I'm good for and start using me as the punching bag I am meant to be. And for some reason, the idea of taking a thumping from Noah hurts my heart more than I know his fists and feet will hurt my body.

I shove away my still half-full plate of hash browns as the thought kills my appetite. I know I'm going to have to redouble my efforts to get Noah to leave me alone. I won't be able to live with it if he doesn't.

I fall asleep on the couch with Sam. We're supposed to be watching some new police drama movie with Geena Davis and Scott Evans, but I can't keep my eyes open. The excitement of the day has been too much, so incredibly good, that I doze off with my head on

Sam's thigh. I awaken when he lifts me from the couch. I wrap my arms around his neck and rest my head against his thick, solid chest, thankful again that my own personal Superman decided all those years ago that I may be poison, but I'm not Kryptonite.

Sam sets me on my feet beside my bed and ruffles my hair. "Don't forget to brush your teeth, sleepyhead."

I nod sleepily, pulling my shirt over my head. "Sam?"

"Yeah, buddy?" He turns at the door and smiles at me.

"Today was awesome. Thank you." I busy myself with my belt buckle so I don't have to see the expression on his face. My sudden shyness with him doesn't make much sense to me, except that I'm afraid I don't tell him thank you often enough.

"It was great for me, too. Well, ya know, except the part where I lost every single race to my bratty little brother."

He laughs but I already know he's joking. Winning has never been an obsession with Sam. He enjoys the competition much more than the victory—for himself, anyway. But he always, always makes a big deal out of my victories, even if they are at his expense.

I grin at him. "I got lucky on the last one."

"Yeah, sure. Lucky. You beat your new friend, too. That had to feel good. Gotta be getting tired of beating me."

I shake my head and drop my jeans. "He's not my friend."

Sam's brows draw together in confusion. "He's not?"

I step out of the pool of clothes at my feet, deliberately leaving them there until I come back from the bathroom. Then I'll put them in the hamper in my closet, but I will not fold them. I haven't folded my dirty clothes since Sam took me out of state custody. It's less rebellion against Carl than unlearning a bad habit—or so I tell myself. "He's just someone I know."

I look up from putting paste on the toothbrush to find Sam watching me from the bathroom doorway, a quizzical expression on his face. "Aves…I know you don't have many friends…"

I look down, suddenly uneasy and somewhat sad. "I can't have friends, Sam," I whisper.

He reaches out and gently squeezes my bare shoulder, causing my gaze to find his in the mirror. "You do have friends. You have me and the K's and Molly. I think you're safe to let this one in, too, little bro. What's his—Noah clearly wants to be your friend."

I shake my head and try hard to quash the rising panic. "I can't."

Sam smiles and squeezes my shoulder again before pushing off the doorjamb and walking away. His words drift back to me. "Take a chance. Talk to Kendall about it. I don't think you're gonna have much choice."

Chapter 6 - December

My shift on Thursday went by without so much as a passing sighting of Noah Yates, not that I was keeping track. Today, however, he's outside when I go out for my lunch break. He's sitting in his usual spot across the alley from my bench. He must have noticed the surprise in my eyes because he grins sheepishly and puts down the smallish piece of wood he's been messing with.

"I swear, I'm not stalking you," he says.

I shrug and sit on the bench. "I'm beginning to think you live in this alley."

He laughs. "It must seem that way. We're pretty slow at the moment. Not too many people wanting delivery this close to Christmas."

I nod, not really sure how to respond, or even if one is necessary. I take a drink of my ever-present Frappuccino and study the pavement between my feet. As often as I look at it, one would think I'd be able to see the differences in it from day to day, but, really, it's just an intriguing mess of cracks strewn with an assortment of tiny and little rocks.

Noah clears his throat and my eyes dart to his solid chest. Once again, he's wearing that blue plaid flannel shirt that has become my favorite. Does he know that? Does he wear it so often because of that?

I roll my eyes at the ridiculousness of my train of thought and tune back in to his words.

"...It was very impressive."

Confused, I ask, "What was?"

"Your driving the other day. Man, I never would have expected that crazy good driver to be you. You're very aggressive out there."

I blush but can't keep the smile from my face. "Thanks. I love it. You were pretty good, too."

Noah laughs and the sound warms me from the inside out. "Not as good as you, apparently. We'll have to have a rematch sometime. Let me get my honor back."

My gaze slams to the concrete again. The warmth of a minute ago turns to a chill in an instant. I should have known better. He thinks I humiliated him. Of course he's going to want revenge. The sudden violently cold breeze causes tears to flood my eyes. "I'm sorry," I whisper, knowing it won't be enough but hoping with everything in me that Noah Yates is actually the man he pretends to be. My pulse kicks up and my breathing shallows, preparing my body to run.

"Don't be sorry. You won fair and square."

His words and tone are calm and reassuring, but it's too late. I feel myself hit flight mode. I have to get away, but my legs refuse to heed my brain's commands. I stare at Noah's chest, tears rolling down my face, just waiting for his next move, the one that will punish me for winning on the kart track.

Instead of coming at me, though, Noah stays completely still. Only his chest moves, rising and falling with his breath and his words. "Hey,

hey. Don't cry. It's not that big a deal. I get beat on the track all the time."

His words should make me laugh and I honestly believe that's what he's trying to do, but I don't understand why. Why is he being so nice about this? Why isn't he making me feel bad for winning or for crying like a baby? None of it makes sense and, in my confusion, my tears come harder.

"Breathe for me, Avery. Just breathe. It'll be okay. I'm not going to hurt you. That's it…in…out…slowly…in…out…"

After a few minutes of his composed coaching, my fear recedes with the tears and I'm mostly just wary and wrung-out, my usual state of being. I venture a quick glance into those amazing hazel eyes and see only sincere concern.

"I'm sorry," Noah says softly. "I thought we were past this by now. I keep forgetting you're sometimes still afraid of me. But I promise I will never, ever hurt you."

Don't make promises you can't keep! my mind screams at him, but I only nod and concentrate on breathing. Perhaps one day I'll be able to trust him, but I haven't reached that point yet and I may never.

"That's my guy," Noah says softly and even I recognize the pleased tone in his voice, the smile I'm too embarrassed and shy to look up and see. "Another win."

A few beats of silence pass before he speaks again. "So, Christmas is coming up pretty soon, huh? Do you and Sam have big family plans?"

I shake my head, forcing away all the images that try to fill my mind. Christmases long past: a couple of good ones, but mostly selections of bad and worse. "We don't have any family," I answer quietly.

Noah brings his knees up, leans his chest on them and wraps his long, strong arms around his shins. I notice with fascination that as his shirt obeys the call of gravity and falls away from his chest, I can see a sprinkle of golden chest hair shimmering against his smooth, tight skin. I want to look away, but I'm fascinated by the thought of how that hair and that skin would feel against my fingers.

I feel heat race in my face at the track my thought are taking. I know I have to get those thoughts out of my head. It's far too dangerous to have them out there where any change in my demeanor could alert Noah to them. I take a quick drink of the slowly warming Frappuccino and try to pull my mind out of the gutter.

"I'm willing to share my family, if you want some more. My little brother's a pain in the ass right now, but he's a good kid. I guess it comes with being fourteen. I thought I knew it all then, too."

I grimace at the thought. Plenty of fourteen-year-old punks have been in and out of the bookstore. Not a single one of them would I want to claim to know, much less be related to.

Noah laughs. "You know, it might be perfect. You'd never have to speak again. We can't get Luke to shut up."

I giggle, thinking of Sam at that age. There was only one sure-fire way to get him to shut up—and to blush fiercely. "Ask him about girls."

The sound of Noah's answering laugh is cut off by the noise of the store's back door opening. Still giggling, I look up to see Sam staring at me as he comes out the door. His gaze quickly takes note of Noah sitting across the alley laughing. The stunned and confused expressions that cross Sam's face, especially when compared to the mental image I'd just had of the guilty, embarrassed expression on his fourteen-year-old face, cause me to dissolve into a genuine giggle fit. I'm beyond help; I can't control it.

Sam steps fully out the door and stares at me like he's never seen me before. Then he strides over to Noah, who is laughing harder now, probably because of my giggles, and offers his hand. After a quick glance my way, Noah shakes Sam's hand but remains seated on the cold, cracked concrete.

"Noah, right?" At his nod, Sam continues. "It's nice to see you again, I think. What did you do to this one," he indicates me with a toss of his head, "give him laughing gas?"

My giggle fit intensifies as Sam looks back at me, totally mystified.

Noah grins up at him. "Honestly, I have no idea. We were talking about Christmas and my little brother and he just started doing this." He looks at me again and his laughter starts anew. "I don't know, man, but I'll take it."

Sam gapes at me for another minute before a smile finally chases the confusion from his face. "You know what?" he says to Noah. "I'll take it, too."

While those two talk about whatever it is they talk about, I attempt to end my insane little fit. I take great gulps of air and really concentrate on blowing them out slowly, bringing some regularity to the rhythm. Just when I think I've got it all worked out and under control, a loud hiccup starts the giggles racing again. It's the giggle, hiccup, "ouch," giggle, hiccup, "ouch," pattern that starts both of the guys into their own second round. Eventually the "ouch" becomes painful and I have to start the calming process all over again.

Finally, I mostly succeed and stare innocently up at Sam, trying desperately to ignore the occasional twitch in my lips. Oh, they want to go again, but I won't let them, silly things.

"Are you done?" Sam asks with far too much amusement in his voice.

I nod soberly, afraid I'll hiccup again if I so much as open my mouth.

"Good." He shakes his head, still fighting disbelief, I think. "Are you ready to go?"

"G—*hic*—o?" I parrot—sort of—and frown at the offending diaphragm spasm.

'Yeah. It's Friday. Time for your appointment."

I shake my head. "No. She's out of town so I'm off the hook, remember? I'm free until Monday next week because of the holiday, then Wednesday."

Sam nods. "Oh, that's right." Then he grins mischievously. "Although, from what I've just witnessed, you could use a session today."

I roll my eyes at him. "Laughter is the best medicine. *Reader's Digest* says so."

"Well, here are ten things *Reader's Digest* won't tell you—"

"Wait," Noah interrupts, moving to his knees. "Are you sick?"

And just like that, the joy of the moment is murdered in cold blood. My eyes find the concrete between my feet again and I study it hard, as if my gaze was forced there by a magnet. The last thing I want to talk to Noah Yates about is my need for, or the progress of, my therapy sessions. It's not that it would come as a surprise to Noah that I'm all sorts of messed up—he has met me—but I'm ashamed to admit to one more flaw before this man. He's so perfect, I can't imagine how he could possibly understand how the rest of us have issues that require outside intervention, even if it's a hopeless case like mine is. Despite Sam and Kendall Moorhead's best intentions, I cannot change who and what I am. I clamp my eyes shut, focusing on the fireworks behind my lids and shake my head.

"Avery?" It's Noah again, the alarm in his voice rising.

Another pause I refuse to fill. Finally Sam says, "He's in therapy."

The sound of Noah resettling into his usual spot allows me to reopen my eyes, but I dare not look up from the concrete.

"Therapy can be very useful," he says. "My brother and I went after our dad died a few years ago." Noah clears his throat. "My mom's a psychologist. I've learned a lot about people from listening to her. I mean, she didn't talk specifically about her clients, just about how we all have mental scars and how the different theories of treatment work for various issues. Uhm, anyway, therapy can be tough stuff, but I know that without it, I wouldn't be sitting here today."

Shocked, my gaze cuts to his. I drink in those hazel depths while trying not to think about what his words might really mean. The thought of Noah feeling the way Joey did is almost a physical pain. Before I can even process the thought, I whisper, "I'm glad you're here."

One of his coworkers chooses that moment to call his name. Noah groans. "Looks like they've found me. I gotta get back. Do you wanna go in first?"

I nod vigorously, glad to see the end of this suddenly too heavy conversation. I grab my Frap bottle from the bench next to me and get to my feet.

"Wait, Noah," Sam says, surprising me. "If you're not doing anything else or could carve out some time, Avery and I would love it if you'd come over for Christmas."

I gape at him, my mind at an absolute stand still. Never once would I have expected that invitation.

Noah grins broadly, first at Sam and then at me. "I'd love to," he says. "But only if you're okay with that, Avery. I'm pretty sure that would mean we're friends."

I look to Sam who encourages me by widening his eyes and nodding almost imperceptibly. My gaze flicks to Noah who waits patiently, not moving a muscle. I realize suddenly that I want this, too. Before I can change my mind, I nod and rush back inside the store, leaving the two big boys to figure out the logistics. *What have I done*, I wonder.

***

Sam won't let it go. Every chance he gets, he brings up Noah Yates. He grins as I stutter and stumble uncontrollably at the mention of Noah's name. Sam's not being mean, I know that much. He claims it's cute. I've never once in my life been called cute. Well, not to my face. I remember that's how Molly said Noah described me that first horrible day, but I'm sure that doesn't count.

Finally I've had enough. I throw a pillow at Sam, who's reclining on the other end of the couch. For all that it's called a "throw' pillow, it doesn't sail through the air very majestically. Of course, that could be because I throw like a three-year-old, but still. No aerodynamics at all. Fortunately, with the element of surprise, one doesn't need aerodynamics.

Sam peels the thing off his face and pretends to glare at me. "What was that for?"

"What is your obsession with Noah Yates?" I huff.

Sam quirks an eyebrow. "What's yours?"

"I don't have one."

He chuckles. "Oh, but I think you do."

"Seriously, what were you thinking inviting him here?"

"Avery, you were *giggling* when I found you with him. When's the last time you giggled about anything?"

I shrug, my impatience rising at the implication. "I don't know, last week?"

Sam rolls his eyes. "Try never in all the time I've known you. I didn't even know you *could* giggle. I mean, I like to think I'm a pretty funny guy sometimes, and you've *never* giggled at anything I've ever said."

"Maybe not to your face."

"Exactly."

I growl my frustration. "I can't be his friend, Sam. He's too big. Those muscles are designed to hurt people. I can't do it."

Sam sits up and runs a hand through my hair like I'm five years old again and grips my neck, bringing our foreheads together gently. "Of course you can be his friend. Haven't you noticed the way he is around you? He gets it, without you ever saying a word. He knows you already."

I pull back and shake my head, denying the truth I hear in Sam's words. If I refuse to acknowledge it, it can remain unknown, right? "He doesn't know a thing about me. He's no different from any of the rest of them, except that he'll hurt me worse than Tommy ever could, worse than—" My eyes drop to my lap as I finish the thought only in my head. *August. Worse than August.*

"Or he could be the next best thing that ever happens to you."

With a chilling certainty, I suddenly know what this is about. While terror gathers in my heart and tears pool behind my eyes, I look deep into Sam's eyes. He stares back with a curious expression, but I see my answer there. He's found his out.

Silently, I extricate myself from the couch and go to my room. Ignoring Sam's calls, I quietly latch the door behind me. I sit on the bed and bring shaking hands to my face. Sam intends to pawn me off on Noah so he can marry Kira guilt-free. I take a shuddering breath and move to the sanctuary of the closet as the tears come violently.

Chapter 7 - December

"Why do you feel that way, Avery?"

Sam's betrayal was so brutal it was all I could think about the entire weekend. After an extremely quiet two days around the apartment, it was the first thing I said to Dr. Moorhead when the session began.

My gaze flicks up to hers in disbelief. Did she not just hear me? "It's—it's obvious, isn't it?"

She frowns. "I don't know. Why don't you tell me?"

I clasp my hands together in my lap again, the anxiety level rising as I think it through. It's as clear as the freckles on my nose. Sam wants to marry Kira. He may not have said it in so many words, but they've been together so long it's easy to see they belong together. The only stumbling block to that plan is me. Sam won't want to leave me on my own unless he's absolutely sure I can handle it, which is why I'm here talking about my life to a shrink like I'm some lab experiment. But just in case this therapy stuff doesn't work out, he'll need a backup plan. Enter Noah Yates, Knight in Pilling Plaid Cotton.

Somehow, Sam has got it in his mind that Noah can replace him, be the new fake big brother. Not only is that ridiculous, but, if I'm honest, it hurts like hell that Sam could discard me when he's ready to move on.

I explain all this to Kendall and finish with the thought as it occurs to me. "The only difference between Sam and Mom is that Sam's never hit me."

"Don't you think that's unfair to Sam?"

I shake my head sharply. "No, it's the exact same thing. Mom had to get rid of me so Carl would marry her. Sam has to so he can marry Kira." The tears spring to my eyes as I realize that my entire relationship with Sam has been something completely different to him. Not all of it; not our time in state custody. Just the last couple of years since Kira came along and became his number one priority. Since then, he's been trying to figure out how to get rid of me, just like Mom did.

I haven't felt this kind of soul-ripping emotional agony since Joey died. Maybe now's the time. Maybe it would be best for everyone if I just join Joey. That way Sam and Kira can have their life together without Sam worrying about me. And I'll get to be with my best friend again. As for Noah, well, he won't have to break my heart by breaking my bones.

Who am I kidding? I'll never have the nerve to do what Joey did. I'm terrified of screwing it up. As much of a burden as I am to Sam now, I could never let him live with the guilt I know he'd feel if I botched a suicide—and I would; I screw up everything. Just my luck, I'd only be aware enough to know I failed and not be able to do anything about it.

But another thought skitters through my brain. I like Noah, I realize with some surprise. It's rare that I allow someone to get close enough to form that much of an opinion about them. Usually people fit into one of two categories: those who terrify me or those who will only cause mild anxiety. Sam, Molly, Kira, and the K's all fall into the third, exclusive category of people I like. Somehow Noah managed to cross the barrier from the terrify group into the like group.

"I would like to suggest you discuss this with Sam, Avery. Perhaps he has a different perspective on it. I'd venture to guess he thinks you building new friendships goes along with therapy, different but coordinating ways to help you become a healthier young man. If you don't feel safe talking to him about it one-on-one, I'd be happy to invite him in so you can discuss it with me here."

I scowl. "But he knows I don't do friendships. Sam's the only person I can really trust—and now I can't even trust him!" I'm selectively leaving out Molly and the twins because they don't count in this situation. I know I'm about to work myself into a genuine panic attack, but I can't seem to pull myself back. I stare out the office window and think about air flowing over my bare skin, try to force myself to believe I'm free and fine. But I can feel the World's Lumpiest Couch beneath me, the walls surrounding me. I close my eyes and breathe deeply for several minutes until the tide of panic seems to slowly recede.

I'm still keyed up and on the verge of completely losing control, but my grip on that control is stronger than it has been since I figured out Sam's plan. For the very first time, I look Kendall Moorhead in the eyes—hers are hazel, too, I realize, but a pale imitation of Noah's—and force steel into my voice. "You have to help me, Kendall. I'm not going to let Sam pawn me off on Noah, but I can't lean on Sam anymore either. I have to learn to cope on my own. I have to be strong enough."

Kendall smiles slightly. "That's always been the goal, Avery." She turns to her desk and begins writing while talking. "Okay, I'm going to give you some homework to do over the holiday. Our next appointment is the twenty-eighth. That gives you nine days to complete it. Are you ready?"

I take a deep breath, silently ask Joey for help, and nod.

***

I've been trying to avoid Noah since Sam's invitation five days ago. I've not taken my breaks outside, which irritates me because even if it is stupidly cold outside, it's *outside.* Inside, I've been amazingly successful at dodging him. The three times I saw him in the store, I managed to hang back in the stockroom or break room until he left. I should have known he wouldn't allow it for very long. The man's like a bad rash or a dandelion—he just keeps popping up again and again.

Even as his business seems to be slowing because of the impending holiday, the bookstore gets busier and the demands of the customers grow more and more bizarre and esoteric. I'm dealing with one of our more eccentric regulars when the chime above the door sounds for the four thousandth time of the morning. Annoyed by the sound, I glance up from my conversation with the exasperating Mr. Warner to see Noah beaming a huge smile in my direction. I hear myself stumble over a few words and take a calming breath, trying in vain to put Noah Yates and his kissable lips out of my mind.

"As I was saying, Mr. Warner, the 1911 *Encyclopaedia Britannica* is not something that is currently being published, nor is it something that anyone would just randomly turn in to us for our used book drive. I strongly suggest you contact collectable book dealers. You might even try eBay."

The aged and increasingly senile Mr. Warner draws together his incredibly bushy white brows and frowns at me. "So when can you get the entire collection for me?"

"I'm sorry, sir, but I won't be able to get it for you."

He narrows his rheumy eyes. "Then I want to speak to Molly. She's a sensible girl. She'll get it for me."

I sigh. "Molly won't be able to get it for you, either, sir."

He bangs his cane against the counter before me and I flinch but stand my ground. I don't have to be *too* fast to outrun a gimpy octogenarian, and I'm quite sure I can disarm him before he gets in more than one good strike. "I want Molly!" he demands brusquely.

Suddenly, he blinks at me and I recognize that he's somehow come back to himself. "Well, young Avery." He smiles widely. "How are you doing, young man?"

I cock my head at him as I return his smile. "I'm fine, Mr. Warner. How are you?"

He nods gamely. "Oh, fair to middlin'. Did you get that new Harry Potter book in yet?"

"That series ended already, sir, remember? Just seven books."

"Oh, of course. In a book store, ask about a book. I meant the last movie."

I smile. "Yes, sir. If you'll wait right here one moment, I'll go get it for you."

Mr. Warner waves dismissively. "Nonsense, young man. I'll just wander around a bit, maybe have a cup of coffee while I read a bit of my old friend Shakespeare. I'll get the movie on my way out."

"Make yourself at home, sir." He hobbles slowly away and I smile after him, more than slightly confused with the interaction with him, as usual.

I look over to see Molly executing a very un-gothlike bounce-and-skip over to me, a huge grin parting her black-painted lips. Inwardly I groan, knowing the cause of that expression on her face could be none other than Noah Yates.

She drapes herself across the counter dramatically. "Your boyfriend's here."

I roll my eyes. "I saw him."

Molly giggles—something else very un-gothlike. I wonder why she even keeps up the pretense. "So you admit you're interested in him."

"Give it up. It'll never happen."

She rolls onto her side to prop her head on her hand. "It could if you'd let it."

I turn my gaze to my feet, not really interested in having the conversation, but knowing it has to happen sooner or later. "Molly, there's absolutely nothing about me that would interest a man like

Noah Yates. The only thing he could possibly want me for is a punching bag."

"He's not like that."

I sigh but nod slightly. "No, he's not. At least I don't think so. But I can't really take that chance, can I?"

Molly frowns and stands up straight. "Avery, you're so wrong this time. I'm gonna get you to see it, I promise."

"Please leave it," I beg.

"Not a chance." She swings her long skirt around her ankles girlishly and looks at me through heavily-gooped eyelashes. "It's time for your lunch break. Noah's waiting for you to tell him it's okay to join you."

"*What?*" I squeak, feeling my heartbeat kick up.

"Don't worry. I'll hold your hand. Walter and Brian and Maya can handle the floor."

I shake my head as the blood leaves it. It's not that I'm afraid of Noah so much as that I'm afraid to be in that tiny room with him. Outside is fine. Even here on the sales floor is okay, if he keeps his distance. But that break room is so small—and Noah is going to take up so much space and air.

"Avery." The low, soothing sound of his voice washes over me like warm water. "It's okay. You know you don't have anything to fear from me, don't you?"

I nod. Somehow I believe it to be true, despite the voice in my head screaming about massive muscles and the sheer size of him. I mentally hush the frightened young boy in my brain and look up at

Noah's chest. "Don't you own any other shirts?" I snap, irritated more at myself than at him.

I can tell by the way he looks down at himself that my question took him by complete surprise. Then he laughs. "I have three exactly alike. They're my favorites. Don't you like them?"

They're my favorite things he's ever worn, aside from that one pair of jeans I absolutely will not think about. I take the chance on eye contact. His are literally sparkling with amusement and, for some reason, that irritates me even more. I shrug and look away. "They're okay, I guess."

He chuckles again. "Maybe someday I'll tell you why I wear them so often. So what do you say? Lunch?"

My eyes track back to his and I see the hope in them. How ridiculous is that? *Hope for what?* I chide myself. *That you'll break bread with him?*

"Consider it a trial run for Christmas," he offers with a smile.

That seals it. I have to do it now. I'll be able to use the time to convince him he shouldn't come for the holiday. Silently, I nod my acquiescence.

"Win!" he crows triumphantly. I throw him what I hope is a dirty look. Apparently I'm bad at them because he just laughs.

***

It isn't as terrifying as I thought it would be. The room is small, yes, but Noah chooses a seat at the far end of the table, leaving me the spot nearest the door. I don't know how he just instinctively *gets* these things about me—keeping his distance, trying to minimize his size, leaving me an option to escape—but there's no question that he does. Perhaps one of these days I'll feel comfortable enough to ask him. In the meantime, I listen with half an ear to the mindless conversation Molly has engaged him in while I pretend to concentrate on my beef enchiladas warming in the microwave.

I notice Molly has some weird vegetarian lasagna thing already warmed up, ready to go. She's digging in with gusto even as she peppers Noah with questions. I turn to see what the big man is having for lunch and sigh when I see two cold cut sandwiches on white bread, a small bag of chips, and a single-serving container of tapioca pudding.

When the microwave signals, I take my meal to my seat and sit down, covering my lap with a couple of paper towels. I glance up to find Noah staring at me with a goofy grin on his face. Immediately I go on the defensive. "What?"

"I feel like a grade-schooler here. You both have hot lunches and I have—" he indicates his disgusting lunch "—this stuff."

I frown. "Can't you cook?"

He laughs. "Nothing anyone would survive eating! No, that's not true. I can make pretty good chocolate chip cookies. But man cannot live on cookies alone. I know; I've tried."

Molly giggles and I laugh. Pointing to his supposed food, I ask, "Is this what you have for lunch every day?"

Noah shrugs. "Usually. Sometimes I have fast food or a can of soup or something like that."

Molly looks up from her grazing. "That's really a shame, Noah. You should take better care of yourself. Avoid meat. It's cruelty to animals. Plus, it makes you smell."

Noah blushes slightly. "Do I stink?"

"Ignore her," I jump in. "She's always trying to convert people to the vegetarian lifestyle."

She smacks my shoulder. "I am not. Well, maybe. But the point *is*, Noah obviously needs someone to look after him."

"What's that have to do with avoiding meat?" I challenge.

She crosses her eyes at me. "It doesn't, okay? I was just saying that one of the ways he can do better for himself is to not eat meat, especially that processed crap that passes for meat these days."

"I need lots of protein," Noah inserts.

Molly nods enthusiastically. "There are plenty of ways to get the protein you need without meat."

I look up in time to see the pained look on Noah's face and laugh. "Molly, the man likes meat. Leave him alone."

Both of them choke on their food. It takes me a minute to figure out why, but when I do my face heats fiercely. I stare down at my enchiladas like *they* did something wrong. Despite Noah's hearty laughter, I'm supremely embarrassed. I *never* make sexual innuendos, so this one was completely unplanned. I have no idea how to react, where to go from here. "I'm sorry," I mumble, still staring down at my food.

Noah struggles to stop laughing. "No, it's okay. I know you didn't mean it that way. But you're right in both cases."

I shiver suddenly as the confirmation of Noah Yates's sexuality washes over me. I've suspected that might be where some of his interest in me originated, but I've never been sure. Of course, just because Noah's gay doesn't mean he thinks of me that way. He could just think, wrongly to be sure, that I'd make a good friend for him.

I glance up as Noah takes a bite of his pathetic sandwich and shudder for a completely different reason. *No more*, a voice in my head says, and I completely agree.

Molly polishes off her veggie concoctions and goes to the refrigerator for her customary after-lunch ice cream. Not for the first time, I wonder about her affection for the dairy treat, but I'm not about to ask her how she justifies it. Either I don't understand vegetarianism or I don't understand her version. Regardless, I'm not in the mood for a full-on discourse about it. She sits back down around the corner from me and points between Noah and me with her spoon.

"I think it's really great that you're going to spend Christmas with Avery, Noah."

I blanch at the reminder, but Molly just plows on in her usual oblivious way. "He would never admit it, but he likes you a lot. And Sam and Kira are great. I think you'll have a terrific time."

Noah laughs in that easy way of his, even as I pray for my chair to swallow me whole. "Well, unfortunately, I won't have the whole day to spend with them. My grandparents and little brother and I are gathering for lunch at my mom's. But after that, I'll be free."

"Noah, Sam wouldn't want to take you away from your family," I rush to interject, seeing my chance. "You really don't need to abandon them just to see us."

"Oh, it's fine. After lunch the ladies go play cards down the street and grandpa and little brother will sleep away the afternoon pretending to watch football."

"But still, wouldn't you rather have the whole day with family?" I wince and yell "Ouch!" as Molly's boot connects with my shin.

Noah just shakes his head and smiles. "You're not getting away from me that easily. Besides, I already think of you as family. I'll be there with bells on, buddy. Count on it."

Chapter 8 - December

I have a memory of a Christmas at my grandparents' house from before my dad died. It's not really a memory of events so much as a sense memory. I can smell the old house. Houses built right after the Second World War have a peculiar smell to them. I don't know if it's the wood used to construct them or the particular varnish used in that era or what, but it's a truly special smell. It hints of permanence, of stability, and of happiness. I don't remember what my presents were that year, but for some reasons I remember sitting at the table with my mom and dad and his parents. In this misty, watercolor memory there are two things on my plate I can't get enough of—and one thing I never want to see again. The bad was stuffing, which was just too freaky for my little boy brain, mushy but crunchy at the same time, all while tasting suspiciously like wood.

But the two things I loved most I could only vaguely remember. Never once in the years of state care were we ever served anything like them again. So when Sam and I were preparing for our first Christmas after the group home, I searched the internet cooking sites furiously for hints about those two dishes. The only thing I had to go on were vague recollections of apples and oranges. I didn't find the recipes that first year and Sam was absolutely no help. I think he secretly felt I'd finally gone off the deep end. With that motivation, I was determined to find them before that second Christmas rolled around.

Finally, just after Thanksgiving that year, I found them in a church cookbook at the local library. I made the "apple-banana salad" that following Christmas, much to Sam's delight. It was the only homemade dish amid a bunch of Chinese food. The salad consists of apples, bananas, chopped walnuts, and maraschino cherries, all tossed in a sweet and tangy mayonnaise-based sauce. Sam loved it so much he will sometimes ask me to make it with no holiday in sight. The second dish I call Orange Fluff. It's a tapioca pudding-based dessert with whipped cream, mandarin oranges and a couple packages of Jell-O pudding. Sam wasn't so sure about that one since Mandarin oranges aren't his favorite thing. But I love it even more than the apple-banana salad. Its deliciousness brings back the good feelings and vague memories of being part of a loving family. Those dishes make me feel safe and cared for, even if I have to make them myself.

Seeing the blissful expression on Noah's face as he savored each bite of his tapioca pudding cup at lunch on Friday convinced me that he'd probably love the Orange Fluff. I refuse to look too deeply into why it's so important to me that he enjoys it. I'm chalking it up to being a good host. I may not really want him here today, but since he is so bound and determined to show his face, the least I can do is be sure there's something on the table I think he'll like.

Unlike the Orange Fluff, which I made yesterday and left in the fridge to set up, I have to make the apple-banana salad today. I'm not about to take a chance on serving Noah discolored fruit. The stuff the man shoves in his face is disgusting enough, he needs to see that cooking for himself is not only the healthier choice, but isn't difficult. Not that whipped cream, lots of pudding and mayonnaise are healthy, but I tell myself they can't be as bad as processed meats and white bread. Here I am, Mister Limited Menu, trying to turn someone else on to home cooking. Irony's not a very nice woman.

Of course, I'll never get the dang thing done if Sam doesn't stop swiping apple pieces. I smack his hand as he reaches into the bowl for the fortieth time. "Samuel Jackson Kenyon, I will cut off your hand if you do that again," I warn in my sternest voice.

Sam gapes at me like he's afraid, then smiles and ruffles my overlong hair. I really do need to get that mop cut, but I just hate, hate, hate people touching me, even that much. "Geez, Aves. Uptight much? Relax, buddy, Noah's going to have a great time."

I glare at him and throw a whole apple in his general direction. He lunges to the right to catch it. I shake my head and resume cutting, wondering why things never end up where I aim them. "Stuff that in your mouth, brat," I grouse around a hidden smile.

Sam takes a big noisy bite out of the Red Delicious and talks around it. "You're cute when you're nervous about a guy."

My knife stills instantly and I stare up at him, praying he won't see the pain in my eyes. He's starting the pawn-Avery-off stuff earlier than I expected. I figured he'd at least wait until the end of the day, after he'd seen how well or not Noah and I get along, but apparently that doesn't matter to his plan. "You invited him. Now I have to try to make him feel welcome."

Sam nods and takes another bite of apple. "Does it bother you that I invited him?"

I sigh heavily and push away from the table, needing space. I pretend I'm not freaking out, covering my tracks by retrieving a bottle of water from the refrigerator. "What's done is done," I say noncommittally.

Sam regards me for a minute, his head cocked to the side slightly. "Are you trying to tell me you don't like him?"

I shrug and pick up the small bag of walnuts that needs chopped. "He's okay."

Sam grins around a fresh bite of apple. "He's okay. Hmm." He turns to check the progress of the turkey in the oven. Why Sam has taken on the particularly unpleasant task of cooking the bird himself, I have no idea. Apparently the whole traditional holiday thing is really taking root in Sam's psyche, which is just another reason why I have to make this therapy thing work, or find a fool-proof way to be with Joey. Unfortunately, as far as I know, there is no fool-proof method. I'd find a way to mess it up, even if there was one.

"He seems really taken with you," Sam says, taking the last bite of his apple. He tosses the core into the trash like he's playing basketball.

I frown into my chopped walnut mess. "I don't know what you mean." My chest clenches and stars sparkle at the edges of my vision. He's really going to make me do this. Here in the kitchen, with me in sleep pants and a t-shirt, he's going to push the Pawning Avery on Noah subject. I'm so not prepared for this, not when I'm going to have to play nice with the both of them for the rest of the day.

Sam scoffs slightly. "C'mon, little brother. You have to admit he's different from everyone else. He understands how to interact with you in a way that not only doesn't scare you but puts you at ease. Well, as at ease as you are with anyone who isn't me." I refuse to look up when he pauses, but I hear the smile in his voice as he continues. "Face it, buddy, the guy's into you. You just have to decide what to do about it."

The starbursts increase. My shaking hands gather the finished walnuts and sprinkle them in the bowl. Tears spring to my eyes as my voice deserts me. "Please," I whisper. "Please stop pushing me at him." The pain of Sam's rejection slams into my chest, tightening the fist clamping down hard on my heart.

"What?"

Sam may be able to pretend he doesn't know what's going on, but I can't, not anymore. It's been tearing me apart for more than a week. I can't let it go now. I can't keep pretending it's not happening or that it's okay. He's taking away my one safe zone and it's killing me inside. My arms wrap around my waist, the way I wish Sam's would, except I'm the only person who can comfort me now. I feel the wet splat of hot tears on my arms and hate myself for being so weak.

Sam's warm hand covers my shoulder and I flinch away. I force my eyes open to see him kneeling beside me, shock losing the war with concern on his face. He leans forward to draw me into the safety of his arms, but with a shattered cry, I skitter away, coming to rest across the kitchen from him, the pain oozing from my heart and eyes.

He sits back on his heels. "Avery, what's wrong?" He sounds genuinely perplexed, and maybe he is because I'm sure he didn't expect me to figure it out so soon.

"D-don't pretend!" I beg.

"I don't know what you're freaking out about, buddy. All I wanna do is help like I always do. What's going on?"

The hollowness inside is so intense I feel like I might explode from it, just shatter into a million pieces. I'm not even sobbing. The numbness inside is so great the tears are simply flowing from my eyes. "You can't just hand me over to him," I cry.

"What? Aves—"

"You can't be like my mother! If you don't want me around anymore, then say so, but you can't just turn me over to Noah like Mom did."

Sam's eyes nearly bulge out of his head. "What are you talking about? Avery, I would never not want you around! You're my little brother! Jeez, I wouldn't know what to do if you weren't here with me."

I want to believe him. I want that so much, but his words don't explain his obsession with Noah and me. And there's Kira, too. I hug myself tighter and shake my head. "What about Kira? I know you want to marry her. Then I'll be on my own. I can do that, Sam. I don't need or want Noah to replace you. I'll be able to take care of myself, I promise."

Sam sighs as I cry and I think for the first time that I could actually hate him, not like I hate Carl or Tommy, but I could definitely hate him for doing this to me.

"Whoa, sailor, just slow down a little. Finally you're making sense." Sam draws his hands down his face like he does when he's completely exhausted and heaves another sigh. "Well, sort of." He stands and crosses the room to place his hands on my shoulders. I try to shrug him off, but he won't have it. "Listen very carefully, okay?" he commands, his voice that soothing tone that always calms me. When I nod he continues. "Yes, Kira and I will probably get married someday. I haven't asked and we haven't talked about it lately." I stare at his torso, halfway down, letting the rhythm of his even breathing steady me. "But we have talked about you. We're agreed that you always have a home with us, Aves. There is no way I would ever not want you to be with me if that's where you want to be. I love you, in case you've forgotten. You're as much a part of me as my right arm. Besides, we figure Uncle Avery equals a built-in babysitter when the time comes."

Sam's finger under my chin tilts my head back and I hesitantly meet his eyes. "As for Noah, I can see he likes you a lot. I think it's more than just like, but I don't want to freak you out any more right now. And, Aves, I know you like him, too. Kaleb says he's a good guy, and I can tell he treats you well, or he would if you'd let him. You deserve to love and be loved. Yes, in that way." I cringe and he laughs softly. "So if I'm pushing you toward Noah, it's not to get rid of you. It's because I can see the two of you could be happy together, if you would let him in."

Again, I shake my head. "That's not possible for me, Sam. You know it's not."

"I don't know anything of the kind and neither do you." He looks at me for a long moment during which I try to convey to him with my eyes everything I can't say with my tongue. Sam knows me, knows my history better than anyone. He should understand exactly why what he's proposing cannot happen. That's not who I am; it's not part of my destiny. I'm not fated to be some character in a gay romance novel-like love story. As much as that hurts—because wouldn't that really be nice?—I know I'm much more like the Beagle dogs laboratories keep in kennels for testing purposes. My purpose is much more to be used and abused for someone else's enjoyment than my own. Finally Sam sighs, seeming to deflate just a little. "At least try to be his friend, Avery. You could always use another friend, especially one who makes you break out in random fits of giggles. Promise me you'll try."

Hesitantly I nod, wondering what the heck I'm thinking. For all Sam's good intentions, we both know that a distant friendship is all I'm capable of where Noah's concerned, and that might even be stretching the limits of my abilities.

"Good," he answers with a smile and pulls me into a tight embrace. Sam places a kiss in my hair and squeezes me once before he lets go to look me in the eye. "Remember I love you, little bro. When there's nothing else in the world you can count on, you'll always have me. Nothing and no one will ever change that, okay?"

I smile around fresh tears. "I love you, too, Sam."

He grins and steps away. "I know you do, buddy." On his way out of the kitchen he swipes a few more pieces of fruit from the bowl. I just shake my head and resume chopping walnuts.

Alone in the kitchen I ponder Sam's words. He was as genuine as I've ever seen him, but I'm still not sure. The fears of abandonment and rejection are almost overwhelming at times. As far as I know, Sam has never lied to me, but his interest in seeing Noah and me together is far too convenient to only be about finding me a new friend. My hands shake with uncertainty so I abandon the last of the unchopped walnuts, throwing them in the waste bin. The last thing I need is to lose a finger because I can't stop thinking about Noah Yates.

Even after the conversation with Sam, I know with certainty that I have to recommit to making this therapy thing work, and that I can't let my fears ruin the day. With great determination, I shake off my melancholy mood. There will be too many people around today; I have to make the best of it. Thankfully I'll have a few hours to get myself under control since Noah won't be here until late afternoon. We'll have lunch without him since he isn't sure when he'll be able to get away from his family.

Kira arrives just as I'm putting the apple-banana salad in the refrigerator to chill. She gives Sam a glancing kiss on the cheek and hurries into the kitchen, her arms full of dishes, grocery bags swinging dangerously from her arms.

"Aves!" she exclaims upon seeing me. "I brought those cinnamon apples you loved at Thanksgiving."

"Thank you," I say with a genuine smile, helping her unburden her arms.

"You're welcome, sweetie." She groans in relief as the last of the bags make it to the counter. "I brought pumpkin and apple pies, extra cool whip, the cinnamon apples and enough potatoes to feed Dublin." She winks at me and I can't help but laugh.

"That's terrific. We'll make a shepherd's pie kind of thing with the leftover turkey and potatoes. That should feed us all for a week or two since Sam bought the biggest turkey he could find."

Sam wraps an arm around my neck and runs the knuckles of his other hand over my head playfully. "Hey. A man provides for his family."

I poke him in the ribs, the only sure way to get away from him when he has me like this. He skips away and puts Kira between us, his hands on her shoulders keeping her as his shield.

She eyes me carefully, her smile almost frozen in place. I can tell she's waiting for me to break down. I'm used to Sam's ribbing, though, so we're all safe from an outbreak of melodrama. I smile back at her and point to Sam with what I hope is a threatening expression. "Sleep with one eye open, big brother."

***

After the Kira as Shield episode, I retire to a long, hot shower, trying to repair the damage the conversation with Sam has done to my psyche. I am relieved to realize I truly believe he spoke the truth, that he doesn't plan to get rid of me or pawn me off on Noah as I'd suspected.... But I can't let that change my plan. As much as he says Kira is okay with me hanging around after they get married, I know I'll be in the way. Marriage is for two people, not two people and a damaged little brother who isn't even blood relation. Under the hot spray, I reaffirm my decision to work with Kendall Moorhead to get healthy enough to handle life on my own, even if that means therapy for the next twenty years.

The afternoon passes at a snail's pace. Kyle, Kira's single brother, arrives shortly before lunch is ready. He's a great guy with a fun sense of humor, so I almost welcome the distraction. He and his twin Kaleb have always been good to me. When I'm at the go-kart track and Sam's racing or off doing something else, one or both of the brothers hovers in the near distance or keeps me occupied somehow. I know Sam and Kira have explained some of my history to them, but I don't mind. Kyle's like another protective brother to me, where Kaleb flirts unmercifully but harmlessly. I'd forgotten Kyle was coming over today, though, so seeing him at the door surprises me. Their parents have decided to take a long overdue second honeymoon cruise to the tropics, so all three of the siblings are on their own. Kaleb and his boyfriend took the opportunity to go to Josh's parents in Florida for the holiday.

The first few times I'd met them, Kaleb's flirtation freaked me out, but Sam assured me it was just hiss way of being friendly. As we spent more time at the track and I was around Kaleb more, I understood how true Sam's statement was. I'd lay odds Kaleb didn't even realize he was flirting with me. Still, I am relieved it's Kyle who's spending the day with us and not Kaleb because I just couldn't handle his particular brand of holiday levity today.

Kyle musses my hair as he walks in with a couple of six-packs of Sam Adams and I smile up at him. "I'm glad you could come, Kyle."

"Me, too, squirt. And I'm really glad Kaleb and Josh won't be here. I get enough of his ugly mug at work." He winks to show he's joking so I decide to play, too.

"I thought you were going to say 'in the mirror.'"

He pretends to scowl, but ends up laughing. "I think I liked you better when you didn't speak."

I smile innocently and step back as Kira comes to give her brother a hug. Then it's all kinds of craziness as Sam takes the turkey out of the oven and the three of us start transferring food from their pots and pans into table-ready serving dishes. Kyle watches from the doorway, sipping his beer, a bemused expression on his face.

At last we all sit down at the table and watch with amusement as Sam tries to carve the bird with his brand new electric knife. After the third time the blade grinds to a halt scant centimeters past the crisp golden skin, Sam yanks it out of the turkey and tosses it in the trash. Grabbing old-fashioned hand-powered knives from the drawer behind him, he glowers at the trash bin. "I don't get it. I watched the people at the group home use those things every year and they never had a problem. Remember, Aves?" At my nod, he physically shakes off the memory and brandishes the new manual cutlery. "Never fear! We shall have succulent dead bird slices momentarily!"

"Nice," Kira rebukes with a shudder.

Sam merely grins back at her and attacks the turkey with both knives. After he's practically dismantled the thing and passed around white or dark slices, he puts the remainder of the carcass back on the counter and fills his plate. I feel almost guilty that I made Kira put the Orange Fluff back in the fridge, but I made it for Noah. It wouldn't be as special if all the rest of us had already taken gigantic helpings of it—and that is the only way to eat that, in gigantic helpings. It's far too good to show restraint.

Sam, Kira and Kyle carry on a lively conversation filled with sibling teasing. I content myself with the food and listening to their banter. Sam's turkey actually is succulent, not dry at all like I'd feared after watching the knife's blades stall repeatedly. Those glow in the dark apples are just as delicious as I remembered from a month ago. My apple-banana salad is crunchy goodness, the potatoes are whipped to buttery perfection, and Kira worked wonders creating the gravy.

All in all, life's pretty good at the moment. Especially since Sam and I have cleared the air about Noah and Kira. I don't know how she could possibly want to share a home with her husband's not-even-adopted little brother, but if Sam says it's true, then it is. He has no reason to lie. And that thought brings my mind back around to Noah Yates. Just because Sam wouldn't lie about him and Kira doesn't keep his little theory that Noah and I could ever be anything but friends from being sheer insanity. Heck, I'm not even sure I can handle a friendship with Noah.

He is so…huge. His presence, his personality, his physical body are all out of proportion to me. I'm the small guy who fades into the background, the one who hopes no one notices him. Noah is the big, beautiful man who draws everyone's eyes like an irresistible magnet. He doesn't mind being the center of attention. In fact, I suspect he rather likes it. He handles the spotlight and people well, even me. He's insanely charming, ridiculously good looking and undeniably sexy. In short, he's way out of my league, even if I wanted to play, which I don't.

But still, there's something about him that makes it impossible for me to tell him no, some small *something* that draws me to him. The man can't even cook himself a proper meal, for Pete's sake. I'd never have suspected that sort of not weakness, really, but something akin to it, from Noah. He's so enormous and muscular and he obviously takes care of himself. But it *is* nice to know the man isn't as perfect as the package appears. Oh, lord, his package. That's a whole different thing I certainly can't afford to think about. Yet somehow, my treacherous mind already has a picture of what the man looks like naked … and ready. A thrilling little tingle buzzes down my spine at the image. I realize I've gasped audibly when the dull background noise of the conversation abruptly stops.

I flush mightily, as if the other three can read my thoughts, and furtively look at each of them through my long bangs. Sam's wearing a smirk but the other two are gazing at me expectantly.

"What?" I ask, hoping to confuse them all.

Sam bursts out laughing and I feel my cheeks flame again. "Did you really tune out that entire conversation?" he asks.

I look down at my mostly empty plate, unsure of the best answer. "I guess I did. I'm sorry. Did I miss anything important?"

Sam's smirk returns full force. "Kyle was just telling us about a good friend of his who works at the kart center sometimes. He's been mooning over some guy for weeks, but the guy won't give him the time of day."

I look back at my brother, waiting for the point.

"Well, this friend told Kyle yesterday that there's finally been a breakthrough. Apparently he's been invited to spend today with the guy he's been going crazy over." He looks at me hopefully.

I glance over at Kira and Kyle who wear matching smiles. I frown and shake my head a bit to clear the fog still there from that image of Noah naked. And wet now! Oh, lord, what's wrong with me? "And?"

Sam cocks his head at me, a confused look on his face. Our expressions must match because I have no idea why he felt the need to tell me about one of Kyle's employees. "It's Noah."

"What's Noah?"

Sam laughs. "The guy, Avery! Kyle's employee is Noah. And the guy he's been mooning over is you!"

Slightly panicked, I look to Kyle for confirmation. His huge smile is all I need. I feel light-headed and slightly queasy. "Noah's just— I'm—" I gulp lungsful of air and pin my gaze on Sam's. "Friends," I whisper around the rising panic.

Sam grabs my hand where it still rests against the table. "Aves," he says slowly, "calm down. It's okay. Kyle says Noah's a good guy. If all you can give him is your friendship, he won't push for more."

He's holding something back. I can tell by the tone of his voice. It's the same tone he used six months ago when he had a really bad day at work—and, oh yeah, some cranked-out drug dealer had shot at him. But as much as I'm trying to figure out what that *something* is, it has to take a backseat to keeping control of myself. As much as I want to spin out and let the panic chase me down the hall to my room, I recognize this as the first true test of my new-found determination to stop living in fear. If I'm going to be well enough to be on my own when Sam and Kira decide to get married, then I have to start now. Somehow, starting down that road because of something related to Noah seems appropriate on a multitude of levels, none of them comfortable.

***

Kyle leaves shortly after lunch so he can go open Go-Kart World for the Christmas Day crowds. I almost wish I could go with him, but I have a feeling the crowds would be way too much to handle today. Instead, I let Sam and Kira talk me into playing another Scrabble tournament. For someone who's always surrounded by books, I'm lousy at the game.

Noah shows up about four o'clock, arms laden with gift bags, a string of ringing sleigh bells around his neck. *He really is a dork*, I think, unable to hide my smile. I watch his arrival from the kitchen doorway, a strange mix of emotions racing through my body. On one hand, I'm relieved he's finally here because the anticipation and dread have been killing me. On the other hand, holy crap all six foot four, two hundred twenty pounds of Noah Yates is now in my house, my sanctuary, smiling at me from the entryway as Sam helps him with the bags. On the other hand, the twinkle in his eyes and that wide smile combined with the ridiculous sleigh bells spread warmth through my body. On the other hand, holy crap all six foot four, two hundred twenty pounds of Noah Yates is in my house! *Wait, how many hands was that?* I shake my head, waiting for the fear to grip me with its icy talons. But much to my surprise, I feel nothing more than a mild anxiety *for* Noah, not *because* of him. What really catches me off guard is the hope that Noah enjoys being here. Suddenly, Noah having a good time is the most important item on the day's agenda.

I smile at him. "Merry Christmas, Noah," I say quietly as I move further into the room.

"Merry Christmas, Avery," he replies gravely, then gives me a dimpled smile that sets off explosions of tingles all over my body. Before I can contemplate or freak out over that, he extends a medium-size gift bag to me. "Don't say I didn't contribute to the everybody-get-fat theme."

He chuckles as I take the bag and look inside. Nestled amongst red and green tissue paper is a Ziploc bag. I look up at him and laugh. "Cookies?"

"Hey," he says, bringing a hand up to his chest as if I've wounded his heart, "don't mock me. I told you they're the only thing I'm good at in the kitchen. Give 'em a try. I dare you."

Sam laughs. I'd forgotten he's there. I glance at him and he holds up a hand in surrender. "I'm just hanging up the man's coat. Don't mind me."

Noah grins wider. "Sorry about the presentation, but I realized too late I didn't have a pretty party platter or anything and I wasn't sure I could carry everything with one anyway."

Kira waves away his apology as she comes over. "Don't worry about it. We don't stand on ceremony around here." She gives him a hug and I remember belatedly that our cozy little group all knows each other separately from me. "It's good to see you again, Noah."

He returns the hug but doesn't take his eyes off me. "Good to see you, too, Kira. It's been too long."

"It has. But I don't think that will be a problem anymore."

I swear I hear an innuendo-laden wink in her voice. My cheeks light with a fire of embarrassment. Before anything else is said, I vanish into the kitchen, grateful to be out of the spotlight.

A few minutes later, I've just finished arranging the last of Noah's cookies on a platter when I hear his soft voice behind me.

"Have you tried one yet?"

I turn to see him standing just inside the doorway, not blocking it closed but near enough to it I hesitate trying to get around him. "No, I—" My gaze flicks up from the smile on his luscious lips to his eyes and I'm instantly lost and found at the same time. The way he looks at me, it's like I'm the only one in his world, the only one who matters to him. I know that look from Sam and Brian. It's the way they look at Kira and Molly. It should frighten me more than it does, but instead, I'm flooded with a sense of calm. It takes me by such surprise that I can't speak. I simply stare into the most amazingly beautiful pair of hazel eyes I've ever seen. I know I can do that, can look Noah in the eyes because what I see there makes me think Sam might be right, that Noah will never, ever hurt me physically. I feel it in my bones. I know it's as true as the sky is blue. The realization zings through my body like a live current. "I was waiting for you." My cheeks color at the different ways that statement can be interpreted—and on the many levels I mean it.

"Were you now?" Noah's smile turns to a grin, like he's just read my mind.

"Well—I, uhm—I didn't mean *you* specifically," I stutter.

"Mmhm." He nods to the platter. "Better bring 'em in then," he says, then rolls away from the wall and disappears back into the living room.

I take a few breaths to steady my nerves and push the chaotic anxiety to the back of my brain. I can't deal with Noah and these new thoughts about him at the same time. Since thoughts are easier to boss around than Mt. Man-Everest out there, they get to take a hike for a while. Besides, I'm certain to have much more to think about as soon as Noah leaves.

***

"These are the most amazing things I've ever put in my mouth." Kira shoots a look at Sam. "No offense, honey."

Sam's so busy making orgasmic sounds around his own mouthful of cookie that he just waves away his girlfriend's comment. Noah, however, almost chokes to death. He coughs and sputters around the cookie in his mouth.

I glance between Kira and Noah and the half-eaten cookie in my hand. As ridiculously delicious as it is—Mrs. Fields, Little Debbie and Sara Lee would all be jealous—Kira's comment has kind of put me off it. Regretfully, I fold my napkin around it and put it on the coffee table. Noah's still coughing, so I cross the room and hand him his glass of milk. He looks up at me with watery hazel eyes, his surprise and thanks evident in them. He takes a sip or two, wetting the pieces in his mouth and making them easier to swallow correctly. Once I know he's not going to die on us, I retake my seat in the armchair across the room from him. Kira and Sam are sitting together on the couch.

I feel curiously detached from the moment. As much as I try to shut them down, I can't stop the Noah-centric thoughts from zooming around my head. He's here in my home, sitting six feet away from me and I feel no fear, only the usual mild anxiety, but even that's dulled. I've felt more anxious around him in the book store than I do here, in the one place he absolutely should not be. Even Kyle's earlier revelation that Noah's been "mooning over" me, and my physical reaction to him in the kitchen a few minutes ago are more fodder for contemplation than fuel for fear. And really, that's what bothers me the most.

The man is beautiful and undeniably sexy. He's funny in his own way and obviously smart, though why he uses his muscles more than his brain is a question for another time. So why would he be the least bit interested in a guy like me, with panic and social anxiety issues enough to write volumes about? What could he possibly find attractive about me? Perhaps I should suggest he see Kendall Moorhead. The man clearly has more issues than I gave him credit for.

I watch him surreptitiously as he gets himself under control again after the near death-by-cookie experience. He really is a fine specimen of manhood with all those hard muscles and that blond hair, those glorious hazel eyes surrounded by long, thick lashes. *All that and as gentle as a kitten.* I sigh quietly and drop my gaze to my hands in my lap, reminding myself that even kittens have razor-sharp claws. If only I were a different person, someone who could ever be worthy or capable of receiving love I would let him pursue me until I caught him. The squeeze of pain in my chest startles me so much I let out a little gasp. As much as it might hurt to see, I have to convince Noah he needs to go moon over someone who deserves his affections. The great question is how to do that.

"Noah, those really are delicious cookies." Sam's voice drags me from my painfully circular thoughts and I look up at him. He's looking at Noah while tearing of and feeding himself pieces of what must be his fifth cookie.

My gaze flicks back to Noah in time to see his eyes move from me to Sam. How long was he watching me, I wonder, hoping the pain my thoughts had brought hadn't shown on my face.

"Thanks, Sam. It's my grandmother's recipe. When I was ten Kaleb convinced me to jump off the roof of his house. I broke my ankle and spent almost all of summer vacation in a cast."

"Oh, I remember that summer!" Kira interjects.

Noah nods. "I spent a great deal of time with my gran in the kitchen. She taught me how to make these." He chuckles ruefully, undoubtedly picturing that summer in his head. "She tried to teach me other stuff, too, but this is the only thing that really stuck." He shrugs and a surprising bit of color touches his cheeks. "Well, I guess I can still peel and whip potatoes with the best of them."

"If you can make these, you can make real food, too." The sound of my own voice surprises me. I hadn't intended to speak, but now that my gums are flapping, I may as well continue. "You should see what he considers lunch, Sam. It's gross."

"Hey!" Noah protests, sounding surprised and slightly affronted.

"White bread!" I warm to my subject now, glad to have anything else to think about than how delicious Noah looks in that dark brown turtleneck sweater. If that blue plaid shirt was a favorite, it's now a very distant second to Noah in a turtleneck. "And processed lunch meat!"

"It was lean!"

I roll my eyes and look to Sam. "You should thank me for not letting you go to work with stuff like that."

Sam grins at me and shrugs. "Maybe he just needs a boyfriend who cooks."

I gape at him, the idea causing yet another squeeze of pain in my chest.

"Do you cook, Avery?" Noah inquires "innocently" around a small, sly smile.

I narrow my eyes at him. "You know I do."

"Convenient," he smirks. "I don't have time to learn. Between work and school and the gym, I hardly have time to hit the grocery store. And when I do try to cook I usually end up setting off the smoke alarms because I forget what I'm doing. I have a very short attention span when it comes to food."

But not when it comes to me. And isn't that just the weirdest thing.

"Maybe you should cook for him, Avery," Sam suggests oh, so helpfully.

My wide eyes cut to Sam's. It's not like the idea hasn't been in the back of my head since I saw Noah's sad, sad lunch, but I've been forcefully keeping it there, afraid of what it would really mean if I let that particular genie out of the bottle. It would mean spending time with Noah, spending more time thinking about him. It would mean doing something for him that I only do for Sam and me. "I—I don't think that's a good idea," I finally stutter.

"Actually, it's a brilliant idea," Noah enthuses. "Aves, I could pay you per meal. You could do like ten to twelve meals a week, if you wanted to go that far, and I'd never have to rely on white bread and processed lunch meats again!"

"You don't even know if anything I cook is edible!" I protest.

Noah frowns a little. "You just said you can cook. And I saw what you had for lunch the other day. It looked delicious." He shrugs and pops the last bit of his cookie into his mouth. He thoughtfully chews while the rest of us watch him in silence. "But if you don't want to, Avery, I understand." He grins. "I won't even try to guilt you into it."

I roll my eyes and sigh. "You're all just going to gang up on me anyway."

"Hey!" Noah protests.

"Not true!" Kira says.

Sam, however, just smiles lazily at me as he pops the last of his cookie in his mouth. "I don't know why you're fighting it, Avery. You've already started doing it."

"You have?" Noah's grin makes me tingle with heat, but I'll blame it on the blood rushing to my face in embarrassment. He wasn't supposed to know I made the Orange Fluff specifically for him.

"No." Catching Sam's look, I hastily modify my denial. "Well, I mean, not really." Noah's grin widens and I'm quite sure I hate him. "I may have made a dessert with you in mind."

"May have or did?"

"Oh, definitely did," Sam interjects with a laugh. "He wouldn't even let the rest of us sample it for lunch."

Noah's eyes go wide. "Really? Wow. Aves, that might be the nicest thing anyone's done for me in ages. When can I have some? What is it?"

I turn to him from scowling at Sam who simply smiles back and cuddles in closer to Kira. "With dinner. It's nothing special, Noah. It's not Bananas Foster or anything."

"I have no idea what that means, but if you made it for me, it's special." He rubs his big hands together. "So when's dinner?"

Sam and Kira laugh but I roll my eyes again. I swear Noah is just an overlarge kid. "In a couple of hours," I tell him, feeling very much like the only grown up in the room.

Noah pouts momentarily but then breaks into a grin again. He turns to Kira and stage whispers, "Help me break him down, okay?"

Kira giggles, Sam pretends not to hear and I groan.

"So what're we gonna do until then?" Noah asks like he's done nothing wrong. "Strip poker? Yahtzee? Scene it? Twister?"

"As cute as you are, Noah, I have no desire to see you naked," Kira says with a shudder. "It would be like seeing one of my brothers that way."

"But I'm very good. I'd probably be the only one left with clothes on." He thinks for a minute. "I'd bet Avery would be the first one naked."

"What?" I yelp, the very thought of being naked starting the anxiety rising in a rush.

"Honey, you have a very expressive face. You'd be horrible at poker."

I flush uncontrollably at the off-handed endearment. I'm sure it means nothing, just Noah being Noah, but it does nothing to stem the rising tide of anxiety. I push up from the chair. "I-I-I'll be—" I gesture down the hall towards my bedroom and move that direction before I completely lose the ability to speak.

As I turn I see the look of alarm on Noah's face. I can't stop to explain. I know I must look stupid running off down the hall to my bedroom over nothing, but this whole day has been one long test of my nerves. I've done really well, I think, but now I need a few minutes alone to rest and recharge, especially if Noah's going to be here for the rest of the evening.

I close the door behind me and lean back against it, careful not to mess the poster of Rogue that covers the full-length mirror there. I take a deep breath and let it out slowly. It's shaky and I laugh at myself a little. *Noah*, I think. *It's all about Noah.* From telling him a few weeks ago that I couldn't be his friend we've sure gone a long way in the opposite direction. How he's sitting just a few feet away, in my house, spending Christmas with me and Sam and Kira. And now with all these revelations floating around in my head, I'm desperately close to forgetting who and what I am. I need a reality check.

I sigh and push away from the door, already dreading what I'm about to do, but knowing I have no choice. I move to the dresser and, concentrating on looking only at what my hands are doing, I carefully lift away the heavy black shroud covering the mirror. I fold it neatly and put it down on the dresser top, staring at its blackness intently, bracing myself for what's to come.

With fumbling fingers, I pull my Henley over my head from the neckline. I repeat the neat folding and gently place the blue atop the black. *Fitting, that,* I think. Now if only there were some purple and green and yellow to go along with it, I'd have the entire rainbow of bruise colors there to look at.

Closing my eyes, I breathe deeply and face the mirror. I sweep my long bangs from my face with a trembling hand. Finally, I force my eyes open to take in the horror that is my bare-chested reflection. As usual, the sight brings a sharp pain to my eyes as they're flooded with tears. Savagely blinking them away, I force myself to take a long hard look.

I mentally check off each one of my catalogue of reminders as I take them in. Yes, there is the destroyed right eye socket, the one that's been broken so many times it's no longer the usual shape. It's the reason I grow my hair long and make it hang down over my face. It's not pretty, but then it shouldn't be. I take in the way that eyebrow is interrupted three times by scars so that the four pieces of the brow no longer line up properly. My long, narrow nose is crooked and off center from my mouth from three—or was it four?—breaks. Yes, four. Twice from Carl, twice from Tommy.

I thrust out my right arm, fleshy side up and have no trouble finding the three oval scars from where Junior and Darrell attacked me with my mother's curling iron. The smell of burning flesh stings my crooked nostrils as fresh in my mind as it was that day, the day after I'd had the cast removed.

There are similar scars on my left arm, also from my supposed step-brothers, but those were made by their cleats as they stomped me into the wet grass of the back yard.

I look at my chest now and see the jagged six-inch seam where my young flesh had caught on an exposed nail when they threw me in the doghouse that last time. Tracing the ugly red and white length with a trembling finger, I whimper, much like the dog they always claimed I was. I remember the horror of dealing with the oozing infection that came with it, on my own, of course, because no one else cared enough to help.

I take in other, smaller marks across my torso, their stories mostly blending together in the misery that was my torturous childhood.

This is who you are, Avery, I remind myself. *You can change your name and your location, but these will never change. Whatever fantasies you're entertaining about Noah Yates in the back of your twisted little brain, remember this is you, the failed abortion, the human punching bag, the kid no one wants. Tucker or Avery, it doesn't matter. This is all you're worth.*

And finally, I let the tears flow, the truth of those words a pain far worse than any of the physical assaults that have left such vivid reminders on my body.

***

A light tap on the bedroom door rouses me from a fitful slumber. I force my gritty, aching eyes open with a groan. I can't believe I actually cried myself to sleep. And with Noah Yates in the next room.

Well, if he had questions before about what kind of emotional wreck I am, he should have all the answers by now.

"Aves?" The tap sounds again and I squawk a "yeah" past my parched throat.

The door opens slowly and Sam pokes his head around it, a look of concern adorning his wonderful face. I feel awful. Somehow it always hurts Sam when I have these meltdown moments. I know he sees something good in me, although I have no idea how or why, so these times when I check back in with the truth of who I am upset him.

He comes fully into the room and closes the door behind him. "Are you okay?" he asks as he crosses the room to sit beside me on the bed.

I shrug and take in a shuddering breath. "I didn't mean to fall asleep. How long was I out?"

Sam frowns and reaches out to brush away the salt tracks on my cheeks. "I'm more worried about this. Why were you crying?"

I look away, causing Sam's hand to fall away, and then close my eyes against the returning pain. "I can't be something I'm not," I whisper.

"Who wants you to be anything but you?"

"You do. You *all* do." I look back at him, begging him to understand. "I know who I am, Sam, what I am. You all pretend I'm just like you, but I'm not."

"Of course you're not like me, buddy. Everyone is unique because we all have different experiences and you've had some truly hellacious ones. But I'll tell you this: what those people told you when you were a kid are nothing but poisonous lies." He stops and brings my face around with a gentle touch. "Look at me, please."

It takes great effort and quite a while, but my suddenly wet again gaze finally meets his.

"Avery, you are a wonderful, worthwhile human being. You've been my best friend since I was eleven years old. There's no one in this world I love more than you, including Kira. It hurts me that you still believe those hateful things your abusers told you because I know they're absolutely not true. But worse than that, it hurts *you* that you still give them that kind of power over you. I've never told you this before, but as much as I hate your mother for what she put you through, I am so thankful to her for dropping you at that fire station. If she hadn't, we never would have met. And I know that without you my life wouldn't be one-tenth as good as it is." Sam draws a finger down my still salt-streaked cheek. "You have so much love bottled up in that little body, Aves. It's just bursting to get out. And I'm eternally grateful that those bastards weren't able to kill that part of you. But, buddy, you have to learn to accept love, too—from someone other than me. You *are* worthy, I promise you."

My tears spill over again and Sam gathers me in a hug as the sobs take over. "You've had a really tough road," he says into my hair. "Harder than you deserve, for sure. It's your goodness they were so afraid of, that they tried to beat out of you. But guess what? They lost and you won. You're still good—so much better than anyone else I know. So please, little brother, please stop letting those voices in your head tell you you're less than, that you are not worthy. Because if you aren't worthy, than the rest of us damn sure aren't, okay?"

I feel Sam's face pressing into my hair and hug him tighter. I want so badly to believe what he says. I know he believes it without a shadow of a doubt, but it's so hard to overcome so many years of programming, especially with all the physical reinforcement. Carl and Mom and Tommy and the boys not only believed what they said about me, they actually drilled it into my flesh with lasting reminders, forcing me to believe them too. I can't promise Sam what he wants, but I can try to learn to forget. I want to be worthy of someone's love and I know Sam believes I am, which is why he cares for me so unconditionally. We've been down some of the same roads. He knows everything about me. Our shared history is a powerful bond. I want to be worthy, but I know I'm not, period. Then again, Sam cares for me, so maybe I am. But if my own mother, the one person in the world who is virtually required by biology and the law to love me, chose Carl over me, then how can I possibly believe someone would or could care for me of his own free will? And that's what it all comes down to—if she couldn't, even with the supposed "maternal bond" between us, then there's no possible way anyone else could.

It takes a while, but eventually my tears dry up again. Sam extricates himself from our hug and hands me a Kleenex from the box on the nightstand. When we can both breathe again, he smiles at me. "I know you probably don't believe everything I just told you, Avery, but I swear on my life it's all true. You're my best friend and the best little brother an orphan could hope for." I can't help but laugh a little at the absurdity of the comment and Sam smiles back at me, clearly pleased he's gotten me to laugh. "Okay, are you ready to get cleaned up and have some dinner?"

Reluctantly I nod. I feel better than I did before my reality check, and now that I'm grounded in reality again—despite Sam's pep talk—I'm ready to face Noah again.

"Good." Sam pats my denim-covered thigh twice before standing up. "Go wash your face, brush your teeth and find a shirt. Dinner will be ready by the time you're done." He winks and heads for the door. "Don't take too long. Your man's out there waiting for his dessert."

"He's not my man," I argue immediately.

Sam smiles back at me from the doorway. "Yeah, he is. You just have to claim him."

When I come out of the bathroom, I notice that the shroud once again covers the mirror. I touch it lightly on the way by and send Sam a silent thanks.

***

I emerge into the living room after my ablutions and the first place my gaze goes is to Noah. He sits in the chair I vacated earlier, one that allows a view down the hall. It feels like a protective move and I offer him a wan smile. He smiles back but I see the worry written on his face. A magic marker would be subtler.

"Sorry about disappearing like that," I say to the room in general.

Kira gets up from the couch and presses a kiss to my forehead. "It's okay, kiddo. We understand."

I smile my thanks and turn my attention back to Noah. Kira moves into the kitchen to help Sam, affording our guest and me at least the illusion of privacy. I move to sit on the arm of the couch nearest him. I take in a deep breath, preparing to try to explain, but Noah's soft, gentle voice derails my train of thought.

"Did I do something wrong?" he asks. "Was it the strip poker comment? Because if it was, Aves, I'm really sorry. I thought it would be obvious I was joking."

"No, it wasn't that. It wasn't you at all, really." I expect to see some relief cross his beautiful face, but instead the concern only grows. "Sometimes…." I take a breath and try again. I'm not used to explaining my meltdowns, so it's a challenge to do it without revealing too much. "Holidays are harder for me than other days, Noah. And you've seen how well I cope with those." I shrug. "I can't really explain it aside from saying that I have some issues." I try a smile but it trembles at the tips. "But you should have figured that out by now."

Noah nods. "We all have issues, Aves. Maybe not as big as yours, but they're there. The important thing is that we work on them, chisel away at them until we realize they're not the insurmountable mountains they appear to be, but just a pile of rocks we can move around and get over."

In spite of myself I smile at him. "Does your mother know you're a philosophy major?"

He grins and winks. "Psychology, actually, but yes, she does."

I file that information away for future use and point at him. "No diagnoses over dinner."

This time he laughs and the lightened expression on his face eases something within me. No matter how miserable my own life has to be, there's no way I want to be the cause of his.

***

Nervously, I drag the Orange Fluff container from the fridge and set it in front of Noah. When I pull back the lid he looks at it like it's radioactive.

"It's orange, Avery."

"Yep." I stare at the Jell-O, suddenly afraid this was a horrible idea.

"I thought you said it was tapioca."

"It is tapioca. Look, you can see the little frogs' eyes."

"Gross, Avery!" That from Kira.

"Frogs' eyes?"

I grin. "That's what my grandmother called 'em."

"And you ate it?" Kira again.

"Of course!" Sam offers excitedly. "Dude, frogs are cool! Especially to little boys."

Kira shudders and points to Sam's crotch. "You're only allowed to produce girls, do you hear me?"

"Hey!" Sam protests, covering himself protectively. Noah and I dissolve into fits of laughter.

When he recovers, Noah picks up his spoon and gamely loads it with his dessert. He shakes his head once. "For little boys everywhere!" he says before shoving the spoon in his mouth.

I watch with a growing grin as the flavors burst forth on his tongue. Cool whip, mandarin orange, vanilla pudding, tapioca pudding. Noah closes his eyes and moans so erotically I swear half the gay men in town stand at attention, me included. He chews the orange, swallows and lets out a lusty, "Oh my god."

Sam and Kira dive for their spoons but Noah is quicker. Before they can get their greedy hands on the bowl, Noah snatches it up, cradling it like a football, his spoon-laden hand out like a blocker. "Mine!" he snarls and I can't help it. I collapse to the chair in giggles, picturing him sitting alone in the corner of the kitchen, cradling his bowl, snarling and snapping at anyone who steps foot in the room.

Eventually I recover and dinner continues, but that bowl is never far from Noah's reach. Sam and Kira only get a single large spoonful. Noah is much more generous with me, though. He allows me three overlarge spoonsful for making it and promises a lifetime supply of cookies if I make more for him to take home. Sam, of course, is all over that, offering to run to the store immediately for ingredients. I stop laughing long enough to assure Noah he'll have a fresh batch for New Years and that if he'll just slow down, he can take the leftovers home with him.

He regards me seriously across the table. "Pinky swear?" he asks holding up his hand, the digit in question extended.

"What?"

"Avery, you have to pinky swear or I'm going to camp out in your kitchen until you make more."

I laugh and shake my head.

He turns to Sam. "He thinks I'm joking." Back to me, he says, "Aves, I like to camp, but I warn you now, I get ripe after a few days. So…pinky swear?"

As ridiculous as it is, I almost believe him. I glance at Sam who gestures emphatically at Noah's hand. "I'm the only one allowed to get ripe around here," he says. "Pinky swear with the man!"

Kira buries her face in her hands. "Why do I hang out here?"

Sam places a sweet kiss to the top of her head. "Great sex and Avery's cooking."

"Oh yeah." She shrugs and looks up at me. "Swear, Avery! There won't be any great sex if these two get into a smelling contest. Save us both. Please."

"You're all crazy," I pronounce, looking at each of them in turn. "I'm not pinky swearing."

Sam shoves back from the table. "I'll get the extra blankets. I'm taking *your* pillows, bro."

"Okay, okay," I laugh, more than half believing him. "Fine." I slowly bring my hand up to Noah's, knowing full well this will be the first time I've touched his skin to mine. I curl my pinky around his warm, rough, much thicker one and he squeezes back and hangs on. I feel the current jump between us and my gaze jumps to his hazel one. Quickly, I jerk my hand away before our fingers are melded together by the heat of his flesh on mine. His eyes won't release mine though and I see the emotion flame in those hazel depths. I shiver from the intensity of it, torn between fear and the first real flush of desire I've ever experienced from touch.

Hastily I tear my gaze away and fumble for my water glass, my eyes not daring to look anywhere but there. I bring the drink to my lips, the glass and the cool water reacting against the hotness in my body. *Too much, too much, too much*, I think.

I flinch when Kira drags the almost empty glass from my lips. "Shh, relax," she whispers, smiling indulgently at me. I peek at her long enough to tune back in to the moment. Sam and Noah are already deep in conversation. I heave a shaky sigh and Kira smiles at me, patting my hand where it rests on the table. I smile back and chance a glance at Noah. He winks at me and takes another bite of the dessert I made just for him.

***

After Noah leaves and Sam and Kira retire to Sam's bedroom, I curl up on my bed with my sketch pad. I usually only drag it out after a session with Kendall, but this has been an emotional day and I could really use the wind down. As usual, I grab what's left of the black pencil and start with that. Tonight, I only make a few horizontal lines, some thick, some thinner, then a few vertical ones of alternating thickness to intersect with them. Once those are complete, I stare at the image and pick up the blue pencil. I shade around each of the black lines, then make blue lines following the same pattern as the black ones. It's when I pick up the green pencil to finish the job that I realize what I've done.

I laugh at myself and silently curse Noah. I've just drawn that blue plaid shirt he wears so often, the one that has somehow become my favorite. The man is entirely too far into my brain, but how will I ever him out of it?

Chapter 9 - December

Three days later, it's my first scheduled therapy session after the holidays. My hands shake the pages so badly I can hardly read the words I've written on them.

"It's okay, Avery. Just read what you've written. We'll get into the details later."

I want to roll my eyes because if that was supposed to make me feel better, Kendall went way wide of the mark. I don't do it, of course, because of the lessons well-learned and catalogued on the paper in my hand. Setting the paper on my lap so it will stop shaking, I take a breath before beginning. "I'm going to do this kind of chronologically, okay?" At her nod, I continue. "Memory: My dad's funeral. What I learned: Mom hated me after that, but I don't know why. It seems like she didn't before that, but I only have a few memories from when my dad was still alive, so I can't be sure."

I take one more deep, steadying breath. I have to get this all out. I thought writing it was bad, but it hurts so much more saying these things aloud. Even though I've known them my whole life, they sound so much worse, more real almost, in my own voice.

"Memory: Carl beat me for not cleaning my room good enough or for walking in front of the television or for tracking mud in the house. What I learned: No matter how hard I tried, he would always find a reason to beat me. But I still tried to be good. I didn't want him to hit me. I wanted him to love me—or at least like me.

"Memory: Mom told me I was an abortion that didn't work, that she wished I'd never been born. What I learned: That she hated me, that no matter what I did, I'd still have been born.

"Memory: My mother dropped me off at a fire station six days before my eighth birthday. What I learned: Even my mother, who was supposed to love me unconditionally, wanted me gone enough to just leave me at the side of the road. If she didn't love me enough to choose me, neither would anyone else."

"Good, but that's only four. Did you have a fifth memory?"

I look at her in astonishment. "Wasn't that enough?"

She nods, as if in agreement. "Okay, can you give me one good memory then?"

My shaking has slowed but this memory thing still hurts like mad. I've spent all week trying to catalogue the bad memories into a top four worst list and now she wants me to find a good one? "I—I don't know. I suppose there is one."

She smiles like she knew there would be. "What is it?"

My mind casts through the recesses of my memory, desperate to find my first good memory. My heart swells with love. "The day I met Joey."

"Okay, and what did you learn from meeting Joey?"

"That I wasn't alone." I swallow hard around the tears of loving and losing him so quickly in succession. "Except then I was because he died."

"Are you angry at him for leaving you?"

I shake my head, not wanting to talk about him. If I keep him inside where no one else can get to him, he's still safe and still mine. "No. I wanted to be, and I think I was at first because he'd left me alone in that house with them, but I'm not anymore. If I'd thought of it, I might have done it first. It was the only way he knew to make it stop."

"What would you tell him if you could talk to him now?"

Emotion chokes me. "That I love him. That I miss him every day and that I understand."

Kendall nods and makes notes on her yellow legal pad. "Talk to me about those other memories."

I close my eyes and swallow against the swell of pain. "My mom hated me. Her boyfriend hated me. His kids from a previous relationship hated me. They made sure I knew it every day. The only bright spots at home were the two little boys mom and Carl had together. They were too young to know to hate me, but I'm sure they would have eventually."

"Are you angry with your mom for leaving you at the fire station?"

"I—I don't know. No, I'm not angry. It makes me sad and confused. I wish I had been good enough for her to love me, but that wasn't ever going to happen. I just wanted to be good." Angrily, I grab a tissue and press it to my wet eyes. "I just wish she could have seen how hard I tried, that it would have counted for something. I didn't want to be bad. I swear I never meant to be. Why couldn't she see that?

I've never understood why she hated me so much. What could I have possibly done wrong at that age for her to hate me?"

"Avery, you have to understand that her hate wasn't about you; it was about her. I firmly believe that she started out loving you—she may love you to this day—but something got in the way of her being the best mother she could be and she had no idea how to handle it, so she directed it at the person least able to hurt her or defend himself—you. Some would say her greatest act of love was getting you out of that house, getting you somewhere she thought you would be safer."

I boggle at her. "What? She loved me so much she dumped me at a fire station? She loved me, so she hit me and kicked me and made me lie about her and Carl breaking my bones? That's not love. That's hate. She hated me for being born."

"That's also possible, but, again, you have to realize that's her fault, not yours. You didn't do anything to create that hate or to perpetuate it, and you certainly didn't deserve to have them physically or emotionally abusing you."

I stare out the window and try to absorb her words. They make no sense. "I can't talk about this anymore."

"Okay, tell me about your holiday. Noah was coming over for dinner, wasn't he?"

I take a few minutes to put mom and Carl out of my head, then I give her a rundown of holiday events. I try to leave out the meltdown, but the woman is too dang good at her job. She makes me drag the whole thing out so she can examine it piece by piece.

"We have to do something about your self-talk, Avery. The way we talk to ourselves is, in many ways, more important to our mental health than what other people say to us. We are the ones in our own heads, the only ones who are able to constantly reaffirm our self-worth and build our self-esteem. That's another thing we need to work on."

"I don't understand what that has to do with anything," I answer honestly.

She brushes her long red hair behind her shoulder and leans forward. I watch as the strands slowly retake their previous position. "When Sam told you he loved you, did you believe him?"

I frown, knowing the "correct" answer, but unable to say it. "I know he cares for me, yes."

"That wasn't the question. Do you believe he loves you?"

"I—" I turn to look out her window, hoping it looks like I'm trying to compose an answer, but in truth, I shut down my brain. I can't go here. I can't examine my every interaction with Sam like this. Yes, he cares for me. Yes, he *takes* care of me. But that other word...that's not part of my world.

"Avery?" she prods after long moments of silence.

"I'm not—I don't deserve his love."

"Why not?"

"Because of who I am."

"But, Avery, everyone deserves love. Everyone deserves a chance to be happy. Don't you think that applies to you, too?"

I shake my head, fighting against the tears. I wish what she says is true, but it isn't, not for me.

"Sam loves you, Avery. It has to be true or he wouldn't have stood by you and protected you in the group home. He wouldn't have come back for you, and he certainly wouldn't be living with you now if he didn't love you. Isn't that right?"

"I don't deserve it," I say, finally breaking down. "One of these days he's going to figure it out, just like they did."

"They being your mom and Carl?"

I nod.

"But what if they were wrong, Avery? What if all those horrible things they told you and called you weren't really about *you* at all? Then what?"

I can't stop crying and I can't form sentences either. The thought of losing Sam hurts so much worse today than it did before Christmas because now I can feel how empty I would be inside if he stops caring about me—even being pawned off on Noah would be better than that.

Kendall hands me a paper cup of water. Irrationally, I hope these things aren't being added to my bill or I'll never get her paid off. "Drink this," she instructs kindly. It's amazing how taking in water stops the water from flowing out. Neat trick.

When I've collected myself, Kendall smiles back at me from her chair. "I want you to repeat after me: 'Sam loves me and I am deserving of love.'"

I shake my head almost frantically. "No."

"Why not?"

"I can't. I just can't."

"C'mon. 'Sam loves me and I am deserving of love.'"

"No!"

"It's a simple sentence—well, compound actually, but that's neither here nor there. Say it with me then: 'Sam loves me and I am deserving of love.'"

"NO!"

She leans forward, almost aggressively. "Why not, Avery? Tell me why not and I'll leave you alone."

"Because no matter how many times you say it, it doesn't make it true!"

Kendall smiles widely and relaxes back in her chair. "Exactly, Avery! Exactly! And no matter how many times your mom and Carl and the boys from the group home reinforced their lies and venom and hate with their fists and boots, it didn't make them true either. It just means they left a more lasting mark on your psyche. So our job is to figure out why you're still holding on to t*hose* lies so tightly you won't let any good, positive truths into your head and your heart."

***

Sam pushes his plate away and leans back, his hands on his flat belly. "Thank goodness that's the last of it. I am so sick of turkey."

I laugh and poke his belly. Unlike the Pillsbury doughboy, Sam doesn't giggle; he grunts and doubles over protectively. It's even cuter, really. "It's your own fault. I offered to make you something different."

"I know, I know. But that would have meant turkey tomorrow and I *am not* starting off the new year with that dang bird."

I laugh again and gather our plates for the dishwasher. “I guess next year you won’t buy the biggest bird you can find.”

Sam groans again. “Definitely not. Next year it’s back to Chinese. Wait, does Noah like Chinese?”

The forks in my hand clatter to the sink but I refuse to give him more of an answer than that. Noah's likes and dislikes have been frequent topics of conversation with Sam in the last six days. “It’s New Year’s Eve, Sam. Give it a rest.”

Sam gets up from the table and ruffles my hair on his way past me. “I’m gonna go take a shower. You’d better get ready. Kaleb’s party starts in an hour.”

“Sam….”

He stops in the doorway and pins me with a look. “Don’t even start with that, Avery. You promised Kaleb you would go.”

I hang my head. A party, any party, is the last place I want to be, even though he’s right; I did promise Kaleb. “Fine but I’m taking my own car. I don’t want to be there all night.”

“Nope. We’re cabbing it tonight, champ. Neither one of us is driving on Amateur Drunk Night.”

I nod. “Good point.” He grins and heads down the hall. “But you’re paying!” I shout after him.

I turn back to the dishwasher and load the pans I used earlier to make Noah's lunches for the rest of the week. I still can’t believe I let them all rope me into it, but it actually feels good to be doing something for him—for someone else, even if he is paying me for it.

Of course, I'll never, ever admit it. Okay, maybe on my death bed when everyone else is too deaf with old age to hear it.

***

For all the money Kira's family has, Kaleb's quaint little house is just that—small. He and Josh bought the house together as their second anniversary present to each other. They chose it, Josh told me once, because it had a big beautiful back yard they could entertain in and rooms small enough to feel cozy. It's also a post-war craftsman, so of course I fell in love with it the first time I stepped into it and noticed that glorious old house scent. I felt instantly at home, which never happens outside my own home. In fact, it took several months of living in our apartment before I stopped feeling like a guest in it, even though Sam and I moved in at the same time. Or I should say we moved him in, I carried in all of my worldly possessions in a duffle bag and my spanking new bedroom set was delivered by a furniture store—not the one Noah now works at.

At New Year's Eve, of course, it should be too cold to utilize the back yard Kaleb and Josh love so much. But they live for gatherings like this, so there are six tall outdoor heating towers spread evenly around the yard, bringing the brisk thirty-three degree night air up to a comfortable level. When Sam and I step through the back door, the first person I see is Noah.

He breaks into a broad grin and waves at me but continues his conversation with a man I don't recognize. I wave discreetly back at him, feeling a heat not from the towers rising inside me. I try to convince myself it's just embarrassment, but even I'm not buying it. Since the touch of his flesh on mine on Christmas day, he is practically all I can think about. I know it's pointless and insanely scary, but I can almost feel my flesh reaching out to him, wanting to feel that frenetic flash of desire again. I won't let it happen, though. At least, not while I'm awake. Just as I can't control the nightmares that I cycle through every few months, I can't help that I've woken with his name on my lips more than once in the last six days.

Determinedly, I shake off those thoughts and follow Sam through the yard to greet Kaleb and Josh where they hold court in a very cutely designed seating area tucked off to the left side of the yard. Though they're not near one of the heating towers, the small group is kept warm by a blazing fire pit. The flickering light from the flames seems to alternate highlighting first Josh, then Kaleb and then the two of them together as they lean close to share a private joke. Perhaps because they've been together since long before I met them or maybe because such things have never been so forcefully at the forefront of my mind, for the first time I wonder what their story is, how they found each other and became a couple.

Sam starts to call for their attention, but my hand on his arm stops him. He looks down at me curiously, but I just incline my head toward the couple, hoping Sam will follow my wordless lead. As I really watch Kaleb and Josh together for the first time, it's the little things that strike me. The way Kaleb's hand drifts to Josh's knee and gives it a light squeeze. How Josh reciprocates with a caress along Kaleb's back when he leans forward to laugh at a photo on someone's iPhone.

It's the way Kaleb leans back against Josh's chest without appearing to ever question that his man will be right there to catch him that finally cinches it for me. This is what real, true love between two people looks like. It's not the constant tension or the begging for forgiveness or the threat and follow-through of physical violence that characterized my mother's relationship with Carl. I cannot imagine any situation where these two men would raise a hand to the other.

The shiver that races down my spine is not from the cold. No, it's from the quite unexpected fire of longing that flashes to brief life deep in my belly. Even before I fully recognize what it is, I snuff it out with a firm reminder that this is not meant for me. I can and will take vicarious pleasure from Josh and Kaleb's happiness but I cannot and will not be fool enough to allow myself to want something similar for me.

I make myself shrug off the encroaching black mood and step forward to get the couple's attention. Josh sees me first and, flashing a big smile of welcome, nudges Kaleb.

"Avery!" he exclaims, springing from the bench to engulf and lift me into a spinning hug. With Kaleb, flirtation and exuberance are always right at the surface, waiting for any reason to burst forth.

I laugh and slap at his broad, muscular shoulders. "Put me down, you nut."

He does and holds me at arm's length by the shoulders. "Aves, you look terrific. Happy New Year, buddy. Would you like a beer or some wine or something?"

"I'm fine, really," I assure him, hoping he'll let me go soon. Several people I don't know have taken in the show and are staring openly.

"Okay, well, it's time to refill the cooler anyway. Why don't you come with me and lend a hand." Kaleb smiles in that wicked way he does and I surrender to the inevitable. He grasps Sam's hand and pulls him into an affectionate, brotherly hug. "Hey, Sammy. Good to see you, bro. Sorry about bailing on Christmas, but Josh wanted to go to Florida to see his parents. Hey, he's got a beer or two left. Claim my seat and make him give you one. Aves and I will be back in a few."

Sam laughs a "Sure thing, Kaleb," even as Kaleb wraps a long arm around my shoulders and turns us happily back the way I've just come.

Inside the house it's warm, cozy and quiet. In the kitchen, Kaleb's demeanor changes from almost hyper to calm and relaxed. It's clear the house soothes him in the way that being off-stage must relax an actor. Kaleb gestures to the table, so I take a seat. He opens his beautiful French-door refrigerator and pulls out two Sam Adams. He pops the tops and offers me one of the bottles. I've probably had a total of ten beers in my life, but I accept this one with thanks and a smile.

Kaleb sits across from me and takes a quick sip. "So talk to me, stud. What's going on?"

"What are you talking about? I don't know. I just got here."

"No, no. Not here. I've got that covered. What's going on with you? I haven't seen you in a while, well not to actually have a decent conversation with you."

I smile, wondering how long he'll let me get away with it. "Nothing's new. I go to work and come home."

Kaleb begins to peel the label from his bottle. "See, that's not what my sources are telling me at all. I hear one of my best friends is enamored with you and even spent Christmas at your house."

I shrug. "I'm not encouraging him, Kaleb. I don't know that he wants anything more than friendship from me, but if he does, he's not going to get it."

Now Kaleb frowns. "Really? That's a real shame, Aves. You're a sweet, lovable guy and Noah is one of the best men I know. He would definitely treat you right. You could do much worse."

Hastily I defend Kaleb's friend. "Oh, don't get me wrong. Noah's shown himself to be a good guy so far. But Kaleb…" I look to my lap where I hold the untouched beer tightly with both hands. Any more pressure on that sweating bottle and it's likely to shoot up like a rocket. Deliberately, I loosen my grip until the danger is abated. I feel ashamed to have to say this again for the second time in a week, but what I told Sam on Christmas Day is still true. "I can't be who he wants me to be. It's just not me."

"Who do you think he wants you to be?" Kaleb questions quietly.

"I don't know. Someone like you or like Josh."

Kaleb takes that in for a moment before responding softly. "Avery, it's not my story to tell, but when I met Josh he had been through some really horrible things. He didn't turn up in my life just like the guy you see now. It took a lot of hard work for him to put all those things in the past and to learn to live in the present. Even now he has occasional bad days when it all sneaks back up on him. But he knows now that he deserves to and can be happy." I look up to see Kaleb smiling sweetly at me. "I suspect that's something you still have to learn, but trust me: you deserve it, too. When you really come to accept that, there's no one in this world who will be better at reminding you and showing you than Noah."

I smile sadly and nod. "It's not that easy, Kaleb. I wish it were. I wish I could be normal, but I'm never going to be."

He exhales air through his teeth. "Normal is relative and not exactly a goal I aspire to. I hate to sound all Hallmark-slash-Army, but we all just want you to be the best Avery you can be. Sam and Kira and Josh and I care a lot about you, Aves. We would love to see you happy because you deserve it. Noah sees that, too. All I ask is that you don't write him off because you don't think you're worthy of the big lug's love, because you really and truly are." He smiles at me and puts his now empty bottle on the table. "Now give me that beer before it gets too hot to drink."

Blushing brilliantly and blocking a barrage of thoughts, I gratefully hand him the bottle. "Thank you for the talk, Kaleb. I'll think about what you've said, but I really can't promise anything."

"That's all I can ask, buddy." He takes a swig of the beer and grimaces. "You're just a little heater, aren't you? I think I just wasted a beer!"

A few minutes later, Kaleb goes back outside to play good host, but I stay behind to gather my wits. It seems everyone wants to see me happily coupled with Noah Yates. Everyone but me, that is. Yes, he's a dead attractive guy. Yes, he seems to be a genuinely nice person. Yes, I feel pulled toward him, but meteors are pulled to the moon, too, and look how that turns out for either of them.

Despite Kendall's words from our last session, deep in my soul I know that Carl and Tommy and Mom are all correct. Nothing in my life thus far has disproven them. Even if a tiny piece somewhere deep inside me still wishes that fact were untrue, the rest of me knows better. So what possible good would it do me or Noah to even pretend to entertain the idea that we could be more than friends? I wouldn't have the slightest idea how to be in a romantic relationship. Worse than that, though, is the thought that stops my breath and kick starts my heart: Noah would want to have sex. With me. Sex with me. The phrase reverberates around my brain painfully.

No, no, no! I bury my face in my hands and fight against the panic. I picture open sandy beaches and never-ending oceans to stave off the trapped, claustrophobic feelings. My breathing comes in shallow, rapid-fire lurches around my palms. I can't think about that. I cannot deal with the images of Noah's gigantic naked body atop mine, surrounding me, pinning me down, invading me, smothering me. Unable to hold back the panic, I stumble through the dining and living rooms, past the front door and out into the middle of the front yard. I stare up at the sky, arms extended from my sides, feeling the slight breeze rush over the fabric. Impatiently I push my sleeves up over my elbows, allowing my skin its fill of fresh air. Eventually, my mind blanks out into a black void and I lower my tired arms to my sides, hugging them around me to ward off the sudden chill.

Some small noise directs my attention back to the house. Noah sits there on the steps watching me, his long muscular arms wrapped around his knees. I hadn't noticed them when I saw him earlier, but now the moonlight reflects off a pair of stylish eyeglasses. Their presence changes his face from pure jock to square-jawed intellectual jock. It's a stunning transformation, one that sends tingles through me. I hate that my body is so physically aware of him. It's a betrayal to my brain, which screams "run," to have my body yearn for just the opposite.

"How long have you been sitting there?" I snap churlishly.

Noah's lips twitch upward. "Not long."

I stand my ground, a brave guy fifteen feet away from him. It's my head start if things go wrong. "Why are you spying on me?"

He nods, as if agreeing he deserves that. "I was afraid Kaleb had upset you. Looks like I was right. I just wanted to make sure you're okay."

"I'm fine." Why does he have to look so amazing? He's all decked out in yet another turtleneck—cream colored this time—and brown slacks. The sleeves hug his huge biceps and strain against mile-wide shoulders. I'm sure his square pecs and flat stomach will be beautifully highlighted when he stands. And those pants are without question cut to show off his below the waist assets. No matter how much I fight it, the very sight of him sends forth the tingles again.

Noah grins. "I see that. So what did Kaleb say to start you down Panic Attack Boulevard?"

"Nothing."

"Can I guess?"

I shrug, not sure what else to do. I don't want to talk about it, but I can't pull myself away from this man either. It's a ridiculously confusing mental space to be in, unable to go but unwilling to stay.

"I'm going to venture Kaleb wanted to talk to you about us. He wanted to throw his support behind the 'Noah and Avery as a couple' idea, right?"

I nod, the bad juju rising again.

Noah sighs. "I thought so. Why does that idea scare you so much, little one?"

"You don't know me," I croak around my suddenly restricted throat.

"I know you well enough to know I like you a lot. I know you've been through some very troubling, very traumatic things in your past. I know you carry scars inside and outside. But, Avery, you're a beautiful soul. When I'm with you, I can't get enough of you. When we're apart, you're all I think about. I can't get you out of my head. And, honestly, I don't want to."

He smiles and beckons me to him with one crooking finger. I can't stop my feet from moving in his direction. As if watching from above, I see myself moving across the yard to the porch where Noah sits patiently, hand out, waiting.

"Give me your hand, Avery," he commands gently.

Without wanting to and fighting it every inch of the way, I slip my hand on top of his, palm to palm. I shiver at the touch, eyes closing, stopping just short of rolling back in my head. Despite the night chill, Noah's hand is warm and rough against my own soft skin. He rotates his hand around and slides his fingers between mine, lacing us together loosely. I open my eyes to drink him in, knowing the panic can't be far behind.

Instead of speaking, Noah just gazes at me softly, a gentle smile curving his lips. He squeezes my hand lightly and I return the gesture, surprised to feel the panic settle and recede. Behind his eyeglasses, his hazel eyes are clear and sparkling, even in the dim moonlight. I take the few remaining steps that bring me to his side, separated by the stair rail. His arm must be uncomfortable, the way it's draped over the wood, but neither of us moves to disentangle our fingers.

In slow motion, I watch as Noah's other hand comes toward me. His smile deepens and those dimples pull me under his spell even more. I'm immersed in Noah but I've never felt safer. His long fingers brush my jawline as his thumb strokes my bottom lip. My eyes close again and I hear a sound emanate from my throat. Fire spreads through my body from where his thumb caresses my mouth. Unconsciously, my tongue moves to wet my lips and I taste him. That sound comes again, but this time I know it isn't from me. He tastes salty and warm and foreign but wonderful. My tongue darts out again for another quick sample and this time it is me who makes that low, keening sound. His thumb moves to my chin and I slowly open my eyes, drunk from his touch.

"Win," he whispers roughly and flashes those dimples again under heavy-lidded eyes. "You're safe with me, little one. You always will be. You know that, right?"

I nod because I know somehow, somewhere deep inside that it's true. Physically, Noah would never harm me, not while there was breath in his body. But emotionally? That's something else altogether. I drink in the warmth and emotion in his eyes and take a step back. He lets me go without protest, that dimpled smile steady.

"Go back to the party, Avery," he says quietly. "I'm gonna head home. But next year, I want my New Year's kiss."

Still drunkenly numb from the touch and taste of him, I merely nod. Touching tingling fingers to my lips, the spot he had caressed, I grin stupidly as I take a few steps back. With one last look into those hazel depths, I dart into the darkness and make my way back to the party through the gate at the side of the house.

Chapter 10 - February

I prop my head on my fist and stare out the break room door. Noah should be here any minute for lunch, but until then I'm bored. It's hard to believe it's the first of February already. The ubiquitous Valentine's Day decorations hanging and sitting all over the sales floor are enough to make me forever and always hate the color pink. And seriously, what's so romantic about a book? Walter, as usual, has ordered more *Kama Sutra*-type books that, frankly, squick me out. It's not hetero sex that does it, per se, just the idea of what those books are going to be used for when the purchasers get them home—if they even make it home. Last year I found more than a few of them sticky and discarded in the bathroom. I shudder at the thought. Poor books.

I'd wager my next paycheck Noah wouldn't need a book like that. His hormones probably provided him with the perfect instruction manual as soon as he hit puberty. The way he walks around with so much confidence, I just know the man's never struggled or been lonely in bed. Of course that brings images of Noah spread out in a big bed in just boxers. I close my eyes to see the image more clearly, even though I realize it's a supremely stupid thing to do. I've never seen him naked, not even with his shirt completely undone, so how could my mental image of him be anywhere near the real thing? And why would I want to see the real thing? Unless—unless I was planning to have sex with him, which I absolutely am not.

Instead of the tsunami of panic that thought should—would normally—bring with it, the only things that rise are my temperature and the constriction level of my slacks. I shake my head hard to clear it of these flights of fancy and laugh a little awkwardly at myself.

We've spent quite a bit of time together since New Year's Eve. It's kind of hard not to when I'm cooking for him as much or more than I'm cooking for Sam and me. Cooking for Noah has been more fun than work, something I never would have expected. I've taken advantage of my employee discount more in the last thirty days than I have in the entire time I've worked at Flip the Page, and for cookbooks, of all things. So far, Noah has been eager, grateful and complimentary of my concoctions. I've only repeated one meal—sausage goulash—because he asked me to.

In thirty days we've smiled and laughed and talked about everything from our favorite colors—his is blue, mine came out "hazel" and I blushed furiously while he flashed those dimples at me—to world events, to my progress with Kendall.

In thirty days he hasn't tried to touch me again.

In some ways, I'm beginning to wonder if I imagined the whole scene in Kaleb's front yard, but then I remember the taste of him and I know I wouldn't have made that up, not like the images of him in his boxers.

Kendall has worked me hard in the last month, but she insists that we can't rush the type of emotional healing I have to do. I'm sure she's right but I've never felt more alive than I have these last thirty days. Kendall keeps trying to prepare me for a crash, but how much further could I crash than where I was in November? Even that was progress from August—but August was an aberration. I feel more like myself than I have since then. What happened in August took me straight back to the depths of hatred I'd lived in for seventeen years, before Sam rescued me from state custody. I lived through that before—barely, but I did it. I know I can do it again, even if Kendall is right and I do crash.

I've never seen Sam so proud of me. Now when he comes home if there are worry lines in his face, I know they're from the job, not me. As bizarre as it sounds, I've realized I need Sam to be proud of me, to see that all his care and sacrifice haven't been for nothing. I need him to know I'll be okay so that he can start living his own life, for him and Kira and the family they're going to be someday soon.

It hasn't been easy. Kendall's a hard taskmaster. She still gives me homework, things to think about and to write about so the poison slowly drains from my brain and heart. I'm not there yet. I may never be. I still hear Mom's and Carl's and Tommy's voices in my head telling me what a worthless waste of skin I am. But I believe them less. When Sam spends the night at Kira's, I can even sleep in my own bed. Well, it's only happened twice and the first night I lay awake all night, but it was on my own bed, not in the closet. The second night, I actually did sleep for a few hours.

The drawings have come easier, too. They often leave me feeling creative and happy instead of empty and frustrated. The one from yesterday is my second favorite so far—right behind the rendering of Noah's blue plaid shirt, which is now framed and sitting on my nightstand. The one I did yesterday is actually a picture of something instead of just impressions of my emotions—or some cotton cloth. I sketched a closet with a bed pallet. Although the clothes in there aren't mine, the pallet is. I drew the pallet half out of that sanctuary. It's an accurate representation of the fact that I find myself needing it less to escape into and more for just a place to store clothes. I'm making slow but steady progress and that fills me with hope and happiness.

"So what's on tap today, little one?" Noah asks with a smile as he comes through the door.

I smile all the way up at him and take the lid off his main dish, keeping the small one covered. "Grilled lemon chicken with wild rice and green beans." I bring the still covered dish closer to me. "And if you're good, a dessert."

His eyes go wide like the smile on his face. "Orange Fluff?"

I shake my head. "Nope. Something new."

Noah shakes his head and sits down. "You're too good to me, Aves. When I asked you to cook for me, I never expected this."

I shrug and wait for him to take his first bite before tucking in to mine. "It's nothing. I enjoy it."

He chews, issuing an appreciative moan that warms me from the inside out. After swallowing, he says, "I'm glad you're enjoying it because I know I am. I haven't eaten like this since I left my mom's house. And honestly, I'm not sure her cooking could compare."

I feel the heat in my cheeks. I should be getting used to Noah's easy praise by now, since he's so liberal with it, but it always surprises me. In all the months since we met, I've never heard him say a negative thing. Even when talking about accidents that have happened at work or his own father's death, Noah finds something positive to pull out of the situation. I've never known anyone like him.

I've never tasted anyone like him either. The color returns to my cheeks at the thought and when I glance up at him a little smirk crosses his lips like he knows exactly what I'm thinking about. Truth be told, it's been almost all I can think about since the moment it happened. As crazy as it sounds, even to me, I wish it would happen again so I can savor the moment. I know it's not likely to ever happen again. I know Noah was trying to comfort me and show me that I actually can trust him. He can't possibly be interested in a relationship or even just sex with me. He's positively the most handsome man I've ever seen, tall and masculine and confident in a million ways I'll never be. He's sexy with all those muscles, not too much, just enough to show he works hard with them and he knows they look good on him. He's sweet and kind and gentler than his hulking size would indicate. So what would he want with me?

I sit my fork down and look into my lap, overcome with a tidal wave of desperate longing. I haven't let myself realize until just this very moment how much I really do want Noah to want me. But the problem is, even if he does, I'm incapable of giving him what he wants. It's another abject failure on my part that I can't ever measure up to what he wants, what he needs. And it hurts more than I ever could have imagined.

Noah's hand gently covers mine where it rests on the table. I blink away the threatening tears but I don't move my hand away. I need his touch right now to lessen the blow to my heart. Perhaps he knows everything because when he whispers, "Aves," I could swear I hear pain in his voice, too.

Noah's thumb caresses the pulse point on my wrist and I watch through watery eyes, lashes and too-long bangs. "It's okay, little one," he soothes. "Whatever's going on in that head of yours, you know you're safe here with me, right?"

I nod even though right here with him is exactly where I shouldn't be. I want it too much, whatever it is we're doing. I know that being with him will only make it worse, make me want it and him more. So why can't I pull away and put distance between us? Why does the thought of not seeing him at lunch almost every day make me want to hold on to him like I would Sam?

Slowly, I turn my hand palm up and straighten my fingers. Noah manoeuvers his hand so his thick fingers slide between my thin ones and he closes them over me protectively. I grip him fiercely for a moment before letting my hand go limp. "We can't," I whisper.

His thumb continues to stroke the back of my hand. What is it with his thumb? Always his thumb. "Of course we can," he says lowly.

I shake my head and pull my hand from his. He lets me go without resistance and I can't help but hope his grip on my heart will relent as easily. I push back from the table and take my plate to the trash where the scrape of stainless steel across ceramic is the only sound in the room. Silently I rinse and dry the dishes and stow them safely away in the carrier I bought specifically to bring our lunches. I feel Noah's eyes on me the whole time but only when I'm finished does he speak his nickname for me again in that low, gentle voice.

"Little one…."

"Eat your dessert and go, Noah, please," I whisper.

"Tell me what's wrong."

"I can't."

"Okay," he says. "There's no rush, Aves. We do everything on your timetable."

I turn to look at him and he holds his hand out to me. Just like that night, I'm drawn to him by a power greater than me. I slip my fingers between his and close the distance between us. When I'm close enough, he leans his forehead against my stomach and inhales deeply. I stare down at his head of handsome blond hair, aching with the need to run my hands through the short strands. Somehow the feel of him against me grounds me again, sets the hope free and banishes the fear. He turns those deep pools of hazel bliss up at me and smiles tenderly.

"This is nice," he almost whispers.

I give a shaky laugh and move to sit back down so he won't notice the effect his touch has on me. If I'd wondered if my body liked the feel of him, I had the answer now and it was a resounding, tingling yes. With fumbling fingers, I uncap his dessert and push it toward him.

He looks in at the overly generous helping and flashes those dimples at me again. "I love cherry crisp."

"I know," I answer, the blood rushing to my face again, where it is much safer.

"How?" he asks, offering me the other spoon.

"Kaleb told me."

Noah takes a bite and closes his eyes with pleasure. I swear the man loves dessert more than any child. He swallows and fixes me with that hazel stare again. "Delicious. That settles it. There's only one thing for you to do."

I swallow my own much smaller bite and smile back at him. "What's that? Make more?"

"Nope." He grins and digs in again. "Become my personal chef for life."

***

Two nights later, I finally relent to Sam and Kira's endless cajoling and agree to accompany them to a pre-Valentine's dinner and movie. They claim they're still going to do their own thing on Valentine's Day; they just want to have a little quality family time with the three of us. Walking back into my room from the shower, I nearly jump right out of my skin at the sight of Sam rummaging through the clothes hanging in my closet.

"What are you doing?" I snap, struggling to secure the towel around my waist.

Sam jumps and looks at me guiltily. "Just looking for something nice for you to wear. When's the last time you updated your wardrobe?"

I frown at him in confusion. "I can dress myself, you know. Besides what difference does it make? We're going to a movie. It'll be dark and no one's gonna care anyway."

"Dinner first, remember? C'mon, champ, dress up for me. When's the last time you did that just for fun?" He resumes pawing through my clothes.

"When I was two. What's going on?"

"Nothing. I just want my favorite people to look nice and feel good about themselves tonight, that's—ah, here we go." He holds up a bright blue button down he'd gotten me for Christmas last year. Inwardly I cringe but paste on a half-smile. I've never worn that shirt outside the house. It's far too bright and attention-seeking for my liking.

"Okay, fine," I say, knowing I'll need time to prepare myself for all the unwanted stares and remarks I'll be getting. "Can I get dressed in peace now?"

"Sure thing." Sam studies the shirt for another moment before draping it carefully over the bed. "Wear your black jeans with that. You'll look amazing."

"Jeans?" I question in surprise. "I thought I was supposed to dress up."

"How many times have you worn those jeans, Aves?"

I shrug. "I dunno. Two or three times."

"Exactly. They're still new. Good enough." He stops to ruffle my wet hair on his way out the door. "You need a haircut. Get dressed."

He snatches my towel before I can stop him. Laughing, he throws it back at me, where it lands on my head.

***

Kira and I are laughing at some stupid joke of Sam's as we walk into the restaurant. It's Sam's favorite steakhouse so I know dinner will be delicious and, for once, something I didn't cook. And then I notice Kira walk right into Noah's open arms. He looks over her head at me and winks.

"What are you doing here?" I ask before I can stop myself.

Sam's hand lands on my shoulder and gives it a squeeze. "We invited Noah."

I turn and look up at him as it all falls into place, the dressing up, the insistence that I come. "Why didn't you just tell me?"

He gives me that look that means he knows I know the answer to a very simple question. "Would you have come?"

I see Noah and Kira involved in a conversation but Noah's concerned hazel gaze is still on me. I turn back to Sam. "I don't know, but I should have been given the choice." I frown at him. "Sam, Noah and I are never going to be more than friends, so if that's what you're aiming for, forget it."

Sam holds his hands up in surrender. "Hey, hey, no ulterior motives on my part, kiddo. We just thought the four of us could have a nice dinner and enjoy a movie together. I know you sometimes feel like a third wheel, so now we have a nice, balanced four."

I sigh and feel myself relax a bit. Without the extra pressure of Sam and Kira trying to create a love spark, I know I'll be able to enjoy the evening. It'll be just like lunch at work, only at night, in a nice restaurant, with Sam and Kira watching, and with Noah in yet another turtleneck. Heaven help me.

The smiling hostess shows us to our table, thankfully not a booth, and the two big men follow in the small wake left by the petite Kira and the even shorter me. I feel outmaneuvered and undersized. At the table, the men quickly move to put Kira's back to the door with me opposite her, Sam to my right, Noah to my left, and a garishly decorated half-wall to my back. I know Sam, being the cop he is, usually likes to face the door or the larger area of the dining room so he can surreptitiously watch the goings-on around him. More than once over the years, he's hustled me quickly out of a place when he's seen suspicious activity, usually suspected drug trades in bathrooms or when he's expected violence to break out. In his current seat, Sam's back is to only two booths and the corner where the restrooms are discreetly tucked away. It means traffic will pass behind him, but I know he'll be alert enough to know exactly who or what is coming his direction. I also know he's deliberately given up to me the seat he'd prefer, so that I am bracketed on each side by his and Noah's tall, muscular masses. I have without question the safest seat in the house, with Kira's being a close second.

As our server comes to deposit glasses of ice water before each of us and hand out menus, I smile my silent thanks to Sam who winks in response. A slight sadness passes through me, but I quickly shake it off.

Yes, I'll miss the effortless way Sam takes care of me, even in this seemingly safe situation, but that emotion is for later.

I listen to the three of them discuss the merits of various cuts of meat as I peruse the menu, looking for something Avery-sized to eat without resorting to the hated children's menu. I'm not exceptionally hungry and steakhouse portions are notoriously too much for me. Shortly after Sam had rescued me from the group home, he brought me here. Because I'd been unsure of the cuts of meat and ignorant to the size of portions here, I'd let Sam order for me. While he'd polished off almost everything and even ordered an ice cream dessert, I'd taken the remains of my dinner home and had two more meals out of it.

I tune back into the conversation just in time to hear Noah say, "Really? That's great. Congratulations, little one."

I flush hard at the use of his nickname for me in front of Sam and Kira and then harder when I realize I have no idea what he's talking about. As is becoming his habit more and more lately, Noah seems to read my mind.

"Sam just told me Walter offered you the bookkeeping position when Brian leaves next month. That's a really exciting opportunity."

His praise lights my cheeks again and I look at my lap to hide my embarrassment. "Thanks," I mumble.

Much to my surprise, Noah's index finger slides under my chin and raises my face until I look him in the eyes. "Hey, don't be shy," he says softly, that finger on my skin still drawing all my attention. Unable to maintain the intense eye contact, my gaze drops to his lips and then jump back to his eyes, because no matter how discomfiting it is to look into those hazel pools, watching the man's lips move is far, far worse. "We're very proud of you."

His easy praise warms me as much as the heat from his skin and I smile tremulously and nod, breaking contact with his finger. "I know. Thank you," I offer softly. "I don't think I'll take it, but it was nice of Walter to ask anyway."

Noah smiles, obviously pleased about something. "You should give it some serious thought before you turn him down. I think you'd be terrific in the role. Talk to Kendall about it."

Our server returns with drinks—a Cosmo for Kira, Crown and Coke for Noah, and iced tea for Sam and me since he has to drive later and I'm just not fond of alcohol. As he distributes the drinks and takes orders around the table, I can't help but notice he's flirting with Noah. I feel my eyes narrow in irritation as I take a good look at him for the first time. I have to admit, he's not bad looking. Medium height and build, more jock than bookworm probably, he has a classically handsome face and a pleasant smile he's using to try to charm Noah. Even with all that going for him, the word I'd use for him is average. He's certainly out of my league, but he's nowhere near Noah's. No, the guy Noah ends up with needs to stand out in a crowd as much as Noah does. He needs to be vibrant and dynamic and have a wicked sense of humor, because there's very little more beautiful than Noah laughing. This guy, he's vanilla bean ice cream, maybe Neapolitan with his clothes off, but Noah deserves Baked Alaska.

I'm frozen yogurt, a pale imitation of the real thing, but really, that's okay. As much as I've started to yearn for more from Noah, I know it's not possible. No matter how many times Kendall makes me say it, I know I'm not capable of being loved in the same way others are. I've never been bothered by it before now. But now...now, Noah makes me wish I could be more worthy. It's something else I'll have to learn to live with.

Sam nudges me with his knee and I check back in. "Kaleb's up at the bar. I'm going to go say hi."

"Me, too," Noah says, rising from the table.

Sam leans over to press a kiss to Kira's lips before getting up. It's something he always does, but this time it breaks my heart a little.

"Avery." I hear my name as almost a low growl in my ear. I turn my head and look up to find Noah's face just inches from mine. Before I can think to move away, he moves in, sliding his mouth over mine once, twice. He draws back, licks those incredible lips of his and winks. "Win," he whispers, breaking into a radiant grin.

As he and Sam move away, I notice Sam slap Noah on the back and bend his head to say something to him quietly. My gaze slides to Kira, who sits there staring back at me, the fingers at her lips unable to hide her smile. I try to focus, to breathe, to say something, but all I can do is replay the moment in my mind. The moment Noah Yates kissed me.

I meet Kira's gaze finally and she erupts into laughter. "Yes, it really happened. Noah just kissed you right in front of Sam and everybody."

I nod, dumbfounded, and look down at my shaking hands. *My first kiss*, I think, bringing my trembling fingers up to my tingling, smiling lips.

***

By the time Sam and Noah return from no doubt giving Kaleb a hard time, I'm almost calm. Almost. My old friend panic never had a chance to freak me out, clobbered over the head as it was by excitement and surprise and an overwhelming sense of glee that Noah would not only want to but actually would kiss me. I fear I'm on the verge of hysterical giggles.

"Kaleb says hello. He's meeting a new kart distributor or he'd come over," Sam says as he sits.

Noah resumes his place to my left and I feel my cheeks glowing with heat. Airliners could use my face as altitude beacons, although that would be disastrous for everyone. I'm overcome by a shyness laced, perversely, with a streak of rebellion. I risk a glance at the first man to ever kiss me. The open affection in his winking gaze shoots unfamiliar desire through me. I shiver at the force of it, hoping for anything else to capture everyone's attention.

Noah smiles at me and turns to Kira. "Your brother said Kyle's seeing somebody?" His knee brushes mine and I know he's read my mind again. He's diverting attention away from me.

She laughs. "Oh, he's seeing someone alright. Hillary Redman, of all people. You remember her, don't you?"

Noah visibly winces. "I'm not likely to forget her. She chased me relentlessly through three years of high school. I even talked to my dad about transferring."

Everybody laughs, but I'm intrigued by this new facet of Noah's personality. I've never seen him anything but controlled and confident. Somehow it makes me feel better to know that even Noah had trouble with high school, if only because of the incessant advances of some teenage trollop.

"You wouldn't recognize her now," Kira says. "She's pulled herself together, calmed down. She's a nurse now. That's how Kyle met her again. He almost sliced off his thumb doing something stupid to his own kart. Hillary tended to his wounds and it was something at first sight. I don't think Kyle's ready to call it love after three weeks, but whatever it is, it's hot and heavy."

Noah nods. "I'm glad she got herself together." He laughs. "She sure scared the heck out of me. I think the time she tried to kiss me by my locker sophomore year was the instant I figured out all those weird feelings I'd been having for Kaleb meant I was gay. Maybe I should thank her."

My heart leaps to my throat. Kaleb. Noah has feelings for Kaleb? Of course he does. Kaleb's his match in every way. Except, what about Josh?

Kira and Sam laugh. "Probably not a good idea, bro."

"Yeah," Kira adds. "I can't think of any woman who would appreciate a guy telling her she made him realize he was gay. That's not something that would make her feel sexy, for sure!"

Our flirtatious waiter arrives with our food and I surprise myself by wanting to growl at him when he puts a hand on Noah's shoulder as he places his plate before him. It all happens in an instant, I see server boy's hand on Noah's shoulder, I stifle the growl and I feel Noah's knee brush against mine under the table. My eyes cut to his. I should know by now: the man misses nothing. Even with the waiter still moving around him, Noah's amused gaze is focused solely on me. I flush for the seven hundredth time of the evening and turn my attention firmly to my own food. I can't help the small victory smile that tugs at my lips. Waiter boy touches Noah and Noah still has his eyes on me. That is not a development I would ever have expected, but it feels good.

***

The movie can't hold my interest. Between the lethargy brought on from a stomach full of succulent steak, the darkness of the theater and the safety of being sandwiched between the two big men, I'm slowly giving in to the lull of sleep. The third time my head pops up when I wake, Noah takes pity on me. He wraps his arm loosely around my shoulder and pulls me to him. I glance up at him and relax at the sight of his gentle smile.

"Lean against me and go to sleep if you want. It's okay," he whispers.

I hesitate. It's one thing to hold his hand in the break room or Kaleb's front yard. It's something else entirely to essentially cuddle up to the man in a public theater. I look over at Sam to see him smile at me and nod, Kira similarly wrapped up under his left arm.

Even with Sam's apparent blessing and my newfound comfort with Noah's touch, the little voice in my head screams at me to do anything but what Noah suggests. I shake my head at him. "I can't."

He nods and offers me a lopsided smile. "You can, you know. You're perfectly safe with me. But I won't push. We do this at your speed." His hand lifts from my shoulder to muss my hair before falling once again on the back of my seat.

I lean forward, elbows on knees, chin in hands, determined to stay awake and maybe make sense of this movie by the time it's over. But try as I might, I can't concentrate on the storyline. As compelling as the shield-throwing superhero might be, he pales in comparison to that last sentence of Noah's. "We do this at your speed." Just what is *this* and what is my speed?

My mind wanders back to that look in Noah's eyes back in the restaurant right before his lips touched mine. Those incredible hazel pools had been filled with some intense but unnamable emotion that had caught the breath in my throat. My lips tingle again at the memory and I bring my fingertips to them once more, scarcely able to believe it really happened. The sensation of fingers on my mouth draws me back to that incredible moment at Kaleb's when Noah's thumb had so gently stroked my lip, the moment I'd gotten my first taste of him. It hadn't been enough then, despite how bizarre it seems now, and I wonder if the memory of Noah's taste and touch ever will be.

I glance back at him to find his watching me with a lopsided smile. Ignoring the voices in my head, I sit back in my seat and curl up next to him, my head in the crook of his shoulder. I feel his biceps flex as his arm around my shoulders gives me a light squeeze. I hear him whisper, "Thank you," just before his lips brush my hair. My heart races and my body tingles in response. I allow myself to breathe in that special scent that is all and only Noah and relax against him.

Seconds later, a tap on my forehead startles me awake. My head jerks up from where it rested against Sam. Surprised, I stare into his blue gaze before looking quickly around for Noah, who is conspicuously absent. The house lights rise quickly, bathing us in their harsh glare.

"You missed the whole movie, sleepyhead," Sam accuses with a smile.

I shrug and fight back a yawn. "Sorry."

Sam ruffles my hair. "Don't apologize to me. Apologize to your boyfriend."

I glare at him sleepily but I know the effect is ruined by the rush of blood to my face. "Shut up. Where's Noah?"

"He had to go unload that gallon of Pepsi he drank. I figured we'd let you sleep a few more minutes while he waited in line."

I nod and my jaw cracks with the force of my yawn. I duck my head in embarrassment.

Sam laughs again and I even hear a quiet giggle from Kira, who looks just as sleepy as I feel. Apparently the movie was only good for the two big boys. "C'mon, let's get you home so you can dream about your boyfriend."

"Stop that," I say, embarrassed again, even as my lips tingle with the memory of Noah's kiss.

Sam stands up and looks down at me with a grin. "You'll be okay, Avery. I really believe that. With or without Noah Yates, you'll be fine." Then his grin turns teasing and his eyebrows dance obscenely. "But with him I can tease you mercilessly about all the crazy sexual stuff you two will get up to. I think I'm looking forward to that the most."

I can only gape at him as a thousand scenes overlap on my mental view screen. Thankfully Kira is there to give Sam's butt a much needed swat.

***

I look shyly at Kendall through my mess of dark bangs and fit another puzzle piece in place. It's been two days since Noah kissed me and it's almost all I can think about. I was an absolute wreck at work yesterday, zoning out in the middle of ringing up customers, forgetting answers to the most basic questions. I'd even caught myself trying to shelve a book about Greek statuary in the relationship improvement section. Thankfully, I hadn't needed to try to hide my scattered thoughts and emotions from Noah because it was his scheduled day off. Several times I found myself wondering if that was another example of him knowing what I need before I know it myself. Sam was right months ago when he said Noah knows how to handle me. Well, Sam said Noah "gets" me, but I don't think anyone can truly "get" me. Even Sam has a hard time with that sometimes, and he was right there in the group home with me all those years.

I've replayed Noah's kiss in my head so many times in the last forty-some hours that I'm not even sure it's real now. No, that's not true. I remember vividly the feel and taste of Noah's lips against mine, but I wonder just how much too much I'm reading into it. Kendall looks back at me expectantly, not even pretending to work the puzzle with me. She just plays with the piece between her fingers, a bemused smile on her face. She's known throughout the session that something new is on my mind. It's taken me forty minutes of our fifty minute session to be able to voice it.

Finally I can't hold it in anymore. I twist my fingers together nervously in my lap. "I have something to tell you, but only if you promise not to ask how it makes me feel."

Kendall laughs throatily and finally slots her piece into the puzzle. It'll be beautiful when we finish. It's a fifty-three inch by thirty-eight inch, four-thousand piece picture of Neuschwanstein Castle. I haven't missed that the handsome King Ludwig II of Bavaria, the builder of Neuschwanstein, was very eccentric, suspected to be insane, and supposedly gay. Clever, clever Kendall. "Well that's sort of my function here, Avery, but I'll try to come up with a more original question."

For a moment, I relive the way Noah's lips brushed over mine once, twice. I see again the hundred different ways he smiled at me that night at dinner, the way he encouraged me to rest against him during movie, and that awkward goodbye after when he hugged Kira, shook Sam's hand and tousled my hair. If I'm not completely honest with myself, that's the part that confuses me most: the tousling of the hair. It's an affectionate gesture, yes, but it's so brotherly that, coming on the heels of a kiss, I don't know what to make of it. But if I *am* completely honest with myself, it's the kiss that totally blows my mind.

"Noah kissed me," I blurt out, unable to contain it anymore.

Kendall nods, a half-smile playing at her painted lips. "Okay. Would you like to give me more details?"

I blanch. "No!"

Kendall laughs again. "I'm sorry. I should have been clearer. I don't mean give me details about the kiss, although that's fine, too. What I'm really asking is that you paint the scene for me: where were you? How'd it happen? Did you enjoy it? Do you want it to happen again?"

I swallow hard and try unsuccessfully not to think about how unfathomable Noah's eyes were so close to mine. I fill Kendall in on the details of the surprise double date, the unsavory server, the follow-the-leader mimicry that led to my first kiss. I can't stop the smile any more than I could force my fingers from touching my lips for the nine hundredth time since Noah did.

Kendall leans back in her black, high-backed office chair and regards me with a smile. "Congratulations, Avery. Not only is this a big moment in your life, but you seem to be handling it well. Or did I miss the panic attack?"

My eyes grow wide with the realization. "There wasn't one."

Kendall's smile grows wider. "You see? Your hard work is paying off. If Noah had tried to kiss you in November, what would you have done?"

I shake my head in wonder, unable to imagine it. I know I would have freaked right the heck out. I probably wouldn't have left my bedroom closet for weeks.

"So here is the important question: do you want Noah to kiss you again?"

Chapter 11 – March

"Oh my god!" I cry, running across the living room to where Sam has just walked in the front door. His left eye is swollen almost closed, colored ugly shades of purple and green. His bottom lip is stitched and I can see he has bled down onto his uniform shirt. Gently, he removes tissues from deep in both nostrils. I pull myself up short. I want to touch him, but I have no idea where else he's hurt. "Are you okay? What happened?"

Sam smiles tiredly, wincing when the action pulls his stitches in his lip. His tongue and fingers reach the spot at the same time and he shrugs slightly before toeing off his shoes. "I ran into an old friend tonight."

"Friend?" Clearly one with a different friendship with Sam than I have.

"Yeah." He pulls off his gun belt—I will always think of it as a utility belt—and stows his weapon in the safe inside the coat closet. "We got called to a brawl at a bar called the Finish Line. It used to be a sports bar, but now it's mostly a biker bar with assorted losers thrown in." He eases himself down on the couch, grimacing as he holds obviously sore ribs. "Anyway, when we got there, the first guys on the scene had mostly calmed things down, so I was just doing another walkthrough to make sure we hadn't missed anything." He trails off, probably reliving it.

Trembling, I very carefully sit down on the couch next to him. "And?"

"And I was walking down the hall to the bathrooms when our old friend Tommy Blevins came out of the men's room. I don't know if he recognized me or just decided to run from the uniform, but he took off back into the bathroom. I ran in after him. That's when he clocked me the first time." Sam shakes his head. "I have no idea what happened, but it was like the instant I saw him, all my training went out the window." He gestures at his face. "This is my own fault. If I'd followed procedure, I wouldn't look and feel like this. But it was just…," he pauses, then practically spits the name, "Tommy Blevins."

The first mention of the name had caused my breath to seize in my lungs, but this time I feel the panic rising. Tommy Blevins. I can see him clearly, even after all this time. It doesn't take much for my body to remember the feel of his fists and feet on me. I close my eyes as a ripple of fear courses the length of my spine. I look up to see Sam staring back at me with his one good eye.

He puts his hand on my shoulder. "Don't worry, champ. He's not going to hurt you. He's locked up for assaulting an officer plus various and sundry weapons and drug charges. With his history, he'll probably get time again."

I nod, not quite believing it, still perched on the precipice of panic, and move cautiously under Sam's raised arm. I lean against him and try to keep calm. But…

Tommy Blevins. My own special demon.

***

I wake from the nightmare, breathing hard and crying. It wasn't the worst one I've ever had and I should be grateful. I'm not screaming my fool head off, but having them back again hurts and fills me with a sense of dread. How long will they be around this time? How bad will they get? Is this the crash Kendall keeps warning me about? And how is it possible that Tommy Blevins has this much power over me still, so much that the mere mention of his name—okay and the evidence of his fists on Sam's body—can cause these horrific dreams to come back?

Although I feel like I've just run a marathon, not tried to sleep, I know I won't find peace in slumber again tonight. Carelessly, I toss back the covers and climb out of bed. Glancing at the clock, I bite back a sigh. It's only 3:30, another six hours before I have to be at work. Gritty-eyed, I pull on a t-shirt to compliment my sleep pants and pad barefoot into the kitchen. I look longingly at the cabinet in which the Ambien resides, but knowing I don't have the full eight hours they require, I pull a cookbook from the cupboard instead. Perhaps I can find something good, but not too complicated for my sleepy state, to make Noah for lunch. I already have his meal for today prepared, but I may as well get started on the rest of the week.

***

"So what's on tap today?"

My head shoots up toward Noah, who walks through the door without a care in the world. Luckily, I'm on the opposite side of the room, but I still back up against the counter, putting as much space between us as possible. I notice absently that he's wearing another turtleneck today, but my gaze goes no higher than his neck.

I look at him, but have nothing to say. I still haven't slept, so even if the specter of Tommy Blevins hadn't just turned my life upside down last night, my nerves would still be buzzing dangerously.

"Aves?" Noah asks again, gently this time. "What's the matter?"

"N-nothing," I whisper, unable to put sound to the air leaving my throat.

Noah's movements slow like a man trying not to spook a wild animal. He moves to a chair farther from the door but not necessarily closer to me. I know he's giving me the option of escape and I can't believe the amount of gratitude that fills me at that simple gesture. He sits down quietly and folds his hands together atop the table, keeping his big body strangely still.

The chime of the microwave startles me, but I pull myself together enough to retrieve Noah's food and put it on the table before him. It's a large steaming bowl of chili with a heap of shredded sharp cheddar cheese melted over a few pickles. Noah glances up at me with a gentle, melancholy smile, but I quickly shift my eyes away. I can't afford to see the emotion on his face or I'll completely lose my composure.

I place a sleeve of crackers in front of him and carefully step backwards to warm my own food, not turning my back on him, even though the rational side of my brain reminds me I'm safe with Noah. I watch the bowl go round and round on the plate and think that's my life. Just when I think I'm breaking free from my past and the reality of who I am, something sends me careening back to it. I'll always be the same, no matter how much I try or what I do differently.

And just as one day my life will end, so does the microwave cycle. Blinking the tears from my tired, aching eyes, I reach in and rescue the metaphorical me, setting the bowl on the table across from Noah. Normally I would sit around the corner from him so we could be closer, but today I desperately need the distance the table provides.

Noah has prepped his chili with crushed crackers and stirred them in, but he waits until I catch up to take his first taste. "Pickles?" He laughs. """Little one, you're a genius. I never would have thought of that, but it's amazing."

I smile wanly and mumble my thanks, keeping my attention on my own food. Regardless of what Noah says, I can't taste anything but fear.

A few moments later, I hear Noah sigh. I cringe, knowing what's coming. "Is this because of the kiss, Avery?" he asks softly.

My startled gaze immediately jumps to his wounded one. "No!" How could he think that? That kiss was the most amazing moment of my life, wildly beating out that night on Kaleb's porch. I take a deep breath and focus on the tabletop between us. "I'm sorry, Noah. I-I don't mean to be weird."

Noah chuckles softly and stretches his hand toward me on the table. All I have to do is move a few inches and we'll be touching. I can practically feel the warmth of his skin against mine. “Tell me what’s wrong,” he coaxes gently.

I close my eyes and can’t stop the twin shudders of revulsion and terror that race up my spine at the thought of Tommy Blevins. I don’t want to talk about him, but somehow I know Noah deserves the truth. He can’t change anything, but at least he’ll know I’m not freaking out about his kiss. “When-when I was in the group home, before Sam came….” My voice cracks against the tears in my throat, but I force myself to continue. “There was a kid—Tommy—who used to beat up the younger kids. Joey and I got it worse than the rest and more often.” I risk a glance up to find Noah gone completely still, his eyes on me, an unreadable expression on his strong face. “When Sam came, he pretty much forced Tommy and his gang to leave us alone, but sometimes he’d get to us anyway.” I try a wan smile, but it dies on my trembling lips. “I have only seen him once since I left the group home. It was my fault. I was where I shouldn’t have been.” I shake the memory to the back of my mind. “Anyway, Sam ran into him yesterday on a call. Tommy got in a few punches before Sam could subdue him.”

Noah's index finger gently strokes the back of my hand. I don’t remember sliding it closer to him, but I must have. His touch soothes my ragged mind.

“One of your worst nightmares shows back up in your life and you’re a little freaked out. It’s perfectly natural, Aves.” Noah's hand moves mine so his thumb gently caresses my palm. “Just remember I’m not here to hurt you, sweetheart. In fact, I’d give anything to make sure no one and nothing ever does again.”

Immediately and involuntarily, my downcast eyes fill with tears. I know he means every word. It means more to me than he can ever fully understand. With Noah, I don't have to pretend to be strong. With Noah, I actually have someone other than Sam to lean on. There's not a molecule in his body that believes the terrible things Mom and Carl beat into me with words and fists. Noah genuinely cares for and will protect me. And that last thought is my undoing.

Without embarrassment or shame, I allow the tears to flow. They're pain and hate, fear and self-loathing, relief and release, but ultimately they're healing. It is long moments before my mind recognizes the feel of wet cotton against my face. It is only then that I recognize the strong bands of Noah's arms around me, holding me to his chest. He croons softly into my hair as he caresses my neck. Contrary to every instinct I've ever had, I allow myself to lean into him, absorbing his undeniable strength. Incredibly, I recognize the lyrics to the pop song he's marvelously singing to me. I first heard the Christina Aguilera song in a temporary foster home on one of my rare stints outside of the group home. Mrs. Garcia played it for us at least once a day, but the words never seemed to apply to me before. But now, as Noah sings them in that gorgeous, deep voice of his, I believe that Noah thinks I am beautiful in all ways.

I squeeze my eyes tight against a fresh onslaught of tears and allow my arms to encircle him. I tilt my head up to look at him. He smilingly sings the chorus again and I fall deep into those hazel eyes. When his words die away, he caresses my cheek gently then leans down to press a kiss to my lips. My mind sighs with some alien but wonderful emotion and I allow myself to kiss him back. Before it gets too deep, Noah pulls back and presses pecks to my nose and forehead.

"All better?" he asks.

I can only nod and smile goofily at him as my chest explodes with the most wondrous feeling. I have no name for it, but it feels suspiciously like happiness.

***

Spring arrives before I realize it. One moment we're having the biggest blizzard on record—on Valentine's Day, no less—and the next moment the grass is that fresh, beautiful green, the trees are getting their leaves back and the birds are singing rapturously. The days get longer and brighter and I can't help but compare them to my mood.

With Kendall's help and a lot of ugly, painful hard work, I'm almost back to where I was before August. I feel like a normal person again. It's almost unsettling. Of course, I still have setbacks, still have days I'd rather spend sleeping the day away in my closet, but I resist that temptation, and, thankfully, those days are fewer and farther between than they've been for years.

Naturally, Noah plays a part in all of this, too. The day I allowed him to hold me as I cried over the reappearance of Tommy Blevins changed something fundamental between us. For the first couple of days afterward, Noah was almost tentative around me. It was the first time I'd ever seen him unsure of himself. Seeing him that way made me unsure, too. I spent far too much time wondering if he regretted kissing me or if he would ever do it again. I wanted to put back up the walls he so successfully destroyed between us because I was afraid he would up and disappear one day, realizing I am far too much trouble for him to bother with.

Instead, Noah shows me he has no intention of going anywhere. He invites me to meet him at the kart track to defend my victory from months ago. Now how am I supposed to say no to that? It takes three weeks to sync our weekends off, but finally it happens. Because I'm still nervous about being there with just him, we make it a foursome. Kira and Sam come along and entertain us for a while, but sometime after the second race, they vanish.

Noah feeds me so much cotton candy I swear I will be buzzing for two days. He thinks it will be enough to distract me from the race, from kicking his pretty round behind out on the track, but he sorely underestimates my competitive nature.

I'll never forget the way he stares down at me, eyes narrowed, hands on hips. His posture might have intimidated me if Kaleb weren't massaging my shoulders. Well, that and the goofy grin on Noah's face pretty much takes away the fierceness of his expression. We've just finished our fourth race and we're all tied up, two apiece.

"Double or nothing, winner takes all," he dares me.

I laugh. "Noah, we haven't bet anything."

"Don't distract me with semantics." He scowls around a grin he can't contain. "Okay, so we bet now."

"Watch out for this one, Aves," Kaleb faux-whispers in my ear. "He's up to something."

I smile up at him from the corner of my eye. 'He's *always* up to something."

"Hey!" Noah clasps his hands to his chest just over his heart and staggers back a few steps. "That hurts."

I laugh again and take in the moment. I honestly can't believe I'm here with *him*, doing *this*, literally without a care in the world. This…*happy*…is such a foreign emotion, but it feels so amazingly good. This is what people write songs about, what they take drugs to simulate. But for me, all it takes is being with a teasing Noah at an indoor go kart track. Five months ago I never would have believed it possible for me to feel so totally unburdened, so free, so happy. And five months ago I never would have believed Noah Yates would be the catalyst for it all. I push down the uncomfortable thought of exactly what that means and soak up the sights and sounds and energy of it all. I want to be able to tuck this memory safely away, to be able to pull it out and enjoy on one of those bad days.

"Name your terms, Goliath," I tease.

Kaleb's rumbling laughter behind me vibrates through me where he's kneading my shoulders. "He's got your number, Yates. You'd better quit while you're ahead."

"But I'm not ahead!" Noah pouts. "We're tied!" he shakes his head. "Fine, but you just remember you forced me into this."

"I what?"

"Tut!" He makes a shushing motion with one hand, bringing the other up to wipe the grin from those beautiful, tasty lips. "Okay, if—*if*—you win this race, you can give me a consolation kiss."

If my eyes could widen any more, I think they would fall right out of my head. "I—what?"

Noah smiles innocently and continues. "But when—*when*—I win, you agree to go to dinner with me somewhere nice, just the two of us. No chaperones."

I gape at him, but he isn't finished.

That cocky grin of his reappears as he slowly walks toward me. The pitch of his voice changes to a sexy rumble that vibrates my entire body. "And of course I promise you can give me a victory kiss."

Involuntarily my eyes roll back at the incredible promise in his voice and I hear a whimpering sound issue from my suddenly constricted throat. At the sound, my eyes pop back open and I lock my knees where they've threatened to buckle.

Kaleb's hands have stilled on my shoulders and I look back up at him. He's wearing the most astonished expression, eyes wide, mouth slightly agape. Suddenly he comes back to himself and looks down at me. He squeezes one shoulder and steps back, swallowing hard. "Honey, if you don't take that bet, I will." Then he winks, smacks my butt and walks away.

I turn to stare at Noah who gazes back at me with a serene smile. "Whaddya say, baby?" he asks. "You interested?"

I growl and shove him hard in one shoulder. He barely moves. "You're such a jerk. Of course I'm in." I put my hands to my hips and give him the death scowl. "I'm gonna wipe the floor with you."

He actually chuckles. "Are you sure that's what you want, little one? You'd settle for a hollow victory and a kiss?"

I move to point at him to reinforce some argument I'm about to make, probably that he's a presumptuous jerk, but he captures my hand and brings it to his lips. All rational thought ceases. I can almost feel the switch in my brain flip. All power to the auxiliary! Ridiculously intense tingles spread through my body in response to Noah's touch.

"Mmm, that's what I thought," he croons lowly. Turning my hand over, he presses a licking kiss to my wrist and my whole body shudders. "Cotton candy," he whispers with a wink and a lick of his lips. As his lower lip slowly slides free of his teeth, I finally regain breathing function and look reluctantly away. He chuckles again and slides past me. "Go get ready for me, little one. You're gonna eat my dust."

Twenty minutes later he leans down so I can give him his victory kiss. I avoid his lips, placing a tender peck on his left cheek. I whisper into his ear, "We're still tied, you know. That first one still counts."

His big hands goose me where he holds my small waist. "It's still a *win* for me," he whispers back and I know he's not talking about racing anymore.

***

The end of March rapidly approaches and with it comes the decision I have to make about the bookkeeping position. Walter talked me into doing the training for it while Brian could still teach me, with the understanding that, in the end, I still might decide it's not something I want to do.

Although I'm still unsure about taking on the responsibility, I've discovered that I love the job—the ordering and invoicing systems were a piece of cake to master. Brian's a good teacher and he's careful to explain the whys of everything we do so I understand. Even though I was painfully trained by Mom and Carl to blindly obey without question or hesitation, my brain works best at tasks for which I comprehend the reason. Perhaps it's because there seemed to be no rhyme or reason behind half the things that happened to me as a kid and I always tried to think one step ahead to avoid being in trouble—not that it did any good. In the concrete world of numbers, I find reason, flow and order. It's a revelation. For me, the best part is trying to find a discrepancy in the numbers. It's like a mystery with few clues, just waiting for me to solve it.

I only wish my feelings for Noah were like that. If I could divide them by nine and figure out where they got transposed, I would be a happy guy. Well, that might not be true, but it would be one less thing to worry about.

I cook him ten meals a week, lunches and dinners, for which he pays me a ridiculous amount of money, but I would do it for free just to see his reactions. I've hit on a few key favorites, ones he asks me to make again and again, and I'm broadening my skill set tremendously. Sam has been enjoying the fruits of my experimentations, too. He took to calling me the Good Wife until he got meatloaf three days in a row. Now he calls me Chef Champ, which cracks me up. I'm neither a chef nor a champion, but it makes me feel good to be able to please the two men in my life.

And as much as I have fought it, there is no question that Noah is in my life to stay. It absolutely petrifies me to think he wants more from me than friendship, food and a few kisses. Really, there is no thinking to it; he's basically said it.

March Madness is some eons-long college basketball tournament that apparently happens every year. I remember vaguely hearing about it before, that it's a really huge deal for college sports lovers. I've even heard that the President of the United States talks about it. I don't get it. Basketball is so supremely boring. I can't understand the point of watching ten giants running from one end of the field—*court*—to the other throwing an orange ball through a hoop in the air. I guess it's better than golf, but so is watching paint dry.

Of course, both Noah and Sam are obsessed with this tournament. When Sam stops by the store one day while Noah and I are eating lunch—tarragon chicken with sautéed string beans and wild rice, with cranberry nut dessert—Noah invites us to his place to watch the UK play KU. When I ask why the British are coming, both men laugh, then Noah presses a sweet, somewhat condescending kiss to my forehead and says, "Ah, honey, the University of Kentucky, not the United Kingdom."

"Oh," I say, cheeks flaming with embarrassment, and that's the end of my basketball discourse.

When the day comes, Sam insists I tag along to Noah's place to watch the game. I pretend not to go willingly, but as much as I am uncomfortable stepping into Noah's personal space, I'm almost equally as curious about the place he calls home.

In the end, it takes two days of cajoling from both of them and a blessed valium, but I put on my big boy pants and step into Noah's lair. I almost laugh at Sam, decked out in KU attire, until Noah answers the door in very nearly the same stuff—except my heart skips a beat and all my blood rushes to my face and my groin when I see Noah.

Where Sam wears a polo shirt with the university letters and bird logo, Sam is only half-dressed, clad in a tank top jersey and shorts. A tank top—which means those amazing arms I've felt around me and fantasized about in my most private moments are now laid bare in all their smoothly muscled glory for my eyes to see. And those shoulders! He greets Sam jovially with a handshake that rivets my eyes to that incredible bicep as it flexes and bunches and whatever the heck muscles like that do when they're putting on a show. My mouth goes dry and I have to work to swallow in order to squeak out a hello.

Despite the valium, my breath comes in shallow bursts and I excuse myself to the bathroom for a minute alone to get myself together. I've never had such a reaction to someone's physicality, his sexuality, before and it's dang frightening. But even more than that, it's *exciting*, which is a whole new level of discomforting. I reach my shaky hands out to turn the tap—cold water on the face, good—and bump against the counter. I gasp, realizing I have an erection. My heartbeat kicks into overdrive with embarrassment. I hope to all that is holy that Noah didn't notice. I mean, I'm a short guy, but I'm not little everywhere and, looking at myself in the mirror, the bulge is pretty obvious. I have to force myself not to untuck my shirt.

I compel myself to calm down, breathing slowly until both my heart rate and my treacherous groin are under control. Pushing down the panic that this might happen again, I splash my face and the back of my neck with cold, cold water. Then I catch sight of myself in the mirror and almost let out a laugh of relief. I brush my hair aside and focus on my ruined eye socket. No, there's no chance of that erection coming back now. And even if it did, one look at my full face would have Noah running for the hills. I breathe a sigh of relief and blink quickly to empty my eyes of self-pity water, as Carl would call it.

I open the door to find Noah leaning against the far wall of the hallway. I nearly jump right out of my skin, a neat trick if I could do it.

"Oh! You scared me." I notice his blond chest hair glistening in the light and resolutely turn my eyes to the floor.

"Are you okay?" he asks gently.

I nod, my eyes traveling up part of the long length of his exposed lower legs, desperately trying not to notice the shimmering blond hair there, too. I swallow hard once again and force my voice to work. "I'm fine. I'm sorry."

He pushes off the wall and then I feel his finger under my chin, urging me to look up at him. "What are you sorry for?" he asks in that same patient tone.

I tilt my head up but keep my eyes down, newly conscious again of how I look, of who I am, and how insane it is for me to have these feelings for anyone, much less a man like Noah Yates. "I shouldn't be here," I whisper.

Noah's hand cups my cheek, his thumb gently stroking my full bottom lip. It's a gesture I'm more than comfortable with after a month of his kisses, because his thumb on my lips always means his lips will soon follow. "You absolutely should be here," he whispers back. "I would love for you to be here all the time. You belong here."

I try to shake my head, but he won't allow it. Instead, I murmur, "No."

"Yes," he answers. I can feel him moving closer, his mouth readying to join with mine. "You belong with me, little one."

I feel like a volcanic mess inside, torn up, on fire, conflicted in a million ways, but I know I have to be strong enough to stop this madness before my heart erupts. "No. Whatever you think is going on, Noah, it can't happen. I can't be that guy." I put my hand to his chest to push him away, but he's so warm and solid and sleek beneath my fingertips. I close my eyes, in defeat or defense, I'm not sure, but it doesn't matter.

"It's already happening, sweetheart. It has been for a while," he whispers just before his mouth makes contact with mine. He keeps the kiss slow and easy, not demanding or asking for more than I can give, just gently pursuing like always.

I can't help it; I can't stop myself. He feels too good, too strong and solid and *real.* I moan and lean into the kiss, clutching at the silky material of his shirt to bring him closer.

His arms come around my waist and urge me closer. He lets me take the steps to bring our bodies together, never forcing, only requesting. But when I do take those steps, he groans and deepens the kiss, his tongue asking mine to play. His arms hold me tight against him and I feel safer, more secure, and more complete than I ever have.

Finally he breaks the kiss and rests his forehead against mine. He smiles softly at my shuddering breath and I can't help but mirror the expression. He brushes my bangs away from my face and I slam my eyes closed, going absolutely rigid in his arms, waiting for the rejection, hoping it won't hurt too much, but knowing it will.

He places soft kisses on my closed eyelids and one on my destroyed socket. "You're beautiful," he whispers. "I mean it, Avery. You are beautiful to me." His lips rest against my forehead as he completes his thought. "I know you need time and we'll take this as slow as you need. Even if it takes years, I'm still going to want you to be mine because you *are* that guy. You may not believe it yet, but you will." He presses a kiss to my forehead again, then cups my face in his gigantic, rough hands and kisses my lips once more. "Get yourself together and then come watch the game with me, okay?"

I can only nod as he gently releases me and strides down the hallway.

Eventually, I make my way out to the living room to see what all the ruckus is about. Both of my guys are cheering wildly and talking excitedly about some play or another. They try to explain it to me, but even with the replay they watch in absolute silence, save for the final moments when some giant in blue stuffs the hoop with the ball, doesn't make it any clearer. I simply smile and nod and say, "Go UK."

"*KU!!!*" they yell in horrified unison.

When I merely smile impishly, Noah gathers me in his arms and gives me a gentle noogie, followed by a smacking kiss to the top of my head and pulls me down to sit beside him on the couch. I giggle a little and curl into him under his arm, resting my head on his insanely sexy chest. While he and Sam animatedly watch the game, I watch the play of light highlight the smattering of hair across Noah's chest.

I have a lot to think about, but here, in the circle of Noah's arms, with Sam across the room, I've never been more content. Maybe it's the valium finally kicking in. Maybe it's something more. Only time will tell.

Noah wakes me from an embarrassingly drool-filled slumber at half time and I go to the kitchen to make baked nachos mariachis. I'm spreading refried beans on the last of the chips when Sam wanders into the room, eyebrows buried high in his hairline. He leans against the counter and waits, slowly drinking his Sam Adams.

"What?" I finally ask, moving to spoon the drained, browned hamburger across the two cookie sheets of chips.

Sam smiles triumphantly. "I told you."

I frown and keep working. "Told me what? Make yourself useful and drain that can of black olives, please."

He hops to, still grinning like the fool some people take him for. "He's a good guy. I approve."

I put the empty skillet in the sink next to him and pick up the tiny pieces of green pepper, working the same magic with them. "What do you approve of, dear brother?" I ask, not at all wanting to hear his answer.

"Oh, no, you're not going to get me to say it. But if you two haven't said it yet, I don't know what you're waiting for. It's completely obvious."

I sigh and fix him with a glare. "What is this, 'Fiddler on the Roof'?"

Sam laughs. "More like 'The Mirror Has Two Faces.' You're a lot more than you let anyone see, Aves. But Noah sees what I see in you, no matter how hard you try to hide it."

I snatch the olives out of his hand and try to hide my embarrassment under what I hope looks like disgust. "Geez, which one of us is gay? You just referenced a Barbra Streisand movie *nobody* watched."

"Uh huh. Defensive isn't a good look on you, little brother."

"And gloating isn't on you, either."

Sam laughs. "Yeah, but you know what does look good on you?"

"What?" I ask, already dreading the answer.

"Well-kissed lips."

I almost drop the can of olives. "Out!" I order, pointing and blushing madly. "Out of my kitchen!"

Chapter 12 - April

Three weeks after the basketball game, Noah presents me with a shiny new Jayhawk key ring.

"Uhm, thanks?"

He laughs. "I didn't think that would impress you much."

"Oh. It's lovely," I say quickly, hoping I haven't hurt his feelings. The very last thing I want to do is hurt Noah.

He takes my hand and presses a kiss inside my wrist. I have no idea why, but every time he does that my heartbeat spikes. He's dressed casually today. Even though he isn't scheduled to work because of classes, he still came to the store for our lunch date. I know he could save time and energy eating on campus, but it's nice that he still wants to share his meal with me. I don't understand why, but the man wants to be with me whenever he can. It makes resisting him harder. He never demands, always requests, never pushes me much farther than I'm comfortable with, just enough to leave me with my head spinning in a most pleasant way.

From his pocket, he retrieves a shiny silver key and deftly fastens it to the ring. "This," he says as he holds it up proudly, "is a key to my apartment."

My eyes widen and I jerk my hand back. "No, Noah." I shake my head. "I can't take that."

He smiles patiently. "You're gonna need it, Aves. I'm taking the rest of April and the first half of May off from the store. It's the last push before finals and graduation. I'm going to be super crazy busy getting everything done on time. I have my final papers to write and then exams to study for on top of classes." He grins. "I'm counting on you to keep me fueled up so I can give it all my best. That means I won't be able to be here for lunch all the time, so I'll need you to deliver to my place. Can you do that for me?"

I don't know what to say. The idea of being responsible for a key to his place scares the heck out of me. If this were anyone but Noah, I would refuse flat out. Some people still look at me as some trouble-making foster kid. They assume because I wasn't raised by my "real" mom and dad that I'm some sort of delinquent—a liar or a thief or worse. Accepting this key from anyone but Noah would be the first step in being accused of doing something illegal. What if Noah's place is broken into and robbed after he gives me a key? I'll be a prime suspect. It makes me feel paranoid, but I've seen it happen before.

"Noah, I—I can't."

He sighs and puts the key on the table. "Sam said you wouldn't take it. I had hoped he was wrong." He turns pleading eyes to mine and I almost immediately drop my gaze. "I guess that means we won't be seeing each other very much."

"I-I can bring stuff when you're going to be there. That way I won't need a key."

"But I want you to have it, little one. I want to know you can get in whenever you need. Heck, I want you to be there whenever you want to be." He sighs. "I don't want to have to miss you, Aves."

Tears of awe and sadness and regret fill my eyes. Awe that he would trust me so much, sadness that I won't be seeing him every day, and regret that I looked at his gift as a trap and had hurt his feelings. I close my fingers over the key. "I'm sorry I hurt your feelings, Noah. I don't want to miss you either. I'll try to time your food deliveries for when you'll be there, but I'll take the key just in case." I glance up and am gifted with a wide, dimpled smile of happiness.

"Ah, the fine art of compromise. It's a deal." He leans forward and presses a quick kiss to my lips. "Okay, I gotta run if I'm going to make it back to class on time." He smiles, and then snaps his fingers as if a thought just occurred to him. "You're off tomorrow, right?"

"Yes."

He stands up but I keep sitting, something I wouldn't have dared to do months ago. Sometimes it surprises me how comfortable I've gotten with Noah in these few months, although I suppose with him kissing me all the time, it was bound to happen.

"Earth to Avery."

My gaze snaps up to his and I flush. "Sorry. What?"

He grins at me in that way he has, like he enjoys indulging me. "I said I have a full day on campus tomorrow, so why don't you grab Sam or Kaleb and give that key a dry run. I know you'll be freaked out about being there alone the first time, so bring some company. They've both been there before, so it should be fine."

I swallow and shift my eyes away, still not on board with the idea of being in Noah's house without him. His enormous hand on my cheek, his thumb at my lips brings my attention back to him in a hurry. I look into his hazel eyes and gently nip his thumb. His eyes darken and the breath catches in his throat. Where I'd only meant to tease him, apparently I'd hit some sort of secret sexual hot button. Note to self: no more nips. Oh and doesn't that just bring up a pretty picture of what I can only imagine his bare chest looks like. Dang it.

Noah leans down until his lips are only a fraction of an inch from mine. "If you do that for me, I'll leave you a very special gift." My eyes close as a wave of heat suffuses my body and it takes a long moment to realize he's talking about going to his apartment tomorrow. Silently I nod and am rewarded with the tenderest of long kisses.

He draws back, winks and moves to leave. I let him take a few steps before I find my voice. "Noah?"

He stops and turns, giving me his full attention, as always.

"Why do you keep kissing me?"

He smiles and comes back around the table, urging me to stand with a gentle tug on my hand. His arms go around me and his mouth is on mine again, checking to be sure my tonsils are still in place. When he draws back, he smiles down at me. "I kiss you because you are the most adorable man under the sun. And because you taste delicious. And because I like it. Do you want me to stop?"

I sigh and lean into him, my chin on his chest, still holding his gaze. "No," I say simply.

"Good," he answers, cupping my face and kissing me breathless.

***

"He must really care for you," Kaleb says the next day as I slide my new key in the lock.

Noah was right. I feel better having our friend accompany me on my maiden voyage to his empty apartment. That's not to say that the phone call to ask Kaleb to come with hadn't been weird for me. But like always, Noah seems to have planned three steps ahead. Kaleb was expecting my call and agreed almost immediately.

I twist the nob and turn to Kaleb as the door slides slowly open. "He wants food," I say, reaching for the three big casserole dishes he's holding.

"I've got 'em," he says, shouldering his way inside and heading for the kitchen.

I take the time to look around like I hadn't dared to the night Sam and I came over for the ballgame. Like most rentals, the walls are a stark white, but Noah has taken the time to personalize his space. Here and there, in artfully arranged groupings, are floating shelves containing not knickknacks but books, anchored solidly on each end by matching candleholders that must be of some heft if they double as book stops. There's also a five-shelf bookcase almost full of more books, thrillers and mysteries, but also some whose titles betray Noah's field of study. I run my fingers over the unbroken spines of several volumes and wonder what it must be like to collect things, especially something as solid and sturdy and adventure-laden as books. A flicker of envy flares but I quash it swiftly. Noah had a better start to life than me; he's destined for great things. He deserves to be surrounded by the things he cares about. The library is much more like the younger me: temporarily on loan to this family or that agency.

I notice a couple of framed jerseys hanging side by side above another floating shelf. On this one rest a baseball and what I can only assume is a hockey puck. Both are autographed and sitting in cute little stands. I glance up at the jerseys and see they, too, are autographed by people named Tkachuk and Freese. I shrug. With my knowledge of sports, those names mean nothing. If Carl's boys hadn't found it amusing to use me as target practice, I wouldn't know the difference between a baseball and a softball.

I move on to the soft brown suede couch where Noah and I cuddled during the game. I smile stupidly, remembering, and run my fingers lightly over the material. There are two matching armchairs and, mounted on the wall, the enormous LED television.

I notice an 11 x 14 photo on the table near one of the chairs and pick it up, studying it carefully. My fingertips have just outlined Noah's slightly less rugged, teenage face when Kaleb's voice behind me makes me jump and almost drop the thing.

"That was taken when Noah was seventeen. It's the last picture he has of his dad."

I nod and take in the family, frozen forever in time. His dad seems healthy, if a little tired. The love and pride he has in his family shines through his eyes and the radiant smile that flashes dimples identical to those of his elder son. "What happened?"

"Aneurysm in the shower. He and the boys had just gotten back from an afternoon of golf. Luke took it hard, but nowhere near as hard as Noah. His dad was his hero."

I nod silently, hoping Kaleb will go on. Noah's little brother looks like a seven-year-old version of Noah, full of mischief. Their mother, her shoulder-length dark hair elegantly arranged, stares out of the picture with kind eyes and an indulgent smile.

The family portrait is so different from anything I've ever known that my hands start to shake. Hastily, I put the frame back down before I manage to break Noah's family, too. I clear my throat nervously, shove my hands in my pockets, and turn to find Kaleb regarding me with a solemn expression.

"I-I better get that food packed way," I stutter, moving past Kaleb into the kitchen.

"Aves—"

"It's just food, Kaleb," I say. I open the refrigerator, hiding my flaming face, and look for things to move to make room for the dishes I brought.

"Then explain this," Kaleb challenges.

I pull my head out of the fridge and see Kaleb brandishing a white box with blue ribbon. I shake my head in denial for both of us. "I don't know what that is."

"It's for you. It was on the counter."

I shrug and look away, busying myself with one of the casserole dishes. "Oh. Probably cookies and a shopping list. Noah said he'd have a surprise for me. You know he can only make his grandmother's cookies."

"Does this look like a box of cookies to you?"

I make myself look again, even though I know the box is nowhere near big enough. "No." I feel myself pale and start to shake. What has Noah done now?

"You better sit down before you wreck the place, Aves."

Nodding once, I slide into the chair Kaleb pulls out from the table. He grabs two bottles of water from the fridge before sitting down opposite me. He uncaps one and hands it to me. It's all so déjà vu it's scary. The last time we did this was in Kaleb's house at New Year's. Four months later everything and nothing has changed. Noah and I know each other better, we're friends who kiss now. I drink deeply from the water as Noah's words from the night of the ballgame come back to me: "*It's already happening, baby. It has been for a while.*"

Nervously, I look at Kaleb. "Is that what I think it is?"

"I think so," he answers with a slight frown.

I shake my head. "I can't take it, Kaleb.... Why? Why would he buy me something like that? I'll just break it. I break everything." *And everyone*, I finish silently.

"I don't know, Avery. Maybe he thinks you'll like it? Maybe he thinks you deserve it?"

Suddenly the box starts singing. It's the song Noah sang to me the day I told him about Tommy Blevins. I stare between Kaleb and the box, panicked.

"You better answer it."

Frantically, I fumble with the ribbon and the box, unable to separate the two. Another chorus goes by before; finally, the ribbon comes off, only to stick to my fingers. I shake them ineffectually. Kaleb laughs and Christina keeps singing.

Suddenly, it's silent. I stare at it beseechingly but nothing happens.

"Down," Kaleb says. I put the box on the table and he laughs again. "Not you, dork. The song. I was finishing the lyrics."

"Oh," I say, picking it up again in trembling fingers. I lift the lid and stare down at its contents, dumbfounded. As I carefully reach inside, Christina belts it out again. I almost throw the thing I'm so surprised.

I look at Kaleb again. "Well, answer him," he says, shoulders shaking with suppressed laugher.

Quickly, I fumblingly extract the new white iPhone from its packaging and slide my finger across the screen the way I've seen scores of much cooler people do for years. I tap the answer button and bring the phone to my ear. "Hello?" I squeak.

"Hey, sweetheart," Noah's voice coos. "Surprised?"

"Uh—very." I can't even put two words together I'm so freaked out. Surprised? That's an understatement.

Noah's low laughter reaches my ear and somehow the sound of it starts to calm me. "Good. Now before you start in with the 'I can't accept it' speech: yes, you can. It's my gift to you for everything you do for me."

"Noah—"

"Avery," he mimics.

"I can't afford this. *You* can't afford this. I can't pay a bill like this!"

"Baby, it's paid up for two years."

"*What?!* Noah, no—"

"Shh. It's okay. Mom asked me what I wanted for graduation and this is it. I want us to be able to contact each other whenever we want. I wanna send you texts and funny pictures when I'm bored in class. And I want you to be able to do the same. Your little prepaid didn't even do text! Please, please just accept it. I know you think it's too much, but I worried about you all winter with your car and that phone you never bothered to get more than a handful of minutes for. Please, Avery. For me?"

I look to Kaleb for help, as if he can hear the guilt trip Noah's laying on me, but he just smiles and nods. "This is Noah. You know it as well as I do."

Finally, I heave a sigh of defeat. There is no winning this argument. "Okay, you win. Thank you for the overly-extravagant gift."

Noah growls his victory and I practically melt into the chair right in front of Kaleb. How embarrassing. "You're welcome, little one. Listen, if it makes you feel better, you can make me some Orange Fluff as repayment." He laughs.

I glance at the counter where a new batch is already waiting for him. "We'll see," I hedge. "Honestly, Noah, are you sure? If I accept this thing I'll probably wind up breaking it in the next two weeks. I'm a klutz, remember? I could break things professionally!"

Noah laughs warmly. "No worries, little one. It's fully insured. Take it. Enjoy it. I've downloaded some music to it. Oh, and Words with Friends. We'll have to play that. It's fun."

"Uh, Words with—okay." I have no idea what that is.

"Okay. I gotta run back to class. Can I see you tomorrow?"

"Sure. You want me to bring lunch to the store? Won't that run you short of time?"

I hear him pause and I brace myself. "Actually, I was hoping you'd want to come over for dinner tomorrow. I'll grill steaks. Bring Sam and Kira, if you want."

My heartbeat thunders in my ears. "Sam works tomorrow night."

"Oh," he says. I can practically see his expression, the way he bites his bottom lip when he wants me to do something outside my comfort zone.

"I'll ask Kaleb. Maybe they're free."

"Excellent! But if not, will you come anyway?"

I can see by the expression on Kaleb's face that he knows exactly what's going on and that he and Josh now have unbreakable plans they didn't have ten minutes ago. I tell myself it's okay. It's just Noah. We've been alone together dozens of times in the last four months. I know I'm safe with him. We're friends. Friends who kiss. "What time?" I ask, hating the tremor in my voice.

"Seven o'clock?" he asks.

"It's a deal," I say before I can convince myself otherwise.

"Yes! It'll be fun, you'll see. But I really gotta go now. I'll text you later. Listen to the music! Bye!"

I hear the call drop and stare at the screen of my brand new white iPhone. *What have I just agreed to?*

Kaleb clears his throat and I quickly look up at him. "So you're seeing each other now?"

"What? No! We're just friends." Friends who kiss.

"Friends who kiss?"

I stare at him wide-eyed. "Sometimes," I answer painfully.

"Friends who do more than kiss?"

I blush furiously and avoid his gaze by putting the phone back in its protective box. Maybe if I carry it around like this, I won't break it. "No," I answer, barely above a whisper.

"But you want that, don't you, Avery? You want more from Noah than a friendship with a few kisses?"

"I can't," I say after a too-long period of silence.

"But you want to? ...Avery?"

"No!" I get up to attend to the food. "I can't! I'm not—Noah knows, okay? I'm not leading him on. He knows I'm different. He knows I—can't." Inexplicably, tears sting my eyes. I've never wanted to be intimate with anyone before. I've never allowed myself to dream anyone would want that with me. I've always known what I'm useful for and it's certainly not that, but lately.... Lately, I have wondered what it would be like to be with Noah that way. I've allowed myself to imagine it and dream about it. Thanks to his infinite patience and my progress with Kendall, it doesn't seem like such a far-fetched idea. I know he would be gentle and that feeling his strong, naked body against mine would be much more than I've ever imagined, but I'm not there yet. I may never be and that thought hurts and disappoints me more than I expect it to. Part of the problem is that I know what I look like naked. I'm no one's idea of attractive, much less sexy.

Not like Noah. Noah's almost everyone's idea of sexy. He's blond and built and beautiful. He can have any guy he wants. All he has to do is flash those dimples and turn on the charm and guys must be begging to jump into his bed.

I'm not one of those, though. I can't afford to be. The thought slams into my head with such force I almost drop Noah's Orange Fluff container. It's what he's going to expect from me if I keep letting him kiss me. I choke down a sob and keep my face buried in the cool air of the refrigerator. It was going so well, this friendship with kisses.

As if echoing my thoughts, Kaleb says, "You're going to have to make a decision pretty soon, Avery. Noah deserves to be with someone who is more than just his cook."

I close the refrigerator and nod in agreement, avoiding Kaleb's eyes. "I'll sort it with him. I promise."

Kaleb cups my cheek in his hand. It feels strange not being Noah's hand. I miss the caress of his thumb on my lip. I look up at the man who's like another brother to me. "You deserve all that, too, you know?" he says softly. "You're a wonderful guy, Avery. Noah could do a lot worse. Hell, he *has* done worse. But you need to believe you're worth it, that what you two could have together could be magical. I can see it. I think you two were made for each other. But if you don't think you can do it, you need to stop it soon before you both get hurt."

"I will," I whisper, the very thought of hurting Noah rips through me like a knife.

Kaleb's hand drops to his side. "Wrong answer, kid. Way wrong answer." He shakes his head sadly. "Get your stuff together and let's get out of here before we're both - late for work."

Swiftly, I gather the iPhone in its box and follow Kaleb to the door. I know Noah will call or text the new phone tonight after I get off work. I'll find a way by then to make sure he knows our friendship has to go back to "without kisses."

***

Noah answers my knock on his door and my mouth goes instantly dry. The Sahara Desert has more moisture than my mouth—but only for half a second. Then it starts watering so much I have to swallow before I can gurgle out a "hi."

The man is going to be the death of me, I have no doubt. I'm used to the plaid button down Noah or the sexy turtleneck Noah but nothing prepares me for this. The most beautiful man in the world stands before me, dimples flashing on each side of his wide smile. He's dressed in painted-on blue jeans and a tight, black tank top that emphasizes the immense breadth of his shoulders and the power in his biceps, not to mention how lovingly it hugs his square pectorals. Atop his blond head sits a black baseball cap, jauntily angled and backwards, of all things. To make matters worse his nipples aren't his only attribute that are clearly outlined under his clothing.

"Aves! You're right on time!" He leans forward to brush a kiss to my cheek before I can remember how to work my tongue to form words. He looks at me for a moment, that dang smile widening and I know he has somehow accessed every naughty thought in my head—and there are so many I don't have the first clue how to get them out of there.

He grabs my hand and gently pulls me into the kitchen, talking a mile a minute about the meeting with his advisor at the university. I try to focus on his words so I won't notice how his shoulders, chest and arms flex as he prepares the steaks and potatoes for the grill. It's a lost cause. All I can do is watch him and swallow frequently.

Dang that Kaleb. If he hadn't pushed so hard yesterday I never would have noticed things like the outline of Noah's…of Noah in his super-tight jeans. How can he even move in those things? Isn't he afraid of pinching himself if he moves wrong?

"…and then the unicorn turned purple and I thought to myself, 'Avery has to see this!'"

"What?" That last sentence does not compute. Purple what?

Noah laughs and leans across the bar to press a light kiss to my lips. "You zoned all the way out. I thought I'd see what it would take to bring you back."

I flush and study the countertop between us. "I'm sorry."

"Don't be. I know this is outside your comfort zone. But you're here! That's a huge win for both of us."

I shake my head, some of the tension draining from my shoulders. "How many wins is that? I've lost count."

The grin Noah sends my way makes my toes curl. "Every day I get to spend with you is a win." He leans in to kiss me again.

I laugh and grab his head, turning it to the side.

"What are you doing?" he asks.

"Looking for the corn! It's going to start running out of your ears any minute!"

He pulls away and pretends to pout. "You wound me, sir."

I laugh again and lean forward for his kiss. "Aw, I'm sorry. If it makes you feel any better, your ear looked really clean."

Noah barks a laugh and shakes his head. "And to think I once believed you were a nice, quiet boy."

I look at him through my lashes. "Oh, I was," I reply honestly. "But you ruined that a long time ago."

"And thank goodness for that!" Noah smiles and picks up the platter of steaks and potatoes. "Care to keep me company while I cook for you for a change?"

I follow Noah outside onto the postage stamp-sized patio, bordered by a six-foot high privacy fence. The space is as generic as it gets, but in the unseasonably warm spring evening, in Noah's company, it somehow seems homey and wonderful. I watch quietly as he deftly places the steaks and potatoes on the grill. He keeps up a rolling monologue about the day, throwing in an occasional joke to make me laugh or to be sure I'm paying attention, I'm not sure which.

It's fascinating to watch him like this, though. For as hopeless as he claims to be in the kitchen, he's clearly comfortable with a grill. It's apparently another one of those *man things* I missed out on learning.

Sam and Kaleb both love to grill, too, but I've never liked them. I feel a stab of jealousy, but only for a moment. Everyone needs his own place to shine. Just because mine seems to be in the kitchen cooking for Noah instead of outdoors cooking for Noah doesn't make it any less valid. In fact, come the zombie apocalypse, Kaleb, Sam and Noah will all be sitting ducks while I'll be safely indoors, happily cooking and baking away. Perversely, the thought of watching these big men fighting off brain-starved walking corpses makes me giggle.

Noah glances at me, eyebrow raised and I laugh again. "You don't even want to know," I promise.

He ambles toward me and I edge around one of the deck chairs, putting it between us. It's hopeless, I know; he'll catch me soon enough. But I also know he'll kiss me into submission, not beat me bloody. A shiver of thrill races down my spine in anticipation.

I see the twilight glitter in his eyes, watch the smirk come to his sexy lips as he catches on. He stalks closer, hands flexing at his sides. Just a few months ago, I would have run screaming in terror; now I fight against the smile twitching my lips.

I feint right and go left, putting the Plexiglas-topped table between us. A feral grin blooms on Noah's mouth and I laugh.

"You're gonna get it," he warns, tossing the deck chair behind him.

"You gotta catch me first."

"Oh. Think you're that quick, do you?"

I bite the tip of an index finger, pretending to think. His gaze tracks to my mouth and my heartbeat kicks up. "Nah. You're just big and clumsy."

"You little brat!" Noah laughs. "I'll show you big."

As if I haven't been seeing it in his jeans all night. The thought distracts me long enough that he's almost on me before I notice. I let out a very manly squeal and dodge as his fingertips nearly get a grip on my shirt sleeve. I put the other deck chair between us, panting a bit from my near escape and the mental image. My gaze involuntarily goes to his crotch and I flush. I would swear it's bigger now.

"Are you done?" Noah asks teasingly. My eyes find his, hoping he hasn't noticed where I've been looking. "You have nowhere else to hide, baby. You're all mine now."

I look around frantically but there is nowhere go to. All I can do is take a few steps back until my back is pressed against the door to his apartment. Covertly, I reach for the handle, but he sees me.

"Na-uh," he says, simply stepping over the chair. His long arms reach out, grab me and pull me against the solid wall of his chest. "No more running, baby," he whispers against my lips before claiming them in a needy kiss.

I kiss him back for a moment before Kaleb's words crowd into my mind. I push Noah away, leaning back in the circle of his arms to look into his lust-glazed eyes. It's then I know for sure Kaleb's right. Either I decide to go all the way with Noah or no more kisses. And as much as the idea of sex with him should make me weak in the knees with desire, it still scares me. Kisses are one thing, but sex changes everything. I can't. Not yet.

I drop my forehead to his chest. "We can't do this anymore, Noah. It isn't fair."

His lips graze through my hair. "Can't do what?"

I push away until he finally releases me from his embrace. I can't stop now but I can't quite bring myself to meet his gaze. I watch the hypnotic rise and fall of his chest instead. "We—you—" I take a deep breath and run a trembling hand through my hair. I should have worked out how to phrase this before now. I don't want to hurt Noah's feelings, but I've never exactly had this conversation before, so I have no idea how to do it now. "We have to stop the kissing."

He was still earlier, letting me sort through the argument in my head, but he positively freezes now. "We do? Why? Have I made you uncomfortable? Have I pushed too hard?"

I shake my head. It's the opposite of what he thinks, but it doesn't surprise me that his first thought is that he's upset me somehow. "No, not at all."

"Then what?" He cups my cheek in his calloused hand and as always, I'm putty in his hands.

"It isn't fair to you," I whisper, eyes closing as his thumb finds my lip. It's like a magnet or something.

"It sure *seems* fair to me," he rumbles. "I get to kiss the sexiest guy in my world and he seems to like it enough to kiss me back. What part of that is unfair?"

I look into his hazel eyes again, insanely pleased by his obviously hyperbolic compliment. "I'm not ready for more than that, Noah. I might never be. Kaleb says—"

"Baby, don't you worry about Kaleb. He wants to see us both happy, but he doesn't get to decide what's best for us." Noah smiles and tweaks my nose. "So I hope you don't mind if I keep on kissing you. I know you're not ready to go beyond that and I'm more than okay with that. We do everything on your time table. I just want to be with you, keep getting to know you." He grins wickedly. "And taste you every now and then. Are you okay with that?"

I nod, relieved and overwhelmed at once.

"Good." He nods and flashes that grin again. "Besides, how many other men have you let kiss you?"

"None!"

"Exactly." He presses a sweet kiss to my lips, then licks a line to my ear. He takes the lobe between his teeth in a gentle bite and whispers, "Win."

I shiver and laugh at the same time, turning my head to accept another deep kiss from the most amazing man I've ever known. Noah swats my behind and steps away. "Time to turn the steaks. You like yours medium rare, right?"

"Yes, please." I stare after him, almost confused. That's it? After all the freaking out the conversation with Kaleb caused me, Noah's going to dismiss his best friend's concerns just like that? I watch him flip the meat before voicing my doubts. "Noah, are you sure? I mean, Kaleb is right about it not being fair."

Noah frowns over his shoulder at me, closing the lid on the grill. "Kaleb isn't part of this." He strides confidently back to my side and frames my face with his hands. "You and I are the only two people who have a say in whether or not we're friends with kisses, or friends with benefits, or anything else. I'm perfectly happy the way we are. If you're not, then we should talk about that. I don't want to hurt you or force you into anything you don't want to do. But if I'm going too slow, you should tell me that, too." He tenderly caresses my bangs away from my eyes. "So? Should we talk or can I kiss you again?"

I'm not stupid. I know Kaleb's assertions are valid. Noah will want more than I can possibly give him. It may be next week or next month or even six months from now, but that day isn't today, apparently. Instead of living in fear of the consequences of every thought or action, in this one instance, I'm going to ignore that cautioning voice in my head. Being with Noah is worth whatever heck I'll have to pay later. Smiling, I wrap my arms around his neck and bring my lips a fraction of an inch from his. "Kiss me," I whisper.

To my surprise and relief, we keep up a friendly banter all through the rest of the preparation and consumption of the meal. It's only when Noah starts making noise about dessert that I realize I should have brought something, should have contributed more than just a healthy appetite. And I have eaten heartily. The marinade he used on the steak added a sweet and tangy flavor to the meat that my mouth fell in love with. The salad and potatoes were good, too, but the steak was among the best I've ever had.

"I should have brought something for dessert," I say, my face heating with embarrassment. "I'm sorry. I didn't think."

Noah's hand covers mine on the table and he smiles at me. "It's okay, little one. I've got this covered." He takes the two steps from the table to the counter that divides the room and picks up his phone. It's identical to the one he gave me yesterday. I pat my slacks pocket protectively to make sure mine is still there and safe. He texts something and puts the phone back down.

He smiles at me again and extends his hand. "Let's go watch a movie. I picked up *Wolverine* the other day. How does that sound?"

I give him my hand and let him pull me upright and into his arms. They close around me as his lips descend on mine. I moan into his mouth and lean against him, realizing just how far we've progressed from that first meeting. Instead of terrifying me as he did then, this big man wrapped around me makes me feel safe and cared for. It's a feeling I could come to like very much.

I push him back. "Too much," I pant, staring at his rapidly rising and falling chest.

"No, baby," he coos. "Not nearly enough. But it's okay, we'll slow down." He presses a kiss to my forehead and steps away toward the living room, pulling me along by the hand.

I look at our joined hands and give in to the dopey smile that spreads across my lips.

In the living room, I sit gingerly on the edge of the couch, suddenly nervous. How will this work? Will Noah want to cuddle again like we did the night of the basketball game? Or will he sit in one of the chairs by himself? I feel the tension threading through my body as he fiddles endlessly with the Blu-ray and its player. Maybe this isn't such a good idea. We've had a good night, or at least I think it has been. Perhaps I should go now before things get really awkward.

The sound of Noah's doorbell slams through my brain like a shot, scattering all thoughts, coherent or otherwise.

Noah rises from his spot in front of the television. "That'll be our dessert." He smiles so big at me I almost miss the slight coloring of his cheeks. He holds a hand out to me. "Come get the door with me. I may need the extra hands."

I narrow my eyes at him, suspicion edging the corners of my mind, but I slide my hand into his and follow him to the door. The color in his cheeks tells me he's up to something, but I haven't the foggiest idea what it could be. As he reaches for the knob, the bell sounds again, making me jump. Impatient clod, I think.

Noah opens the door with me at his side and I'm immediately bowled over by the disjointed chorus of "Happy birthday, Avery!" that erupts from the motley crew in the hall.

I'm so stunned it takes me a minute to realize Kira is standing there holding a large rectangular cake, festooned with blazing candles. Behind her, jostling for position are Kyle, Kaleb, Josh, Molly and Brian. The only one missing is Sam, but I know he's at work.

I hear Noah chuckle beside me and turn to stare up at him through watery eyes.

"Happy birthday, baby." He laughs down at me, clearly pleased with himself.

I launch myself at him to stem the tears, wrapping my arms around his broad shoulders. "Thank you," I whisper into his neck. "How did you know?"

He hugs me back tightly. "I asked Sam a while ago, then put this together a couple of weeks ago. Except for you. I was afraid you wouldn't come by yourself. But you did!"

I draw back to look up at him in wonderment. Sam is the only other person who has ever made a big deal out of my birthday. Aside from him—and the K's since he started dating Kira—no one has ever cared. My birthday. I've always hated it because of what it means—it was the start of all the hatred that has come my way. Mother, of course, never celebrated the day with me after Dad died. If anything, it was cause for worse treatment: more bruises and a broken bone or two, those were my usual birthday gifts.

But Noah…Noah sees it as cause for celebration and a bit of a party. Heat suffuses my entire body as a glorious but unrecognizable emotion spreads through me. I grab his face in my hands and bring his lips to mine, hoping, praying he can tell from the kiss just how much this means to me.

"Okay, lovebirds," Kira breaks in, "this cake is getting heavy and I really don't want to set the place on fire. Break it up already."

Reluctantly, I pull away from Noah and turn to the hallway full of my friends, my family—people who, I understand now, truly care about me. I wonder if I'll ever stop smiling. A giggle escapes me and I clamp a hand over my mouth, eyes wide.

Everyone laughs as Noah moves to take the cake from Kira. "Come on in, everybody. I want to get a couple of pictures with Avery and the cake, then we'll dig in."

I accept hugs from everyone as they pass, too overwhelmed to be nervous about it, and follow them all into the kitchen. Noah makes me pose with the cake and I laugh when I get a good look at it. It's Rogue driving a go-kart out of a book. It couldn't be more perfect.

Once they've all blinded me with camera flashes, Noah cuts into the cake and Kira adds scoops of ice cream to everyone's plates. I settle on one of the barstools, listening with a smile to the fast and furious banter between the K's and Noah. Brian and Molly join in where they can, but it's clear they don't know the other four as well. As usual, Josh just takes it all in, smiling indulgently at his more gregarious husband. Kaleb has hinted that Josh endured a painful past but neither of them has ever spoken of it more specifically. I wonder how much we have in common there and hope, for Josh's sake, that it isn't much.

I feel Noah's hands on my shoulders and turn to smile up at him. He beams down at me and my breath catches in my throat at the happiness in his eyes.

"Good surprise?" he queries, flashing those dimples.

"Very."

"You're not mad?"

I blink. "At what?"

"At me. For inviting all these people to interrupt our quiet dinner together."

I shake my head and smile again. "No." My gaze falls to his chest as emotion rushes through me. "Noah, no one has ever done this for me before."

His hand cups my cheek, caressing my lips with his thumb. Like Pavlov's dog, I'm well trained: I'm already anticipating his kiss. "I figured," he says, his smile dimming a bit.

I hate to see his happiness drain away. "Don't get me wrong; Sam has always celebrated with me. He says it's something brothers get to do for each other." I try for a joke. "I think it's just an excuse for more cake." His dimples flash again and my heart skips a beat. "This is the best surprise ever. Thank you."

He leans forward to kiss me. He tastes of chocolate cake and caramel-coconut frosting. "I'm glad you're happy," he whispers. "Happy birthday, baby."

As he kisses me again and the catcalls start—again—I blush with embarrassment and the realization that Noah's right. In this moment, right now, I'm the happiest I've ever been.

An hour or so later, as everyone else is getting ready to leave, Kaleb steers me into the kitchen. "Have you two talked about our conversation yesterday?" he asks, seeming almost uncomfortable.

Still on an emotional high, I study my friend carefully. "Actually, we have."

Kaleb looks at the floor. "Listen, I really need to apologize. I spoke out of turn. It's none of my business how you and Noah conduct your relationship. Josh is plenty pissed about my meddling." He grins at me sheepishly. "He said I wouldn't get any again until I apologized to you." Now he looks aghast and I almost laugh. "Not that that's why I'm apologizing. Shit. This isn't going at all like I planned."

This time I do laugh at him. "Kaleb, you don't need to apologize. I know you only have Noah's best interests at heart—"

"Yours, too," he quickly interjects.

"Thank you. I know that, too. You made some good points that I'm going to be thinking about for a few days, but Josh and Noah are also right: this isn't any of your business. I say that with love, I hope you know that." At his nod and smile, I continue. "I don't know what's happening between Noah and me. I know we're friends and I know he wants more, but I also know I'm not quite ready for that. You've said Josh had a painful past you had to overcome. I'm sure that took time, right?"

"A damn long time," he admits with more than a hint of residual frustration.

I laugh. "You made it through it; that's the important thing, Mr. Impatient. I'm still coming to terms with my past and what that means about my future. I care for Noah very much and I never want to hurt him, but what that means for us as friends—or anything else—I just don't know yet. You have to let us figure it out on our own, in our own time."

Kaleb grins. "I just want you both to be happy. I can see how perfect you are together. I can't help it if the way you're dancing around each other drives me insane."

I roll my eyes, thinking how proud Kendall will be when I tell her about tonight. "It's a short drive, Kaleb. You're just going to have to circle the block a few times."

He barks out a laugh and pulls me into a hug. "Happy birthday, little brother. For the record, I'm sorry if I caused you any distress yesterday. I love you both, you know?"

I squeeze him for a second and step back. "I know. We love you, too. Now go home. And thank you for coming tonight. It means more than you'll ever know."

***

Noah shuts the door behind the last straggler just as my phone rings in my pocket. I'm not surprised to hear Sam's voice on the other end. "Happy birthday, little brother," he says. "I'm sorry I couldn't make it to the party tonight."

I laugh. "Thank you. I wish you could have been here. It was amazing. I can't believe you guys pulled it off without me ever suspecting."

Sam laughs. "Hey, it was all Noah. The rest of us just knew when and where. Unfortunately, some idiot decided to go the wrong way on the interstate or I'd be there, too."

"Oh, no," I gasp, imagining carnage. "Is everyone okay?"

"Mostly," he hedges. "It isn't as bad as you're probably imagining. But never mind that. I just called to say happy birthday. I love you."

"I love you, too, Sam," I answer, the words coming easy now.

We hang up and I replace the phone in my pocket. I watch as Noah comes back into the living room from the kitchen, something hidden behind his back. "Another piece of cake already?" I tease.

"What? No." He blushes and sits beside me on the couch, still hiding his hands behind him. "It's time for presents."

"Pres—? What?"

"Well, present, really. It's only one." He pulls a small rectangular box from behind him and hands it to me.

I stare at the beautiful burgundy wrapping paper with a silver loop of ribbon, more than a little breathless. "You didn't have to get me anything. You've done enough. This is the best birthday I've ever had."

"I know I didn't have to, but I wanted to. I saw it and I knew you had to have it. Open it," he encourages with a grin in his voice.

I take in the beautiful man before me, then carefully unwrap the package. Inside the paper is a black velvet box that I recognize is for jewelry. "What is it?" I whisper, unable to make myself open it.

He laughs softly. "Open it. You're making me a nervous wreck."

I glance up at him again and notice that his cheeks are a little flushed and the pulse point in his neck is fluttering wildly. Gathering all my courage, I close my eyes and lift the lid carefully.

"Baby, you have to open your eyes to see it."

Embarrassed, I slam my eyes open and gasp. Lying on the black velvet lining is a gorgeous silver dog tag-shaped pendant on a black leather cord. "Noah," I whisper in awe.

"Read it," he says, reaching up to stroke my hair.

"'With the courage to be myself, I am beautiful,'" I read, choking up on the last word. I look up at him through tear-filled eyes. "Thank you. It's beautiful."

"So are you." He leans over and brushes his lips across mine. He lifts away from me, his thumb caressing my bottom lip. "You've shown so much courage the last few months, working through your therapy, taking those online classes *and* a new job." He smirks." Learning to become comfortable with me touching and kissing you. You just amaze me every day, Aves. I couldn't be more proud of you." His mouth claims mine again and he touch between us is electric, sending tingles racing through my body. I slip my fingers into his hair, anchoring him to me, the only signal he needs to deepen the kiss. I get lost in the feel and taste of him like always. This gorgeous, sexy, tender-hearted man means so much to me, so much more than I ever could have imagined five short months ago. I want it to be like this forever, this simple and pure and easy, but I know deep in my heart it can't. One day soon I'm going to have to make a decision to be as courageous as Noah believes me to be, or to live safely and not cross that next boundary of fear. When he touches me like this, I want nothing more than to be the man he sees. I just hope he really sees me and not just someone he hopes I can be.

Moments later, far too soon, he pulls back, breathing hard, and presses a kiss to my forehead. "Let me put it on you."

I watch as he takes the leather cord from the box and clasps it carefully behind my neck. The weight of the leather and the silver feel heavy and foreign, but I love it. It's the second greatest gift Noah has given me, the first being himself.

***

Two valium pump through my system and still I'm a nervous wreck. I pull the dog tag from under the collar of my shirt and stroke it, willing my legs to keep walking down the hallway. All I want to do is run as far and as fast as I can away from here, but I know how important this is. On one side of me, Noah takes my hand. I flash a trembling smile his way, hating how weak I am. On the other side, Sam squeezes my shoulder in reassurance and I take a deep breath, exhaling slowly.

"Are you ready?" he asks.

I close my eyes and nod. I have no choice. It's now or never, hopefully literally.

"You don't have to do this, you know. We can watch the CCTV feed."

I shake my head. "No. That's only television, like another episode of *Law & Order*. I have to see him with my own two eyes. I have to watch him while the judge puts him away."

Sam nods, a proud smile teasing his lips. "Okay, let's go."

He pulls open the door to the courtroom and I almost bolt for freedom. If this is how I feel just being an observer, I can't imagine how actual criminals feel. Sam and Noah lead me to the first bench and we slide in to wait. I fidget nervously, still fingering the dog tag. There is nothing I want more in the world than to see Tommy Blevins put in prison, but the idea of actually seeing him, being in the same room with him freaks me out. Even though I know he'll be in handcuffs and ankle restraints, I can't imagine any way he wouldn't be able to get to me if he wanted to badly enough.

Tommy has pled guilty to felony assault on a law enforcement officer, felony possession of methamphetamine with intent to sell or distribute, unlawful possession of a firearm by a felon, possession of firearm with altered serial numbers, and the commission of a violent act while in possession of a controlled substance. He's going away for a long time. The only question is how long the judge thinks is long enough.

I lean forward, head in hands to control my breathing. I'm confronting the second greatest ghost from my past today. Once it's all over I'll be able to feel pride in that, but right now it's all I can do to sit calmly waiting. I feel Noah's hand rub calming circles on my back and I close my eyes, allowing myself to remember August, the last time I saw Tommy Blevins.

That day was hot and humid, even by August standards. Everything stuck wetly together, especially clothing and skin. People were limp with exhaustion and short tempered from the weeklong heat wave. I'd had the day off, so I took myself out of the apartment with its insufficient air conditioning and went to the mall. I knew that despite the heat from other people moving around there seeking relief from the heat, it would be cooler than our apartment. I was sure I could find a nice quiet corner in a bookstore, sip an iced coffee and enjoy the frigid air in peace. Why I didn't just go to my own store, I'll never know.

I didn't often venture out on my own, especially to the mall, but the oppressive heat obviously short-circuited my better senses. I'd been at the store for a couple of hours, drank a couple of iced coffees and was really getting into a Bart Yates book I had purchased when I had to go relieve my bladder.

As the bookstore didn't offer public restrooms, I had to traipse halfway across the mall to the massive one just off the food court. I'd just finished my business and zipped up, my new book between my upper arm and my ribs, when I heard the sound I'd hoped and prayed never to hear again.

"Tucker," Tommy Blevins spat at me, calling me by the only name he knew.

I jerked my head toward the sound of his voice to see him and two other men standing just inside the doorway. *Always with a posse*, I thought irrationally, even as his name escaped me on a shocked, frightened whisper.

"So it is you," he growled. "What are you doing in here, you little faggot? Looking for some cock to suck?"

The cold steel of the first cubicle wall pressing against my back was the first indicator that I'd been backing up even as Tommy slowly advanced on me. The only escape route lay behind him, guarded by his two thugs. "I-I just needed to p-pee," I stuttered out, the fear I felt skyrocketing to panic at the menace in his words.

Tommy smiled at me, baring blackened, uneven teeth. He looked different, older of course, but harder in the eyes, softer in the belly. My book slipped from my grip and hit the tiled floor with a small thump. "I owe you and that piece of shit Sammy a thank you for getting me out of that group home." He took three more steps toward me. I trembled with terror and loathing. I hated him, but I hated me more for putting myself in this position.

Tommy cracked his knuckles like some lowlife out of a movie and his thug gallery laughed. I heard one of them slide the door's deadbolt into place and I knew it was all over but the pain. Pain I deserved for being so monumentally stupid as to come here alone, for being me, for continuing to draw breath long after I should have stopped.

"Think you can deliver a message to little Sammy for me, Tucker?"

It wasn't really a question and this had very little to do with Sam. Tommy's fist connected with my gut, much harder than any punch he'd ever thrown as a teenager. I doubled over in pain and my eyes closed just before his jeans-clad knee smashed into my face.

I cried out in agony and terror, begging him to please stop. He'd always wanted me to beg before but I'd refused. Now I did it easily, not for me, but for Sam. I knew I was born to take beatings like this, it was my purpose in life, but I didn't want Sam to answer the eventual 911 call and find me like this. It didn't matter anyway. I pleaded until I couldn't draw breath enough to speak. Just like before, Tommy took his time and enjoyed himself, showing off for his cheering buddies before leaving my bloody, bruised and broken body on the filthy tile floor. His last act of humiliation was to urinate on me before calmly washing his hands and walking out the door laughing, clasping his buddies on the shoulders.

I don't know how long I lay there, semi-conscious in agony, before some unsuspecting father and his small son found me. I awoke hours later in the hospital to see Sam's worried face staring down at me. Only then did I let myself cry. I cried at the pain, the humiliation and the cruel, spiteful destiny that was mine, to forever be the punching bag for the dregs of society.

It had been a cruel joke to give me the previous five years with Sam, slowly learning how to be a different, better person, one who wasn't always the target. Just as I was about to forget my role, Tommy reminded me.

The rattling of a door at the front of the courtroom brings me out of the nightmare. I suck in a breath and sit upright, swiping away the tears on my cheeks. Today isn't Tommy's victory, though; it's mine, mine and Joey's. Finally the bastard is going to prison for a long time. I grab Sam's hand, squeezing for dear life as the sheriff's deputies escort Tommy in. I feel the weight of Noah's hand on my thigh and cover it with my own, my tension slowly sliding away. Tommy looks thinner and more bedraggled than I remember. His longish blond hair is a dirty, ratted mess around his head. The orange jail jumpsuit and shackles remind me he won't be able to hurt me now and I slacken my grip on Sam's hand. Tommy doesn't look up from concentrating on walking with the shackles, but I can see his face.

I had expected to be terrorized upon seeing him, but instead a strange sort of peace radiates through me. The second greatest demon of my childhood is about to be vanquished.

Those of us in the courtroom rise when the judge enters. The last minute legal speak is nothing but a buzz to my ears as I continue to watch Tommy stand at the defendant's table. Finally I look at the judge for the first time as he begins to speak to Tommy.

"Mr. Blevins, you have appeared before this court three times previously. Each time I have allowed your counsel to persuade me that with adequate drug rehabilitation and counseling, you can be a contributing member of our society. However, that will not be the case this time. Your appearance here on the most serious charges of your criminal career indicates to me that, while you may not lack the capacity for change, you lack the will to do so. Therefore, this court sentences you to the maximum allowable sentence for each count against you. That is a total of seventy-six years, Mr. Blevins. You could very well spend the rest of your natural life in prison. I suggest you spend the time before your first parole availability in…" I watch in awe as the judge searches through his papers. "…seventeen years to learn how to be the contributing member of society your counsel believes you can be. We're done here."

In stunned silence, I watch as the judge rises from his bench and disappears through a door at the front of the courtroom. Tommy's lawyer bends to say something in his ear as the deputies pull him from his chair.

It's over. My Tommy Blevins nightmare is over. I'm free of him. I look at Sam, still wearing the shock on my face.

He grins. "How's that feel, champ?"

"It's really over, isn't it?" I search his face for any sign I might be wrong and find none. I turn to catch a glimpse of Tommy being led back through the door whence he came. I look at Sam again and then at Noah, my face nearly cracking with the size of my smile. I want to cry with relief, but I will shed no more tears for Tommy Blevins—never, ever again. "Ice cream. I need ice cream to celebrate!"

My guys laugh and lead me from the courtroom, matching smile lighting up their faces.

Chapter 13 - May

I'm a miserable failure. I'm not wallowing in the "miserable" so much as the "failure." After listening to Kaleb's concerns about my relationship with Noah and then trying and failing to get Noah to admit that our friendship would be better without kisses, I will admit only to myself that I'm glad Noah didn't budge on the issue. Noah's kisses are wonderful and amazing and they're practically all I can think about when he's not around. I think I must be getting better at them because he seems to want to kiss me more often now. I'm not complaining.

He's gotten busier in the last three weeks. We hardly ever see each other now unless one of us makes a special effort to do so, and so, of course, we do. As much as I love spending time with him, I know he's working himself to the bone with his school work. It seems like every time I talk to him he's either between classes or headed to or from the library or a meeting with one of his faculty advisors.

Today is another of those marathon work sessions for him. Last night he said he needed to spend the whole of his Saturday finishing his research. Most of his paper is finished, though, so what he's doing today is fact- and reference-checking.

Last week was my first official week as bookkeeper of Flip the Page. Because Walter has paid for and enrolled me in some online classes with the local community college, it seems I'm going to be working extra-long hours for the foreseeable future, which further limits the amount of time I have to spend with Noah. Exactly when that time with him became so important to me, I refuse to think about, just as I refuse to analyze my growing feelings for him. All I know is that when I'm with Noah, I feel like I could conquer the world. I feel normal, worthwhile and cared for in a way Sam never could—or should—make me feel. Sam is my brother; Noah is most definitely not.

It's early when I arrive at Noah's apartment. As he kept hounding me weeks ago until I finally agreed, I slip my key in the lock and go on in without knocking first. "This is your second home, Avery. You shouldn't have to knock on the door to your own home," he told me then. A smile teases my lips as I think about that conversation. If mom could have seen the determined look on his face, heard in his voice how much he wanted me to feel at home there, she probably would have passed out. Noah sees good in me, even when I don't. Noah wants me around, even when I'm desperate to escape my own head. It's shocking, amazing and something I will never take for granted.

Lights are on in the kitchen and living room, but I don't see or hear Noah, even though he should be hard at work on his last paper. It's due by five o'clock Monday. Perhaps he's gone out for breakfast or to the gym to free his mind for a while.

"Noah?" I call, just in case. The preternatural silence of the apartment spooks me. I know it's just because I expected to find Noah bent over his laptop working furiously before heading to the library later. Nothing seems out of place or even different from the other times I've been here, but I can't deny that it just *feels* weird. "Noah?" I call again.

I walk into the kitchen and see his wallet, car keys and cell phone sitting on the bar. Wherever he's gone, he's not going far. Bracing myself, I move to the mouth of the hallway. There are only three doors down the hall: the bathroom, Noah's bedroom and a smaller bedroom he keeps for his brother, Luke.

I call his name again and this time I'm rewarded with what sounds suspiciously like a groan. Not a good, happy moan, but a noise borne of pain. Immediately my mind jumps back to all the times I've made similar noises. My knees shake like they're teaching my hands how it's done and I practically fall into the wall when I take a step forward. My mental view screen flashes ridiculous images of Noah lying on the floor, covered in blood from a beating he doesn't deserve. I force myself down the hall and peer into his bedroom for the first time.

Noah lays supine atop an enormous unmade bed, dressed only in blue boxers, one arm thrown over his eyes. He's pale against the caramel-colored sheets, but otherwise seems unharmed. Although he's not covered in blood, he is covered in sweat.

"Noah?" I call again.

He rolls in my direction and peers at me as though he doesn't really believe he's seeing me. "Aves?" he croaks weakly.

With only the slightest hesitation, I cross the room to kneel beside the bed. "Are you okay?" I ask, putting my hand to his forehead. He's burning up. I jerk my hand away in surprise then slowly put it back, gently brushing the damp strands of his hair from his clammy skin.

Noah groans again, his eyes closed already. The rush of emotion almost overwhelms me. I have no idea what to do for him but there's no way I can leave him to his suffering. Seeing the big man felled rattles me. Noah has always been so strong and confident, almost like he's immune to the everyday troubles of life. I know that's not true. I know he's as human as the rest of us, but he's such a tank—big in size and in personality.

I think back, dredging the depths of memory for a clue how mom or a foster caregiver had helped me or one of the other boys in a similar situation. The only thing I can think is to get Noah's fever down before his brain boils. I have no idea where that appalling thought comes from, but it scares me into action.

I stumble away from him and dash into the connecting bathroom where I search cabinets for a washrag. Finally finding his neatly-folded multicolored stash, I wet the cotton under the cold water tap, ringing it out and rewetting it in hopes of getting more, even colder water in it.

When I place the cloth on Noah's forehead, he groans and shivers and I'm convinced I've just killed him. He rolls onto his back and tries to take the cloth away, but I grab his hand and bring it back down to his flat belly where I hold it loosely. "Shh," I soothe. "It's gonna be okay. You're gonna be fine."

I wish I knew that were true. I wish I could believe me, but I have zero experience with this. Sam is never, ever sick and when I have been, it's never been like this. I get head colds. Whatever this is that has Noah flat on his back groaning in pain is no head cold.

Gently, I move the cloth around his face, trying to spread the coldness. My hand trembles and at times I fear I'm barely making contact with his skin. Noah groans again as I reach his neck and I realize the cloth has grown warm from our combined heat.

Thinking ahead for once in my life, I rush into the kitchen and fill one of Noah's large mixing bowls with ice and water. Thank goodness the man likes to bake, I think with a slightly hysterical giggle.

Back at Noah's side, I place the bowl on the nightstand and refresh the cloth. The cool pressure on Noah's forehead causes him to gasp and I jerk away, out of my depth now more than ever. The image of his brain boiling behind those hidden hazel eyes is the only thing that keeps me applying the cold cloth to his face and neck. I continue my ministrations with one hand and frantically dig my iPhone from my jeans pocket with the other. I fumble with the blessed thing until, at last, I find the right contact. Looking back at Noah, noting how unnatural it is to see his long thick blond lashes resting against his cheek, shuttered over those beautiful eyes, I punch the key. I force myself to keep calm, to keep moving the cloth along Noah's stubble-studded cheek while the phone on the other end rings and rings.

After what seems an eternity and a half, Kira's annoyed voice greets me in the usual way.

I take a deep breath and it comes out in a fury. "Kira, you have to help me. Noah's sick, really sick, and I don't know what to do."

"What? Avery, slow down. What's going on?" Obviously I've awakened her from a sound sleep.

"Kira, please! He's burning up! I don't want his brain to boil, but I don't know how to stop it! What do I do? I don't know what to do, Kira. I don't know what to do to help him." The last comes out on a sob and I consciously reel myself back in. It's not much and it won't last long, but I have to keep it together for Noah's sake.

"Does he have a temperature, Avery?"

I pause. "Uh, I don't know. I think so? He's really hot to the touch—on his forehead—and he's sweating and shivering. I don't want—Kira, we can't let his brain boil! It can do that, right? I know I read it somewhere!"

"Focus, Avery," she snaps, all business now that she's awake. "Noah's brain is *not* going to boil. Get a cold wet cloth and wipe him down. Start with his face and neck and do his torso, too."

"H-his torso?" I squeak, looking down at—oh, man, the most beautiful almost naked male body I've ever seen. The man is ripped and tight in all the right spots, the golden hairs of his chest made dark with sweat, cling to his skin in swirling patterns. The rippled dunes of his abdomen capture my attention for a moment before I force my mind back to the reason he's splayed out naked before me like a buffet.

"Yes, his torso. Keep it together, Avery. It'll be okay. Is he awake? Has he told you what's wrong?"

"He's burning up! That's what's wrong!" I huff, exasperated at both of us. My eyes stay glued to the rhythmic rise and fall of his chest. Noah's chest. His naked, tanned, golden-haired chest just a few inches away.

Through the phone, I hear Kira's keys scrape across some table. "Keep up with the wash cloth, Aves. Try to wake him up and give him some ibuprofen or Tylenol to start lowering his fever. Then get him to sit in a cold bath. I'll be there in a few minutes. Just hang on, champ. You're doing great."

Ibuprofen? A cold bath? Yes, that's brilliant. Why didn't I think of that? Dropping the phone to the floor, I rush to Noah's bathroom and start the water filling the tub, thankful I don't have to search around for a plug for the stupid thing like the one at my place. Here it's a lever I switch. I put my fingers in the water and hiss at the coldness of it. Noah's really not going to like that. Hoping I'm doing the right thing, I open the warm tap just a little so it won't be so shockingly cold to his heated skin. I pause at the medicine cabinet to retrieve the ibuprofen, then dash to the kitchen for a glass of water.

Back at his side, I try to coax him gently awake, almost whispering in my desperation. "Noah, come on, big guy. We've got to get you in the tub." He's so pale it truly frightens me. What if I should be calling an ambulance? What if his brain really does boil and it's my fault? Desperate fear morphs into desperate anger and my gentle touches become more forceful. "Noah! Dammit, wake up! C'mon. I need you to help me."

Noah groans once again and rolls onto his side facing me. "Good! That's good, Noah!" I enthuse desperately. "Now sit up so we can get you in the bath."

His eyes slowly open. Even if I hadn't been here for the last twenty minutes trying to get him awake, one look at how dull and unfocused those gorgeous hazel eyes are would be enough to tell me he feels like warmed over death. Still, he gifts me with a smile and a sigh. "Avery," he croaks. "Thought I'd imagined you." His eyes start to drift closed, so I grab his legs and pull them none too gently over the side of the bed. Geez, they weigh a ton apiece.

"You didn't imagine me. I'm right here." I pat his cheek. "Noah, listen to me. You have to sit up and help me get you into the tub. You have a high fever."

Noah groans. "Feel like lead," he complains but helps me get him upright.

I shove the pills and glass of water at him. "Take these. You'll feel better in the tub. C'mon, big guy. Help me help you."

Noah slowly swallows the pills. As I place the glass on the nightstand, he slumps forward as if he's more exhausted than any human has ever been. With aching slowness, he shuffles himself closer to the edge of the bed, preparing to make the massive effort of standing. Knuckles pressed into the soft mattress, Noah's arms tremble as he struggles. The man is a foot taller and almost a hundred pounds heavier than me, but I try to help. Bracing myself against the side of the bed, I slide my arm under his and curl it around his ribs. The man is positively slick with sweat. Gripping him tightly, I say, "On three, okay?"

He nods then groans and brings his hand to his forehead. "Dizzy," he explains.

"We'll get you feeling better in just a bit, okay?" When he carefully nods again, I start the count. "One…two…" Noah takes a deep breath and I follow suit. "…Three."

We both grunt at the effort it takes the two of us to get him to his feet. I start to release him but he wobbles so I tighten my grip on his slippery back. "That's the hard part," I pant encouragingly. I gently turn Noah towards the bathroom and take every slow, unsteady step with him.

What seems like ages later, we're in the bathroom. Noah leans against the sink to catch his breath as I turn off the water in the tub. I'd left it running at a fairly slow rate, but it has taken us so long to get here that it's only a couple of inches from the top. I turn back to Noah who is listing to one side, his eyes closed again. Grabbing his wrist, I stop his slow slump. His eyes pop half open again.

"Can you do the rest by yourself?" I ask tenderly, grazing my hand down his cheek to keep his attention. The feel of his stubble sends a shiver down my spine.

"I'm taking a bath?" he queries with some confusion.

"To lower your temperature."

"Oh," he answers, struggling to stand on his own again. I steady him with a hand on each side of his ribs. He blinks at me as if he's not sure I'm really there. With an unexpected flick of his wrists, his boxers fall to the floor.

Oh. *Oh!*

Not quickly enough, I drag my gaze back to his unfocused one and swallow hard, my heartbeat racing, my hands suddenly shaking. A completely naked Noah is the last thing I expected, even though I've just drawn his bath. Right. Bath. Naked. Sort of goes together. But—oh, geez. He's so…naked. And, uhm, *gifted.*

I look away, back to his bedroom and see his unmade bed. Okay, so not helping. I swallow again around a suddenly desert-dry throat and step away, forcibly keeping my eyes locked on the reflection in the mirror of Noah's strongly muscled bare back. He lists forward and I quickly step into him, resuming my previous grip on his back but bringing my other hand to rest low on his hard, flat, bare belly. To guide him better, that's the only reason for that contact. My voice is a croak when I speak. "Okay, big guy, let's get you into the tub."

I guide him carefully the remaining few feet to the bath. Floor space is cramped so I have to watch both of our feet to make sure neither of us steps on the other or trips on a rug. And I will swear by all that is holy that I'm not once distracted by the generously thick length of him curling over his balls. And not once do I almost erupt into nervous giggles when I absolutely do not notice how well-trimmed he is. None of this happens because I keep my focus locked on our feet and the floor. And it's a good thing I'm not religious because I would surely spontaneously burst into flames for lying to myself.

No, instead of getting caught up in the sight of Noah's gloriously naked body, I cautiously advise him to step into the tub with one foot. "Good. Now the other." It's incredibly awkward and for half a second I think he's going to crash us both to the floor, but we manage it. The first touch of his foot to the water makes Noah gasp and jerk back, but I lean on him enough he resumes the mission. Soon both feet are in the tub and we slowly lower him into the water, all the while I pretend I don't hear his whines and curses. Somehow I keep it together enough to continue offering encouragement and praise.

Mere inches from mission accomplished, Noah's foot slips and his body comes into crashing contact with the bottom of the tub. He gasps, eyes wide, and I mimic him as the sudden infusion of Noah's body mass sends a wave of freaking freezing water hurtling over the side of the tub, drenching my shirt, jeans and the bathroom floor.

Checking quickly that Noah's okay, I grab the towel from the rack on the wall and desperately attack the escaped water before it can damage the hardwood. Without more than a sliver of a thought to Noah's presence, I rip the soaked shirt over my head and apply it to the job on the floor, too. Shivering, I finish mopping the water and stash the towel and shirt in a soggy pile behind me. I sit back up on my knees and look to Noah. He stares back at me through violent shivers but wearing a slight smile. His wet hand reaches out and cups my cheek, thumb to my lip as always.

"S-s-so bu-beautiful," he whispers through his tremors.

Suddenly I realize I'm half naked, something I never, ever am when there's the remotest chance anyone will see. I skitter backwards into the corner nearest the door, curling into a ball with my knees drawn up to my chest. I hug my legs, keeping my torso pressed against them, hiding as much as possible. *Please tell me he's too sick to remember this*, I pray silently.

"M-my bu-beauti-beautiful Avery." Noah sighs through chattering teeth, letting his head fall back against the wall. His fevered eyes close. I watch him closely for a minute to make sure he won't slip under the surface of the water, then silently slink away to find something to cover me.

***

When I open the door to Kira, she stops in surprise and gives me a slow once-, twice-over look. I know I must look a fool. In addition to absurdly swimming in one of Noah's blue plaid shirts, my jeans are soaked down to the knees from the tidal wave of water. I know my face shows the stress of worrying about Noah and his possibly boiling brain. I can't help caring about him and I won't hide it from Kira. I don't need to. Still, my get up is a bit embarrassing.

"Uhm, water came over the side of the tub and soaked me," I explain with a blush, ushering her in.

"Uh huh. And so you decided to wear a long-sleeve shirt? In May?"

"It was *cold* water."

Kira laughs and ruffles my hair. The gesture is so Noah-like that tears spring to my eyes. I blink them away furiously. "Show me to the patient," she says.

"He's in the tub," I tell her, leading the way. "Oh, I guess you figured that out." I bite my lip and look back at her. "Should I have called an ambulance? He's really out of it."

She puts a hand to my shoulder. "I'm sure he'll be fine. We'll figure it all out when I see him. Getting him in the bath was a great first step. Did you get the Tylenol into him?"

"Yes, well ibuprofen. I didn't know what to do," I lament, walking into the bedroom. "Sam's never sick. I've never had to take care of someone before."

"You're doing fine," she assures me, stepping into the bathroom. She kneels next to the tub and puts her hand to Noah's forehead. He hadn't seemed as hot when I'd done the same a few minutes ago. "Pretty high fever," she confirms, digging into her purse.

Noah's eyes flutter open and he offers her a weak smile. "Hey."

"Hi there." She smiles back at him. "Got yourself sick, did ya?" She brandishes a digital thermometer from her purse, removing it from its protective case.

Noah groans. "Feel like crap."

Kira nods. "I bet you do. You look it, too. Open up." When he opens his mouth she slides the thermometer under his tongue.

Noah's body temperature has warmed the water enough that he's no longer chattering his teeth. Or maybe the cold water has cooled him enough? I don't know how these things work, but I hope it's in Noah's favor. Watching Kira stroke Noah's slowly drying hair, I'm glad I thought ahead enough to cover his…gifts…with a wash cloth. While I have no idea how modest Noah is generally, I'm sure Kira would rather not see just how well-endowed Noah is, even accounting for shrinkage. A baby's arm comes to mind and I have to stifle a nervous giggle.

Kira shoots a curious look at me over her shoulder, but the beep of the thermometer captures both of our attention. She gently removes it from Noah's mouth and reads, "103.6. That's not dangerous right now, but it is too high." She smiles at me. "Good job cooling him down, Avery. There's no telling how high his temp was before you got him in here."

I smile tremulously back at her. "It was your idea. Is he going to be okay?"

Kira shrugs. "He's sick. There's no doubt about that, but we'll get him through it." To Noah, she asks, "Do you want us to take you to the doctor?"

"N-no." He shivers again, seeming much more awake. "It's just the f-flu. Been g-goin' 'round." He slides back so he's sitting more or less upright. "Have to type my paper." He groans and brings his hands to his face. "Or die. That might be easier."

"Don't you say that!" The vehemence in my voice surprises all of us.

Noah tries to smile up at me, but his lips barely turn up at the corners. "I'm only kidding. I think." He shivers again. "Can I get out of here now?"

Kira frowns. "Your temp is still really high, Noah. We need to get that down." She thinks for a minute and turns to me. "There should be some ice packs in the freezer. Wrap two of them in separate dishtowels and bring them back. We'll get him settled in bed and use those to lower his body temperature. We'll also need more Tylenol and some Gatorade. Do you have any, Noah?"

He nods miserably.

I nod, too, but hesitate. For some reason I'm reluctant to let her help him out of the bath. It's more than not wanting her to see his nakedness, although that's a huge part of it. Strangely, it's not about shielding her from him. It's that I feel I should be the one to help him, the only one to help him. Somehow Noah's nakedness is something special just between us.

It's a ridiculous thought. I know that. After all, how many men has he taken to his bed before? Any one of them could claim far more familiarity with Noah's body than I could ever hope to, but I would fight off every one of them, too. As stupid as it sounds, Noah belongs to me. Not really and not forever, I know that, but right here, right now, he's mine and I have to see him through this.

"Kira—" I start and stop because, really, how do I even explain these very weird, possessive emotions?

She looks back up at me and smiles in understanding. "You want to help him to bed?"

"I-I'm already wet. And, well, he's…you know."

She smirks. "Naked?"

I nod and avert my gaze, blood rushing to my cheeks.

Surprisingly, Kira gets to her feet and pats me on the shoulder as she passes. "I'll see you in a few minutes. Call me when you have him covered up or if you need help. Nice touch with the wash cloth, by the way." I can't tell if the laughter in her voice is nervous or mocking, but I decide I don't care. She may have known him her entire life, but he's mine now.

In the tub, Noah gathers his strength to try to stand, but fails. He gazes at me with misery in those gorgeous hazel eyes, his breath coming heavier from his struggle. "Can't," he says.

Before I can even think about it, my hands frame his beautiful face and I press my lips to his, offering comfort and support and strength in a kiss, only the second kiss I've ever initiated between us. I draw back and press our foreheads together.

"Gonna get you sick," he mumbles.

I kiss him again. "I've had my flu shot."

He half smiles and kisses me again. "Good. So good."

I chuckle at him. Even in his weakened state, he's all about the kisses. "Roll over on your knees. I can help you up more easily that way." He tries to smirk like I've said something naughty but he can't quite manage the expression. "Yeah, yeah," I say around a grin, moving away to grab a fresh bath towel from under the sink.

Once he's on his knees, I lean in and wrap my arm around his ribs. Together, we slowly get him to his feet. He breathes heavily into my hair for a few minutes before straightening fully. I step back and hold the towel up for him to step into when he gets out of the tub.

Even those few steps seem to exhaust him. He leans a shoulder heavily against the wall. I take pity on the poor sick baby, tenderly rubbing the towel across his broad, muscular shoulders, down his long powerful arms. This should scare the hell out of me, I think. I can see up close and way too personally how powerfully built the man is. But I feel something entirely different from fear: tenderness, empathy and something more I absolutely refuse to acknowledge. Sweeping the towel down the vast expanse of golden-haired chest, past pebbled nipples that practically beg to be suckled, I feel blood pooling in my groin. I glance up to find Noah watching me intently, his eyes riveted to my face. Quickly swiping down his faintly-chiseled abs, I switch to his back to avoid his heated gaze and marvel at the musculature beneath my fingertips. I feel the heat of him through the towel. My breath catches in my throat as I'm confronted with the firm roundness of his glutes. My hands shake as the towel glides over them. My eyes nearly roll back in my head as the incredible sensuality of my actions hit me full force. I have never touched another person so intimately, never ever wanted to, but now I don't want to stop. With the towel between our skin we're not really touching, but I could swear I feel an electric current pass between us.

It boggles my mind how much I want to step forward and press myself against Noah's nakedness, how hard it is to not press my lips to that spot high on his back between his shoulder blades, to not wrap my arms around his narrow waist and explore his flat stomach and hard chest with my hands.

I take a deep breath and force myself to continue drying him, down his thighs. *Perving on a sick man. What the hell is wrong with you?* I curse myself, nearly yelping aloud as I accidentally pinch the throbbing erection in my jeans as I drop to my knees to do his calves. Speaking of erections…oh, please, no, Noah. Please don't…oh. Oh!

Shallow breaths rush into and out of my lungs as I knee-walk around in front of him again and see I'm not the only one with blood flow problems. His eyes are closed but his head is still tilted down as if watching me through his eyelids. Up one leg, then the other I swipe the now sodden towel, thrilling internally at the power harnessed in his thick thighs. And then…then all that's left is….

I look up at him again, hoping, praying, dreading that he'll spare me this, that he'll reach for the towel. His body tenses but his eyes remain resolutely closed, his face blank, almost as if asleep. The lump in my throat has grown to the size of Connecticut, but I force my trembling hands to press on. I look away, but push the towel between his thighs, sliding up…up…up.

The heat of his balls against the back of my hand startles me and I force my eyes back to the job. Obviously I can't dry him there without seeing what I'm doing. I swipe the towel between the juncture of legs and torso and then gently cup it around his balls, rolling tenderly, tugging slightly. I wrap my toweled hand around his length, carefully moving back and forth, pretending with everything in me that I don't feel him lengthen and thicken even more under my fingers.

My breath comes in hard, short puffs but I can't…can't bring myself to release him, because then I'll have to look at him, stand beside him and help him to…to bed. A shiver races down my spine and it's enough to break the spell. I release my hold on Noah's…very, *very* generous…thickness…and wrap the towel around his waist, anchoring it above his left hip. I clear my throat so the lump is only Rhode Island-sized and dare to look up. Noah's heated gaze meets mine and I swear I positively dissolve into a puddle at his feet. With so little blood actually flowing to my brain I have no idea how I flush as furiously as I do.

"C'mere," he commands gruffly and there's no one in the world—or at least the room—who could disobey. I'm barely steady on my feet before his arms wrap around my waist and bring me tight against him. I feel his erection against my belly and moan into his fierce kiss. One of Noah's hands grips the hair at the back of my head, angling my mouth just how he wants it. The other anchors me firmly to him at the waist. Mine are splayed against his chest, feeling those golden hairs and that solid wall of soft, heated skin beneath my palms at last.

The kiss is unlike any we've shared before. There's a hunger, a desperation there that he's never shown before. Noah's tongue delves quickly into my mouth and I push back aggressively, something I've never really done. Sure, we've played with tongues before, but I've mostly followed his lead, learning as I went. He moans into my mouth and bends me slightly backward. My arms slide around his neck and I rise to my toes, giving as good as I'm getting. Finally, Noah drags his mouth away to nuzzle my neck—something else new—as we both gasp for breath.

"So much," he whispers against my skin. "So much."

I nod against his chest, not sure what he means, but agreeing anyway. That kiss was so much more than I could have believed before. As the world slowly settles back on its slightly more tilted axis, I realize he's trembling against me. I'm flooded with remorse for forgetting what we're supposed to be doing. "C'mon," I mumble against his skin. "Let's get you to bed."

"You look good in my shirt," he mumbles.

I flush and stare at the floor. "Are you ever going to tell me why you wear this one so often?"

"Easy," he says, falling into the bed. "You talk to me more when I wear that one."

I stare at him in disbelief but he doesn't notice; he's already passed out.

***

While Kira tends to Noah in his bedroom, I escape to the kitchen with a riot of confused thoughts struggling for dominance in my head. My physical reaction to Noah is most easily explained. I've never been that close to a naked man before, especially not someone I care about. And I do care about Noah. He's a wonderful person. He's incredibly kind, infinitely patient, endlessly intriguing and ridiculously generous. And he kisses like a dream. The fact that he wants to kiss me, of all people, still surprises me. He could have his pick of men to kiss and…more.

I close my eyes against the deep slice of pain in my chest that thought brings. I don't want him to kiss someone else, much less the more. I slap a hand to my mouth to stifle the startled cry that issues from my throat. Tears pool in my eyes and I bend over as if taking a blow to the stomach, because the realization hits me with a physical force.

I'm in love with him.

It's absolutely, positively insane, but it's unquestionably true. I want to be with him all the time and when I'm not, the mere mention or thought of him causes a giddy smile to spread my lips. I want to make him laugh and take care of him. I want to hear about his day and what he thinks about his classes. I want to help him achieve his dreams, even if it's just by making sure he has enough of the right things to eat. And I want him to kiss me, to hold me, when the world seems too messed up to survive another minute. Noah makes me feel safe and…like I matter…in ways I've never experienced before. He makes me *feel.*

I take a moment to savor the exquisite joy the revelation brings, trying unsuccessfully to stifle a giddy giggle. I'm in love with Noah Yates, the most beautiful man I've ever known. Of course he's sexy as all get-out, but it's his internal beauty that has brought us here. I've seen good-looking men around before, but none of them have possessed the generosity of spirit that Noah has. None of them ever cared to look past my fears and scars to see what Noah instinctively saw in me. And none of them made me want to be a better person, to overcome my fears and my past. None of them could ever be Noah.

I want to rush back to his bedroom and smother him with kisses, a thought that makes me giggle again, somewhat uncomfortably. The poor man's sick. The last thing he needs is some lovesick idiot mackin' all over him.

I plunge my hands into the hot water in the sink and wash the dishes left over from Noah's dinner last night, carefully razing all thoughts from my brain. I can't afford to examine them now. Noah, the man I'm in love with, needs me to help him get well.

***

The man has the worst handwriting on the planet. I'd swear it on my father's grave, if I knew where it is. Trying to decipher his flat lines and curlicues is nearly impossible, but I have to do it. He wrote his final paper for Behavioral Psychology longhand and the final, polished project has to be presented to the professor's secretary by Monday. I have to transcribe it, because if he doesn't get better in time to do it himself, it will earn him an Incomplete, meaning he won't graduate. I can't let that happen, even if he does write in something resembling Arabic.

I glance over at Noah sleeping peacefully beside me. I'm torn between wanting to smack him upside the head for never learning penmanship or curling up next to him and holding him while he sleeps. The last option is almost enough to catapult me off the bed and into the living room, but when I tried that earlier, he'd shuffled slowly down the hall, wrapped in a sheet to sleep on the too-short couch. He wanted me near him while he slept, he said. My fingers card through his short hair and a smile pulls at my lips. How could I possibly turn down the request of a sick man, even one with atrocious penmanship?

With a contented sigh, I turn back to the paper and the laptop. I don't understand a lot of what Noah has written, but some parts make me gasp with their familiarity. He's not talking about me at all, but those certain instances do a lot to explain how he has always known how to approach and deal with me. If it were anyone but Noah using these techniques to get me to trust him, I know I would feel like a lab experiment, but I know Noah's heart. He would never look at me that way.

We've come so far together in these seven months. If anyone had told me in November that I'd be sitting on the slumbering giant's bed with him next to me, I would have...well...I probably would have run and hid. But here I am and there he is, making soft snuffling noises in his sleep, battling to get well.

Fighting myself even as I do it, I sit the laptop and the paper aside on the nightstand and stretch out atop the covers. He's asleep. He'll never know. And if he wakes, I don't think he'll mind. Slowly, carefully, I move up behind him. Resting my head on my crooked arm, I slide the other around his waist. It's only seconds before Noah's fingers thread through mine and he slides our joined hands under his chin. He sighs contentedly and whispers my name. I press a tender kiss to the back of his still-heated neck and close my eyes, letting his clean scent fill my lungs. Eventually I drift off with him, the very sick man I love.

***

Four days pass before Noah feels well enough to kick Kaleb out of his apartment. I get the phone call on my way home from work. They've all taken turns taking care of him when I've had to work. Kaleb, Kyle, Kira, and even Sam have taken shifts sitting with the patient. Each has reported increasingly irascible behavior which has pleased me no end because it means Noah is feeling better. So when Kaleb calls, I'm ready and relieved, except Kaleb is far too gleeful. He laughs uproariously as he describes in great detail how red-faced Noah was just before almost physically tossing him out.

"Kaleb," I say on a sigh, signaling a change in lanes so I can go by Noah's place instead of going home to shower first, "the poor man's been sick. Did you have to bait him so much?"

"Hell yes!" Kaleb laughs. "He's fine, Aves. I swear to you. He's just milking it so you'll keep taking care of him. One of you is going to have to make a move soon or you'll be at this stalemate forever. Well, not forever because I'm about done watching you two dance around in circles. Don't make me kick your asses. Tell the man how you feel."

With a gasp, I jerk the car into an empty parallel parking spot and nearly drop the phone. "What are—what are you talking about?" I'm not ready for anyone else to know. I haven't even told Noah I love him. I'm not even sure I know how to tell him.

I can hear the smirk in Kaleb's voice. It is *so*not attractive. "Uh huh. Friends who kiss. Friends who nurse each other back to health. Friends who decipher his abominable handwriting so his paper isn't late and he graduates with honors."

The sound of my racing heartbeat in my ears almost drowns Kaleb's voice, but I hear him loud and clear. "Yes. Friends. Nothing more."

Kaleb sighs and the mirth is gone from his voice when he speaks next. "You can lie to yourself all you want, but you can't lie to me. I've seen you together and I've seen you apart. I was in Noah's shoes once, remember? Never—listen, you know you can talk to me about anything, right?"

"Yeah."

"And that I won't judge you and will always love you as my brother from a really shitty other mother?"

I can't stop the chuckle. Kaleb, Mr. Blunt. Love him or leave him, you'll never change him. "Yeah, I know."

"Alright then. Go see your boyfriend. He's jonesin' for some Avery time."

"He's not my—"

"Yeah, yeah. Shut up. Love you, buddy."

"Love you, too, Kaleb." And I do, almost as much as I love Sam, which is how I know I'm in so much trouble when it comes to Noah. My feelings for him are off the charts, totally different—and growing. I sigh heavily—because what the heck else am I gonna do?—and nose my old rattletrap Honda back into the traffic that will take me to the man I'm hopelessly in love with.

***

He crushes me to him when I walk in the door, his mouth finding and devouring mine before I can even say hi. As hellos go, this is definitely the best on record. When he finally breaks away, I flush and look down, then quickly to the right when my gaze encounters evidence of his arousal straining his sleep pants. So it wasn't just a one-time occurrence. I'm simultaneously pleased and terrified. It's one thing to wonder if kissing me pushes his buttons, it's entirely something else to be presented with the throbbing evidence. I push away. "Miss me?" I ask in a leaden attempt to lighten the mood.

"Maybe a little." He smiles that dimpled smile he knows gets him anything he wants.

I tap him hard in the middle of his chest. "You've been told on."

He holds his hands up in surrender but doesn't even have the grace to look abashed. "It was all Kaleb." Now he turns on the puppy dog eyes. "I'm a sick man and all he was doing was harping on me. He could have set back my recovery by weeks! Months even!"

I can't stop the laugh that bubbles out of me, but he knew that. He always knows. I let him encircle me in his strong arms once again and I breathe in the fresh, clean scent of him. I rest my forehead against his chest and smile when he presses a kiss to my hair. "Why am I the only one you don't fight tooth and nail?"

"Because you're the only one I want or need to take care of me."

It would be so much easier to be cross with him if he weren't so flipping wonderful. Oh, he's not perfect. The last several days have proved that. He can be irritable and snappish and whiny, but he's my irritable, snappish, whiny, handsome, hulking mountain of a man. And I love him, more than I have a right to.

I push away and head for the kitchen, hoping he doesn't notice as I wipe my eyes. "Have you eaten yet?"

***

"I can't go, Sam. Stop arguing with me!"

Sam rolls his eyes like a petulant child or a fed-up older brother. "You *are* going and that's final. Go get dressed. *Now.*"

I narrow my eyes and prepare to argue back when he interrupts, well and truly angry. As angry as I've ever seen him. If he were anyone else, I would be behind a locked door and in the back of the closet by now, but it's Sam and while I know he's angry *at me*, I also know he won't take it out *on me*. "I don't know why you're being so selfish about this, Avery. This is Noah's big day. He specifically asked us to come. You'll be surrounded by your friends and family. No one's going to hurt you with me and the twins there, so just take a valium and get a move on already. We're close to being late as it is!"

"He wants me to meet his mom!" I don't mean to tell him. Heck, I've been counting on Sam's protective nature to get us in and out of Noah's graduation ceremony with as little social interaction as possible in a space with a panic-inducing two thousand expected attendees. But then Noah dropped that bomb on me two days ago and it's been the only thing I can think about. Noah's mom. No, just…no.

"Oh," he says and drops into the kitchen chair behind him.

"Yeah, 'oh'," I mimic sarcastically.

Sam looks up at me, all the fight gone from his face, replaced with a double dose of his usual worry for me. "That's a big step. I didn't realize you were there yet."

"What do you mean 'there'? I'm not 'there.' I don't even know where 'there' is! We're just friends, Sam. Why do I have to meet his mom if we're just friends?" I'm practically panicking already and we haven't even left the house yet. I glom on to the "just friends" label because, although I know we're far more than that, it's the only thing I have left keeping the panic at bay.

Sam fills a glass of water from the tap, grabs a pill out of the bottle in the cabinet by the stove and shoves them both at me. He looks as shell-shocked as I feel and I won't deny taking some satisfaction in that. I hastily swallow the pill and will it to start working right the heck now. Instead, I start to hyperventilate. Sam grabs me and pushes me into the chair, shoving my head between my knees. "I—can't—meet—his—*mom*!" I pant.

'Of course you can," he soothes. "Avery, not everyone's mom is an abusive piece of sh—work. You've met Kira's mom. She's a wonderful woman. I'm sure Noah's is, too."

"Haven't—met—her—mom."

"Really? Didn't you meet them at Easter?"

"No!—Focus!"

"Right, sorry."

I feel Sam's hand rubbing my back comfortingly. Between that and the most uncomfortable position known to mankind, I finally get my breathing under control. I sit up slowly and stare at my brother. "What am I going to do? This is the only thing he's ever asked of me and I can't do it. I told him I would, but I can't."

Sam hands me the water and I drain the glass. That determined look he gets when he knows I'll argue takes over his face and I want to scream. "You can do it," he says calmly. "Noah and Kaleb and I will be right there with you. It'll be okay. You were gonna have to meet her sometime anyway, Aves."

"No I wouldn't."

He looks at me with a 'stop the bull pucky' expression. "Avery, everyone knows you can't plan a gay wedding without the mother of the groom."

"We're just friends!"

"Uh huh." He reaches out to touch the mark on my collarbone, a gift from Noah last night, something new again. "And I suppose this is from Noah's curling iron."

At my glare, Sam dissolves into laughter.

***

The ceremony is interminable. Despite the valium coursing languidly through my bloodstream, I can scarcely sit still. I curse Noah for having a last name that starts with Y. What kind of name is Yates anyway?

I don't realize I've asked the question aloud until Kaleb whispers in my ear, "It's English. Settle down."

It isn't until Kaleb clamps a hand on one knee and Sam the other that I take control of my fidgetiness and put it to good use, chewing my fingernails, something I haven't done since Mrs. Garcia, one of my first foster caregivers, laced them with Tabasco sauce.

"Jesus, Avery, calm down," Kaleb says into my ear. "You're driving me to drink and I don't even have my flask!"

Kyle surreptitiously hands him his and I bark out a laugh.

Finally, Noah's name is called and the entire row jumps to our feet in applause and deafening whistles, courtesy the twins. I climb onto a chair in time to see Noah shake his head and laugh at something an older man handing out some book-like thing says. He's grinning the entire time and I know I wouldn't have missed this for the world. This is Noah's moment, our chance to celebrate his achievement. I'm so proud of him I could burst.

I glance at Sam and he ruffles my hair, beaming a smile back at me.

When the last name is called—three after Yates—we make our way out of the big arena thing where the football team plays and stand around on the grass waiting for Noah to arrive. It's a maddening crush of people, some in cap and gown, but mostly supporters and family, like my own little group. Kyle, Kira and Sam, Kaleb and Josh, all huddle around me talking about the party Kaleb is throwing for Noah later tonight. Kaleb, always the party animal, plans to get Noah puking drunk.

"Not gonna happen, buddy," Noah says with a laugh behind me.

I turn to look at him and the breath catches in my throat. My mountain of a man has never looked as handsome or happy as he does in his bright blue cap and gown. The deep, rich color shouldn't bring out the sparkle in his hazel eyes, but it does. He looks at me and his smile widens, dimples flashing. He holds out his arms and I'm in them before I can tell myself no PDA.

His arms tighten around me and his lips are in my hair and I couldn't possibly want for another thing in my life. Noah leans back, tilts my head up and gifts me with the sweetest kiss, his tongue tracing my teeth before coaxing my tongue to play. I hear a moan and a low growl and know we both feel the perfection of the moment. I break away for breath, ignoring the catcalls from our own peanut gallery. "I'm so glad you're here, little one," he whispers in my ear. I nip his in response, causing him to gasp. "Careful or somebody will think you like me," he whispers with a chuckle and a squeeze of his arms.

I pat his chest, the gown silky under my fingertips. "Well, what they don't know won't hurt them." I smile at him and accept another peck of a kiss.

I turn back around to face our group, surprised when Noah's arms slide around my waist from behind. I smile up at him and receive a wink back. My hands come up to rest on his and he twines our thumbs together. I lean against him and stare at the ground as the conversation flows around me. Up until now, Noah and I have kept our displays of affection for just us, behind closed doors or when no one else is around. Having all of them know that Noah and I are friends who kiss—and I know they all do because they gossip with each other like it's their purpose in life—is much different than having just put on a show for them and anyone else who happened to be walking by. Seven months ago I would have run and hid before the possibility could arise. Heck, even last month I would have begged Noah not to kiss me in front of our friends. But now? If our peanut gallery comprised of three hulking men and a badass chick hadn't been present, I would have freaked. But with these people, my family, I know I'm safe, protected and cared for. And if Noah wants to kiss me in front of them, I'll kiss him back.

I glance up at Sam. He smile and mouths *you okay?* I nod and try to smile back at him.

A few minutes later, Kaleb seems to notice we're all still rooted in the same spot. "What are we waiting for?" he asks with a self-conscious laugh.

I hear a warm, tinkling laugh answer back. I know instantly who it is. I launch myself from the incriminating circle of Noah's arms. "I do hope you're waiting for me, Kaleb," says the voice that goes with the laugh.

From my spot between Sam and Kyle, I see the woman as she steps into the group. Kaleb's genuinely pleased, "Mom!" is immediately drowned out by choruses of welcome from Kyle, Kira and Noah, who looks at me with a cautious expression. I start to think maybe this is the K's mom until she makes them all wait until she's hugged Noah before enveloping them each in a hug in turn. No, this is the woman from the photograph in Noah's living room. She's a bit older, but just as stylish, decked out in a figure-fitting dress of a contrasting color to Noah's gown. They'll look lovely in a picture together, I think.

She greets the K's warmly, engaging each in a short conversation before standing in front of Sam and me. Her smile is warm, but I cannot meet her eyes. I wonder if she knows what her son and I have been doing. I wonder how completely she disapproves if she does know. Sure it's innocent, just kisses, but a woman like this must have plans and expectations for a son like Noah. And I have no doubt that him playing around with someone like me is far, far from those plans. "Who have we here, Noah?" she asks lightly. Her voice sounds too polite, too interested to be genuine and I pray silently for the earth to open up and swallow me whole.

Noah comes to stand to my left side and drops what I'm sure is meant to be a reassuring hand on my shoulder. I tense and he squeezes lightly. It's his first misstep in "handling" me and I'm disappointed it comes when I most need him to make the right moves. "This is my very good friend Avery and his brother, Sam. Sam's dating Kira, and I've told you all about Avery. Guys, this is my mother, Maggie Yates." I really want to know what that means, that he's told her all about me, to be able to see the truth in Noah's eyes, but I'm too terrified to move.

In what seems like slow motion, Noah's mother brings her hand out, waist high, for me to shake. Waist high because any higher and I would interpret it as a prelude to a slap, I wonder? Noah and I haven't talked in depth about all that's happened to me, but I know he knows more than the little I've told him. The Gossip Group couldn't have failed to warn him against getting involved with me. And Noah most certainly would have warned his mother. I force my hand to hers and grip it firmly as briefly as possible. "Pleased to meet you, Mrs. Yates," I somehow croak out.

"Oh, honey, please, call me Mom like the rest of the kids do," she offers with another warm laugh.

"No thank you, ma'am," I hear myself say.

For a second she looks stricken and I see her glance at Noah, then she looks back at me. “Of course, honey. I’m sorry. That was silly of me. Please call me Maggie.”

I nod, just to have the conversation over. I won’t call her anything and we both know it. I step slightly away from Noah and behind Sam as he shakes Mrs. Yates’s hand.

“So you’re the young man who’s swept our Kira off her feet. It’s lovely to finally meet you. Kira’s kept you to herself for far too long. It’s about time she lets her second mama get a look at you.” She steps forward and hugs Sam. “Whatever you’re doing, keep it up. I’ve never seen our girl so happy.”

“It’s very nice to meet you, Mrs. Yates. I’m doing my best and I promise to keep trying.” Sam’s never met a grown woman he couldn’t charm, even someone’s mother. For the first time, I envy him that easy confidence.

Mrs. Yates and Sam exchange a few more words I can’t make out over the blood pounding in my ears. I take a step away, but Noah's fingers lacing with mine halt me where I stand. I’ve never been more ashamed. Noah's mom is nothing like my own mother. She can’t be, not having raised a man like Noah. I know I’ve embarrassed him in front of the woman who gave him life and then cared enough to raise him into a wonderful man. I just can’t help my reaction.

Noah's fingers squeeze mine and I turn to see him staring down at me with a sad half smile. “I’m sorry,” I whisper, wanting nothing more than to run.

His other hand comes up to cup my cheek and caress my lip with his thumb. "You did fine," he says softly. "I know that was huge for you. Thank you for meeting her. It'll get easier the more you see her, but right now I'm so proud of you I could kiss you silly."

"Wouldn't take much," Kaleb interjects lazily.

"I know where you live, Kaleb," Noah warns with a smile, never breaking eye contact with me.

Kaleb laughs and clasps both of Noah's shoulders. "I know, bro. It's where you're gonna puke your guts out later. Now go take your boyfriend someplace quiet before you start making out in public again. Mama Yates doesn't need to see that yet."

"I'm not—"

"Shut up and get out of here before I change my mind about being your distraction."

With a wicked grin, Noah gently tugs me away from the group toward the event parking area.

***

Several hours and another valium later, my mind is a kaleidoscope of faces and names, none laying claim to the other. Kaleb's party is in full swing and Noah has been dragging me all over the place introducing me to anyone and everyone. The early ones were rather daunting until I realized no one cares who I am or what my name is. More recently, people have been lubricated enough by the freely-flowing alcohol that I know they won't remember much in the morning anyway.

The entire group seems young, masculine, carefree, and happy to have graduated or to be out of school for the summer. It's not my style of crowd, not by a long shot. But then, no crowd would be my style. I feel Sam's eyes on me frequently throughout the night and he checks in often, making sure I'm not freaking out with both the sheer number of people and being Noah's tag-along. Surprisingly, I am doing okay. No doubt the valium gets a great deal of credit, but I know my work with Kendall has paid off here, too. Tonight, despite the increasing drunkenness of the crowd and their overwhelming maleness, I don't worry I'll end up someone's punching bag. Noah's friends and the people Kaleb has invited into his home all know the score, as it were. They're all either gay or female or very comfortable with gay people or some combination of the above. There's not a Tommy Blevins or Carl-type in the bunch.

There are, however, a certain mother and younger brother I studiously avoid. I feel their eyes on me periodically, too. I can practically taste their curiosity, smell their disapproval, but this is Noah's night and none of us is going to ruin it. Or so I hope.

Kelly Clarkson's "Stronger (What Doesn't Kill You)" pounds from Kaleb's impressive sound system and I catch myself actually applying the lyrics to my life. Although the song's "you" is, presumably, the singer's ex-boyfriend, I see that person as my mother. And yeah, I realize that the day she left me was really my beginning. I am stronger now, and I am beginning again, surrounded by these people who care about me even though they have no reason to. And the most amazing thing of all is that I've discovered I have the ability to love someone so much I'm willing to face down mothers and little brothers, two of the most terrifying creatures ever to populate the planet.

All night Noah either holds my hand, has an arm around me, or holds me close the way he did at his graduation, with his arms around my waist letting me lean back into him. He holds *me*, the guy who recoiled violently when he first tried to introduce himself all those months ago. Tonight I'm his anchor, the one he introduces to everyone and doesn't want to stop touching. I know it's not alcohol making him so touchy-feely. I've monitored his consumption all night, but he's been sipping from his bottle and, much to Kaleb's chagrin, is only on his second beer in three hours. I've never seen him happier. I knew before tonight how hard he worked at his classes, but I don't think I understood before this party just how much completing his degree—with honors!—meant to him.

I look up at him, so proud I think my heart will burst with it. He glances down at me and flashes that dimpled smile. I don't even try to stop my fingers from tracing the crease of it in his cheek. He looks back down at me, clearly startled by my touch. Quickly he excuses himself from the conversation and pulls me by the hand through the crowd into Kaleb's kitchen.

Thankfully the room is empty so he leans against the counter and pulls me into his embrace. "You still doing okay?" he asks, concern flashing in his gorgeous eyes.

I lean into him and reach up to press a quick kiss to his sexy lips. "I'm so proud of you," I whisper, my throat closing with emotion.

"Yeah?" He beams a smile. "Thanks, baby. I'm pretty proud of you, too."

That startles me. "Me? Why?"

Noah strokes my long bangs back from my face, letting the soft tendrils of my hair caress his hand as they fall through his fingers. "You have faced all kinds of demons today and you haven't flinched once. Oh, baby, you're doing so well." He kisses me slowly, deeply and I wonder if I'll ever get used to how amazing his kisses are. Somehow I doubt it. When he draws back, his eyelids stay closed for a few seconds, as if he's taking extra time to savor the feeling. It's insanely sexy. Finally, he opens them and reaches out to caress my bottom lip with his thumb. I think it's almost a habit for him now. "I could kiss you all night," he says with a smile. "Promise me we'll try that someday."

Instead of answering, I bury my forehead against the solid mass of his chest.

Noah strokes my hair and presses a soft kiss into it. "I didn't mean to push you, little one. I know you're not there yet. It's okay. I promised never to hurt you and I intend to keep that promise."

I smile tremulously up at him. "We need—"

An index finger to my lips cuts me off. "Shh. This is way too serious a conversation to have tonight. We have all the time in the world, baby. Let's just enjoy it, huh?"

I shake my head in disbelief. "You always know, don't you?"

He smiles and kisses me lightly. "It's my job to know."

"You're insane. You know that, don't you?"

He wiggles his eyebrow. "All the best psychologists are." I groan and he laughs delightedly. "Whaddya say we blow this Popsicle stand? We can go home, pretend I'm sick again, and fall asleep in each other's arms."

I can think of nothing more wonderful than that. Alas. "I think you've had too much to drink."

He laughs again and pats my buttocks. "Just drunk on you, baby. Just drunk on you."

Chapter 14 – August

"I just want to jump in there with him," I whine, staring longingly at the lucky white duck nonchalantly swimming in the pond. I have no idea what possessed Noah to think that August would be a great time to go for a hike in the park, but here we are, strolling along beside the pond, sweating to death. It's been two and a half months since his graduation. Noah has finally fully regained not only his healthy pallor and all his energy, but a deep, even tan that turns his skin a stunning golden and leaves sun-bleached streaks in his blond hair. He's breathtaking.

"Funny you should mention that…."

I look at him askance. "Funny because we're both sweating enough to make our own sweat pond or funny because you were thinking the same thing?"

Noah laughs a little and looks at the ground. "Uh, well either of those, I guess, but…."

Holy cow! He's nervous! Noah Yates is nervous! I take half a second to savor the moment before my enjoyment crashes and burns. If the ever-confident Mr. Yates is letting nerves get to him—nervous being a synonym for fearful, after all—then I should be flat out terrified. I feel every muscle in my body tense as Noah slowly looks up at me, a question in those hazel eyes of his. "What is it?" I whisper.

He grins a little shyly. "So, uhm, Mom and Luke are going out of town for the next two weeks. They're going to visit my dad's folks in Maine. We haven't seen them in a couple of years and, you know, they're getting up there and don't travel well anymore, so yeah. Mom and Luke are going there."

"Why aren't you going?" The narrative flood of words aside, it seems unlike Noah to pass up an opportunity to see his grandparents.

"I didn't get the time off work. It was either this trip or the time for finals. I'm gonna try to see them for Thanksgiving." He smiles and wags a finger at me. "Stop distracting me. I have a point here."

I lift one eyebrow at him and maybe kinda smirk a little.

"Okay, so it's hot. And Mom has a pool. So I think we should take advantage of it. She already told me to invite the K's and you and Sam over, but I figured it would be easier for you to go while she's gone. I know it still freaks you out to deal with mothers, or my mother, or whatever. So what do you say? Wanna go swimming with me?"

I stare up at him, completely speechless. Swimming? With Noah? "I-I—" The image of him climbing from the bathtub, dripping wet and naked, flashes in front of me. I've seen him half-dressed since then, of course. Any time the man plays outside, be it a pick-up basketball game with one of the twins or lounging around the house on his day off, Noah favors basketball shorts and no shirt. I can't say it bothers me anymore. I've grown used to his casual nudity, even come to look forward to it, especially when he presses that spectacularly sculpted chest against me when he kisses me. But swimming would require me to disrobe, too, and that isn't happening. "I can't," I finally say.

Noah grins and wags a finger at me. "See, I knew that would be your first answer. But I don't think it's the one you really want to give me." He takes my hand and tugs me over to a nearby bench, thankfully well-shaded by a giant of a tree. Oak? Elm? Redwood? How does one tell the difference? My thoughts collide when Noah brings my hand up and presses one of his licking kisses to the inside of my wrist.

I yank my hand away and frantically look around in distress. The area is deserted, as has most of the park been. Noah's chuckle brings my attention back to him and I give him my fiercest scowl.

He smiles back innocently. "So, care to tell me why you said no?"

"Not really. I don't like swimming."

"Uh huh. And?"

"What 'and'? There is no 'and'. I don't like to swim, Noah. Can't we just leave it at that?" I look away, back out at the ducks on the water, wishing I could fly away with them.

"I think you're scared of something, baby, and we won't be able to fix it if you don't tell me what it is."

I swallow hard. "Stay out of my head, Noah. I'm not your patient."

"No you're not. And you know I've never thought of you that way. But I do happen to care about you a great deal and I hate to see you deny yourself something out of a misplaced fear. Is it the water?"

"No."

"My mom's place?"

"No."

"Is it me?"

I swing around to him with a laugh. "I haven't been scared of you since I saw what a big baby you are when you're sick." It's mostly true, although I haven't been physically afraid of him for far longer than that.

He frowns. "It is me, then. Help me fix it, Aves. Talk to me."

"It isn't you, Noah. I told you: I don't like to swim."

Noah laughs suddenly. "Yeah, okay. Look, baby, you don't have to wear a speedo or anything—although I wouldn't argue if you did. You can be as covered up as possible without drowning."

I shake my head and look at my feet. "How?"

Noah moves to sit on the back of the bench, directly behind me. His nimble fingers begin to massage my stiff shoulders. He leans forward and captures my right earlobe gently between his teeth. "I told you it's my job to know," he whispers, bussing my temple. He sits back up and continues the slow, sensuous massage. "So a t-shirt and board shorts ought to cover it. Do you have a pair?"

I shake my head, wondering if I've just agreed to his silly plan.

"No worries. I'm sure Luke has a pair that'll fit you. Or we could go buy you some now. Get into a mall and out of this heat."

"I'm not swimming with you, Noah."

"Fine. You can be the beer babe."

I cough out a laugh. "I am not your hired help, Noah Yates."

"Who said anything about paying you?"

"Oh, you'll pay. One way or another, you'll pay."

Noah bursts out laughing. "I look forward to it."

***

Several heatstroked hours later, I lay on Noah's living room floor, my face pressed up against the cold air conditioner vent. "Turn it back on," I whine pitifully as the air stops moving.

Noah just laughs from the kitchen. "You know, you could just go take a shower. I'll put your clothes in the wash. You'll feel a hundred percent better."

I give the idea serious thought for half a second. "What will I wear in the meantime? I'm not parading around naked in front of you."

"Oh, now that's too bad." The tone of his voice tells me he's not really joking and doesn't that thought just blow my mind. I know I'm nothing at all to look at, even with clothes on, not like Noah. And knowing what my clothes hide, I'm even more determined to keep them on, which means no shower and no swimming.

I reluctantly raise my head from the still-cool vent cover and peer in his direction. "Are you even doing anything or are you just standing in front of an open refrigerator?"

"Hey, you get cool your way, I'll get cool mine," he says around a laugh.

I shake my head sadly and slowly get to my feet. The heat of the day really has worn us both out, but neither of us was willing to cut short our day out. Even dehydrated, overheated and exhausted, I have to admit it's been the perfect day. The long, meandering hike, the pond at the park, the Frisbee golf I've never played, still don't understand, but am apparently good at, and best of all, Noah's company make it one of the best days of my life. It amazes me how he can somehow coax and cajole me into doing things that are completely outside my comfort zone and I end up enjoying them. I know it's his company I really appreciate though. I'm doing my best to savor every bit of time we have together.

I make my way into the kitchen, still turning that thought over in my head. He really is staring blankly into the refrigerator soaking in the cool air, so I sneak up behind him. As per usual, he's shirtless, having stripped off the sweaty thing as soon as we walked in the door. I think I'm going to goose him and run like the wind, but instead I find my hands sliding around his waist to his flat, slightly ridged belly. His breath catches on the intake and he straightens to stand upright. I press my cheek against the smooth warm skin of his back and close my eyes. I sigh contentedly, my fingers lightly tracing the contours of his belly. I love the way his stomach muscles contract when I touch him, the smooth warmth of his skin against mine.

"Whatchadoin, baby?" Noah questions lazily. I hear the smile in his voice and my lips mirror it.

"Just feeling you. Is that okay?" His stomach is sprinkled with golden blond hair in a six-inch wide swath from points south of his waistband, slowly widening as it reaches his chest. He keeps it carefully trimmed so it's not too dense or too long to enjoy. I do love the sort of slightly prickly feel of it against my soft palms.

"More than okay," he answers, standing completely still as I explore. I smile again and turn to press a kiss between his shoulder blades. My hands slowly glide up his ribbon of fur until I reach the bottom side of his pectorals. If Noah's rippled stomach is lovely, his chest is insanely so. He has deep, square pectorals that swell and round slightly with muscle. I'm glad they're not well-developed but flat like some men I've seen. Noah's chest makes a fantastic pillow, mostly, I think, because of that wonderful swell. Inadvertently my thumbs encounter his nipples and Noah sucks in a breath as they pass over them. They're gorgeous too. They're hard now and I can't resist sliding my thumbs across them again. Noah jerks at the contact. I smile against his skin. A wicked thought bounces through my brain and for a minute I resist, afraid it's too much, but when Noah leans slightly back against me, I give in. Encircling his pebbled nipples between thumbs and index fingers, I slowly, carefully roll them while simultaneously licking a few inches up his spine.

Noah gasps, spasms, moans and reaches up to capture my hands. He shudders a couple more times and brings my hands down to his stomach, encouraging a southward exploration.

I close my eyes, take a deep breath and admit to myself just how much I want this, how much I want to feel Noah's naked skin against my palms. Like this, with him compliant and facing away, I'm safe to let myself experiment. Slowly, my trembling hands move on him until they encounter the elastic waistband of his basketball shorts. My fingertips edge under the silky material and he groans.

"Is this okay?" I whisper against his back.

"More than," he answers huskily.

Emboldened, I slide my hands further, feeling the heat increase as the texture of his hair changes slightly. Our breaths come fast and shallow and I can't decide which of us is more aroused. I'm painfully hard and can feel him pulse against the thin material of his shorts. Pressing a kiss to his spine again, I move my fingers outward to brush against his shorts so I don't accidentally poke him with my fingernails.

My hands move on and I finally feel him against my fingertips, so soft and so rigid all at once. It's magnificent. Noah gasps again as my fingers close around his thickness, groans my name as they slide toward the head of his shaft. My mind is awash in emotion. I'm scared and elated and so incredibly turned on.

I allow my other hand to continue on, to find Noah's balls, even as I gently stroke my thumb over the wet tip of his throbbing erection. I've handled mine more times than I can count but it's never felt like this. One hand slides slowly up and down Noah's shaft as the other one finally cups and caresses his testicles.

Without warning, Noah moves quickly to shove his shorts down to past his knees, giving me freedom to work—and to look. His arms go to the tops of the still open refrigerator doors and I feel his stance change slightly as he leans against them. I move to look around his ribs and shudder at the sight of my hand caressing his manhood. "Oh, Noah," I moan, my own husky voice surprising me. "So beautiful."

"So good, baby," he whispers back. "Please don't stop."

Encouraged, I grip him more firmly and stroke a little bit faster, only slightly embarrassed to realize my hips are mimicking the motion, thrusting my denim-covered erection against his thigh. The hand caressing his sack moves up his torso in search of those sensitive nipples. I can't look away from my hand on him. It's the most incredible sight I've ever seen. I increase my speed, just because I can, because suddenly nothing is more important in this moment than making Noah happy.

The quiet, erotic noises he makes as I change grip, angle and speed turn me on in ways I can't even comprehend. As my fingers close around his nipple in a slight squeeze, I lick another stripe up his spine. Noah's head falls back and he moans loudly as his orgasm overtakes him. I feel his shaft swell in my hand and I move to watch as ribbons of cum fly powerfully from his long, thick cock. The sight triggers my own release and I whimper against him as I come in my jeans.

We both sag in relief for a moment before I'm overcome with embarrassment. I move swiftly to disentangle from him but Noah's quicker. He grabs my hands, stilling me, then turns in the circle of my arms, which promptly drop to my sides. He takes my face in both his hands and tilts it up to look at him. I search the hazel eyes and find a mix of emotions that darkens the green and highlights the flecks of brown.

"I'm so sorry," I whisper, unable to hold his gaze.

"Please don't be. That's exactly how I want you to touch me," he rumbles huskily, closing the distance to kiss me slowly, searchingly. My arms come around his shoulders and his go to my waist. Swiftly, he moves forward, lifting me so I'm only barely sitting on the counter. Noah's kiss turns tender, almost teasing, and I moan into his mouth. He breaks the kiss to smile sexily down at me. Slowly he brings my hand to his mouth and gently but thoroughly cleans his spend from my fingers, watching me watch him do it. My eyes roll back in my head at the sensation of his tongue on my skin and the knowledge of just what he's doing.

"Kiss me?" he queries.

Painfully hard again in the wetness of my boxers, I press my lips to his. When his tongue invades my mouth, I groan at the incredible new taste. Noah pulls me to him and I wrap my legs around his hips, my arms around his neck, unwilling to break the most erotic kiss of my life.

When finally we break for oxygen, I bury my face in his chest, panting like a marathon runner. I feel his lips in my hair as he says, "That was incredible and completely unexpected. Thank you. Are you okay?"

I have no idea how to respond. I don't have the first clue if I'm okay or not. That was the most awesome experience of my life but I have no idea if I want to repeat it or not. I don't even know how it happened. One minute I was going to goose him, the next he's coming in my hand—and I'm coming in my jeans.

"It's okay to be a little bit shaken, you know. I don't think you expected that any more than I did."

"No," I admit, cringing at the tremor in my voice.

"Do you regret it?" he asks.

I chuckle and look up at him. "No, do you? I thought I would, but—wow."

He laughs. "Wow is exactly right."

My erection has subsided enough again that I'm wet, sticky and uncomfortable. I laugh lightly to myself: my first orgasm with another man present and I come in my jeans. Neither smooth nor bright. I'm right on par with half the teenage male population. "I gotta go get cleaned up," I say.

For a moment he look startled. "Did you…?"

I flush furiously and nod, refusing to look at him.

"Damn, that's sexy," he growls, swooping in for another deep, hungry kiss. He lifts me from the counter. "Go get something to wear from Luke's room. We'll throw your stuff in the washer. Oops," he laughs, pausing to pull up his shorts.

The sight of his resurgent erection causes me to flush furiously. I head for the door to hide that tell-tale redness in my cheeks when a thought stops me. "Noah?"

He looks at me, "Yeah, babe?"

I gesture to the refrigerator, still standing wide open. "You're gonna have to clean the fridge."

He grimaces and laughs. "Well worth it. Go get changed. Then we'll talk."

When I come back a few minutes later, dressed in a pair of Luke's board shorts and t-shirt, Noah is wiping down the vegetable drawers in the refrigerator. I can't stop the idiotic smile that creases my face.

Seeing me standing in the doorway, he laughs again and gestures at the table. "Sit down, little one. It's time we have a talk." He asks over his shoulder, "Would you like some water? Gatorade?"

I slowly lower myself into a chair and stare at his naked back. "Uh, green tea, please."

"Honey, you do my grocery shopping. I don't have green tea."

"Yes you do. Bottom shelf, right corner in the back. I brought some from home the other day." I cringe. "I'm sorry. I should have asked first."

Noah casts me an exasperated look over his shoulder. "What is this place, Avery?"

"Huh?" I'm so eloquent when I'm confused. How could he possibly *not* fall for me?

"This apartment. What is it?"

Oh! I flush furiously, finally following his lead. "My second home."

"Exactly. So why would I be mad if you brought stuff here?" He reaches into the fridge and extracts a Gatorade for himself and the giant can of green tea for me.

"I—because it's your *first* home."

He laughs, shaking his head and sits across from me, scooting the can to me across the small table. "You're silly. I want you to feel at home here. Bring over anything you want: spices, books, music, clothes. Anything. Everything."

I color again and stare holes through my can. "Okay."

Noah takes a couple of long pulls from his drink and I follow the way his Adam's apple bobs with each swallow. My mouth dries with a sudden rush of desire, even after what we've just done. He has a long, sexy neck. I've admired it before, but something about watching the man swallow has blood rushing to my groin again.

He puts the bottle on the table and winks at me with a crooked smile, like he knows exactly what I'm thinking. And knowing Noah, of course he does. I pointedly look down, opening my can as he relaxes back in his chair. He waits for me to swallow a sip before speaking.

"I think we're comfortable enough around each other now that I can just say this and you won't try to run away from me." I look into his hazel eyes wondering if I should prepare to flee. Probably, but he has ever so cleverly put me in a corner, literally. Or maybe I did that. Either way, I don't really feel the need to run yet.

"If my little display over there didn't make it obvious, I want nothing more than to take you to bed and make love to you." I start to stutter a protest but he presses on. "I know you're not ready for that and that's okay. I told you we'd take this at your pace and I still plan to do that. I won't rush you and I won't hurt you. I think you know that by now or we wouldn't be here like this."

I can't look away. It's like he's a traffic accident I can't help rubbernecking. "Why?" I hear myself ask.

"Why what? Why do I want to make love to you?" He continues with a smile when I bob a nod. "Because you're irresistibly beautiful and crazy sexy and I know when we get it right, we'll make the planets align."

I stare at him, wide-eyed, fifty shades of red. For the life of me, I can't string two words together to make a sentence. Even one seems out of reach. Crazy sexy? He thinks I'm sexy? Wait. "I can't, Noah."

He nods. "I know."

"It's not that I don't want to." Once the words start, I can't stop them. "I do. I really do. I think about it. *A lot.* You're so beautiful and perfect and sexy, how could I not want to…do that with you? But—I'm scared."

"Scared of what?"

"I can't let you—" The sobs come from nowhere and overtake me. Harsh, ragged sobs of despair. "Fire station," I finally gasp out between them, knowing they make no sense to Noah but trying anyway.

"Fire station?" he repeats quizzically. "Oh, Jesus!" Suddenly I hear the screech of his chair and I feel the steel bands of his arms wrap around me, pulling me onto his lap as I continue to bawl like a lunatic. "No, baby, no. No fire stations. Never again." He presses kisses into my hair. "Don't you know by now? I'm never going to let you go. You're mine, for keeps, forever. You're my little one. Oh, Aves." And then he's crying too. My Mt. Man-Everest holds me in his strong arms, rocking us both, crying with me. I know he understands and I feel my love for him explode. I wrap my arms around his shoulders and sob into his neck. With each heaving, wrenching sob we share, I feel the poison slowly drain away.

Eventually we both quiet down and just hold on to each other for dear life, shuddering breaths and all. I'm not a pretty crier, but when he turns and sweeps my mouth into a slow, desperately passionate kiss, I'm glad I'm not one of those snot-nosed criers. Ugly crying is okay, but snot-filled kisses are just too gross for words. And what he's doing to my mouth is anything but gross. When I break away for breath, I bury my face in his neck. He holds me tighter and I've never felt so close to another human being. Not Joey, not Sam. I feel safe and cared for. It's disconcerting, but I'm too tired, too drained to fight it, so I just settle more comfortably against him and bask in the feeling.

What seems like hours later, Noah lifts me from his lap to stand before him. He groans as he climbs to his feet, mumbling something about hard, wooden floors. He takes my hand, smiles, and asks, "Do you trust me?"

A lump forms in my throat so I just nod silently.

He swoops down to press a quick kiss to my lips. "We need to recover from this conversation before we have dinner, don't you think?" I nod again and smile slightly, whole-heartedly agreed. "Okay, right now I need to hold you and I think you need to be held. Am I right?" A shudder of longing, of gratitude passes through me and I nod again. I feel like a bobble-head doll, but I can't speak around the obstruction of emotion in my throat. "Holding and sleeping, that's all, okay?"

This time I find my voice. "Okay." Well it's somebody's really husky, very quivery voice.

Noah presses my hand to his lips. "Let's go lay down on the bed where it's comfortable. Please?"

Nothing he could have said would make me say no. He's right. I need to be held by him, to recover and to rest. No other place but his bed would suit that purpose. I step out of the way and let him lead me down the hall and to his bedroom.

He lets me get settled in the middle of his big bed, on my left side with my back to the door—the first time since I was a small child, before the beatings began. He climbs in behind me, pulls a blanket up to our waists and spoons up against me, his arm around me. I lace our fingers together and bring them up under my chin, just as he did when he was so sick.

As I drift off, safe and secure in his arms, in his bed, I hear him whisper, "Forever and for always, little one. I promise." The small smile on my lips says I want to believe him.

***

I awaken with a start and scamper off the bed, looking back at it frantically. I heave a great sight of relief that the bed is empty. As comforting as it was to fall asleep in the circle of Noah's arms, I'm grateful for the few moments alone to compose myself now. The scene from the kitchen floods over me and I collapse onto the bed with a groan.

I can't believe how brazen I was, first to begin to tease him like that, then to actually jerk him off in front of the refrigerator like … like I knew what I was doing. But oh, he had felt so good in my hands, so strong and powerful and all mine. Seeing my hands on him, hearing and feeling how much he liked what I did to him was worth everything. The heady sense of power at being able to bring him to such an explosive climax was enough to make my head spin even now.

But as great as my very first sexual experience was, I'm lost now. I have no idea what to do next. I groan again and drop my face to my hands. If I'm going to pretend to be a fully-functioning grown up, then

I have to act like one. And the first step in that direction is out the bedroom door toward Noah, wherever he is.

After finger brushing the cotton from my mouth with some of Noah's minty fresh toothpaste and wetting down my hair so it doesn't look as slept in as I feel, I mentally brace myself and open the bedroom door. The unexpected aroma of bacon and maple syrup greets me and my stomach growls in response, reminding me we took a nap instead of having dinner. A quick glance at the clock on my iPhone confirms that it's late, almost ten. We—or I, anyway—slept for three hours. I dash off a quick text to Sam telling him not to worry, that I'll be home late. After confirming for him that I'm with Noah, I receive his maddening answer: "No rush then. Have a great time."

Suddenly it hits me and I feel the smile spread across my face. The man who claims he can't cook is doing just that—for me. And judging from the delicious scents in the air, he's doing a fantastic job. My curiosity outweighs my discomfort over having just left Noah's bed and I move quickly to the kitchen door.

I watch him in silence for a few minutes as he deftly turns the bacon and then one of the pieces of French toast. Without a grimace or a sign of uncertainty, he breaks two eggs into the skillet. I feel my love for him course through my body like a live current, setting me atingle. It amazes me that I am capable of feeling this way, but I know I wouldn't stop it even if I could.

Happy laughter bubbles out of me without warning and the most wonderful man in the world turns to me with a dimpled smile and dancing eyes. He comes over, wraps his arms around my waist to bring our bodies together and takes my mouth in a deep, maple and bacon flavored kiss.

"I think I've been hoodwinked," I accuse.

His low rumbling laughter travels through me, bringing another smile to my lips. No wonder people in love smile so much; they can't help it. "Breakfast is easy. I swear it's just breakfast and cookies."

"Uh huh. And burgers and steaks on the grill." I shake my finger at him but the effect is ruined by the smile still lingering on my lips. "I knew I should have checked your spice cabinet before I agreed to cook for you."

Noah laughs again. "Too late now, babe. You're stuck with me."

And yeah, I'm more than okay with that. I'll be by his side as long as he wants me.

The late night breakfast is delicious and I praise him liberally, which causes him to reward me with more of those very special pink-cheeked, dimpled smiles. Our conversation is easy now, as it mostly has been for months.

Together we clean up, laughing and teasing until he leans down to kiss me and I flick soap suds at him. His hands immediately fly to his eyes and he stumbles back a few paces until he hits the cabinets. "My eyes," he groans in pain, fisting them fiercely.

"Oh, Noah! I'm so sorry!" I grab his wrists. I feel horrible. It was just supposed to be part of the game. I never meant to hurt him. "Stop doing that. We need to flush your eyes out."

He shakes my hands off and I take a half-step back. His hands slowly come away from his face and I see a flash of demonic glee in his eyes before he reaches for me and drags me to him, tickling me like a mad man. I giggle and squeal and twist around until my back is to him, which is such the wrong thing to do because then he just leans over and practically pins me in place with his gigantic mass. "Noah! Stop!" I giggle just as he finds the one spot low on my ribs that always almost brings me to my knees. I feel the hot breath of his laughter on my neck and fight even harder. Finally I'm able to break free and I run for the safety of the living room. He's hot on my heels as I dodge around the couch and grab the fly swatter from the table by his chair.

We're both still laughing as I brandish my weapon like a fencing sword, lunging and retreating and teasing. He growls low in his throat and snaps his teeth at me like he's taking a giant bite out of the air.

I stop and look at him, arms dropping to my sides. "You did not just do that."

He blinks at me blankly. "Too much?"

I can't help it. I collapse into a puddle of hysterical giggles right there on the living room carpet. "You are such a dork!" I gasp out.

The big brute picks me up off the floor and settles me on his lap on the couch. I bury my face in his neck and try to stop the giggles, but every time I'm almost calm, I get a picture of him taking a bite out of crime—er, the air—and lose it all over again.

"It wasn't that funny," he deadpans.

I swat his chest playfully. "You didn't see your face!" I sit up and mimic the chomp of nothingness and this time we're both gone. It feels so wonderful, so beautiful, so safe, sitting here with Noah just being silly. I wrap my arms around his neck and press a kiss to his neck, and then another and another, up his neck along his jaw and finally, sweetly to his delicious lips. "Thank you," I whisper against his mouth. I move so I'm straddling him instead of being draped across his lap.

"For what?" he whispers back, kissing me some more.

My hands frame his face and I draw back to look at him, to look deeply into those glorious hazel eyes I'm so in love with. "For being you. For believing I could be more than I was when you met me. For having the patience to let me get this far at my own pace and for pushing me when I need it."

Noah caresses my cheek with the backs of his fingers, a gentle smile on his slightly swollen lips. "I never once doubted you were someone special, Aves. I know you did and you sometimes still do, but you're starting to believe it and nothing makes me happier than seeing you happy. Your smile and laughter give me reason to get up in the morning."

I duck my head, eyes filling with water. I collapse against him, my face in his neck again. His high praise always embarrasses me, but this also fills me with joy and a renewed determination to keep getting better. It would be so easy to tell him, to give in to the urge to say those three words.

Strangely enough, saying them doesn't scare me as much as not hearing them back does. I know he cares for me a lot, but does he love me? It feels like he does, but I have no experience, no history to draw from. Until I can be completely certain, I need to keep that part of me safe still. I hug him fiercely again and scoot back off his lap to stand. I don't have to fake the jaw-busting yawn that hijacks me. "Sorry," I say with a blush. "I ought to be getting home. It's late."

Noah's fingers lace with mine but he remains seated. "You could stay. We could talk some more. You can use Luke's room if you don't want to sleep with me." He half grins. "Or you could sleep with me. No funny business, I promise just cuddles and conversation."

I laugh. "Cuddles and conversation?"

He grins cheekily. "And kisses."

"Going for the full alliteration now, are we?"

He shrugs, still grinning.

It is so tempting to curl up in his strong arms again. I yawn again, no less forcefully. "I really better go."

"Stay. Please."

I weaken momentarily, much to my surprise. Snuggling with Noah does feel good. But no. I'm not ready to spend the night, not yet. "Sam would be here at the crack of dawn. It would be ugly."

He smiles and tugs gently at my hand. I lean over him, bracing myself on the couch on either side of his head. He kisses me tenderly. "You really think they aren't expecting it?"

"What? No!"

He laughs quietly and kisses me again, deeper this time but just as gently. "Baby, they're practically shopping for wedding gifts."

"What?" I yelp, straightening and taking a step back, practically tripping over the coffee table.

"Easy," he coos, hands on my hips to steady me. I shrug him off and search frantically for my shoes, blood pounding in my ears. I know

Kaleb has been none too subtle in his insistence that my friendship with Noah needs to change into something…intimate, but surely the others aren't paying that much attention to us, are they? And what business is it of theirs anyway? That's the problem with having such an interwoven group of friends, they all think they know what's best and—.

My brain and body both freeze at the feel Noah's hands on my face. I keep my head down when he tries to tilt it up. I don't want him to see the tears in my eyes, can't let him read the raw emotions on my face.

"Little one," he croons soothingly. I slam my eyes shut against the effect the endearment has on me. "It's okay. I promise. The rest of them just want to see us happy. They see how happy you make me, so they want to push. It's natural, but…. Look at me." I shake my head. His voice is firmer but his hands ease their already gentle hold. "Please look at me." He waits patiently and finally I gather enough strength to meet his intense gaze. "That's better. Thank you." His thumb finds my lips as usual and I tremble out a smile. "No matter what they want, it doesn't matter, okay? There's only two people in this relationship and we—you and I—we take this at our pace, your pace."

I bring my hands to his strong forearms and realize my lips aren't the only things trembling. I'm practically vibrating. I drop his gaze and stare at the carpet. "I don't know what you want," I whisper.

Noah laughs warmly. "That's easy. I want you—as much as you're willing to give me, for as long as you're willing to give it."

I look at him again and see only sincerity in his eyes. I take a ragged breath that makes him smile. "You deserve so much more."

"Then give me more." He kisses me softly, a kiss I knew was coming since his thumb alighted on my lips. "I only want you, kid. Haven't you figured that out by now?"

"But why?" I ask, genuinely baffled. Of the tens of thousands of men in the city, why would he want me? I don't understand it at all.

Noah brushes my bangs out of my face and smiles again. "You already know, you just won't let yourself see it yet." He grasps my hands and pulls me to my feet with him. "You better go while I'm still willing to let you walk out that door."

I wrap my arms around this enigmatic, patient hunk of man and hug him tight. He presses a kiss to my hair and whispers into it, "So much."

It's the second time he's said that, but I'm afraid to ask what he means. Instead I gather my things and bid him goodnight.

As I drive home, the entire day replays through my head and I wonder if I'll ever sleep again for all the thinking I have to do.

***

I am surprised the next morning when I walk into the kitchen to find Sam sitting at the table eating a bowl of Frosted Flakes. It's not his atrocious choice in breakfast foods that surprises me; I'm used to that. It's his being there at all.

"Don't you work today?" I ask, stopping short.

He motions to his mouthful, chews, swallows and says, “Second shift this week, remember?”

“Oh,” I say, heading for the coffeemaker. “Obviously not. Sorry.”

“So…you got home late,” he fishes with a grin.

I smile into the cup as I deliberately pour the coffee. “Not too late.”

“It was after midnight. Do I need to put you on a curfew, young man?”

The smile in Sam’s voice makes me laugh and almost spill the hazelnut creamer I liberally add to the coffee. “I promise to be a good boy.”

“Not too good, I hope. Are you being careful?”

I take a sip of the coffee and moan in delight. It’s perfect, strong and sugary and warm, sort of like Noah. Then Sam’s meaning hits me with all the subtlety of a freight train. “Geez, Dad,” I say, blushing furiously.

“Well are you?”

I widen my eyes and swing around to meet his gaze. “Sam, nothing’s happening.”

He frowns slightly. “You’ve been dating for months and you still haven’t had sex?”

“We haven’t been—” I can’t finish the denial because, much to my surprise, I realize that’s exactly what we’ve been doing. *Clever, clever Noah.* I laugh. “Yeah, I guess we have been, but no we haven’t.”

“Holy circular thought, Batman!”

I laugh again and sit across from my big brother, clasping the coffee mug in both hands. "Yes to the dating, no to the sex." *Yes to the dating. Mind officially blown.*

"Wow." His expression is truly mystified. Then he smiles. "My little brother is dating—and admitting it. I'm so proud!"

I suppress my laughter only long enough to give him my best glare. "I've only just now admitted it to myself, so no gloating."

"No gloating, I promise. But, why no sex? Don't you want to have sex with him?"

The scarred surface of the table is suddenly very interesting. Sam waits silently, letting me figure it out. "Okay, yes," I finally whisper. My eyes cut to his. "But I can't risk it, Sam. I mean it's bad enough I went and fell in lo—*like*—crap. I like him, Sam. I really do. And, honestly, that scares me enough without adding sex to the mix. What if I'm not good at it? What if I can't do the things he wants me to do? Sex complicates things, even you've admitted that."

Sam frowns and covers my hand on the table. "Sex can complicate relationships that aren't ready for it, but I don't think that's something you need to worry about, and I'm glad for that. You needed to let someone else in. Noah found a way. He's not going to hurt you and he's not going to leave you. He doesn't want to." He grins. "Besides, he knows Kaleb and I would slaughter him if he did."

I smile wanly and take another drink. My thumbnail traces a long scratch in the soft wood of the table. It's new, this wondering what it would be like to have sex with Noah. I've never had a raging sex drive, not like the men I read about or see on the TV. I've always been too conscious of what my body looks like to want to bare it for someone, even a total stranger, maybe especially a total stranger. My scars are ugly, visible reminders of the hell I've lived through, but they're also a plain and clear invitation to add to them. They mark me physically and psychically as one meant to be beaten and abused. I remember the business card in my dresser drawer. Maybe it's time to give some thought to calling the plastic surgeon's office, if only for information.

Ignoring the psychological discomfort of being naked in front of someone, there's the emotional jungle of sex itself. Nothing short of infancy leaves a person more vulnerable. It would mean trusting Noah to not hurt me on a level I can only scarcely comprehend. I told him, sort of, last night that allowing myself to have sex with him only to have him abandon me like my mother did would really and truly kill me inside. He has managed to scale or destroy the barriers I keep between me and other people, and I'm comfortable in the knowledge that Noah will never intentionally hurt me, but having sex with him would open my heart and head and soul in depths I can't even fathom, let alone protect.

I love touching and kissing and cuddling him. I love how just a smile or a look, not to mention a touch or kiss, can create a fire within me that all but begs for more. There's no question that I'm physically attracted to the man or that, if it weren't so complicated and compromising, I would love to find out what it would feel like to make love with him. But it is complicated and compromising and it's asking a lot more than I can give right now. But then again, before February, I never would have believed I'd let him kiss me, and before last night I never would have believed I would stroke him off in his kitchen.

I take a sip of the coffee, find it cold and push it away in disgust. I look up at Sam and sigh heavily. "What am I gonna do, Sam?"

He shrugs and smiles slightly. "This is a conversation you need to have with Noah, little bro. He may be perfectly happy letting you figure it all out on your own time, or he may need you to make some sort of decision pretty soon. But he's the only one who knows what he needs, just like you're the only one who knows what you need."

I nod, a bit shaken.

"What do you need, Aves?" Sam questions softly.

I meet his eyes and, without a question in my heart, say, "Noah."

***

Two weeks later, Noah makes me put Sam on speakerphone and the two of them work together to convince me an afternoon of swimming at Noah's mom's pool is the only way to spend a lazy August day off. I assure them both that I will not be getting wet with them, but in the end, I can't say no to the two most important men in my life.

That's how I find myself sitting in a chaise lounge poolside in the blazing summer heat, wearing a cream-colored t-shirt emblazoned with a logo and dates from Cher's Farewell Tour (Noah's) and a pair of blue-and-white flower print board shorts (Luke's), both of which are at least a size too big. The two giants clown around in the pool, dunking each other, racing laps and tossing a ball back and forth. In short, they're acting like a couple of kids and I can't help but smile slightly as I watch them, my heart expanding in my chest.

"Is it wrong that I find this boyish, playful side of Sam sexy?" Kira asks from the lounger beside mine. Unlike me, she's soaking up the sun whilst I cling to the shade cast by the large umbrella above me. Very unlike me, she's barely clad in a skimpy but not trashy bikini. She's utterly comfortable in her skin and, just like the overgrown boys in the water, she looks fantastic.

I chuckle. "I was just thinking the same thing about Noah, so I'm gonna go with no."

She rolls her head to look at me. Although I can't see her eyes behind her enormous sunglasses, I can read the mild surprise on her face. "So you do see Noah that way? Sexually, I mean?"

I frown. "Of course I do. You've seen him, right? The man's practically a poster boy for sexy."

Kira grins widely. "I knew you'd come around eventually." She nods at the pool and keeps her voice quiet. "I've known Noah since I was six, Avery. I've never seen him like this about anyone before. His feelings for you are very strong."

My eyes cut to the scene in the pool where a widely grinning Noah has just dunked Sam for the hundredth time. I see the expression of surprise flash across his face seconds before he disappears beneath the water. Sam surfaces and lets out a triumphant "Ha!" and I laugh at their antics. I look back to Kira and smile. "I don't understand what he sees in me or why he puts up with me, but he's an awfully terrific guy."

She nods. "And he's all yours. How does that feel?"

A liquid head radiates out from my chest. "Scary but incredible."

Kira laughs. "That sounds about right. Oh, Avery, I'm so happy for you two. You've both needed someone to love you for so long. I'm so glad you found each other."

I blush fire engine red and look away, embarrassed. It's one thing to know I love Noah, but it's weird hearing it from someone else. I desperately wish I could talk to her about what I feel for Noah and what that means, but it feels wrong to confess my love for him to someone else first. Noah deserves to know before anyone else does.

Luckily I'm saved from responding by the men climbing from the water. I watch, transfixed, as the muscles in Noah's arms, shoulders, chest and abs bulge and flex as he lifts himself from the pool. Rivulets of water cascade down his glorious, tanned skin. The urge to lick the water from his skin takes me by surprise in its intensity. It's almost a need. He flashes a dimpled smile and moves toward me, his predatory gaze never leaving mine. He dips to press a quick kiss to my mouth and I lap at his lips, tasting a bit of the water on his skin.

He grins, eyes dark, and, without moving away, shakes his head like a wet dog, spraying both me and Kira with water. We yelp protests but he just laughs.

Noah sits at the end of the lounger and hands me a bottle of lotion over his shoulder. "Would you do my back, please?" I know the innocence in his tone is purely for Sam and Kira's benefit. Feeling their eyes on me, I swallow hard and reach for the bottle. My mouth dries and my hands shake in anticipation of touching Noah's sun-warmed skin.

Sam clears his throat, breaking the spell. "Uh, Kira and I are gonna go inside and make those sandwiches now," he says, dragging Kira to her feet and scampering off.

Noah just chuckles and leans back a little. "Think we scared him off?"

"You know darn well you did," I admonish him.

Noah laughs again, turning around to drag me into another kiss. His forehead resting against mine, he whispers, "You're so cute when you almost curse."

I narrow my eyes at him. "You're not funny."

His grin tells me he knows better. "Sorry. Are you having a good time?"

I shrug, our foreheads still touching. "I'm okay. Looks like you and Sam are trying to kill each other out there."

"Nah." He smiles, flashing those dimples again. "Just a little roughhousing between friends." He pecks my lips again and draws away to lay face down on Kira's abandoned chair. "If you want to come in, I promise we'll keep it to a minimum."

I shake my head climb on top of him, straddling his hips. "That's awful nice of you," I say innocently. Before he can respond I squeeze a line of lotion up his spine, the cold against his warmed skin causing him to arch his back and hiss.

"Brat," he says.

"Jerk." I laugh and bring my hands to his back. It is so easy to touch him. Feeling his muscles under all that smooth skin is almost addictive. I take my time rubbing the lotion into his back and shoulders, enjoying his soft noises of appreciation. The feel of his skin against mine, even this innocuous touch, ignites that increasingly familiar desire in me. Out of sheer spite, I rock my hips a few times against his buttocks, laughing at his answering growl.

***

The next day, when it's just the two of us, Noah is in full-on convince Avery to strip and swim mode. He's gentle about it, begging and cajoling and teasing without making it feel like I have no choice. Truth is, I would love to get in the water. It called to me all day yesterday, but with Kira around, I wasn't about to chance her seeing through my shirt to the ugly scars beneath. I don't want Noah to see them either, but they're part of me. They're evidence of all I've been through, who I was, how I was treated. I don't want to see the change in Noah's eyes when he sees them, don't want to face the possibility, as remote as it is, that he may reject me when confronted with the physical proof of my past. But I also know deep down that our relationship can never grow beyond what it is now if I'm not honest with him about it.

It's the hardest thing I've ever had to do. I summon every ounce of my courage, all the positive lessons learned from Kendall, and focus on the fact that I love this man more than I ever thought possible. If I lay all my cards on the table, let him see me and actually tell him all of my history… Well, if he turns his back then, at least I'll know now. It'll hurt more than all the beatings, but at least I will know I tried.

"Noah," I croak out around the competing lumps of fear and hope in my throat.

"Hmm?" he lazily turns his head in my direction, eyes still closed as he basks in the sun on the lounger next to me.

"I—we—" I sigh and look away, unsure how to continue.

He sits up and faces me, his long muscular legs entering my view. "Aves? What is it?"

His tone betrays his concern and a rush of love fills me. I smile at him with trembling lips. "Honesty," I say out of nowhere. "I have to be honest with you."

"Okay…."

"We've never talked about…about what happened to me." I can't meet his eyes no matter how hard I try.

"Baby, you don't have to do this."

"I do, though." My eyes fill but not all because of the pain of reliving it in my mind. Most of these tears are of gratitude to this gentle giant who knows me so well, cares for me enough he doesn't want to put me through the emotional upheaval of remembering. How could I have ever thought he would hurt me?

Haltingly, I begin to tell him about my childhood. About the few happy memories I have before my dad died, about mom meeting Carl, about him moving in with us. It's the most difficult conversation I've ever had, as one-sided as it is. Noah watches me, his body still and tense, but he makes no move to speak or touch me. When I tell him about the first time mom hit me and how a thorough beating from Carl followed, the words start tumbling from my mouth before I can think about them. Noah learns about mom dropping me off at the first station six days before my eighth birthday, how she told the firefighter that she knew the law had recently changed and she could leave me with them because she didn't want me anymore. I tell Noah how I cried and pleaded and begged Mom to change her mind, how I promised I would be the best little boy in the world if she just gave me another chance. I told him how she looked at me with disgust and contempt in her eyes and walked away without a word or a look back.

I tell him of the kindness of the firefighters and the Child Protective Services worker who took me to my first foster home that night. I tell him how I cried myself to sleep every night that first week because I missed Mom and Carl and my little brothers so much. I even missed the sound of them yelling at each other over the loudness of the television.

I stumble when I start to talk about Joey. I remember how Joey's big blue eyes lit up when he saw me for the first time. I tell Noah how Joey and I immediately became friends and brothers. Even when we couldn't trust anyone else, it was always clear Joey and I would look out for each other forever. The tears come hard as I describe the first time I watched Tommy beat Joey, how Tommy's sadistic posse of preteens held me tight even as I fought to get to my very best friend.

It was a bitter cold December day. Tommy had only been in the facility about a month when Joey and I took a shortcut through the park between the school and the group home. Tommy and his gang intercepted us. He took his time beating Joey, trying to get him to cry or fight back, but Joey did neither. My brave little friend just kept getting back to his feet and asking—not begging, but, even as blood flowed down his face, soaking his favorite shirt, calmly asking—Tommy to stop. I was the one begging and pleading and crying for Tommy to stop, for his hooligan friends to release me. When Tommy had finally had enough, he turned and pointed a bloody finger in my face. "You're next," he promised and spat in my face. His goons released me and I collapsed to the ground in exhaustion and relief. I crawled over to Joey and we cried together, holding each other. I tell Noah that Tommy made good on his threat the very next week.

I dare a glance up at Noah and see him surreptitiously wiping a tear from his cheek. With that gesture I know telling him about my past is the right decision. He doesn't judge me. He doesn't pity me. Like he has since I've known him, he hurts when and because I hurt and celebrates my successes because they make me feel better about myself. This amazing, wonderful man in front of me is the absolute opposite of my childhood. He's someone who genuinely values me for me, who cares about me regardless of anyone else's opinion. He's the man who has taught me that, even though it is as scary as facing down Tommy again, I can feel love, real romantic love.

Gathering my thoughts and strength, I continue my tale. Joey's suicide trips me up again, but Sam's arrival signals a slight upturn. The boy I was finally felt safe thanks to the man I now call my big brother. I skip forward in the story, past the last few years with Sam as basically normal. I tell him about last August, how I was too afraid and ashamed to admit to anyone that it was Tommy who beat me again. I tell him that Sam knew and tried desperately to get me to press charges but I was too scared. Even though he was there, I tell him how I felt about going to Tommy's sentencing hearing for his attack on Sam and admit how healing it was to see Tommy looking so powerless in his shackles and orange jumpsuit. "And in between August and the sentencing, I met you."

Noah slowly reaches out and cups my wet cheeks in his big, rough palms. "Thank you for telling me," he says softly, emotion making his voice raw. "I can't tell you how much it means to me that you trust me with your past and all that pain." His thumb brushes my cheekbone instead of my lips and it feels like the first stage of rejection. Does he not want to see me now that he knows everything? My chest seizes around the thought of losing him and I deflate, slumping at the shoulders and dropping eye contact.

Noah notices the change in my mood as he notices everything. "Hey, none of that." He tilts my face up so our gazes meet again. "You've survived an incredibly difficult childhood and you've grown into a wonderful, interesting, funny and sexy man. You should be proud of how much you've overcome. I'm extremely proud of you, baby. I'm so glad something in you let me through your defenses. Knowing you has changed my life in so many ways, all of them for the better. I can't imagine my life without you. I don't want to."

Tears spring to my eyes again. Somehow that sounds so much different than when Sam said something similar to me at Christmas.

My hands grip Noah's wrist and forearm and squeeze tight, my capacity for words gone. He leans across the space between us and presses a soft, tender kiss to my lips, then my nose and my forehead. I push him away with a laugh. "Dork."

The man I'm so crazy in love with smiles sweetly. "Let's take a dip and wash all those bad memories away, huh?"

I tense. "I—I can't."

Noah nods. "Okay, tell me."

Once more, my eyes find the concrete beneath us. "I don't remember how to swim."

"That's okay. We can stick to the shallow end. But there's more, isn't there?"

I nod, slightly ashamed. "I—I'm not beautiful like you."

"Of course you are. Avery, you're incredibly beautiful to me." His hands frame my face and tilt it up to meet his gaze again. "No scar is going to scare me away, I promise." When I merely stare at him mutely, he tries again. "That's what it is, right? You have some scars from your childhood?"

I swallow hard and nod again, eyes filling.

"They won't scare me away." His eyes practically beg me to believe him and I really, truly want to. But Noah hasn't seen. Well, he has, but he doesn't remember because his brain was busy boiling at the time, so he doesn't know. I stare back at him, paralyzed with fear.

"Show me," he whispers.

I shake my head within his gentle grip.

"You just told me about all kinds of horrible things that happened to you. I'm still here. I always will be. You can trust me with this, too. I promise it'll be okay."

When his hands move to the hem of my shirt, I'm gripped with terror, torn between running and finally getting it over with. Noah hesitates, silently seeking my permission. With a deep breath, I close my eyes, raise my arms above my head, and let him strip away my last secret with the cotton.

I hear his sharp intake of breath and swiftly cross my arms over my chest as shame floods me. Why? Why did I think it would be okay? Why did I give Noah that much power to hurt me? Why do I keep thinking I can be normal? I'm not one of them. And now Noah knows it all. Blindly I grab for the cloth still in Noah's hand, needing to get dressed and away from him as fast as possible.

"Hey, hey, hey. Easy." His hands on my face still me instantly. I flinch away but he doesn't let me go. Instead, his thumb finds my lip. I look at him then, thoroughly confused, bursting with shame and self-hatred.

"I was right," he says around a small smile. "You are beautiful."

I desperately search his eyes but find no duplicity, no pity, only Noah and the way he always looks at me. He gently pulls my arms from my chest and kneels on the concrete between us. His eyes never leave mine as he leans forward and presses his lips to my red, ragged scar. My breath catches as new tears fill my eyes. Could he really be saying he's not repulsed by me? Could it—?

"I love you, Avery," he says distinctly.

The abilities to speak and breathe desert me. I stare at him, frozen, sure I've misheard.

His big, rough hands cup my face again and he brings our foreheads together. My eyes close in confusion. I lean against him even as I struggle to make sense of the last few minutes. "Did you hear me?" he whispers. "I said I'm completely in love with you." He ghosts his lips across mine. With a sob, I launch myself into his strong, warm arms.

I hear Noah's chuckle, feel it rumble in his chest where our bare skin touches for the first time. I bury my face in his neck and try to remember how to breathe. Noah loves me. The sheer volume of happiness in me forces tears from my eyes. I feel like laughing, too, but one must first breathe to laugh. I press my lips to his skin, reveling in the moment I never, ever would have believed would happen to me. I had hoped, but I hadn't let myself believe it could be true. Noah loves me. Really, truly loves me. My small arms wrap tighter around his broad shoulders and, at last, I laugh giddily.

He squeezes me tighter. "Is that a good laugh?"

I nod into his neck.

"You're okay with me loving you?"

"Yes," I laugh.

"Is it possible you feel the same way?"

"Yes," I whisper against his neck, stupidly embarrassed. I've never said it before. It's like I don't know how. I want to say it, but I can't form the words, can't make myself that much more vulnerable. I've bared my soul and my scars to Noah today. Surely he can wait for my heart.

Chapter 15 - August

"It's one year today," I tell Kendall, nervously fingering a puzzle piece. I don't need to elaborate for her. It's all we've been talking about for the last few sessions, that and Noah.

"Is it?" Her eyes flick up to mine as she fits in another piece of greenery. "How do you feel about that knowing Tommy's in prison for a long time?"

I grab another puzzle piece and try to work that out in my frantic little mind. There's so much more to tell Kendall today. Not just about the one-year anniversary of Tommy's attack on me, but about what happened two days ago. I shove those happy thoughts down with a giddy grin and direct my mind back to Tommy. "It's weird. It's like this is a big day for me." I set the piece aside and look directly at her. "He really screwed up my life a year ago. I was starting to think that I wasn't going to be anyone's punching bag again, but then there he was, making my life miserable just like always." I smile, something I never would have thought I'd do in association with last August. "To be honest, if it weren't for you and Noah, I would probably be hiding in my closet right now, doped up on Ambien and valium, just hoping and praying I could sleep the day away."

"We've made a lot of progress," she answers with a genuinely pleased smile.

"We have," I agree. "I know we still have a lot of work to do, but I'm not the same person Sam dragged into your office all those months ago. I feel like a normal person again. I know that I'm not responsible for my mother's poor decisions. I know I'm not destined to be a punching bag for the cosmos. I'm actually happy instead of being afraid all the time."

"That's fantastic, Avery, I'm very proud of you. But I want to let you know that you are the same person. We've just been able to change the way you think and feel about yourself. This guy you're so happy being, he was always there fighting to get out; there was just a bushel of crap keeping him locked away inside you. We do have some more work to do to make sure you never slide back into that blackness you were in, but I feel confident you're going to make it. Ever since that day you walked in here determined Sam was trying to pawn you off on Noah, you've worked very hard to get healthy. It's paid off quite handsomely, don't you think?" She smirks.

I laugh, catching the reference to Noah. "Quite handsomely, indeed. In fact, I have some news on that front, too."

"Do tell."

I can actually pinpoint the time our therapy sessions became less like torture and more like confidants sharing secrets. It was the day I walked into her office to find a card table set up with a choice of three puzzles to work. Of course, at first I thought it was a trap, but she'd finally persuaded me it would help put me at ease while we talked about difficult topics. I don't know if it's an approved therapeutic tool, but it definitely worked the way she intended. We've worked a lot of puzzles together in the last few months, but my favorite is still the Neuschwanstein puzzle. I think I'll suggest to Noah that we work that one together next. Maybe we can find a place for it on one of his walls once it's finished.

I glance at the current puzzle, of which only the borders and one corner are finished, and laugh. "He told me he loves me."

"He did?" Kendall clasps her hands together and lets out a delighted giggle. "Oh, Avery, that's wonderful! Did you say it back? Tell me everything!"

And so I do. "I didn't say it back. Somehow I just couldn't form the words. I think I was in shock. I mean, I've been thinking for a while that maybe he felt that way, but to hear him say it—especially right then, when I'd just bared my very soul and every scar on my body to him, it was just too much. But I will tell him." The laugh bubbles right out of my unbelievably happy soul. "I want to shout it from the mountaintops, so I'm definitely going to have to tell him soon."

"Are you nervous about telling him?"

I smile. "Actually, no. The one thing I feared was that he wouldn't feel the same way, but we've cleared that up. I just want to make it special, you know? I don't want it to be a throw-away moment for him."

"You have a plan."

"A little bit."

***

I prowl Noah's kitchen like a caged tiger, glaring at the oven timer every few seconds. My mind won't stop, unlike the dang timer, which won't seem to count down. It's been two days since I confessed everything to Noah. Two days since he said he loves me. Two days since he convinced me to bare the marks on my body and soul for his inspection. Two days since he tenderly and sensuously rubbed sunscreen into the bare skin of my back, chest, and shoulders and later took me into the water.

I groan at the sensory memory. Feeling Noah's hands slide along my slicked skin was the most erotic moment of my life, better even than stroking him off in his kitchen. My body reacted to the feel of him, sending blood rushing up to meet his hands then then run tell the tale to my groin, which showed its appreciation by almost making a mess all over the inside of my borrowed shorts. Thankfully Noah stopped his caresses before things got truly out of hand, but I was left dazed and tingling on the lounger while he cut a couple of paths through the water, the laps no doubt calming his own physical reaction to our touch.

Today, my beautiful Noah is attending the first day of his master's program classes, so it's a milestone day for both of us. Finally the timer dings and I fling myself at the refrigerator. I scoured the internet before my appointment with Kendall this morning, hoping to find some romantic recipe to make tonight. After two hours of painfully fruitless searching, I stumbled upon a recipe for coffee-crusted beef tenderloin steaks. Knowing Noah loves his coffee as much as he does a good steak, it seems like the reasonable compromise. Now that they've marinated for thirty minutes, I just have to pan sear them, then bake them for ten minutes, by which time Noah should be home.

Home. The word itself brings a picture of Noah to my mind. It seems strange that in less than a year I could go from being so frightened of him to wanting to spend the rest of my life taking care of him, loving him and being loved by him. It's serendipitous that Sam forced me into therapy at the same time Noah Yates showed up in my life. I've heard people say that some things you can plan for, but the greatest things often take you by surprise. Noah certainly has been a wonderful surprise.

I hear his key in the lock as I pull the steaks out of the oven. I couldn't have planned this better if I'd tried any harder. I place the tinfoil tents over the steaks just as he walks through the door.

"Lucy, I'm home," he teases.

I laugh and almost run into the living room to greet him. He wraps me in a tight embrace and places a kiss in my hair. I stand on my toes to receive the real kiss I've been waiting for all day. It is worth the wait, as it always is. I ignore the tingling spreading through my body like wildfire and pat his tight behind. "Go get a quick shower. Dinner's ready."

He doesn't release me like I expect him to. Instead, he tightens his hold on me with one arm and caresses my lower lip with my favorite thumb in all of creation. "Have I told you today that I love you?"

I slide my arms around his neck and bring him in for another kiss. "Have I told you today that I love you, too?" It's not the way I intended to tell him. I had planned for a lengthy confession of my feelings over dinner. When I see the dimples appear as his grin spreads wide on his face, I know this is better than what I had planned. The simplicity of it is just right. He doesn't need me to make a production out of stating my feelings; he just needs to hear that I feel the same way.

His lips come down on mine in the tenderest of kisses, exploring and discovering like we've never kissed before. It's his way of reassuring me, letting me know without words that everything will be alright. I already know it, but I love that he cares enough to show me this way.

***

After dinner, we take our coffee out to the patio. With the excitement of telling him how I feel combined with a healthy dose of coffee beans on the steaks and now liquid coffee, I'm not sure I'll ever sleep again. Over the meal he raved about, we discussed his first day of classes and my appointment with Kendall. I told him the exciting news that she wants to scale back our sessions to once a week. I've been waiting for that moment, waiting for her to say I'm healthy enough not to need her so often. I feel like I've reclaimed this day, made it a positive memory in spite of what Tommy tried to do to me a year ago.

There's so much in my head I still need to say to Noah. I set my coffee down on the table between our chairs and move to sit on his lap. I laugh silently to myself; I'm so completely saturated with love and happiness. I kiss him tenderly and he reaches up to stroke my dog tag, something that has become his habit within the last few weeks.

"You know, I had this whole speech prepared to tell you I love you," I begin. "But when you came in the door, it just seemed so natural to tell you back. I've wanted to say it for weeks, but I was still afraid. I'm not afraid anymore and I have you to thank for that. When I look back at my life before you, it's mostly just blackness. For a long time I thought I was a parasite on the earth, just waiting for it to kill me when it was done with me. Now I know that the true parasite was inside me, killing me from the inside out. At first, I thought it was the hope I have for a better future or the love I feel for you, but I learned it was the self-doubt and self-hatred Mom and Carl and Tommy were able to poison me with. Sam and Joey, they were my two bright spots in a world of blackness, but even they weren't enough to make me see the truth. But you—Noah, you encouraged me to step into the light, to feel the heat and the joy of the sun. You allowed me to learn and grow at my own pace, to stumble and fall and get back up again. Somewhere along the way, I realized I was worthy of the love I feel for you—and what I feel from you, too. That's something I never thought would or could happen to me. I didn't think I was worthy of it, but you knew all along, didn't you? You chased away the blackness, Noah. You've made me realize I want nothing more than to spend the rest of my life here in the sunshine with you. I love you."

I can't believe how easy it is to say, how powerful it feels to be able to say that to him and have absolutely no fear.

"Oh, Avery, I love you, too. I'm so proud of you. You could have continued to live in that world of blackness and fear, but you chose not to and you've worked damn hard to heal yourself and grow stronger. It took a lot of courage. You're so strong and so wonderful, and I'm the luckiest man on the planet to have you." I hear the emotion in his voice and I know all is finally right in my world. I'm not Tucker anymore, not the kid who was the outlet for everyone's negativity. Finally I'm really and truly Avery, the man Noah Yates is in love with, the guy who has so many friends who care about him he has to use a second hand to count them. But most importantly, I'm Avery who is in love with the most amazing man on the planet.

I frame his face with my hands and smile at him, stroking his lip with my thumb. He presses a quick kiss to it and my heart swells. "I know I haven't been easy to love, and I can't promise that everything is going to be perfect overnight, but I swear I'm going to try." I kiss him long and deep like he has taught me over the last months.

He breaks away, breathless and stares at me for a second, then laughs. "It's about time you figured it out."

"Hey!" I smack his shoulder.

He laughs again. "I love you, too, little one. So much."

I nuzzle into his neck. "Do you think I could stay here tonight?"

I feel his sharp intake of breath. "Cuddles and kisses and conversation?" he asks.

"The full alliteration," I answer with a contented grin.

He stokes my back and I feel the slight tension fade from his body as I relax fully into him. "I wouldn't have it any other way."

About the Author

In addition to his newest release, "Out of the Blackness," Carter Quinn is the author of the novel "The Way Back," and the short stories "I'm Every Goalie" and "In the Crease." Carter was born and raised in a very small Western Kansas town where cattle vastly outnumber humans. Because he's contrary by nature, upon graduating high school, he went East, young man, hoping to find more people like him (shh: the gays!). After stints living in places as different as Omaha, Nebraska, and Ft Lauderdale, Florida, he settled in Lawrence, Kansas, and attended the University of Kansas (Rock Chalk!). Although he still bleeds (Crimson and) Blue, Carter now resides in Denver, much closer to his beloved Colorado Avalanche. He is the paw-picked human companion of the sweetest dog in the world, a Beagle-surprise mix named Yashe.

To experience Orange Fluff for yourself, please visit
carterquinnbooks.com

Made in the USA
Charleston, SC
24 September 2013